.50

TOWER IN THE WEST

Tower in the West

by FRANK NORRIS

HARPER & BROTHERS · PUBLISHERS · NEW YORK

For

E.E.N., E.E.N., Jr., and E.E.N. III

friends and kinsmen

The characters (other than a few esteemed and public ones) and events (other than historic and obviously recognizable ones) in this book are fictional, the book being a work of fiction, and any . . . But no, no; permit a quotation:

> *I say no more, except: God be with you, and may He give me the patience to bear well the ill that a few stiff-starched hairsplitters are bound to speak of me. Vale.*

Miguel de Cervantes Saavedra

Part I

Part I

One

PEOPLE, usually young people, have from time to time asked me how I happened to come by this bit or that bit of general information, or some modicum of experience of which they seek the benefit (not that they often put it into practice). The answer is that I have lived a reasonably long time and I have generally tried to pay attention.

I have, I guess, always been fond of the young, even when I have formally taught them. The very young I like most, for they invite most compassion. They are disadvantaged. They have no money, not too many friends of their own age, and are prey to illusion. I absolutely know the latter circumstance to be true from experience. I have seen the bicycle's horrifying upset, and I have heard the catastrophe blamed on everything except the rider. That is a kind of illusion. Children, I have always thought, are also very adult. They like the best of it and will lie to themselves, in hysteria or otherwise, to get it. Like adults.

But with children there is this difference. Pity and protection given them can evoke a certain kind of compensating love in return, which is not always true among adults. At least that's the way it has turned out for me in one very long-standing association.

This particular one has been an avuncular relationship, and I am prepared to recommend it. An uncle's affection toward a niece or nephew is spontaneous, as toward a friend. Theirs to him may be the same. Actual parents and children are more or less stuck with what familial society they inherit.

I never had any children of my own. But I have had something to do with the upbringing of two other children. These are the son and daughter, Jeff and Mary Hanes, of my late brother Thomas Jefferson Hanes and his wife Mary. My own name is George Washington Hanes. Our father was a great admirer of the Revolutionary heroes (his name was Benjamin Franklin Hanes). But I am no Thomas Jefferson Hanes. He was an artist; I am largely an appreciator. He was a creator; I am a conservator, a curator, you might say. How I loved, revered my brother.

Everybody, or almost everybody, in his profession loved him: Louis Sullivan, Adler, Root, Burnham, Holabird, and all the rest. In those days, no less than now, ours was a pretty savagely competitive business. But they liked Jeff well. My brother was twelve years older than I was.

In the course of trying to help my brother's children grow up properly, after their father died, there came at times orders taller than I thought I could fill, but the tallest of them were never altogether financial. We had a considerable income from the firm during the children's earlier years; our equity in the Tower, of course, amounted to a modest fortune.

As I say, I loved my brother, and never more than on that bright spring forenoon when we topped out the steel work on Tower in the West, the name by which his last and greatest building was until recently called. Its function is not now that for which he built it, but like an old friend, the Tower's form and face while worn remain familiar even though its aging organism, like all others, found no way to swindle time in its continuing passage. What man's insides have not changed along with forty years of fairly hard living? The Tower has lived hard and that long.

Everyone who has set foot in downtown St. Louis knows the Tower. Many students aspiring to our profession are required to know it by heart inside and out. Although rote is not the method

4

that I personally find happiest for learning or teaching architecture, a great deal is to be gained from studying the solutions arrived at by my brother to many complex problems in the plan and construction of that remarkable edifice.

What we might call the arithmetic of Tower in the West is simple enough to grasp and, where desirable, even remember.

The twenty-story building, occupying a rectangular plot of 39,400 square feet on the northwest corner of Eighth and Chestnut Streets, has a volume of 5,132,000 cubic feet. A six-story tower rises above the middle of the Chestnut Street elevation. The building rests on caisson foundations and is of steel frame construction. Ashlar facing and piers are of buff Indiana limestone and exterior decoration is applied in bas relief up to the seventh story and from the eighteenth to parapet. The triple-arched entrance to the hotel on Eighth Street has been repeated with modulations in the entrance on Chestnut Street—flanked by shop fronts —to the theater, offices, and tower. The tower is topped by a full-storied panel, screening water tanks and elevator machinery. Below that there is a recessed loggia on four sides behind which were the offices of T. J. Hanes, Architect. Designs for the project were drawn and redrawn over a period of two years. Excavation was begun January 27, 1914, and the building completed December 9, 1916. The cost of the structure came to just under one dollar per cubic foot.

And so on. The edifice upon completion contained so many guest rooms and so many offices. The hotel, besides such-and-such number of kitchens and service rooms, occupied a kind of shell, surrounding two sides of the theater. In addition to four dining rooms on various floors, there were a banquet hall and a ballroom. The theater ceiling was a series of expanding elliptical arches and their spacing, together with the rise of the parquet, was based on Scott Russel's "isocaustic curve" which had been used in the design of the Auditorium in Chicago twenty-seven years before and was to be followed in the construction of the Chicago Civic Opera twelve years later. You could hear what was being said or sung there to the farthest corner. Air, washed and humidified, cooled

5

in summer and warmed in winter, was circulated throughout the whole Tower structure and distributed from ceiling outlets treated decoratively as patterned bosses, this to the surprise, delight, or irritation of the first guests, tenants, and audiences.

So might the Tower undergo dissection. But even now it is not ready for autopsy. It is a living thing, a being, to this day. Ornament, "the fragrance of building," throbbed with life on every wall and ceiling and floor, and the Tower has not forgotten this. For, not having let himself be so much as brushed by the wrinkled old hand of traditional forms and proportions, my brother invented with wood, plaster, mosaic, stone, and wrought iron his own vocabulary of decoration. His instinctive choice of materials and originality in the use of color and design remain, in spite of the timid simplification or, worse, the ornate vulgarizations of his imitators, ever wonderfully new, springtime fresh, his invention, his creation, his own.

But stand again outside, look up and behold the Tower itself. To welcome more light to the interior, and to grace the exterior, the corner windows are turned; the remainder of the fenestration is equally generous. The eye is drawn upward by strong vertical elements; you look at this structure and, if it says nothing else, your instinct tells you that you can be very sure that the roof will not fall in nor the walls out. And yet there is no sense of brutality in its powerful upthrust. The Tower embodies all the calm natural grace of a strong arm upheld.

"Every building that you see," Louis Sullivan said, "is the image of a man you do not see—the man is the reality, the building its offspring."

The image of a man. That surely is what shines from the Tower, the image of my brother: strength, grace, generosity, imagination, power. The original usefulness of the interior might be, as it later was, terribly perverted. And even the exterior could be defamed by little wretched mountebank tricks. But not the mass, not the whole, not that which was *man*, my brother, who never saw it at all except in his mind and on his drafting board. But he had for good and all done his duty to his clients and their money. Infinitely more important, he had done his duty to himself as an architect and as a man. He had composed a thing of beauty.

I believe that most of us have favorite photographs or even paintings of the people we love, but the portrait can also be pictured in the mind and even more durably, for the emulsion does not fade nor the pigment dim until death. My favorite of Jeff sees him standing, late that Saturday morning, at the top of the completed steel work of the Tower, far above the city. He had on his work clothes, blue flannel shirt, canvas puttees, khaki pants, which were the clothes that he had worn on summer encampments with the Missouri National Guard. He gave the whole structure his comradely approval with a slap of his hand on the nearest I-beam. I was below him, not more than five or six feet, on a ladder. Beyond us to the west ran the long tree-green strip of Lindell Boulevard and then beyond it lay the great grass-green oblong of Forest Park. Sharply below and to the east stood the Mississippi, vast, leathern, and motionless.

He looked down upon me, my brother, with his happy great-toothed smile of a wolf. He frightened other people with that smile. He didn't frighten me with it, ever. I loved him.

Directly below was the roof of the beautiful column that is Sullivan's Wainwright Building. My brother had started to come down, but stopped his descent.

"Do you think Louis topped out that old shack of his?" he asked me and laughed. Of course I knew he worshiped Sullivan. Again he started down the ladder toward me. But the steel boss was coming up the ladder right under my behind and he had a bundle of willow branches beneath his arm. His name, as I recall it now, was Baken, maybe Dakin; a Czech, I think. Anyhow he said: "Waid a minute."

We had topped out without a fatality and this man wanted to fix the appropriate propitiatory boughs to the highest steel.

My brother backed up to the top structure. "Well, if they want sentiment," he said. "Come on up here." With those quick hands of his he wired the branches to the steel, gave the steel boss a

7

stout whack on his back, and then the three of us climbed down twenty-six floors into the bottom of the operational area where Ed Reagan was waiting for us in his tomato-colored car. Reagan and his father had contracted the job and, with us, financed it.

Reagan always liked automobiles, big fast ones. My brother and I usually took the Olive Street trolley car between home and the site. We were living at that time in a house he had rented for himself and his family out on the 2200 block on Westminster Place. It was not much of an inconvenience in those days to ride the car line. We had a Model T Ford, but the two of us never used it very much. We were working. I expect that his wife Mary got some use out of it.

For a man of Jeff's great joy in and knowledge of machinery and construction, he surprised some people with his indifference to the automobile, even to the idea of the automobile. In fact he liked to make fun of the invention—except for the Model T.

I recall that as we passed through the paling gate to the street, climbed into Reagan's brand-new Winton touring six, and started home (Reagan had been asked by Mary to have Saturday lunch with us by way of celebrating the top-out), Jeff got off another of his derogatory remarks about the motorcar. We were out on Lindell Boulevard just about passing that wonderful atrocity, the new fake Byzantine Cathedral (I have an older man's almost totally detailed recollection of these scenes), and he turned his jovial wolf's smile on Reagan. We were all in the front seat of the Winton. My brother jerked a thumb toward the Cathedral.

"That's a good faith of yours, Reagan," Jeff said. I knew how he hated that absurd structure.

Reagan made no reply.

"I mean it's beautifully integrated," Jeff said. "Something for everybody." I don't remember what Reagan said, if he said anything.

"Not like this contraption we're riding in," Jeff said.

"What do you mean?"

"One mechanism to make it run, another mechanism to make it stop." And then he laughed quite a lot. "No sense. No integration.

8

Function's all wrong. Not, of course, that anything can really stop the Catholic Church. I'm just speaking of integration." Jeff could be didactic and sharp. It pleased me, but it could make other people puzzled or angry. (The Model T had a planetary transmission: the same mechanism which made it go could also halt it.)

My brother's modest way of living, for his kind of man, may have seemed to others a sort of inverse snobbism. He and his Ford and his work clothes made him look, as a rule, about like a bricklayer. But that was of course in his way what he was. His time in American architecture was a long generation before the fashion of cost-plus building expenses. You, the architect, stuck to the estimate that you had provided for your client. If your own office costs for revision and redesign of plans went above what your original agreement had specified, you were in turn stuck with them. Jeff's frequently did. He was always determined to put up the best building that he could. "It doesn't really make a great deal of difference what's in the cash register," he said. He was in the business of being an artist; he was not in the business of being a particularly rich man. The Reagans he had picked up to do the Tower job God knows where. They were of course bricklayers, too; but they liked money. To every arch there is but one keystone. Jeff was mine.

We sat down to lunch—Mary, the two children, and the three of us—in about as tranquil an atmosphere as anybody could ever be in Jeff's company. Then Jeff began to talk about furniture for that section of our building devoted to the hotel.

"Beds," he said. "Got to be soft enough to sleep in, hard enough to make love on. Place in Chicago has 'em. George found out." He looked at me and gave that savage and somehow blind laugh of his. "Form follows function. And vice versa."

But I wasn't looking at him for more than an instant. I was looking at Reagan and Mary. The movies, the good ones, do better at observing and recording these scenes nowadays than writing can; with careful direction, expressions on the actors' faces tell you all you need know about the emotions of the characters

9

in a given situation. The camera eye, however, is after all no quicker than the human eye. Mine was accurate enough on that occasion. Reagan looked at Mary and Mary blushed. And I began to guess why.

I used to play a little golf. No, that's a silly evasion. I used to play some very good golf. And I played it, when Jeff didn't need me in the office, on Saturdays at the St. Louis Country Club some years before Jones won the National Amateur there.

Jeff said that he was going to take the afternoon off downtown. We had a nurse to toddle little Jeff and Mary over to Forest Park. Reagan offered to drive Mary out to the Club to play cards. I drove off before them in the Ford. I had a pretty good nine, 35–36 maybe; I could usually do it in those days.

When I came in after the first nine I naturally went up to the terrace to see my sister-in-law. She and Reagan and two other people were playing auction bridge, and we talked together awhile.

It was almost dark when I came in from the second nine to look in on them again. I wish I hadn't. Ed and Mary were not on the porch and nobody else was. The two of them were in the card room, inside. There wasn't anybody else there. He had some kind of a colored cocktail in his hand, I suppose it was one of those new ones like a Pink Lady, and just as I watched them he took it from his mouth and passed it to hers. She looked up as she handed the glass back to him and, seeing me, showed me that particular curl on a guilty woman's mouth that is a smile which rejects judgment, defies criticism, and pleads mercy, all at the same moment. It was the first time I ever saw it. I have seen it since several times. I gave them a wave and went on down to the locker room. Naturally I kept my mouth shut about what I had seen. Jeff would have killed Reagan.

Jeff's business that Saturday afternoon, I was told by the steel boss, Dakin or whatever his name, was to climb up to the topping of our building and unwire the willows.

I still have them, withered gray and in the shallow glass case that was made for them, back in my home in, now, Missouri. What an antisentimentalist *he* turned out to be.

In the fall, the building almost completed, Jeff took Mary for a motor tour in Scandinavia, that being the only place in Europe accessible to tourists from neutral countries. It was the beginning of the time when I had the children in my care.

Two

THE news that Jeff was dead came to me on another Saturday.

We were getting up the proscenium arches above the theater of the building (people worked on Saturdays in those days) and Margaret Carton had taken little Jeff and little Mary out to the Florissant Valley Club with their nurse to have a tea party. It was a nice little old place, nothing much more than a farmhouse with some big old maples around it. The membership consisted of only a couple of dozen families and was chiefly maintained as a retreat where the elder males could meet comfortably for an evening of highballs and poker. In the daytime, occasional parties of children brought out from town by their keepers could be seen scampering around the premises, chipmunks quite unaware that they frolicked at the mouth of a nocturnal bears' den. Margaret was the kind of girl who seemed to like all children but in fact outrageously played favorites; since Jeff and Mary had been away she and the kids had given themselves a whirl, Florissant being one of the hot spots.

So Margaret was out there with them and I was on our site when the cable came in. It said that Mary was alive. Jeff was killed. The cable was sent by our Minister at Oslo. They used to make quite a thing of tragic cables in those days. You'd think that I.T.&T. was the next of kin. They got the bad news to you extra fast. With the added services of Western Union, of course, which relayed the signal with a special black triptych on it. The Pentagon does most of that kind of commiseration now, but with the assistance of the same old Western Union.

A small boy dressed in a steel-gray uniform with seedy leather puttees, having dismounted a beat-up company bicycle, brought to me, where I was working in the engineering shack, my tragedy. From time to time, looking at those double-page advertisements in *Life*, I wonder which one of the up-from-the-ranks vice-presidents he became. I hope he is a good one. I hope he's happy. He certainly didn't bring me a happy message. It was not his fault of course; Western Union must have made millions of other people happy.

Unlike so many of my countrymen in this century, I have never set my foot on the continent of Europe in anger. The crowd that I was with in the old war was stationed at Harwich, and so far as military history is concerned a pretty obscure crowd it was. You will look a long time in the books before you find any reference to American Naval aviation in that passage of arms. But we were there, above the French as well as the English coasts, fluttering around looking for German submarines.

And when I say fluttering I mean fluttering. The implement of war that I had charge of was called a hydro-aeroplane, had a wing-spread of fifty feet, and made sixty miles an hour when it was going good. We were officially called hydro-aviators. You first got the thing into action by pushing it out of a tent and into a slough. I was looking in an old scrapbook some time back and came across a fading mimeograph check-sheet that we were supposed to look over before going aloft so as to make sure that everything was shipshape. The first line reads: "Be sure that there is water to cool the radiator." We also had flight equipment to account for: "Four pigeons, with message holders in place, with pencil and pad . . .

Pistols and one box of cartridges . . . Note-book . . . Two pieces of chalk. . . ."

God knows how the chalk was to be used, but, thinking back, I found that I could not kid the old Naval air service or its accouterments, even from this vantage point of time. Every moment of history is its latest; every technology the most advanced. And a younger friend of mine in that long-ago squadron, a boy from Tennessee who happened to be a member of my college dining club, went down into the North Sea and was killed just as dead as you can be killed in any war, no matter how unusual your duty.

Where my brother Jeff died was on a turn of the road bending sharply around and above a chasm which must be skirted before you begin to descend the fjord into the town of Trondheim. Afterward I went there to see the place. It's not hard to kill yourself there, either. I wondered if, at that place and at that terrible moment, Jeff had time for the sardonic reflection that his misgivings about the functioning of the automobile had been finally confirmed. It would have been like him.

I don't know if you were ever present at a Masonic burial service. It is a very moving and beautiful one. I do not belong to the order myself, but Jeff did.

I had gone to New York to take charge of his remains, and to meet Mary. She still wore bandages over some quite serious cuts, but was otherwise in remarkably good shape considering the wreck she survived; it also seemed to me that she was in remarkably good spirits. As she told it to me, the car, European, had right-hand drive so that, when it went over, Jeff caught the whole weight. Mary said that all she remembered was being suspended in the air above the whole scene. I could believe her. The weird effects of velocity in automobile wrecks have never ceased to puzzle me. I once saw a car coming at me in broad daylight and on a ruler-straight road in Indiana. The car wobbled a few times—the steering knuckle had broken, I imagine—and then crossed in front of my car and went into a deep ditch. It turned over twice before it landed bottom down but pointed in the opposite direction. When I got to them, the old couple in the back and the young couple

14

in front were, naturally, dazed, but absolutely unhurt. Their car didn't have a scratch on it, but the front bumper was as precisely detached as though the job had been done in a garage. It lay neatly in front of the car's radiator, and in front of the bumper, also neatly, lay a perfect still-life arrangement of fruit flung from the family's lunch box. Automobile accidents can be very queer. No one could judge from the wreckage what had gone wrong with my brother's car.

The Bellefontaine Cemetery, where we buried Jeff, is a long way out in north St. Louis, beyond the old Maxwelton horse track, later the Maxwelton auto track, and even later the Maxwelton dog track. There is nothing there now except the cement skeleton of a grandstand.

I drove behind the hearse, with Mary, little Mary and little Jeff, and their nurse in our Ford. There were many more cars behind us bearing the other mourners, including Ed Reagan in his tomato-red Winton—a funny sort of car, I remember thinking, for a funeral cortege.

The master of the Masonic lodge, I expect that's what you call him, conducted a brief but to me lovely ceremony over the grave. Jeff's will directed that he was to be cremated, but I couldn't have his body burned. Maybe that was my first mistake about my brother's affairs after he died.

There are some handsome tombs in that cemetery. Sullivan seems to have built a tomb to house the dead of every family for whom he erected a building; for the Ryersons and many others in Chicago, for the Wainwrights in this graveyard in St. Louis. You can see the latter today if you stand where my brother lies. I didn't cremate him as he wished; nor did I later erect him a fitting mausoleum. I compromised. The best that I can tell myself is that the stone is graceful and well designed. Nothing so beautiful as he would have done for me, of course. Mary had told me that Ed Reagan had advised her to leave Jeff's memorial as well as the obsequies entirely to me.

The master of the Masonic lodge picked up a handful of dirt

15

from the side of the grave and letting it fall on the top of Jeff's lowered coffin said, "Alas, brother." The rest of the Masons walked by and did and said the same thing, "Alas, brother."

That was kind of a tough afternoon. I would have liked to have done the same thing myself. Jeff was my *real* brother, but of course I wasn't a Mason. I think that the Masons were the only organization, besides the Militia and the A.I.A., that he ever took time or had the interest to join. He was no church man, or anything like that.

Three

I HAVE never been able to read very far into the Talmud. My brother had read it all. (But he, too, suffered a trauma or so of his own about reading, particularly in the American classics. It was his opinion that *Moby Dick* was far too long, febrile, and boring; that *Leaves of Grass* was the product of an illiterate and crazy fairy; and that *Looking Backward* was the clumsiest fantasy ever to enjoy the luck to be printed.) My brother also knew and savored the Bible, cover to cover. It was he who introduced me to the ancient conception, both from the Talmud and the Old Testament, that it was in some cases necessary for the living brother of a dead brother to marry the dead brother's widow. Old Hebrew law. It certainly was a necessity in our family's case. Or so it seemed to me.

"These Jews had a great lot of sense," he once told me. "A great lot of what you might call heart. Now don't smile. They had lots of basic tribal rules that took care of women. Women, I mean, in trouble: widowed, raped, old, impoverished."

I never thought that my brother had taken time to think or care about women very much. But I guess he had. He thought of a great many things.

"Women," he went on, "require pity. They're vulnerable. Any

17

vulgar or terrible thing that they are required to do is usually what some man makes them do. You know—like making them take off their clothes in burlesque shows? But almost everybody, man or woman, needs pity at some time or another, and here's a point I'd like to make clear to you. Pity, some of the wiseacres would like to tell you, is the acceptance of the repugnant. Don't you believe it. Pity is the quality of mercy, and that can't be too highly praised. Although," and here came the wolf's smile, "it is not an inexpensive sentiment. Pity usually comes high." He laughed. "Anyhow, never do a *woman* a dirty trick—if you can help it."

This next scene is laid about six months after Jeff's funeral. I had come home and gone upstairs to my rooms to wash up after work. Then I went into the nursery and held up little Mary by her heels and busted little Jeff one on the seat of his pants, just to keep them cheered up. Then I went down to the living room to join Mary and cheer her up, too, with a couple of drinks before dinner.

Mary, Jeff's wife, was not a bad-looking woman at that time. She was a blonde whose face, when you paid some attention to it, somehow indicated that she was one of those people to whom not enough attention had ever been paid. And resented it. Jeff, I am afraid, never gave her face or anything else about her too much concern. He never looked very long into anybody's face, for that matter. It was unimportant to him. He was always looking, I believe, rather at some magnificent and as yet unconstructed edifice. His wonderful drawings for buildings that never were and never will be built indicate this well enough. I have those drawings.

Why Jeff married Mary or anybody else is not easy to explain. He picked her up on a job he was doing in Kansas City, literally. She was one of the daughters of a banker who wanted an addition put onto his money mill. She was ten years younger than Jeff and only two years older than I am, so there was always a little twittering among the crones in St. Louis about how Jeff had robbed a

18

cradle. He certainly didn't look the part; he looked and moved like a police dog in top condition, including the coplike smile and remote eyes.

I believe that it had suddenly occurred to him that he ought to have some heirs. He was a busy man accustomed to making decisions about many things, even important things, in a hurry—and there stood Mary, who looked pretty and fecund enough. They were married a few days after he made the decision. It simply never occurred to him, I suppose, to talk to me about his marriage although we certainly discussed everything else under the sun, and of course I never brought up the subject. I was at college at the time of the wedding. So that's about all I know of it. But she was nevertheless the wife that my brother had chosen. She was my brother's wife.

Reagan—the Irish, married Reagan—became her lover not very long after our family moved to St. Louis. That I do know. This night in our living room she told me so. Did she not.

She was sitting there when I came downstairs from petting the kids. She was weeping.

"Now look, Mary," I said, "Jeff's gone and nothing will ever bring him back." That was a good fatuous remark, I realize, and I even realized it at the time.

She kept on crying.

"You've just got to take these things as they come." Another good one. "What is it, what can I do, Mary?"

And then she said, "Go to hell away there's nothing anybody can do not anybody in the world."

"All you God-damned men," was her next remark.

Then she started crying again and after that she wound up with the sniffles, concluding which she told me her bad news. I suppose it should not have been hard to foresee. She and Reagan were going to have a baby. Reagan, true to the faith of his fathers, was going to remain married, if not faithful to his wife and the four or five children that *they* had.

At that particular point of time and space in our civilization, and in that particular cell of society to which she belonged, the

19

quick trip to the illegal surgeon was for most women like Mary not only unthought of; it was unknown.

I ate dinner alone that night. Mary went upstairs to her bedroom to, as she said, "Take a little something to make me rest."

As I say, I shouldn't have been too much surprised at her disclosure after that Country Club business that I had witnessed less than a year before. But I was young and had not acquired those reflexes which prepare worldly men to roll, as it were, with life's expectable and unexpectable punches alike.

After she had taken her knockout pills and I knew that she had put herself to sleep, I thought it all over and it seemed to me that there were only two things to do. First things first.

I called the Reagan house and a maid answered and then old man Reagan answered. Young Ed wasn't home, he said, but was probably playing cards at the University Club, so I went down there. It was a place on Grand Avenue, two or three floors on the top of a lot of dentists' offices. I suppose it is there still.

I went up in the elevator and asked for Reagan and was shown into a card room. He and some other people were playing poker at a round table covered with green baize and it had a shaded light over it. Very professional.

I told him that I had something that I wanted to talk to him about. He got rather shirty and said that if it was business we could talk about it in the morning at the office. I said that this did not come under the head of office business. He said that in any case I had better go away, since I was not a member of the University Club.

Well, that was surely true—not of *that* university club. I said that I would wait for him outside the door in the street, and then he got up from the poker table. Ed was about my weight and age and, I believe, had played on the baseball team at Brown. He then called me a pretty bad name and didn't have the brains to put up a block because when he went over there wasn't a chip left on the table.

Who in the world would call in the cops for a thing like that?

20

But his friends did, and so I spent the night in jail. And a good many more nights, following my hearing.

The judge on my case was Charlie Kleinfelter. He was not a great deal older than I, and he and a couple of lawyer friends of his and I often played golf together.

"How did a business like this happen, George?" he said. "I mean Hanes."

"I can't explain it, your Honor," I said.

"You weren't drunk, were you?"

"No."

"But you broke this man's jaw. That's a terrible thing to do."

I had nothing to say, literally.

"If you can't offer any explanation I'll have to send you back to jail for at least thirty days. You're charged with assault and battery."

"I know. I just don't have anything to say, Charlie—your Honor."

So off again I went to the clink.

Before I was put behind the bars they let me use the telephone to call the home of my friend Junie Neidlinger, who, luckily for me, was for once not out on the town. Junie's father was president of the Teutonia National Bank, the largest on the South Side, and I knew that the elder Neidlinger had a cousin on the board of the *Star*, then the favorite newspaper of the German element in the city. My family were far from being old settlers, but our connection with the Tower had naturally brought us into prominence; when I cooled off a little after my arrest I began to worry about what the papers would have to say and at what length. Junie grasped the situation at once. Always eager for high emprise, he went into action via his father. His father, who had handled the bond issue when we were financing the Tower, got in touch with his cousin. It was the result of the latter's good offices that neither on the following morning nor at any time thereafter did the press make any more out of my case than it would have of any other local fist fight, thus sparing us a scandal so far as the public was concerned. The Irish among our acquaintance did nothing to adver-

21

tise the encounter since it was one of their boys who was beaten up. For exactly the same reason the German and French clans, much amused at the expense of the Irish, were quite forbearing toward me, at the time.

Life in the lockup wasn't so bad as you might imagine. In those days the city jail was an annex to the big police headquarters downtown on Twelfth Street. They kept the prisoners in an enormous two-story room with a double deck of cells back to back running down the middle. A nice open plan. They held the hangings there also, although none took place during my stay.

On the left side as you entered was the dining table, a very long one. Since I was big enough and young enough, the jailor put me up toward the head of the table where the more formidable prisoners ate and where there naturally accumulated the most food. That was good of him because I wasn't going to be there long enough to merit the privilege of having visitors or anything sent in. We had the freedom of the whole room until we were tucked into our cells at sundown. It was then and there that I revived a game which my brother invented and one that I have played ever since. It is called the Anatomy of Boredom. I recommend it to anyone who gets stuck anywhere without anything to read, as for example in a foreign railway station, a subway accident, or a war.

The rules are strict; every game that Jeff thought up had very strict rules. Any number can play, but the beauty of it is that, when stranded, you can play against yourself.

The prime requirement of the candidate to admission in the Anatomy of Boredom is that the person, institution, idea, or even legend was or is tiresome to begin with and has since been heard of far too much and far too often. Mere prejudices do not count. Thus, Franklin D. Roosevelt does not qualify, for even his direst enemies cannot deny that he saved a fairly workable economic system and won a war. Nor does Herbert Hoover qualify for the Anatomy, no matter how strongly his foes may urge it; he was a good engineer and is an honorable man. No, for humans we must turn to such ineffable bores as Hildegarde and the designer Raymond Loewy, who were not much to begin with and, in the lan-

22

guage of show business, have been on too long. That also goes, in the modern game, for: any resurrected letters exchanged between George Bernard Shaw and any woman; any further personal reminiscences of James Boswell; the dull synthetic mythology of Paul Bunyan and (even duller) John Henry. And so on. I'm sure you get the notion.

Anyhow, this pastime helped me kill quite a number of hours while in jail, and after thirty days I was released, not much the worse for the experience.

Then I went home to get my sister-in-law straightened out.

23

Four

THE wedding ceremony which made me Jeff's widow's husband was a very simple one, held at evening in the living room of our home on Westminster Place. Charles Kleinfelter, my golf-playing friend and the judge who had put me in jail, did the job. St. Louis, as you must know, was settled successively by French, Irish, and Germans. The French handled the furs, the Irish handled the boats and the pickaxes, and the Germans made the beer and administered justice, being probably the sanest of the three races that showed up in the nineteenth century on the west bank of the Mississippi where it is joined by the Missouri.

I had thought and hoped that it was to be a simple family affair, and, thinking back, I guess it was just about that. Mary had bidden the guests. She had bidden Ed Reagan, his wife, and their clutch of children, and there they all stood behind the serenely smiling head of the family. ("There's naught, no doubt, so much the spirit calms as rum and true religion," Jeff used to say, by way of Byron.) Well, why not? We and the Reagans were in a sizable building enterprise together. If Ed could forgive me for his broken jaw, I could forgive him for that month in the hoosegow. And nobody could make it look good for Jeff's widow's having an illegitimate child, under the circumstances, except me. At least, that was the way that I saw it.

Not only the young Ed Reagans and the children were present, but also the old boy and his wife showed up, too. This was sort of rubbing it in, I thought. But that wasn't the worst. Mary had also asked Margaret Carton to our quiet little family wedding. And Margaret came, Margaret who had been my sweetheart since we had gone to Mr. Mahler's dancing school together. In the long parade of tastelessness, it occurred to me, the invitation to Margaret deserved an especial float.

Charlie couldn't have been better. He did his job fast, most of the ceremony coming from *The Merchant of Venice* ("Let no one pluck off this ring" or something like that). Little Jeff was my best man. I bent down to him to receive the ring, said thank you to him, then my dead brother's wife spread her fingers on her left hand and somehow I circled the correct one with the ring. There was the proper amount of Mumm, if not Mendelssohn.

The Mumm didn't help too much; on the contrary. For when the kids were shooed off to the pantry for ice cream, some very odd toasts were offered.

Old Ed Reagan said, "May all your troubles be little ones." That I recognized as the product (a) of his generation and (b) of his ignorance. I didn't look at Mary during the proposal.

Then young Ed raised his glass to Mary, and said, "May you always be as happy as you are this day, my dear." His wife and Mary both beamed at this Hibernianism, and for quite different reasons I felt sure.

Margaret Carton lifted a glass to me. "Now you're a married man, George," she said, and suddenly I flinched from the dead finality of her pronouncement.

Everybody seemed to have had enough of the ceremonials after about nine o'clock. Neither Mary nor I had planned on any kind of a honeymoon trip. We'd never even discussed it. This turned out later to look a little queer to some people in town, but I don't actually see why it should have. Our men still had about a hundred thousand feet of interior plastering to put up in the building. The elevator shafts were not even founded. There was plenty of work to do all day and all night to get the Tower opened by New Year's Eve, 1916.

So the Reagans, all of them, and Charlie and his wife said their good nights and little Jeff, the best man, and his sister were tucked away and I left Mary telling the maids how to tidy the place up and went upstairs to my bedroom.

I couldn't possibly remember now what papers I was looking over in bed. It could have been anything from competitive estimates on palm trees for the tea garden to an explanation of why the Otis equipment had been shipped by way of Chicago instead of Indianapolis. But I surely do recall how Mary came in through my bedroom door.

Lubricious. That's a word that always struck me as being just right, sounding just right, for the grimace of fake passion on a fake woman's face. This lady had it.

"Why, George," she said. "You look so surprised."

"I am," I said.

Women used to wear a little more before getting into bed than they do nowadays. At least, so I gather from the magazines. But not a lot more.

"You are?" she said. "Why? Aren't I your wife?"

Jeff had always been impatient with that solecism of hers.

"Am I not your wife," I said. "That's the correct way of saying it, Mary. And the correct thing for you to do is to get out of here and never come in again."

"Oh?"

"And I'll do the same for you."

Whatever it may have been for the Hebrews, that part of the marital arrangement was void in my contract.

And so began and ended our epithalamium.

My brother, fine man and creative artist though he was, gave way to superstition in minor matters. He rationalized it this way: it was his idea that knocking on wood and doing the same routine things the same way, absolutely the same way, every day in the year, would prevent you from making foolish diversionary mistakes. You would be traveling in a safe groove.

He had many other ideas about the steadying influence of super-

26

stition, and he could convince you of them—at least he could and did convince me. I have time after time seen him place a chip and ring it on number nine on a roulette wheel (1889 was his class) and it would almost inevitably come up. That pays 36 to 1 with all the trimmings. But even Jeff did not always win. In the United States at the time that Mary's third baby, this one by Reagan, was born, the national chance of survival for the infant was 1,000 to 11. Nevertheless, this poor baby had to miss it. He was rolled a twelve. And at Barnes Hospital, at that. Perhaps it was all for the better, but I didn't think so even though the child's death released me from any further duty to Mary. And I was not too happy when I heard that the moment she was allowed a telephone, Mary had begun spreading the news that she had suffered a fifth-month miscarriage. I did not deny it however. In another year it would all be forgotten and I would have time to think about my own future.

Five

MARY, big Mary that is, dead Jeff's wife, and I suppose in a way you might say mine, survived the loss of her baby and Reagan's very healthily.

The building was by then completed and opened for business. And what a business it was. She loved it. I remember taking her to the opening night of our theater to hear and see Galli-Curci in something very big in Italian, and later on Mary Garden in *Zaza*, letting the boys all have a look at her very lovely legs as she glided back and forth on a swing to make one more newspaper scandal. We also had Harry Lauder for his fourth or fifth farewell tour. The hotel section of Tower in the West was under excellent management and the best place to stay in town. The old Planter's and the Jefferson were compelled to reduce their rates; only drummers went there now; we offered our hospitality largely to the very well-to-do. The Rathskeller, a vast pillared tunnel of stout Germanic charm well patronized by silver barons from Nevada, oil barons from Texas, and banknote barons from New York, became a celebrated national crossroads. A hundred debutantes with aigrettes and birds of paradise in their hair could be accommodated in the grand dining room; a thousand Republicans with gold pieces on their vests, in the ballroom. The food and service were literally

28

fabulous—people talked about it for years. The grouse were expressed from the State of Washington, the oysters and terrapin from Maryland, the lobsters from the coldest waters of Maine. We had seven men working in the wine cellar. Our own office was reached by a separate elevator to the campanile above the roof, the tower. The Reagans had their place of business below and kept a large suite of rooms on the seventh floor of the hotel, as I recall it, for their clients. It was the fine fulfilling springtime of our enterprise. We had put a lot of money into the Tower, and we were making a lot of money out of Jeff's building.

On New Year's Eve of 1916 there was a party held in the ballroom which even the proletarian *Post-Dispatch* had to take notice of, and respectfully. I brought Mary, naturally, and naturally our table included the Reagan family and some friends and kin of theirs. The band was Art Hickman's, hired east from California, and they played "Rose Room" for the first time I had ever heard it. I remember that fox trot very well because Ed and Mary were dancing to it every time it was played. Old Mrs. Reagan and I also seemed to be dancing to it every time it was played. Hickman had composed it in honor of a ballroom where he was featured in San Francisco, I was told. It's a nice tune; even now I hear it from time to time late at night on my radio. And believe me, I will never forget its association, because it was to these strains that Mrs. Reagan, the elder, said, "I hear you're leaving town soon." That was news to me, and very surprising. Her tone seemed to imply that she knew what she was talking about. I don't know what I said. I was puzzled.

From then on I really began to hear the word.

For several years I had been on the Greens Committee at the Country Club. This was for a couple of reasons: (a) I happened to be the only member of my generation from this club to have been invited to the National Amateur (it was much, much easier to make it in those days) and (b) the senior members needed Dan Pierce and me, who were about the same age, to do the real administrative work with the pro, the grounds-keepers, the caddies, and so on. The old crocks in the crowd preferred it that way. So

29

out I went on New Year's Day to the club expecting the annual committee elections to be nothing more than the usual ceremony of commiserating each other's hangovers, re-election of the committees, and then off to the Tom and Jerry bowl in the bar. Not at all.

Pierce, one of the Irish St. Louisans, was waiting for me under the club's portico.

"Happy New Year," I bade him.

"Not all that happy," he said.

"What do you mean?"

"Don't go upstairs, George."

"Why not?"

"It would just be embarrassing."

So I asked Dan why, and he told me that the governors had already elected the Greens Committee and that I hadn't made the grade.

"I've got the Tom and Jerry down in the locker room just for you and me," he said. "Just for two," he said. "Come on."

Dan had, and always has had, a tight little body, a tight little face, and a tight little mind. Most small people, male and female, I have found to be feists because they are born to resent their diminutive stature. Not Dan.

So we charged into the foaming bowl, and Dan said, "You are not planning to lam out of our fair city, are you?"

I was pretty shocked by the Greens Committee thing coming so soon after old Mrs. Reagan's remarks. Now I didn't know what to say.

"Don't," Dan Pierce said.

"Well, golly, Dan."

"My uncle Tim shot his wife, did you know that? Over on Portland Place. She had the money and they had just been remarried. My uncle Nat got there before the doctor or the police or anybody. Uncle Nat said it was suicide. That was all there was to it."

Well, of course I knew that, everybody in the West End knew it. Nat Pierce was a lawyer and evidently a good one. But I also

30

knew that the kind of tolerance which the Pierce family enjoyed was strictly for the early settlers. The Hanes family, just there to put up a few buildings, weren't in that running. The club governors knew it, too.

"The point is," little Dan told me, "these things blow over. I know. My family has lived in this town a long time before yours." How right; and how wrong of him not to see the difference where Mary and I were concerned. For of course I now saw where the trouble lay.

"There's nothing to blow over, Dan," I said, sounding as stupidly unresponsive, I suppose, as I must have sounded talking to Charlie Kleinfelter in court that day. I could only wonder dumbly how far our ostracism had gone, was to go.

"Well, anyhow," Dan said, after another pull at the Tom and Jerry, "just don't leave." And then, "How am I going to take care of all this work out here and do my own downtown without you? Whether you're on the committee or not?"

I loved Dan Pierce for that.

The next shock came even more unexpectably. St. Louis had about half a million people living in it at that time, but I suppose that everybody except the Germans, who more or less congregated on the South Side and patronized the stores along South Broadway, shopped within a very few blocks of the Central Post Office. Around lunchtime a few days after seeing Dan I stopped by Scruggs-Vandervoort-Barney to buy something or other. When I went in it was raining. When I came out at the Olive Street entrance it was sleeting, the usual miserable winter weather in that town, and there in the crowd waiting for streetcars and taxis was Margaret Carton. I hadn't seen her since the wedding. We extended each other the required pleasantries and then I asked her where she might be trying to get to. She had on a seal jacket and one of the sort of wide-brimmed beaver hats that they used to wear in those days and her eyes, as always, were filled with great kindness. She said that she hoped to get to the Woman's Club, which was a place far out on Lindell, to hear some sort of lecture.

"I'll find a way to get you there," I said, "if I have to carry you on my back right up to the platform."

She smiled and said, "That would probably be the worst idea in the world, George."

"You mean my carrying you? They surely don't mind letting the boys on the premises."

The little laugh that Margaret gave was tactful, not merry. "They might mind you, George. I've got to be running now."

The sleet kept coming down and I doubt if anybody got out to the West End that afternoon very quickly.

Saturdays I always tried to get off in the afternoon with little Jeff. That winter we used to go out to Forest Park to slide down the hill that reaches from the Art Museum to the lake below it, Art Hill. We had a long old Flexible Flyer big enough for a man to lie on and carry a kid on his back. Jeff was the best of pals for almost any kind of fun.

So little Jeff and I took a double belly-flop on Art Hill this Saturday afternoon on a long steep sheet of ice over snow. He, above me, gave a good shriek of joy and I was enjoying it too until I saw that we were going over the stone embankment and onto the frozen lake unless I dragged my right foot so as to throw us and save ourselves. I said to Jeff: "We're going to dump. You roll now before I do." He rolled, and in a small cloud of glittering ice particles we got off and lost the sled over the wall. Jeff wound up just this side of the embankment and I got a fine scraped foot.

Jeff as a child always had a high threshold of pain and lots of guts. Maybe they mean about the same thing. He bobbed up like a billiken.

"Are you hurt?" I asked.

"No, are you?"

"It's just my instep." There was blood coming through the torn front part of the sock.

He was crawling up through the shattered ice toward me.

"Instep? But that's very bad, isn't it, George?"

"Of course not, Jeff. How about yourself?"

32

"But that's what you and mother have both got. That's bad, isn't it?"

"What in the world are you talking about? Aren't you all right?"

"Instep. The kids told me. I'm very sorry for you, George."

Incest.

Mary and I had not even escaped the attention of Jeff's first-grade schoolmates at Smith Academy. They had of course gotten the miserable word from their parents who had in turn gotten their connubial transgressions confused.

Little Jeff's artless revelation amounted to another eviction notice for me and my family. It was all good and plain now. A week or so afterward Charlie Kleinfelter came to my office and he made it even plainer: no old women's insinuations, no old men's snubs, no children's malice. Those people who were not incensed by my marrying my brother's widow so soon after his death, Charlie reported, were outraged in the belief that I had seduced, maybe even raped her and had to marry her. The miscarriage story, it seems, had never stood a chance of being accepted.

"Then there's the other thing. Maybe it wouldn't amount to much by itself, but added all together it doesn't help matters," Charlie continued.

"What doesn't help?"

"When you beat up Ed Reagan." He went on before I could find my voice. "Don't think I fall for any of this, George, although I'll never know why you married her under any circumstances. But everybody knows Reagan and Mary used to be friendly, bridge partners and all that."

I had no idea that a sin as terrible as the one popularly attributed to me would need any further documentation; Charlie's visit introduced me to a new dimension in human nature.

The passage from the Old Testament that Jeff had mentioned to me comes from the Book of Ruth. A group of relatives, talking about a property that a dead brother has left, agree that the brother's widow as well as the property must go to the dead man's living brother. The direction to him reads in part: "thou must buy it also of Ruth the Moabitess, the wife of the dead, to raise up the name of the dead upon his inheritance." I *ought* to know that passage by now, I've read it and thought it over enough: the Hebrew family package deal, as I believe the radio and television people would express it nowadays.

After Charlie Kleinfelter left our office that afternoon, I considered it again. The most important heritage that Jeff had left was the children. And I had to do the best I could by the name of the dead. I knew I had to. What else?

I got up and went over to a mullioned window which gave onto the loggia that surrounded our quarters at the top of the tower. There I did some more thinking. It was a miserable day and so were my thoughts. The city below me looked iron cold. Far to the west and just above the horizon ran a great broad sky stroke the color of iodine. In an architectural rendering the effect is called *morne*, one of those good French words which means exactly what it says and sounds like. Many a student has squeaked through a young and romantic instructor's critique of a weakly designed elevation by using as background this heavy tragedian device.

I heard someone walking into my room. I turned around and it was Paul Eckfield, my partner. I must have looked pretty *morne*, too, because a shadow of sympathy instantly fell upon that round Swede face of his.

"What's the matter, Georgie?" he asked. "You lost your last friend?" I have always hated the nickname Georgie, it makes you sound like a fat, pudding-headed child. Very few people have ever called me that, but I suppose I had neglected to tell Paul about it.

"Not quite," I said.

"Is there anything *I* can do?"

And it occurred to me that if you were seeking an epitaph for Paul, this interrogation would make a fairly appropriate one. He was always using it, often to good effect. An expression of concern seldom makes anybody mad, and Paul was keen to offer his to friends and business prospects alike, in Paul's case both groups being practically indistinguishable. "Is there anything *I* can do?" Whether or not he could or would do anything (I believe that

34

occasionally, if the stricken one's problem required only a mini-mum amount of time and attention, he actually would and did), the proffer was usually appreciated and Paul's use of this gambit was one of his strong professional assets. "Is there anything—?" I can hear him saying it yet. I certainly can.

The philanthropist Paul played a not inconsiderable role in the effort by which I was trying to preserve my brother's company as well as his reputation. I believed that it was my duty to keep the firm going, but I needed help. So in the winter after Jeff's death I went up to Chicago to look for somebody to take into the firm as a business-getter. I wasn't then and never have been any good at that kind of thing. If I meet a prospect and come to like him, I don't want to impose on a friendship to get a commission out of him. If I don't like him I don't want his work anyway. That's why at that time I was trying to scare up a more practical salesman.

I hung around the T-Square Club for a week or more, talking to the boys from various offices who might be candidates for the job or give me a lead to somebody else who might be. No success.

And then one afternoon Paul Eckfield walked into the bar. He was a short, stout man. But he was impressively turned out and what was more, he carried his clothes as though he were not fat at all. You don't see that combination very often. His well-clipped hair was gray, of just that bright steely tone that inspires confidence in the customer.

He spotted me and came over bearing a strong sad smile. "George," he said, "I heard about Jeff, of course. Is there anything that I can do?"

I had run into Paul at several Association meetings and knew of course that he was not only a very capable businessman but a pretty good designer as well. I also knew of his eleemosynary repu-tation. I decided to give myself a little laugh by watching how he would wriggle out of the Samaritan bit.

So I said: "Yes, Paul, as a matter of fact there is."

He never batted an eye.

"What is it, George?"

"You can come down to St. Louis with me and help me run my outfit." It was my impression that he and a partner were doing very well in a small Chicago firm of their own, and that he wouldn't dream of going any place else.

Well, don't you know that his firm had gone bust months before, after his partner had taken to drink and run away with one of the draftsmen's wives? It must have been by the wildest accident that nobody at the T-Square had told me, because architects are a particularly gabby group. Moral: if you're an architect, keep up with the trade press, or at least with the yellow journals.

"Why, I'll be happy to, Georgie," he said.

So here Paul was now, right before me in my own office, on hand with the old first aid as usual.

"Nothing you want me to take care of, Georgie? You sure?"

I told him that I was going home soon unless something important was expected to turn up.

"Leave everything to me, Georgie. Leave it to me," he practically implored. And so for that evening the principals of Hanes & Eckfield, Architects, parted. I had kept my brother's name at the head of the organization, of course.

Taking the elevator down to our entrance I made my preoccupied way along Chestnut Street toward the Rathskeller of the hotel. I had almost reached its shimmering brass revolving doors before realizing that a bitter February gale was blowing, and my overcoat still swung over my arm. It was very cozy indeed when I got inside and descended the few steps to the hospitable rosy tiles, across which I moved briskly to the bar station presided over by Barney Walsh, a great favorite with many of the more frequent guests.

I placed a twenty-five-cent piece before Barney. "Let me have a pair of Manhattans, please, Barney," I said. He nodded, whisked the quarter off the broad gleaming highway of lovingly tended rosewood, and promptly faced me with a small frosted vase of ancient bourbon and the fixings, the second to come at my will. (I insert this little scene, not that it moves the narrative along, but merely to tease the present generation of topers.)

36

God deliver me from a loquacious barber or a taciturn barkeep. Barney was far from taciturn. He always had the five-star final on the local situation and covered the foreign field very creditably as well. Naturally he got around to war talk, the topic of the times. I had often given the matter thought, particularly that afternoon. Barney categorically announced that we would be in it by spring, to which I agreed. His vehemence on this occasion has stayed in my mind, for he used a phrase that I had never heard before but have from time to time repeated since; in my opinion it expresses great conviction. Barney said that we would be in the war by spring "as sure as there is a hole in your so-and-so." He was one of those Irishmen who are dainty-spoken even in the depths of obscenity.

I had the second Manhattan and was about to leave when, anticipating one conversation that I was going to have to undertake that evening, possibly two, I called for an additional single round. For this I paid fifteen cents.

Then I rang up Margaret Carton on the telephone and asked her if she would be at home after dinner and she told me, without any inflection of surprise at hearing from me, that she was not going out any place with anyone in this kind of weather.

Driving home, while the wind almost literally blew the Ford off its wheels, I thought that the storm might be a slight aid to persuading my sister-in-law-cum-wife to let me send her to Pasadena. Not that I really believed that it would take much persuasion. Even in the few years before the publication of such siren songs as "An Orange Grove in California" and "California, Here I Come," and also prior to the really heavy proselytizing for the Golden State, Los Angeles County was already filling up with fruit-growers, movie people, and rubes. Nearby Pasadena was new, too, but you weren't supposed to know it. To the Los Angeles *Examiner*, Pasadena was a society colony like, say, Palm Beach. Most of the Pasadena society people at that time lived in hotels. But this knockabout arrangement did not lower the social tone; in fact, it made it easier for the society people to mingle with the other society people and thus enlarge the colony.

My sister-in-law loved to mingle, and in the summer when

37

Tower in the West was begun she took the children out to Pasadena, returning to report that she had enjoyed a wonderful time. The kids liked it, too. So my proposal to her now might be: Why not consider Pasadena as an all-year-round proposition, and forget the circumstances which make it, or something like it, imperative?

I saw her through the archway dividing the hall from the living room. Her head was bent downward, a strand of her fine blond hair characteristically pulled free from the knot at the back of her neck and hanging across one side of her forehead—the picture of a tired woman washing clothes, a task which you may be sure Mary never undertook. It was just that her hair was of such a delicate texture that she had difficulty keeping it in place. At home, when outsiders were absent, she never tried.

I now saw that she was playing solitaire, and in spite of everything, my heart went out to her. She was always so fond of getting around, and now about all the getting around that she did was to those semipublic balls and parties downtown. What she thought about Reagan and his part in our affairs I didn't know at the time. My guess was that they were sending messages to each other and probably meeting on the quiet. She never mentioned his name to me, however, and I had about decided that on the whole this woman was not really evil, only flimsy and pathetic.

I have always thought that when you have to give somebody bad news, try to be as cheerful about it as you can. So I hopped into the room crying: "Pack the suitcases, momma, the Egyptians are coming!" Perhaps the cry came from Barney's cocktails.

"George! You frightened me so. What on earth are you talking about?" That was the mail-order type of response you often got from Mary.

I went over and looked down at the cards, glistening like Mary's hair under the bridge lamp above them. Pity was in my heart and gratitude for alcohol was in my head.

"Mary," I said, braced, but as tenderly as I could, "I've been getting it from some reliable sources that this town isn't big enough for us two and the other five hundred thousand."

38

"Yes, I've been hearing, too."

"I was afraid you had." At least I was spared recrossing that ugly ground.

"What do you think we ought to do, George?"

"I think we ought to be cleared out of here by spring. I can leave the office in charge of Eckfield, I think, and still retain an interest in it. I suppose we don't have to worry much about the management of the Tower as long as we keep an eye on the figures." This, of course, was thinking and supposing on a very optimistic scale. Absentee partnerships in architectural firms are seldom as sturdy as the Rock of Gibraltar; and the Reagans, father and son, owned as much of the Tower as we did and would surely look out for their stake first. Then I fired my next shot: "I had in mind Pasadena for your place of exile. You liked it so much the time you were there."

"My place?" And here came another Mary, eyebrows and sharp voice both very elevated. "What about you?"

"I'll be in Florida," I said, waiting for the second blast.

It didn't come. I really shouldn't have worried about this part of the arrangements; she didn't want to be anywhere with me once we had left St. Louis, certainly not in Pasadena. She just wondered if I was going to get the better of the bargain, South America or the Orient perhaps.

"What about the children?" she asked, and I thought I heard a little cunning in her voice.

"Why they'll be where they should be. With their mother."

"You're their co-guardian, George Hanes, you know that. Why don't you take them with you?"

Some mother. And *not* flimsy and *not* pathetic.

"I simply can't, that's all."

Then she got keen. "Where is this place in Florida that you're going to?"

"Pensacola," I told her.

"Are there a lot of gay people there? Is that the reason you can't take little Mary and Jeff along with you?"

"There will be a lot of people there pretty soon, I believe, Mary.

I don't know how gay they'll be. It's a Naval aviation training station."

"Oh."

Then I said something which I certainly did not intend to be tricky, but straight from the heart.

"Of course if you don't want to have the children, I know that Margaret Carton and her family would be glad to take them until I get back. You know how fond she has always been of both of them, especially Jeff."

This I believed to be the truth, literally. I had once, some weeks after word of Jeff's death, discussed with Margaret what should be done for the children as the years came on. We were in a mellow mood after the theater, having a nightcap in the Palm Room and sketching, a little whimsically, with the vague delicacy of a fine Japanese print, the picture of our futures. This was before I married Mary, of course. But the complete seriousness of the Mary thing I always brushed aside. It was just a bad nightmare that I had to endure, but like a nightmare, it was not of indefinite duration. It had never been my intention to marry anybody—*really* marry—except Margaret. So the suggestion about her taking care of the children came naturally to mind.

Out roared the tiger-mother, and, I thought, about time. "George Hanes! You must be the stupidest son of a bitch in the world!"

I wondered where she had picked up the epithet. From going around with an Irish contractor, I suppose.

"What," she then asked me, her fury unabated, "would people say about me?"

So ended the evening's first conversation.

Margaret Carton's name represented one of those frequent affiliations between the Irish and French families of the city. She had the skin of the fair Irish and the short nose and nice moon-smile of whatever kind of Irish have those. Her eyes were hazel, the result of the French-Irish cross, I suppose. Her hair, inherited from the Carton side, was coal black and very straight, healthy, coarse, and worn, prematurely for that part of the country at that

40

time, bobbed. Her temperament was her own. Another thing I had decided that afternoon was that we were going to get married not in some vague future but right after I got back and divorced Mary.

It was only a short walk down the hill and across one street from our place to Margaret's; her family lived in the 2100 block on Westminster.

When the door closed behind me and my overcoat was off I said, to start things off on a light note, "You are now practically looking at a sailor boy, a jack-tar you might say." This was calculated to break the ice before diving into the chilly depths of serious business, sound practice according to Paul Eckfield.

"Wait a minute," Margaret said. "Let's go in and sit down before we hear any more of this."

At that time I was not—and, indeed, still am not—a great fan for European case pieces ornamented here and there with decorative metal. But Mrs. Carton's house had some very handsome plain French country fruitwood furniture in it. I am very sure that they had not arrived in St. Louis with the first Cartons. Fur trappers and keelboat men they had been and, by all account, ruffians of the first order. Nevertheless, I had always felt happily at home in the Cartons' house on Westminster Place, and always reasonably pleased to sit with Margaret on the long brocaded pearwood settle to which she now led me.

"Do you wish me to repeat?" I asked.

"You're going to join the Navy? Why that's ridiculous, George. Only tramps and no-goods and runaways join the *Navy*. Are you out of your mind?"

"You don't get me, Margaret. I'm going to Pensacola because they are about to open a flying school there for reserve officers. So when we get in the war we early birds will have an advantage over the rest of them. Bosco O'Fallon, Junie Neidlinger, and several other wiseacres and I have talked it all over. It's the ticket."

"Who says there's going to be a war?"

"Why, Bosco O'Fallon, Junie—"

"Oh, stop it, George," she said wearily.

41

"Well, how about Barney at the Rathskeller?" I asked, trying the light touch again. "You've heard of *him*. Wise as an owl, and he knows it's coming." She gestured hopelessly.

"Okay," I told her. "At any rate I'm going down there. And as so often happens in times like these, I am asking you to wait this thing out so that we can get married when I come back."

She looked at me in horror. "Married! But you're *already* married!"

"I know that and you know why. At least I *thought* you knew why. My part in that show is just about over."

"What did you think I knew, George?"

Come to think of it, how could she, any more than anyone else in town, realize that the whole thing was as queer as a three-dollar bill? Except that Margaret, I had simply taken it for granted, would have understood the situation through her skin since it was I who was mixed up in that palpable mish-mash. And surely she must have noted the odd assemblage of characters at our little wedding ceremony. But apparently she hadn't.

"What did you think I knew?"

The thought that absurdly crossed my mind was that, by God, there can arise in real life—in your *own* life, not just gaslight melodrama—a situation in which the hero's lips are sealed. It's true. Anyhow, in my case it was true.

"I guess we'd better let it go then, Margaret," I said. "I can't tell you. This sounds like something out of a gaslight melodrama, doesn't it, dearest? Not now at any rate."

It occurred to me—and not, as I came to think about it, for the first time—that maybe my jumping in to claim Reagan's baby and save my brother's name had been a gallant gesture that was going to cost me, and continue to cost me, not only more than I could afford but more than I could pay. But what else could I have done? What else could I do now? All of us were still too close together. Enough time had not gone by. At least that's the way I reasoned it there in Margaret's living room that night.

Suddenly great tears filled her eyes. I've never seen anything like it; her eyes would fill, and then without blinking loose their whole quicksilver contents to pour down her cheeks. It was at the same time a terrifying and beautiful sight.

"Go away, George," she said, without the slightest catch of a sob in her voice.

"Can't you even tell me you'll think it over a little, Margaret, until I get back? Mary's going off to Pasadena. You won't even have to see her around. Honestly, this is going to work out, Margaret."

"Please, George, please go away."

A letter from somebody in St. Louis reached me in London in early 1919, just before we were to sail for home. It spoke of a number of mutual friends and how they had done in the war; some news good, some sad. Then it came laughingly to the case of Dan Pierce. It seemed that Dan had gotten no farther from home, by some weird twist of war's dice, than Jefferson Barracks, a reception center at the end of the South Side car line. The letter added that while in service he had married Margaret Carton.

Oh, my brother.

Part II

Part II

Six

WE sang day and night on the transport that brought us home. Returning soldiers must have done so since before Troy. I don't believe that our singing was a hysterical response to our recent release from danger; I think it was induced by a quite different emotion. We had been to a strange place and seen things we had never dreamed of before, and although none of us were overseas long, we all sensed that home was going to be strange now, too. Even if certain reported domestic convulsions such as exorbitant prices, prohibition, and bobbed hair proved, upon closer inspection, to be not too upsetting, the experiences befallen us abroad were such that had home remained as comfortably immutable as a Currier and Ives hearthside engraving, we felt that somehow it would never again look quite the same as when we left it. The least sensitive of us felt this. And so, suspended for a fortnight on an empty sea between two worlds, we raised our loud songs for no better reason than tempts one to shout down a well —to make a noise in a void.

We sang all the songs that anybody could remember; then some scholar in the crowd, one of the engineer officers as I recall, composed a parody on "Good King Charles Is Dead" that became a great favorite, a merry soldier song from another war which few of us knew very much about. The parody was called "Kaiser Bill Is Dead," but the engineer had sensibly retained the old chorus:

> The knavish king is dead, dead, dead,
> We choppèd off his head, head, head,
> And sent him to the Nether Pit.
> We drink, drink, drink a health to it,
> And drink, drink, drink a health to it.

The "drink, drink, drink" refrain especially delighted my friend and fellow townsman Junie Neidlinger, who, in spite of regulations and the penalties laid down for violation thereof, managed pretty consistently to suit the deed to the word. He and I of all the St. Louis bunch who had started out in Naval air were the only two who had managed to stick together. Junie also enjoyed the voyage-long crap game and won a lot of money at it, a great deal more than I did, whenever he could pull himself away from the stud table. In fact, nobody on the boat had a happier time than Junie, confirming once again a conviction I had arrived at as early as ground school that Junie was the kind of man for whose enjoyment war was invented—all phases of it.

Junie, like his older brothers, had gone to Yale, but in the Midwest while the Ivy is rarer the various species of it tend to clump together more closely. Hence, though from the other shop, I saw a good deal of him in the few years before the war; it will be remembered, certainly by me, that Junie was instrumental in cooling off the press when I was put in the stoney lonesome.

All Junie's brothers went into their father's bank, the Teutonia, the one that set up the financing of the Tower. Junie, heartily declaring that if he wished to live in a cage he would apply to the Forest Park Zoo where the air was fresher and the food was free, accepted a connection with the Anheuser-Busch Brewing Company, another South Side concern. As a district salesman he was given the care of about twenty saloons not much more than a spatula's toss from headquarters. The job had almost miraculously found the man. These bars were all owned in part by the brewery so that it would have been unthinkable for the proprietors to pur-

48

chase any other than the Busch product and, industrious men that they were, they worked prodigiously to sell every schooner of it that they could. Where, I at first asked myself, was the need for Junie's services? The answer was that Junie's was a spiritual contribution. Everybody, customer and management alike, was always happier to have Junie around. He might quite as well have left his order book at home, for the accounting department at Busch knew to the quarter barrel what Ernst Mueller or Konrad Epp or Fred Schwartzkopf needed in the way of beers and lagers on any given week in the year. But the soulless accounting department could not be expected to know how to cheer up Ernst, or Konrad, or Fred when, as it must even to the thriftiest and most acute, unforeseen annoyances came to beset them. A grin and a joke from Junie more often than not did much to lessen the distress caused by a patrolman's abusing his prerogatives, a wife's extravagance, a nephew's ingratitude, or feet that hurt. The riddle of who listens to the publican's sorrows was answered with the presence of Junie.

This function of bringing mirth to the aid of the afflicted, however, figured only secondarily in Junie's bonhomous operations. Like Edison, he had the great man's genius for wholly identifying himself with his work. For example, making himself felt at home among his customers and his customers' customers, he would throw into the conversation frequent snatches of German, or what he believed to be German. When he had made use of *jawohl, Katzenjammer, guter Freund, nicht wahr, wie geht's, das ist alles, Prosit,* and perhaps half a dozen other simple phrases, Junie had exhausted his grip on the language. But when humorously interpolated by Junie, they created a very happy effect. There are few atmospheres jollier than that surrounding a good-humored man clumsily attempting a foreign tongue in the presence of those who speak it but like to hear him try. In addition, Junie, as distinguished from my later associate Eckfield, actually did many little favors for people. There was nothing, for example, the purchase of which he was unable to negotiate at a friendly price. And to crown it all, his big, strong, dark German good looks made him a sort of walk-

49

ing avatar of beer drinking. Junie was a great success in the profession of his choice.

You may consider that such attainments in civil life do not prepare a man for waging war, but in Junie's case you are wrong. We were scarcely on station a week on the English Channel before Junie had stocked our mess with more liquor than G.H.Q. owned and was lending out more money than the chaplain. A man of many appetites, he was never bored. To relieve the tedium of our sluggish flying, Junie one afternoon took his sixty-mile-an-hour hydro-aeroplane aloft and, against all the laws of aerodynamics and the intentions of the designers, managed to loop it. The rest of us of course tried to follow suit, with the result that after several smashes peremptory orders came down forbidding the practice on pain of court-martial. About a week later Junie and I were returning to our station at Harwich from a patrol. Below us lay the wide pearl and baby-blue waters of the Goodwin Sands across whose notorious shallows a rowboat could scarcely navigate, let alone a Hun submarine. Nevertheless, Junie gave me a cheery wave and nosed over into a dive. No wireless signal to me or anything. Before I could decide what to do, he straightened out and, kicking the poor old kite into a zoom somehow goaded it not only straight upward but over onto its fluttering back and then into another dive, thus completing the loop. My earphones started to hiss from Junie's signal tapped out on his transmitter: *The incident is now closed. Farragut.*

About the third time that Junie caught me alone in the mess reading a book he decided that I was helpless to make the best of our circumstances. Or maybe he had some Oriental sense of the obligation that one man owes another for the rest of his life after the first man has saved the second from peril (to wit, in Junie's and my case, his quashing a potential newspaper scandal involving me). At any rate he rather obviously went out of his way to look after me, which was unnecessary since I was as big as he and had plenty of resources, so I believed, of my own. After all, I was the head of a successful business back home. What really annoyed me a little was his referring to me as "the professor" after surprising

50

me in the arms of literature. (The book, as I recall it, was *Mont-Saint-Michel and Chartres*, practically a trade text in my business and one which I must have reread at least twice before 1918.) But for the place and period, Junie was almost the perfect companion. He was a good man to go to a war with. However, I would not have discoursed on Junie's life and times at this length were it not that those short months overseas only began a friendship that was a long time ending, and then by no will of either of us.

When we sailed for the States none of us were told what our debarkation point was to be. The home ports were so crowded with returning ships that even the Navy had not made up its mind about us. Judging from the gaiety aboard our vessel you might have supposed that everybody was going to be bitterly disappointed if they were landed any place except Hoboken, hard by the flesh-pots of New York. But most of the boys had by now visited flesh-pots *de grande luxe*; indifference as to our objective equaled our complacency about when we would reach it. Who cared? There was no great hurry. The void was agreeable enough. Since there would be no one impatient to welcome me no matter where I was put ashore, the outcome was no deep concern of mine. Junie said that for his part they could let him off anywhere so long as the natives were friendly.

Where they let us off was Newport News, hard by Norfolk, the Venice of America according to its present boosters. There had been hundreds of us on the transport; there were thousands in the town. But by means of a fantastic number of printed directives issued to all hands, plus a phalanx of signs and notices posted everywhere and explicit enough to lead a blind man to his proper destination, the Navy with a sort of demented efficiency had us all sorted out in a surprisingly brief time. However, certain unexpected novelties did develop.

The transport officer to whom Junie and I reported had gray hair, which didn't seem to go with only the stripe and a half on his sleeve. He presented us each with a Manila envelope labeled "Official Business U.S. Navy" and bulging with more printed

51

matter, our transportation orders, tickets, and so forth. I expect we viewed these burdens in some dismay.

"I wouldn't bother to broach that gear," the officer advised us kindly. "I'll give you the dope by voice signal." We had never heard a man talk so embarrassingly salty in our short Naval careers.

"Now," he began briskly. "Six forty-five P.M. today the sixteenth Danville and Southern coach train to Danville, Virginia. Change at Danville to coaches Southern train forty-one leaving Danville twelve oh four A.M. Eastern time the seventeenth." The salt in his speech had entirely dissolved; here was a man rattling along happily in a language used in a trade that he really knew something about. "Arrive Atlanta, Georgia, eight-twenty P.M. Central Time. Change to Southern coach train nineteen leaving one A.M. the eighteenth arriving Mobile, Alabama, six-thirty A.M."

It seemed to me that we were going to see a lot of the urban South sitting up in the dead of night, but Junie put forward the more important consideration.

"Excuse me, sir," he interrupted, "we're trying to get to St. Louis."

"No, you aren't. You're trying to get to Pensacola. That's where you enlisted, isn't it?"

"Yes, sir."

"Well, that's where the God-damned Navy has to muster you out. Don't ask me why, boys. I've just been a railroad man here in Norfolk all my life." He had a short civilian laugh at the Navy's expense. "That seafaring talk of mine didn't fool you, did it?"

This speech, despite its baleful information, relaxed us to the extent that Junie asked the man where we could get a drink.

"Only hotels and clubs in Virginia."

"What's the best hotel in town?" asked Ensign Neidlinger, now leaning familiarly on the railroading lieutenant's desk.

"None of them's worth a damn, I'd say. You might try the Chamberlain over at Old Point Comfort. Take the ferry from Willoughby Spit."

"Sounds like a long trip for a drink," Junie said.

"Worth it though. Pretty girls, swimming pool, orchestra. You

52

boys ought to make quite a hit. We don't see that kind of uniform around here much." No, the lieutenant was definitely not the kind of officer that we had been accustomed to.

"You don't, eh?" said Junie, a soft purr of calculation entering his voice. "Well, well. Can you tell us how to get to the Navy barge stage?"

The lieutenant spread the palms of his hands in a gesture of the most cheerful ignorance. "Son, I haven't the slightest idea," he confessed.

But a shore-patrol man outside the office gave us directions as well as a curious inspection of our clothes. We wore slate blue in Naval air as everybody in the Navy can now, but it was rare then.

"This is going to be easy," Junie said to me as we walked away from the pier. He patted his fat official envelope. "This stuff has got to get to Admiral Sims over at the Chamberlain real fast."

"The Admiral's in Paris at the peace conference, Junie."

"Good. Then we won't run into him."

It worked. Our brisk manner, our Manila envelopes full of day-coach tickets, and our unfamiliar uniforms not only got us a swift ride across the harbor in a Navy launch but got us one back. The railroad man had not misled us. The Chamberlain did indeed have a swimming pool. It was right off the lobby, made of mosaic, surrounded by tropical plants, and was surmounted by a lofty glass roof that let the fine Virginia sunlight fall upon a bustle of handsome officers, lovely young women, and attentive colored waiters. "Very friendly natives indeed," was Junie's comment on the latter.

I wish that everyone could have had as splendid a homecoming as Junie and I enjoyed, and when some years ago I read that the old Chamberlain had burned to the ground a sudden melancholy and nostalgia pained me more than I would have expected. I hadn't remembered that afternoon for a long time.

The slow train ride to the Gulf was bearable enough once you had made up your mind not to fight the dust and cinders that blew in through the window screens as briskly and reliably as our wheels rolled. It was better to stand in the middle of the open vestibule where you had a more open view of the lovely, shabby countryside as well as some protection from the flying debris.

The redbuds were glowing in the swamps beside the tracks and tender grasses shone in the fields, shaming, I thought, with their innocence the rusty wire fences that held them in. Huge piles of bridal wreath stood on the littered station grounds; farther away we could see crocus and hyacinth and small tulips thrusting their way up from the winter mud of their door yards. In the distance under the still sky even the sober little cedars and ragged old pines looked as though they had preened themselves a bit for the new season. It has always seemed to me that there is nothing quite like the soft warm dream of a homely Southern spring.

When we reached Pensacola the tropical sun had burned all color from the heavens. Whites were worn on the station and the people and the place were already tensed for the flaming assault of the summer.

It was hot enough for Junie and me right then, wearing the last of our sooty, sweat-stained winter-weight uniforms. There was no need for whites where we came from, and we certainly didn't intend to buy any this late in the game. On the other hand, after getting a whiff of the earlier arrivals hanging around the hotel lobby, we also decided against sending our clothes out to the local cleaner, who must have washed everything in straight benzine.

"No Gasoline Gus business for me," announced Junie. So we sent our lockers up to the room and a colored bellhop directed us to his favorite haberdashery. There we each bought a black alpaca suit to harmonize with our regulation black socks and shoes, a Panama hat, some white shirts, and the loudest neckties in the store, this as a gesture of civil revolt against the choke-collars of our uniforms that had sawed our necks for days. The regalia wrapped and paid for, we carried it back to our room and began to get ready to present ourselves to the authorities who would release us from the service of our country.

A good many years after the Great World War a lot of people began shaking their heads disapprovingly at the thoughtless haste in which everybody concerned had jettisoned the nation's forces and armament in 1919. Didn't even a few of us foresee that these might be needed again? Didn't anyone at all pause for a sober moment to consider the threatening disorder of the world if not the lessons that history taught us about the timelessness of human conflict? The answer is no. And it was not because we were hypnotized by the happy babble of the public soothsayers of the day. Nobody was influenced by the doctrine that we had successfully concluded the War to End Wars; nobody that I knew of even listened to it. Nor was there any evidence of mass catharsis, a general feeling of having got a dirty job over with and the hell with it. Not at all. Millions of people had been thinking and working and fighting at war, and then suddenly there was no war. That was all. No past war, no present war, and no future war. The movie of the erupting volcano ran to the end of its reel, whereupon the house lights went up and the audience, not so much as blinking, arose and left the theater empty.

At the actual spot where the war officially and everlastingly ceased, the demobilization centers, the atmosphere was also theatrical but the scene was more like a production by harried amateurs. The show was over: congratulations from relatives were impatiently received and then began the rush to push and pile the sets and properties and temporary chairs into any old corner as quickly as possible so as to leave the hall in some kind of shape for the next lodge meeting but not be the last one left to close the door.

After World War II, again it was deplored that we hadn't kept our military might in being instead of scattering it away like a hurried camper's fire ashes. But there was a difference; this time a "point system" was involved in determining who got out first, attempts were made to persuade the boys to join various reserve programs, and so on. The war that Junie and I went to was very easy to get out of once it was wound up. Nobody wanted to detain you because that would detain him.

I had my own stuff gathered together in about three minutes, nothing more than a small collection of papers and the Colt automatic they issued us in England, only to find Junie still burrowing and snorting around in his locker. When I asked him what he was looking for he said he couldn't locate his gun.

"Where do you think you left it?"

"How should I know?" He gave up his churning among the soiled clothes and got to his feet irritably. "*I* don't want the damned thing, I'll never have one in my hand again. Why the hell should *they* want it?"

So we went over to the quartermaster's office to begin the brief separation proceedings and everything went well until we found out that they did very much want Junie's gun back. He didn't even have the serial number written down anywhere. When it developed that it was going to take quite a while just to arrange for Junie to pay for the missing gun, we agreed that I should go on through with my processing and wait for him at the hotel. There I ran into our friend the bellhop again.

"You gennelmun buy the civvies?" he asked, and I told him we had.

"Being as you has civvies, wouldn't you like to go somewheres get yoselfs a drink?" He gave me a precautionary smile that included just us two. "Don't sell nobody in uniform."

In the short time that we were in school at Pensacola they had worked us so hard that uniformed or not, at the end of the day none of us had enough strength left to lift a bottle of beer, let alone go find one. I asked the colored man if he knew where liquor was being sold and he said he did.

"Bout fo mile down the Mobile road. Nice little place. Nobody bother you."

"How do we get there?"

"Man got a car, he take you. I shows you to him when you ready."

So when Junie came back we were shown the man with the car. It was a Hudson Super-Six, I remember, a very fast and rakish vehicle at the time. Sitting in the back seat in our Panamas and somber suits illuminated by the colorful new neckwear we looked like a couple of Baptist ministers on the loose. The driver was colored, silent, and addicted to speed on the macadam. He was careful, however, when we turned off into two ruts in the sand that ran among some pines and brought us after about half a mile to a clearing where the sand was packed white and hard in front of an unpainted shack. I suppose it had been used before by the turpentine people; the trees all around were chevroned to collect resin. The driver told us that he would be coming out from town with other customers during the afternoon so we could go back almost any time we wanted to. We walked up some steps, crossed a small trembling porch, and entered the shack's one almost bare room where we met our host.

He was leaning over a trestle of planks supported at each end by a sawhorse, a downcast, bony man wearing a gray cotton shirt and trousers that were falling off him. All he needed to make him look like the next client for an electrocution was a slit up his pant leg. His stock seemed to consist exclusively of a galvanized iron bucket of water on the improvised bar and some bottles lying in an old open suitcase on the floor beneath it. This kind of establishment, a venerable if transient institution in the long-dry Southern states, was called a "blind tiger"—why, I don't know.

"Howdy, boys," the man said, without moving his position, "what can I do for you?"

"What have you got, *mein Herr?*" Junie asked, reverting without effort to the sunny manner and lingo of his prewar occupation.

"Whisky, beer."

"Two whisky," said Junie.

"One whisky, one beer," I said.

"Beer?" said Junie, then, "Very well, *ein gutes Glas Bier für meinen Freund.*"

The man produced two former jelly jars and soon we were seated on the porch, our feet comfortably on the railing, drinks in hand. Junie's looked about the color of prune juice. Mine tasted like a solution of bicarbonate of soda and required skillful pouring from the bottle to avoid disturbing the deposit of yeast on the bottom of the bottle. Florida was years ahead of most of the rest of the country in the manufacture of home brew.

"*Prosit*," said Junie.

"*Prosit* indeed," I said.

"What could be nicer than this?"

"Not a thing."

"Nice to get out of that uniform. I mean, to slip into something loose."

Of course we had never worn the old hard collars very often; most of the time our clothing was as unrestricting as you could want, sweaters and coveralls mostly. But I agreed. Presently we heard a car coming and Junie went inside to replenish our glasses "before the rush."

The rush numbered only one man besides our chauffeur. The former went inside, returning with a parcel wrapped in newspaper under his arm and a glass of beer and a salt shaker in either hand. After sprinkling salt in the beer, he drank it off, finishing with a puff and the appreciative remark that it hit the spot on a hot day. When he and the driver and the Hudson had departed, Junie served us another round. I tried the salt cure, which seemed to help.

The sun sank lower in the pines, the car came and went with various customers, the glasses were filled and emptied. The car appeared again with another single customer.

"The animals came in two by two," said Junie.

"What do you mean?"

"We got two this time."

The single man passed us on his way into the shack.

"Just one, Junie."

"Two, I'll show you."

He rose from the chair and fell to his knees. When he tried to get up on one knee he fell over on his side like a log. I remember the humorous expression on his face as he looked up at me. "Funny, *nicht wahr?*" It wasn't funny to me. He couldn't even make his arm push him over on his back.

Junie's fall had shaken the whole house and, in fact, almost instantly emptied it. Our host came out, took one look at Junie, ducked inside, closed the suitcase, and made off with it through

58

the rear window. The customer started running, too. I caught him getting into the car and was going to hold him when the colored man came up. I hadn't noticed his face before, but I did now and was startled to see that it expressed nothing but calm and benignity.

"I come back soon as I can," he said.

"How do I know?"

"I come back all right."

There wasn't anything that I could do with the two of them and Junie laid out on the porch except to trust the driver. So the car went away and I went back to Junie, who now couldn't recognize me. The only thing I knew to do was to get that stuff out of his stomach. Between us we did so by means of his gulping a lot of salted tepid water from the bucket. I put a wet rag over his eyes, as much to keep him from noticing his blindness as anything else. And the colored man did come back.

As we were loading Junie into the car I told the driver to get us as close to the hotel as he could.

"We takes him up to the room," he said.

"That's going to get you in trouble."

"No, it ain't. We takes him to his room."

And we did, through the kitchen entrance and up the service elevator. Junie's speech had now thickened, but he had not lost his sense of amusement at his helpless condition. He chuckled a good deal when the doctor came and flexed his rubbery legs and arms. Then the doctor applied a stomach pump and put a hot compress over Junie's eyes, approximately the treatment I had administered. A lot of people were going to need this therapy for methyl-alcohol paralysis in the next fourteen years and in hundreds of cases they would nevertheless die. But not this tough Dutchman.

A couple of days later we boarded another train, this time at our expense and this time in a stateroom. I found Junie, a sadder and wiser man, in a reflective mood.

"You saved my life, George," he said. "I'll never forget it."

"Can it, Junie. You've gone over that enough."

59

"You saved my life," he repeated slowly. "And I'll never forget it."

I told him again that that was a lot of bull.

He stared out the window for a while and I supposed that he was continuing to brood upon his recent experience when he said, "I don't like this Prohibition thing, George, not a bit of it."

"Under the circumstances I wouldn't think you would, Junie," I replied, hoping to strike a light note.

"No, that's not what I mean. I mean it's not going to work. You can't stop people from drinking what they like any more than you can stop them from eating what they like. It stands to reason."

"It's going to put a lot of people out of work," I hazarded.

"It's already put me out of work," Junie said.

"Oh, I wouldn't say that, Junie. The amendment's almost a year away. Plenty of lawyers are out getting injunctions and so forth. Haven't you been reading the papers?"

He replied with some bitterness that Busch and all the rest of them would be closed down in about six weeks by the wartime regulations against making beer and liquor. Well, that was true, but I had never up to that time given much thought to liquor as a business, or in any other way for that matter. There had been very little time for me to do much drinking even if I had wanted to. Jeff would have considered spending an hour over the glasses about as unreal as devoting it to tatting. From sickness of spirit or self-disappointment or whatever causes it, a good many architects like a good many other artists sometimes drink too much, and Jeff sympathized with their affliction, quoting George Bernard Shaw's remark in this connection that when a patient was undergoing a painful operation it was only natural that he should want some anesthetic. But that was about the extent of his preoccupation with the liquor question, and as I say, I had simply by-passed the idea of liquor as an industry. When Junie asked me how many people and their dependents looked to their living from beer and whisky in St. Louis, I didn't even try to guess.

"About seventy-five thousand," he said, "counting bartenders, truck drivers, and all the rest. You're right. There's going to be a lot of people out of work and real soon, no matter what the lawyers manage to figure out."

Junie the alcohol economist was a new character to me. "Well, anyhow," I said, "you won't be looking for a job, old boy. Your family has plenty of work to let out."

"You know," Junie went on, as though he hadn't heard me, "you ought to be worrying yourself."

"Me?"

"What's going to happen to all those bars and restaurants in the Tower when they can't serve booze?"

"I don't get you. People still have the freedom to eat," I said. But Junie overlooked this reply, too.

"I've been thinking," he said. "That old scarecrow back at Pensacola who poisoned us was on the right track." I didn't interrupt to protest my inclusion as a victim. "Yep, it's the coming business, George." He slapped his knee decisively, the old aggressive Junie suddenly discarding the pall of invalidism.

Now I could see what had been going on in that enterprising mind of his, but I still tried to keep the tone light. "You mean poisoning people?"

"No, no, no. Selling them liquor. Good liquor of course," he added, "so there won't be any trouble. *Nicht wahr?*"

Then he began chattering along thirteen to the dozen about all the bars he knew and all the people who ran them and, if the bars were really closed, all the former customers he knew whose tongues would be hanging out, and so on and so on. And all the time the train was hurrying him closer to home. You could see the season dying a little each hour as we went north.

No one was waiting for me in that great smoking cave of a station at the end of the journey, but Junie's father grabbed him and hugged him with a loud happy sigh as soon as he got down the Pullman steps. I had always seen old Mr. Neidlinger as the typical German patriarch, a square-faced man with just enough of a second chin to indicate solid reliability, a bristle of cropped gray hair on his head, and wearing a salt-and-pepper suit with gold fobs surrounding his convex vest and high, well-burnished black kid

61

shoes. He would lend you a quarter, I expected, if you put up a five-dollar bill as security. I certainly hadn't imagined him going all to pieces, you might say, over a returning younger son. He was very happy, bubbling over. He even beamed at me. "Well, well, Hanes," he said, "so you and Junior came home safe and sound."

Seven

I know that rooms from which you have been away for a while frequently look different, often smaller, upon your return, possibly because while the seeing eye has traveled over new scenes the mind's eye has distorted the image of the familiar place. But neither my eyes nor my visual memory have ever surprised me after an absence from the Tower, any part of it, and especially the lobby of the hotel. I believe that this fidelity of visual imagery was a quantity found in all of Jeff's work, because he was apparently incapable of designing any interior or exterior that might deceive the beholder's first sight of it. His proportions were just and true, impervious and permanent.

What is it that endows a few artists with this ability to achieve perfect balance in space? An inch or so added to or subtracted from a single dimension of that lovely cube that is the dining room at Monticello would destroy its timeless poise. Standing any place within it one has a sensation of pleasure and repose, and not the professional observer alone. I am sure that almost anyone must experience this quiet exaltation which may express itself only in the consciousness of having a "good feeling" about the room. And I am equally convinced that the attainment of the effect, no matter what size the space or for what purpose its use, is architecture at sublimity. No handbook reveals the blessed secret of symmetry to the architect; no more could the mysterious spatial relationships of a lovely girl's face be created by the mere application of a sculptor's calipers.

A good feeling—that is what has always come to me passing through the Tower's triple-arched hotel entrance. The lobby is not large; the average depth of the hotel section is no more than forty-five feet. But it is a room that holds out an unforgettably generous welcome. Jeff had supported the ceiling with a row of piers, divided it into panels by deep beams, and decorated it with stenciled geometric designs. The frieze at the top of the wall was of gilded plaster relief, heavy and luxuriant motifs of intricate foliage, as was the related decoration of the archivolts and soffits of the arches leading to other quarters of the parterre. Around the russet floor of marble mosaic arose a six-foot dado of tawny Sardinian onyx. The room was designed perfectly to surround you in a warm golden embrace.

The city might no longer be home to me; but the Tower, which I had seen rise literally from the mud, was a familiar and agreeable sanctuary for the present.

A clerk I did not recall having met before but who seemed to know me was in charge of the reception desk. His thin face was expressive, his manner one of controlled friendliness, a neat mustache compensated for his scarcity of hair, and when he spoke I heard that he was English. An ideal desk man.

We chatted a little while he assigned me a room—one of the less luxurious, as befitted an owner—and since it was almost lunchtime I asked him jocularly if you could still get a drink around there. He did not bend his head, but his eyes fell to the ledger. It was exactly as though he were attending a funeral ceremony. In a low still voice he said, "You had better get one while you can, Mr. Hanes."

Considering this solemn little scene, I made my way to the Rathskeller in search of Barney. The Tower's barroom, too, looked precisely as it always had: spacious and at the same time intimate, low ceiling, wide expanse of rose tiles, oaken settles with light tan calfskin upholstery, the decorative forms in carved woods and molded plaster tacitly opulent, the lighting soft and directive so as to form glowing islands in the soft surrounding dusk. And, clad in snowy duck, Barney stood doing business at the same old stand. He set down a claret goblet which he was trying to polish into crystal and extended his hand.

"I hope I'm the first to see you back," he said.

"You are. What's the good word?"

"The first of July will be the last of August. That's all they talk about around here. You get it?"

"No I don't, Barney."

"The national act goes in June thirty, everything closes down. Same with Busch, August Busch. What are you going to have, Captain Hanes?"

"Manhattan, please, Barney. I was an ensign, by the way. If I'd been any lower in the Navy they would have had to revive the rank of cornet."

He didn't get that, but refrained from questioning me. Having both stumped each other, I bought him a cigar and he served me the cocktail, the first of its kind to come to my hand, I suddenly remembered, since the evening I had gone to see Margaret.

"Yes," he resumed, "the so-and-sos finally put it over. The short-haired women and the long-haired men, while the boys were overseas." His face showed a smoldering ferocity and I realized that I had seen Barney vehement but never in hot temper before. "While *you* were overseas." That seemed to outrage him even more. "God damn them," he said slowly and deliberately, as though he had chosen that combination of words for the first time. He looked around him as a man might look with awe through the grille of a tomb, as if he could already see the room and the chairs stacked forever on the tables in the locked dark.

"Maybe it won't last long, Barney. The amendment doesn't go in until January."

"How can that make any difference?" He pointed to my glass. "You never needed the stuff, but I don't know what's going to happen to some of these fellows."

I thought of Junie and his proposed rescue mission. And I was also wondering what had been done about a new job for Barney in the hotel, planning to look into it myself, when there was a sound behind me of some people coming in.

"Here's your bunch," Barney said.

I turned around to see Junie and Bosco O'Fallon and a couple of other fellows I knew. Little Dan Pierce led the expedition. There followed a good deal of reunion back-thumping and hand-shaking after which we sat down around one of the corner tables.

"Here's to the last man in!" cried Dan. "I thought I was never going to see you." If I felt that this was an ill-chosen line of conversation, what followed really discomforted me.

"*You* knew Margaret Carton, didn't you? Of course."

"Of course," I said.

"Didn't you use to take her out once in a while?"

"That's right."

"Well, boy, we're married!"

"Got him tied down hand and foot," Bosco told everybody with a laugh. "It's good-by Dan."

"Well!" said Junie. "Congratulations, Dan. How about that, George?" Overseas I hadn't seen any reason to go into that bit of news from St. Louis with him.

It was for a moment as though they were all talking about somebody else, not Margaret; it was as if I had hardly known Margaret at all. Well, ours hadn't been a public "match," that was true.

"Listen," Dan said, "you're coming out and have dinner with us tonight. Here, waiter. Bring me a phone, will you?"

"Not tonight, Dan. You'd better arrange it with Margaret first."

"But I am, you chump." He now had the telephone in hand. "You've got no place—I mean you haven't got anything better to do. She'll be dying to see you."

I could imagine.

But there again I was wrong. Dan announced my return to her, told her to expect me for dinner, and then turned the telephone over to me.

66

"Hell-*oh!*" shouted Margaret. "George, how wonderful!" I couldn't believe my ears. All the people at the table except Junie seemed to have their behavior pitched to a somewhat higher key than I remembered, but Margaret sounded as though she were at a New Year's Eve party. A new and different Margaret.

I told her it was good of them to ask me to dinner and she cried out that I was to be there by six so that we three could have a lot of time together before the other guests arrived.

"Boy," Dan said when I had rung off, "doesn't it feel great being home at last?"

After lunch I called Paul Eckfield, walked around to the office entrance of the Tower, and went up to our place. He seemed a little on the nervous side, too.

"Why in the world didn't you write you were coming?" he asked.

"I wrote."

"I mean write me what day you were getting home." They all kept calling St. Louis my home, forgetfully of course. "Or wire or phone?" he went on. "I could have done something." Then he followed me into my office and I saw what he *had* done, or rather what he had not had time to undo, and his agitation was explained. Under the wide mullioned window that gave on the loggia two draftsmen's tables stood, deserted only since my call from the hotel I guessed. I sat down at my own desk, locked and cleared as I had left it.

"I wasn't sure until yesterday when I actually would get back," I said. And looking over the layout I couldn't help adding, "Did it give you a little surprise, Paul?"

"I'll get this stuff out of here right away, Georgie," he said, settling himself. "We had some rush work to do and I had to call in a couple of extra hands. No place else for them at the time." He got away with it quite coolly, I thought, considering that it was the first overt move toward pushing me out of the nest.

"Never mind, Paul. I'm only going to be in town a few days. How's business?"

He made a hopeless little gesture, the customary beam dimming a bit on that moon face. "Not good, Georgie. Not good at all."

"What's the matter? I heard that all the returning soldier boys were going to get homes fit for heroes to live in. Aren't a lot of apartments going up?"

"Well, yes, Georgie. But it's not easy business to get. These contractors pull their plans out of a book, or let their carpenters draw them, their sister-in-laws, anybody. They're building the stuff out of orange crates and chicken wire and they're coining money, but there's not much in it for an architect."

"Have you tried to get the business?"

"*You* ought to try, Georgie."

Well, I had that one coming to me.

"Maybe you can scare up some work for us when you go back East," he suggested. The deal we had made when I left was that I would open an office in New York or nearby at my expense, and that between what I could do there and consulting on design with the St. Louis office I would continue my partnership in the firm. In 1917, I had drawn around twenty-five thousand dollars from Hanes & Eckfield, and somewhat less the following year.

"I think I'll look around the old jute mill," I said.

"Of course, Georgie, of course. Whatever you wish." By God, he was inviting me to inspect my own place of business as though I were a visitor.

Every company that I have ever known anything about has had a Mrs. Adams. She is the one indispensable hand; when her employers say they couldn't get along without her they are very nearly telling the truth. She has been there forever and if the building burned down and every file incinerated, it would be no irreparable loss; Mrs. Adams knows about everything that has ever gone on, everything. She also has a frighteningly keen sense of what *will* go on. Our Mrs. Adams was Sylvia Freeman Adams. She had joined Jeff as his secretary long ago in Chicago, followed him to Kansas City and then to St. Louis. Mr. Adams had trailed along, too, but none of us would have known about it except that it was reported that he showed up regularly once a year at the annual office Christmas party. You couldn't prove it by me.

By the time that I inherited Mrs. Adams she was worn down pretty thin as far as looks go, and I suspect that she was one of the few of her sex about whom nobody had ever lamented that she was attractive as a young woman. She certainly knew her business, however; that is, our business. She betrayed all the emotion of a concrete slab, but I think she was glad to see me back.

"Anything you want while you're here, Georgie," Eckfield said, "Mrs. Adams will be glad to take care of."

That was another piece of impudence; I had let Eckfield share Mrs. Adams' help simply to make it easier for him when he joined us. But I figured that pleasantry was the best way at the time to pass off his assumed proprietorship of the office handmaiden.

"What do you mean?" I cried in mock surprise. "Mrs. Adams is coming East with me, aren't you, Mrs. Adams?"

"I'm too old to travel any more, Mr. Hanes," she said.

"Oh, come on, Mrs. Adams! You're joking!"

"No," she said, "I think I'd better stay here, Mr. Hanes." And she was *not* joking.

If I had been Eckfield, I think I would have heard the nuance in the tone of her reply, and I would not have liked it.

Walking through the drafting rooms I had another unpleasant surprise: not more than three or four of the men were familiar to me. I wondered which two of the newer ones had been using my room and why, if times were so hard, they were needed in the first place.

Going down in the elevator to the Reagan office I promised myself a talk with Mrs. Adams.

You have seen those father-and-sons group chromos that used to hang, usually in oval rosewood frames, in the parlors of lower middle-class American homes in the days when families were large and such symbols of tribal security were cherished. The father's head and collar, upper right, was repeated in an oblique and ever younger version of same until the viewer's eye rested upon his last important genetic accomplishment, lower left. Few houses on the North Side of St. Louis, where the Irish dwelt, could have been without such a fecund display.

They breed very true, I remember often thinking, whenever I saw the Reagans—father and son—together. Both were full-fleshed men with clublike noses. These were fixed in the middle of faces capable of such rapid muscular flection that one might speculate as to which occurred first, the expression or the corresponding emotion. Neither Reagan had changed very much of course while I was away, either in appearance or attitude toward me. Like so many of the races late to arrive in America and not too heartily welcomed at the time, the Irish often find it hard to accept easily those whose people got here first. The Reagans scarcely tried to conceal their reservations about me.

"And how did you enjoy the fighting?" old Mr. Reagan asked me.

"I didn't do very much of it, Mr. Reagan."

He began to roll himself irritably around in his chair like an old dog too long with fleas. "None of you did. You should have wiped every last murdering one of them off the face of the world!"

I looked at Ed, each strand of his thin black hair combed straight back from his high bare forehead, the top lighting from the window revealing the pink gloss of his scalp beneath. He gave no sign of surprise at the old man's surly violence.

"They didn't come off too well," I said.

"Barbarians! Every baby-killing son of them! Don't you agree? You saw them!"

"As a matter of fact, Mr. Reagan, I never saw any."

"Never saw any? What are you telling me? You lived among the vermin for more than a year!"

Mr. Reagan, I now understood, had been speaking of the English.

"The Germans, the square-heads—ach!" He flapped a gesture of dismissal. "The Germans were *made* to be killed."

"I see," was all I found to say to that. "Well, how have things been around here?"

70

"They've *been* all right," Ed said. "But they *won't* be."

"Of that you may be sure," his father agreed, swerving his great club nose toward Ed. "Hanes is inquiring about the Tower, I take it."

"That's right," I said.

"Apartment houses, now there's a good business," said the elder Reagan, at the same time that a cherub's smile erased the anger from his mobile countenance. "A *nice* business."

"But not the hotel business," Ed amended, sliding me a file of last year's Tower figures across his desk.

Those I knew. There is nothing complicated about calculating a hotel's basic revenue. On food service you expect to break even, so you simply multiply the average daily rental of a room by the number of rooms you have, then again by the days in the year, then again by your current percentage of occupancy. In the case of the Tower it went: 200 x $9 x 365 x 90% = $591,300. The Tower's office space was fully rented on long-term leases and grossed eighty-seven thousand dollars a year. Theater rentals are subject to the ups and downs of show business, but in our worst season we took in six hundred dollars a week for thirty-nine weeks. Thus the Tower's gross income from rentals just exceeded seven hundred thousand dollars. I am certainly not going to bore you with a balance sheet of expenditures, depreciation and interest charges, and so on. Just take my word for it that we operated at a thirty per cent margin of profit on renting space for various purposes. In other words, on the Tower's three-million investment, we were netting from these sources an income of a little more than seven per cent on the money.

But a seven per cent income on first-grade hotel and office operations was not considered good business in those days. Neither the Reagans nor the Teutonia Bank, which held a million and a quarter's worth of the bonds out of a million and a half, so considered it. The happy difference between a lowly seven per cent and a much more acceptable eleven was accounted for by the fact that in three dining rooms, a banquet hall, a ladies' lounge, and a bar the Tower had sold liquor, a hundred thousand dollars' worth of it each year, and at that time selling liquor in a hotel was as close to pure velvet as you could get in a financial transaction without actually stealing.

Ed Reagan leaned across his desk toward me, turned back the Tower statement to the categories under Consolidated Net Income, and pointed a squared-off index finger to the liquor figure. The finger then wagged slowly.

"Not *this* year," Ed said.

"Nor forever after," his father agreed. "Didn't you hear in New York?" he asked me.

"Hear what, Mr. Reagan? I didn't come through New York."

"The Holland House is closing down lock, stock, and barrel the first of the year. Lock, stock, and barrel they are." Anger took over his face again.

"Well, cheer up," I told them. I got ready to leave, having heard enough of this undertaker's talk for the time being. "The Tower is not going to close. Not because some oversized barroom in New York is going out of business."

Neither of them spoke for a while, turning solemn and identical profiles toward a picture of our building on the wall. Although it was only a small familial chromo that they made, it showed that the Reagans had indeed bred true: mean and scared.

A few minutes later I left the pair to their rueful reflections over money and was once more on my way to the ground floor bearing another parcel of food for thought in my own mind.

Naturally I had anticipated that our income from the Tower would for a time at least be reduced by as much as a third. But I was young then and more resilient. I couldn't see any threat of permanent damage to the Tower from Prohibition. We were far from wiped out. For one thing, nobody had even suggested that there might be ways of making money by converting to some other purpose the space no longer used for selling liquor. And I had to smile when I thought of Junie trying to pick up our lost profits.

The honeymoon nest of Dan and Margaret was located just over the county line beyond Forest Park and across from Washington

72

University. The section along Forsyth Boulevard, which faced the University, had sprung up with rather impressive houses in the Georgian and Tudor manner to shelter the matured second or third generations of families escaped from the filth of the old and decaying residential quarters in the city. These families in turn were providing for their own young descendants smaller houses in the oak woods behind them.

Paying off my cab, I took a look across its low budding privet hedge at the home of the junior Pierces. It was a good risk for the fire underwriters: quarry-faced stone construction and slate roof. Like some of its slightly older relatives up on Forsyth, its mode was also Tudor, junior Tudor. The house was lit and ventilated across the ground floor by a series of steel-framed windows of various size, a bow for the dining room I guessed, and of course a picture window for the living room. On the outboard side of the latter stood a glassed-in Tudor sun porch of dependable masonry. Light and air to the second floor were admitted through a collection of gables and dormers, including a small one, to balance the façade I suppose, over the garage wing. Well, the Elizabethans had poked holes out of their garrets when they needed additional living space, why not the architect of Dan's house? And it must have made the contractor happy building in all that expensive groinery.

I crossed the flat lawn and ascended three broad granite steps, presenting myself before a stout, iron-bound door hung to a Gothic arch of limestone into which had been fitted at the proper place the brass mounting of an electric buzzer. A maid admitted me to a foyer whence, since I had climbed three steps up from the ground level to reach it, I could now climb three steps down again to reach the living-room floor, thus experiencing, as the architect intended, the interesting variety of elevation in his plan. A low stile placed in the middle of the entrance hall at base level would have obtained the same effect at less cost. At the bottom of the steps the Pierces awaited me.

Margaret had been one of the first girls in town to cut her hair short. I remembered; she was now one of the first to wear it in a

73

long bob. She looked pretty, very pretty. But as she danced around showing off the house to me, every once in a while giving Dan a pat or a flashing smile, I couldn't reconcile this new vivacity of hers with the old Margaret. She was always fun to be with, always, but she was never professionally peppy.

Instead of being ashamed to be caught dead in such phony surroundings, she seemed to take a positive pride in them.

"Now these," she told me, when we returned to the sunken living room, "are Dan's jewels."

Dan gave a satisfied chuckle as Margaret made a pirouette with both arms lifted toward the walls. These were a collection of large paintings in elaborate gilded frames, each illuminated by museum lighting. I recognized them as undoubtedly the most comprehensive showing of the work of O. E. Gottfried ever to be assembled. Otto Gottfried was a native son who specialized in scenes of the Old West. The ghost of Frederick Remington need not have been disturbed by Gottfried's work, but for some years it had enjoyed a modest vogue in St. Louis. I had been in a dozen homes where one or two small examples decorated halls or dens, but the Pierce living room was a Louvre of the man's art. Wherever you looked, wild horses stampeded over the brinks of vermilion arroyos or naked redskins were chased among the sage brush by cavalry in blue; there were snakes startling cows, cowboys torturing calves, and above the fireplace a careening stagecoach was about to topple its precious load of human freight into a roaring torrent. The effect upon the viewer was that of being caught in the middle of a Buffalo Bill show.

"This guy's painting is going someplace," Dan told me, and I could agree. "I'm holding him for a rise. The bird I bought the house from was dumb enough to throw them in at the price I paid."

"Yes," said Margaret, "we bought the house as was." I looked at her and her expression was for a moment not peppy. Then instantly it was again. "Aren't they simply keen, George?"

"Yes, indeed," I said. "Full of life."

"That's the word," Dan said, "full of life. I'm going to get Otto

74

to do us a mural for the office if he makes the price right, and he ought to, considering all the stuff of his I've got." Little Dan was with his father's real-estate and loan business.

"Well, let's us just get full of life, too," Margaret suggested. She went over to a paneled oak "cellarette" and proceeded to mix cocktails to order. I remember that it was the first time I had ever seen one of those little liquor dispensers in a living room.

I asked Dan how his golf game was.

"I don't get out once a week any more, George," he said. "Too busy making the mazuma. You should have gotten home sooner, boy, to be in on the ground floor. But don't worry, there's still plenty of it laying around."

"Do you know Donald Beeman, George?" Margaret asked. "No, I don't believe you do."

"No I don't, Margaret."

"He's the new manager of Laclede Hardware. Dan says he knows how to make mazuma, too."

"I'll say," said Dan.

"He's bringing a woman named Cox to dinner. I've just met her. She's a widow, isn't she, Dan?"

"She's already *got* the maz—"

"Sh! Dan!" Margaret whispered, for Beeman and Mrs. Cox were on the point of descending from the foyer.

Appearances, as they say, often deceive you, and I was doubly deceived by this pair's appearance. Mrs. Cox had on a long black velvet evening gown with short sleeves to make room for two armfuls of diamond bracelets. By contrast, she proved to be a quiet woman, deferring and well mannered. Beeman, on the other hand, struck me at first as one of those rock-faced characters who would deliberate before giving his opinion on the time of day. Not at all, on very brief further acquaintance. He was in his early thirties—Jeff would have been about his age—and he not only had an opinion about everything, but was going to give it to you whether you wanted it or not. He had a funny way of doing it, too. Someone would bring up a subject and before being allowed to continue, Beeman would interject, "Don't get me started on

75

that!" Whereupon he took up the conversational ball and ran with it.

At dinner Mrs. Cox remarked that she had read in the evening paper something about the proposed League of Nations.

"Don't get me started on that!" cried Beeman. He then, in order: (1) excoriated President Wilson ("a long-haired college professor"), (2) deplored the war (our international loans would never be repaid, (3) praised *Harvey's Weekly* (it had printed a letter of his), and (4) wondered what mess the Democrats would get us into next. His *envoi*, which I later found to be standard with him, was a scornful ripping laugh followed by the enigmatic line: "You never can tell from the wart on a pickle which way the juice will squirt." I wondered what Mrs. Cox thought of her escort and was surprised to see that she hung on his every word.

After dinner we returned to the One Hundred and One Ranch, where the conversation became for a few moments individualized.

"How are little Jeff and Mary, George? You haven't seen them yet of course." And for the first time that evening there was a gentleness in Margaret's expression that I recalled too well.

"I'm going out to California to be with them awhile. We've carried on quite a correspondence, but I'm anxious to see for myself what's happened to them in two years. I expect we'll have some good times together." For some reason I wanted to impress it upon her that it was the children I was going to see, not their mother.

"Oh, of course you will, George. What about schools?"

I really didn't know. I wanted at least to have Jeff near me, but he was still too young for boarding school, and since that afternoon I wasn't too sure where the money was coming from to maintain everybody on my list as well as I would like to.

"I think I can manage to put Jeff in school somewhere in the East next year or the year—"

"Don't get me started on that!" roared Beeman. "None of that Eastern school business for me. I've told Carol that she is going to start in the first grade at Mary Institute in September and she's going to stay right down there on Lake Avenue until they're

76

through with her. A kid that's going to live in the Middle West ought to go to school in the Middle West. I don't want any cranky long-haired ideas put in her head. Girls don't have to know anything but cooking and sewing anyhow, do they, Margaret?"

"Mr. Beeman went to the Rolla School of Mines," Margaret told me.

"One semester, Margaret. I worked my way through one semester. Then I quit and began to find out for myself which end was up."

"I think he's right about prep school," Dan said. "Dead right. My kids," he grinned at Margaret, "are going right out here to Country Day until they're ready for New Haven."

"Well, if you want to do it that way, I guess it won't do them much harm," Beeman conceded.

"It makes sense, George," Dan said. "Were you the one who brought up the school situation?"

"I was just thinking about my nephew."

"Oh, yes, of course. I'd forgotten."

That New Year's noon that we spent together over the Tom and Jerry in the locker room at the Country Club Dan had told me that people were inclined to let other people's troubles blow over. Apparently everything concerning me had been forgotten by Dan, so to the extent of his own memory he had been quite right.

Not much later in the evening highballs were served, along with rueful speculation about how long private supplies of liquor would last.

"Don't get me started on that," Beeman said. This time he really meant it, for, pleading "a big day tomorrow," he presently got his topcoat and Mrs. Cox's ermine, bade us good night, and departed.

Margaret came back into the room after seeing them off. "I don't think I'd like to be little Carol," she said.

"What do you mean?" asked Dan. "Beeman's kid? Why?"

"Oh, nothing."

"Is there a Mrs. Beeman?" I asked.

"She is in ill health," Dan said, and that was all. I wondered what diplomacy might lie behind this restricted report.

"She couldn't come. So Mrs. Cox came," said Margaret, like a small girl reciting her piece. "Now what about a drink, George?" The peppy girl again.

"Not for me, thanks."

"We don't see you every day, you know."

How I wished she did.

The day that I left for California Junie and I had a farewell lunch together at a window table in the top floor dining room of the Tower. As far to the east as you could see spread the immense flat apple-green prairie of Illinois. If I needed anything to make me feel more diminished at the moment, the prairie did it.

We had finished our meal and Junie had called for a cigar, a bottle of Scotch and a siphon. He was going to wait with me until train time.

I could see that the Teutonia Bank had missed a useful executive in Junie. He handled a cigar very impressively; a certain puff or a roll of it could convey a number of substantial attitudes. Right now he and the cigar—he leaning back in his chair, the cigar poked upward to deflect the smoke from his eyes—were together impersonating a solid man ready to discuss a friend's business affairs.

"So you got everything straightened out around here, eh, George?"

"I certainly did, Junie. I did that."

"What's the score?"

"The Reagans are ready to shut down the hotel and my partner has screwed me out of my business. That's about the score."

"Oh, come on, George." He removed the cigar and took a drink from his highball. "*Das geht nicht.*"

"I'm just looking on the gloomy side. Don't worry. As soon as you start up your moonshining business everything—"

"Cut it out." He looked quickly around him to see if anyone was listening. "That's not funny, George."

So he was really serious about it.

"Be sure to write me from California."

"I will, Junie."

"I may think up something for you at that, professor."

I hadn't heard the epithet for some time. Junie was still trying to take care of me.

"I have a trade, Junie. I'm an architect. You'd be down in the street now if I hadn't laid out this floor properly."

He frowned and gave the cigar a reflective chew.

"Trouble is, you got married too soon, George," Junie said.

Eight

THERE is a type of young man that I have always found particularly attractive, even when *I* was a young man. He may be described as the truly advantaged son of a truly successful father. I have often run across this kind of father and this kind of son in the Midwest and the South; I am sure that their kind exists elsewhere, but perhaps not in such a happy concentration as in these regions where family businesses still abound. For a generous spirit and good counsel alone are not sufficient on the part of the kind of father I am talking about. He must be in a position of such authority that he can without hindrance begin to share uncommon responsibilities with the younger man at an early age. In the relationship of which I speak there is no question of clannish nepotism, but a wholesome continuation of the very oldest and best values in the institution of paternalism: the skilled hunter giving with confidence and at his own time a spear into his boy's hand.

It is typical of the son I have in mind that he possesses acumen, reliability, and self-confidence far beyond his years. His fortune is indeed enviable, for the boy has not been made to wait to acquire these qualities little by little and probably crookedly in the grimy forges of corporate competition, so that he escapes the evil, common to those less lucky, of arriving at middle age with his moral and spiritual frame sprung. Tried young, he has the better chance of being integrated young into his world, and therefore his kind is more often than not capable of fun and laughter. He is usually to be found at work or play among his peers and together they can make a most agreeable company.

There were boys like these in the old St. Louis crowd—good sports, hard workers, fellows about my age. My brother Jeff, who was father to me as I have tried to be father to his son, had it in mind to bring me up like that. He certainly always gave me plenty to do on my own around the shop during my vacations and later when I came home from school for good. These early chores might include anything from fetching a hard-pressed draftsman a bologna sandwich to explaining a full set of specifications to a client. Sometimes I was afraid that he was overconfident of my abilities, at which my brother would show me his great wolf's grin and shout, "I don't give a damn if you make a Katzenjammer out of the job. What fool said that you have to crawl before you walk? Just walk! That's what a man is supposed to do. Now go ahead, George, for God's sake go ahead, old boy. You'll win, I know you will."

Jeff felt somewhat the same way about anybody who had won his respect, and he never took anyone into the office who had not won it. He would come bowling down the aisle of the drafting room like a man in a gale (it was a struggle to walk with him), crying, "Liberate the serfs! Liberate the serfs! Strike off your chains! Defy your masters! Do a thing well that they have never even dreamed of. *That'll* teach 'em!"—then disappear into his cubicle with a great bang of the door behind him. Jeff made Hanes what is known in the Navy as a taut but happy ship. Many of the people who had worked there went a long way in our trade.

God knows he left me enough responsibilities after he was killed, and not all of them of a professional nature by a long shot. Jeff had pretty well prepared me to handle the office; it was in my charge when he sailed for Europe that last fall, and of course I carried on, with Eckfield, afterward. But in trying to bring up

81

Jeff's children I did not do so well as Jeff had done by me. I made a terrible mistake in the case of little Jeff's schooling almost the first crack out of the box, and by the time I got around to little Mary she wasn't very little any more and it was too late to accomplish what I would have wanted to.

When he was a tot, little Jeff was the jolliest, dearest little fellow I ever hope to see, and bright and fearless, too. The top floor of our place in St. Louis was the children's. The plan was simple: two bedrooms on one side of a through hallway; bedroom, storage room, and bath on the other; stairway at end down to second floor. He would have been about two, just beginning to talk and understand what was said to him, when he asked his nurse about the storage-room door. She told him that it was the *spare room*. This information he cogitated for about a year. Then one evening before his bedtime when I was visiting him in what he called his "apartment" he asked, "When am I going to see the bears, George?"

"What bears, Jeff?"

"The bears down the hall. Let's go see them now, George."

It saddened me that he had already begun to have nightmares. "Don't worry, Jeff," I assured him, "there are no bears in the hall, not in the whole block."

"Yes, there are, George," he calmly replied, "lots of them. They live in the bear room."

"Where's that, Jeff?"

"Why, next door to the *bath*room of course."

Jeff had passed that door hundreds of times convinced that a den of bears lurked behind, but he had remained entirely serene about it.

He was quite a boy.

On a latter occasion—he couldn't have been older than six—he approached me in the living room and inquired, "Want to be put in jail, George?"

I must have startled a bit because our scandal was now upon us and also because the year before I had indeed been put in jail.

"Don't worry, George," he said, "it's *my* jail. *I'll* let you out."

So he led me down to the cellar and there he had erected in the laundry room a most creditable structure. I had expected something made out of chairs and old strips of carpet. Not at all. Jeff had been taken to see plenty of construction in his time and he was not a builder's son for nothing. He had gotten into the packing room and laid hands on some square wooden crates. These he had not merely adopted in their original forms but had disassembled side from side and with what long labors I could only imagine erected a frame, walls, and roof of the dimension six-by-six-by-six. Observe the interchangeable unities of the paneling. The floor he left as he found it, concrete and therefore perfectly functional for a house of correction. A barrel, or rather I suspected a tower, rose from the middle of the roof. Walking around it, I was surprised to observe that there was no fenestration to this carefully made building nor even a door, and turning to question Jeff about this I discovered that he was trying to hide a face full of mirth behind both his hands.

"This is a jail, Jeff?" I asked.

He nodded vigorously. "It's a *secret* jail," he said.

"Then how do you get in and out of it?"

"That's the *secret*, George, don't you see?"

"No, I don't. Lots of jails nowadays don't have exterior windows. But you haven't got a door. Suppose you want to put a prisoner inside, how do you manage that? Innovation is often commendable, Jeff," I told him, "but it can be carried to the point of absurdity." I was a little disappointed that his able carpentry had been wasted on some nursery aberration. I need not have been.

"It's a *secret* jail. Nobody knows how to come and get the prisoners out." Then he added with the most charming expression of confidence, "but I'll show *you*, George."

With that he whisked up the wall by means of a set of cleats nailed to it that I hadn't noticed, scampered across the roof, and plunged down the barrel.

"Don't forget now, George," he called from inside his revolutionary clink, "it's a secret!" What titanic convulsions of the

83

imagination it must have cost him to arrive at this solution to a major problem in prison security: preventing the break engineered from the outside.

Bright sayings and doings of the kiddies—I know that they are supposed to bore everybody except the immediate family and that to describe them is essentially a tip-off on the ill-concealed egotism of the parents. But I am not actually a parent, you see; I only had the upbringing of Jeff. So I am free to say that he was by all odds the brightest little boy I ever knew. Sometimes friends of mine get to talking about the clever things their kids have said or done (nowadays in my set it's mostly their kids' kids), and I merely smile.

It takes a pretty good man not to get a little nervous when he stops to consider the extent to which the permutations of chance affect his entire life. Suppose that my brother had lived. What a difference his survival might have made to so many people. And of course therein lies the most disturbing part of the whole scheme of fate: the degree to which a rearrangement of one life, however major or minor, can disturb the pattern of a whole series of *other* lives. The bad or the good luck doesn't have to hit you directly; you can catch it off a carom shot, so to speak.

I don't mean to say that all of us are lying supine at the feet of blind circumstance. If you have enterprise, determination, courage—yes, and in some situations caution—you can put up a pretty good show for yourself. But the permutations still place many odds against a winning combination. In the case of young Jeff and myself, but for some unexpectable poor breaks (and I am afraid some faulty thinking) things might have turned out so much better.

The original mistake I made was in choosing the wrong place, when the time came, to send him to school. He was already carrying a couple of handicaps that I wasn't fully aware of, but this one I saddled him with. And the distressing truth is that I had a reasonably free choice of decisions. I shouldn't have let our business situation in St. Louis worry me so much; and to have let the advice of Dan Pierce—prep school in the West, college in the East —tip the scales, that was really ludicrous.

And yet what older and wiser heads were there for me to turn to? My ever-helping partner Eckfield would without doubt have volunteered a capful of mountebank's wisdom. Old man Reagan? I'd have far better gone to Barney the barman. Junie's father I scarcely knew at the time.

No, I was alone with my responsibilities and had been for some years now, and would be for some years to come.

Mary's notions about educating the young, her young, had been conveyed to me in the few letters we exchanged while I was abroad. Characteristically, her ideas conformed closely to those of her chosen environment, to wit, high-style Southern California at the beginning of the twenties. She had placed little Jeff, then almost ten, and his sister, a year younger, in what she described as "the last word" in academies for children, the Montessori school of Pasadena.

I don't know how familiar is the name and fame of Maria Montessori nowadays, but at that time she had a considerable personal vogue, with institutions under her influence scattered in fashionable neighborhoods from coast to coast. Speaking as a sometime educator, I would say that there was no great harm in her kindergartens themselves; the evil that she did lives after her. She was an Italian lady doctor with a heart so overflowing with sympathy for the young that she could not bear to see them taught anything didactically. Let the kids pick it up by themselves or from each other as they toddled along life's highway, that was the scheme: no great burden, as you can see, was put upon the instructor. And so it came about that the doctrines of this sentimental Bakunin of pedagogy gave birth to "progressive" education, spreading teaching methods so lazy and pernicious that today great public universities report as many as half their matriculants unable successfully to read, write, or speak English. Little Jeff and Mary were let right in on the ground floor of the fad.

The two children met me, under the wardenship of a nurse, at the Pasadena station and I must say they showed the gratifying results of sunshine and orange juice. They were not only bigger than I had expected, they were bigger than anybody from the East would have expected, tanned of skin, faded of hair, uncritical of expression. These were Californians. It was very good to see them. Their mother, they told me, was out somewhere with friends but would be expecting me "for tea." The circumstance that their mother was also my wife and might therefore have been expected to be there to welcome me home from the wars had obviously not entered their heads, and for that I was grateful. I had never been their stepfather; I was, as always, no other than their father's younger brother, that fixture of their family known as George. The wedding ceremony which they had witnessed between their mother and me could have seemed to them of little or no consequence beyond installing me as the successor to their father as titular head of the family, for there had been no outward change in Mary's and my relationship. At least the children had been spared that complication in their lives.

Of the two, the little girl had changed more. She was not much more than a rather anonymous baby when we were in St. Louis. Now she had pigtails and a manner of her own. She marshaled the line of march to the hotel, she and I in front, Jeff and the nurse to the rear.

"I hope you've brought evening things," she said. "There's dancing every night."

"Where, Mary? On the green?"

"Don't be naïve, George. On the veranda. Have you an affinity?"

"No, but I've been giving you the once-over pretty carefully." I looked back at Jeff. "Where does she get all this big talk?"

He shrugged. "Don't ask me."

"Jeff doesn't know anything," Mary said. "He can't even swim."

"Well, the ocean's quite a way off, isn't it?"

"We have a delightful pool at the hotel and one at school but he won't swim. Lillie says it's all right though. It's not a personality problem. He'll swim when he wants to."

86

"Who's Lillie?"

"She is one of the teachers at the school," the nurse said. I turned around to see her. She was a presentable looking woman wearing an afternoon dress who might have been employed in a department store, and I told myself that Mary would call her the children's governess instead of their nurse. Jeff had nothing to contribute toward the discussion of him.

"What kind of car will you want, George?" Mary asked. "Mother drives a darling little Scripps-Booth in canary, but I rather like Packards for the men. A phaeton, of course."

"Two-seater," Jeff said.

Mary gave several notes of tolerant laughter. "Just like a little boy."

We had now come in sight of what I assumed to be the birthplace of all this precocity, a huge stucco resort hotel. A wide lawn of closely matted and well-barbered Bermuda grass lay before it, institutionally decorated here and there with pollard plane trees, beds of poinsettia and many couch swings and white tables under large colored umbrellas. No people were about, so that the whole thing looked like a display moved over intact from the Spring Suggestions window of some enormous furniture store.

"Welcome, dear George, to the Miramar," little Mary said.

Jeff was the one I wanted to do business with first, so I asked him to come upstairs with me and help unpack, thus eluding the ladies. He seated himself quietly in a chair, letting me go to work by myself.

His silence disconcerted me, for I had anticipated a torrent of boyish questions about how I won the war. I had even prepared a modest rebuttal in case he had put his older kinsman down as a hero. Not a peep out of him. He watched me attentively, however, and when I had pulled out some old junk that I had brought home hoping he might find use for it his interest seemed to be faintly aroused.

"What are those, George?"

"Goggles," I said, tossing them on the bed.

"Oh."

"You wear them to keep the wind out of your eyes, see, Jeff?"

"I know."

"This is a helmet you fly in. Do you want it?"

"Why, certainly, George, if you don't."

At this point the returning hero permitted the diffidence of his ten-year-old nephew to snip his self-control.

"Listen, Jeff, I couldn't bring you a tin hat. We didn't have them. This is all I've got, this and a map case. It's aviator's stuff, see? For God's sake didn't any of the kids out here take any interest in the war?"

Of course his eyes began to moisten and of course I felt as low as I deserved to feel. It wasn't his fault, it was just that something had gotten left out of him living in this waxworks environment; or something hadn't been put in.

"Never mind, Jeff. It's all kind of beaten up and dirty."

He sprang out of the chair like a jack-in-the-box. "But I want them, George, I *want* them!"

"Well, what—"

"I thought you still might need them, George." He had the things in his arms now with a grip an ape couldn't have loosened. The poor timid little kid. I wondered what the complacent Lillie would have to say about this aspect of his personality. Was this the man who only a few short years ago had dared enter a bears' den? Was this the cunning and indefatigable master-builder of the "secret" prison? What had been done to him?

"Not me, Jeff. You'll do the flying for the family next time out. Tell me about this school of yours. How do you like it?"

Back to the chair in silence, but with the gear clutched to him. I tried him again.

"Maybe you'd rather go off to boarding school, and then to where your grandfather and your father and I went to college."

"Princeton."

"That's right. How about boarding school? Have you got any preferences?"

"I don't know, George."

88

"Well, I mean about going to any prep school at all."

"I don't know."

I don't know. Have you ever set out to tackle a negotiation that you thought might involve proposing a couple of alternatives, neither of them too acceptable but either one practicable, and then discovered that this was not the job in hand at all, but something quite different, much more complex, and, worse, one that would take a tremendously longer amount of time than you had budgeted or could possibly afford? A blueprint for a nightmare, that one.

"Well," I said, and believe me not with too much hope, "we'll talk to your mother about it."

"Yes," Jeff said. He didn't sound too hopeful either.

I walked over to the window to look down on the lawn. The view was now transformed from a large store window into a large garden party.

"Teatime, Jeff," I said. "Where do you think we'll find her?"

He didn't have a chance to say I don't know again because the phone rang. It was Mary.

"Well," she said brightly, "you got here. Is the room all right?" I don't know what I had expected, but it was probably not to be treated as an out-of-towner for whom she had reserved a place to spend the night. I told her everything was all right, plenty of bath towels and so on, at which she giggled.

"Then I'll be right up."

"Wait a minute, is this a good idea?"

"It's the best," she said. "You don't want us to stage the happy reunion scene down here in front of everybody, do you?"

So she came up, entering my bedroom for the second time in our married lives.

The books on proper social behavior fail to cite the etiquette expected of a man greeting after a two years' absence a woman who was his late brother's wife and whom he has married to get her out of trouble—in the presence of her son and his nephew. Does he shake her hand? What are their first words?

In this case Mary's were: "Run along now, Jeff. George, how are you?" Jeff, clutching his new equipment, ran along while Mary

89

arranged herself in an attractive semi-reclining position at the head of the bed, prettily fussing with a number of yards of pale-green tulle around her knees. She was also attentive to a wide hat of laces which, I must say, made a becoming soft frame for her fragile face. I could think only of a large expensive doll decorating a tart's boudoir.

"Jeff's looking well, don't you agree? But rather a problem, the dear little boy." She used "little boy" in connection with Jeff in the same denigrating tone and manner that her daughter did. I wondered if any woman had ever before patronized her own son because of his youth.

"What sort of a problem, Mary?"

"Oh," she swept her arms about her, "surrounded by too many women. Women emasculate a boy." She added, with a faint worldly smile, "When he's too young, I mean."

"Had you thought about some other school for him? I doubt if he's getting very much out of this one."

"That, George, I leave entirely up to you."

As so often happens, I had won a point so unexpectedly that I hardly knew what to do with my advantage, if indeed it was an advantage. The ball was in my court much sooner than I had been prepared to handle it. At any rate I told her that I thought Jeff should be sent to some good boys' school as soon as he was old enough, perhaps next year or the year after. It was impossible for me to make plans more definite at this time, I said, because I was not yet sure where I would set up my own household. However, I was back in the country now and in the meantime I would keep more closely in touch with Jeff, giving him more attention from the male side of the family. Did that fit in with her plan? More or less. Did she believe that it might broaden a boy's viewpoint if he went to school in the Middle West and then to college in the East? She hadn't the faintest idea. Nor, I gathered, much interest in the matter. "Well," I said, "in that case let's talk about little Mary."

"Mary?" She made a little frown. "She has nothing to do with this. A dear, charming girl. My very best friend, in fact." She spoke as though her nine-year-old daughter were a woman of thirty. I had never heard anything like that before either.

"You don't think that she also may be surrounded by too many women, I mean older women."

"How else is she going to learn about life? No, no. Mary is divinely happy just as she is. If you have any idea of meddling in Mary's affairs, George, get it right out of your head. She's *my* daughter."

And nobody, it almost seemed, was Jeff's mother. She shifted the tulle again, a gesture unmistakably intended to close the subject. And so there was nothing to do besides accept the fact that my niece—over whom I had no control except as her trustee, with her mother, under my brother's will—was for the time being at least, removed from my further care.

"Now let's discuss another important topic," Mary proposed. "Isn't this fun, getting things straightened out at last? Let's talk about money."

"That's not a bad idea. We don't have too much of it."

"So I gathered. What do you mean by not too much?"

I began to explain to her what the reduction of earnings by the Tower would mean to our income. Instead of our receiving some forty thousand from that source next year, the figure would be more like thirty unless some means of replacing loss of revenue from liquor sales was found. This news, I noticed, did not surprise her. I went on to say, more out of irony than for any other reason, that the situation had disturbed the Reagans to the point of their hinting at even darker days ahead for the hotel. But, I added jokingly, no date had been set for a stockholders' meeting to consider closing down the place. Mary smiled at this. She began to count on her fingers.

"That would include you, and me, and Ed, and old Mr. Reagan, and Mr. Neidlinger from the bank," she said. "All in St. Louis together. What a party that would be."

"I don't think we have to worry about it for the present."

"No," she said. "No, but we do have to worry about the money."

I had been sending her about a third of the Tower income—which was hers and the children's under Jeff's will—and making some small investments with my own portion. She had also received half of my share drawn from Hanes & Eckfield, to which she was not entitled, Jeff's death having terminated his partnership as my death would have ended mine. On thirty thousand dollars a year a woman and two children could live pretty well in California in those days, as Mary had obviously been doing. On twenty or twenty-five you would still not starve, and I told her so.

"But, George," she said, widening her eyes in mock astonishment, "I never *dreamed* of starving. Not as long as I have a brilliant young man like you to take care of me."

Then I told her about my talk with Eckfield, and the playfulness left her face, leaving instead the expression of a by-passed pickup girl.

"So you let that slick Swede trick you out of your business while you ran off to the war. I never understood why you permitted him inside the office in the first place."

"Eckfield hasn't tricked me out of anything and I had to have him. I'm still the senior partner in the firm. Our earnings are down, that's all, and I won't be in the St. Louis office." Well, that was the story for the time being at any rate.

"Jeff didn't have to have him."

"That's right. Jeff didn't have to have anybody to help him."

She flung herself up from the bed. "Oh, you make me vomit when you talk about him! A tin god! Tin is right."

"Let's go easy on Jeff," I said.

"What did you ever know about him? What?"

"Enough," I said.

"You weren't married to that egotistical maniac! You don't know *anything* about him. *Anything!*"

"I knew enough, Mary. No, I wasn't married to him."

She now had her feet planted wide apart beneath the spreading tulle skirt, her hands belligerently on her hips, her lace hat absurdly agitated by her shaking body.

"You didn't know he drank either, did you?"

92

"This is getting pretty tiresome for me, Mary."

"You didn't know he was dead drunk that afternoon in the car, dead drunk and raving that I was—" She stopped and I thought for a moment that it was from a sudden sense of shame. Then something seemed to change her mind, for in an even higher voice she shouted, "Raving that he was going to kill us both! *Do you hear?*"

In the course of living in the same house with Mary for some years I had become familiar with a certain measure of her fish-wifery. Jeff of course was never exposed to it for I believe that she was afraid of Jeff as a good many other people were. Afraid is not the right word; awed by him. His remoteness made him seem impregnable, impervious; there was no way to reach him easily, to touch him, and that is always a little frightening to others. So that Mary had never in his hearing let loose with one of her senseless tantrums. But she had in front of the children and even the servants. And in front of me as well, to a lesser degree. Her response to the later slander about herself and me, I remembered, was surely irrational. "What would people say about me?" was her impulsive, foolish reaction to my suggestion that she leave the children with the Cartons for a while (a fairly irrational idea of my own, of course) if they would be an embarrassment to her.

But until now I hadn't had to listen to talk like this from Mary. I could only attribute her disconnected malignancy to the pressure of frustrations on her about which I could then only in part guess. Ed Reagan's refusal or inability to marry her was, I supposed, a heavy and bitter one; her ambiguous position as my wife another. She evidently drew a queer sort of comfort from her relation with her daughter, but I could see that little Jeff was a torment to her. I realized that she had plenty to put up with, poor silly inverted woman, and few resources to cope with her difficulties. And so I felt sorry for her, for the terrible things she was saying about Jeff, not angry at her.

"Keep quiet now, Mary," I told her. "You're letting your tongue run away with you." But she did not keep quiet.

93

"No," she ungovernably flew on like an engine with a broken throttle. "No, you weren't married to him. After he was dead you married me, God knows why. Some crazy loyalty to your crazy brother. And what about me? Now you've messed up my life with your clumsy stupidity about money so that I'll be out on the street!"

Her ravings about our marriage struck me at a place where it hurt, and hurt badly. Now she was not desecrating the invulnerable dead, in her malignancy she was clawing at the living. If I could have let myself say the words *you mean walking the street,* I am sure that they would have brought the relief of a drink of snow water to a famished man. Even so, I was not able wholly to restrain my emotions. I allowed anger to misdirect me, for I would not otherwise have chosen this moment to ask her when she was going to give me a divorce.

She sat down on the side of the bed and, holding her face in her hands, burst into laughter. I thought that she had at last broken down in complete hysteria and was preparing myself to go to the phone and call a doctor when she raised her head. She was laughing quite humorously.

"Me give you a divorce, George?" she asked chokingly. "*I'm* not going to marry anybody."

"That's not the point, Mary. There's absolutely no reason any more for us to keep on with this rotten mess. I want a divorce and I want one quick."

"George," she said with a spurious soothingness in her voice. "George, you mustn't let yourself get excited like this. You haven't met anyone recently, have you, George? And of course the little Carton girl got married to one of your best friends while you were away, didn't she, George? You *really* shouldn't have gone away, George. They all took advantage of you."

"I guess you'd better go now, Mary," I said. "As you say, we've got everything straightened out."

She rose and moved toward the door. "Now, now, George. Don't start brooding about setting detectives to spy on me. I don't believe they would do you much good. And anyway, consider the honor of the Hanes name. Isn't it already compromised enough? You'll consider that now, George, won't you? For me?"

Good old George, I thought: he could always be counted on to do the correct thing; or rather never to do the incorrect thing. Or could he?

"Go on, Mary."

She opened the door to the hall. "You're coming downstairs to dinner with me."

"No, I'm not, Mary."

"But of course you are, George. You don't want to embarrass me with my friends. You don't want them to think there's something odd about us, do you? Tha-at's right, George. Uppity-up. That's a good boy."

As we stood waiting for an elevator Mary began to tremble with suppressed amusement.

"They'll all think we spent the afternoon making love," she said.

After dinner, the children having joined us from some refectory of their own, we made a family group seated about in wicker chairs on the veranda, coffee for Mary and me, a small cup of Postum for little Mary, nothing for Jeff. A number of people passed by, some of whom Mary spoke to and invited to sit with us. They paused and I rose to be introduced as "my husband, only just back from France," but none of them stayed. Finally everyone who was going to remain on the veranda seemed to have settled down. There was an awkward silence in our party until my niece, rising to the social necessity, broke the ice.

"You'll play polo, of course, George," she began. "We have our own field here. The Burlingame people came down last weekend and we were quite gay, weren't we, darling?" This last was said bending endearingly toward her mother.

Here Jeff surprised me by letting out a quite normal guffaw. "George can't ride a horse any more than I can," he said. "Golf's George's game. He could beat hell out of—"

"Sledding, Jeff," I hurriedly corrected him. "Sledding's *our* game, don't you remember?"

95

He grinned for the first time in more than two years, according to my reckoning. I felt better about Jeff.

"They never have snow out here, George. Gee, I *miss it* back home."

"It won't seem too long until you're in school back East and there'll be lots of snow."

"I guess so."

"I *know* so. Your mother is all for your going, so that's fixed, see?"

"How's that?" asked Mary, who had been searching the faces of the crowd. "Oh, of course. Our friends are probably inside playing auction."

But one of them, at least, was not. She could be seen making her way toward us from quite a distance, a monstrous old woman with a jeweled walking stick in hand. She was shrouded in violet satin and hung with a museum of beads.

"Mrs. Foraker!" cried Mary, rising eagerly and holding forth a welcoming hand.

"Mary, my dear!" Mrs. Foraker hove to and turned on me a bright iron grimace.

"Mrs. Foraker, may I present my husband, Captain Hanes."

"Captain, how nice!" Mrs. Foraker exclaimed. Without the need for an invitation, she lowered herself, as a ferry to its slip, into a crackling wicker chair. "How sweet," she said. "You two lovebirds all to yourselves."

"George," said Mary, leaning toward me and slipping her hand in mine, "you don't know how wonderful Mrs. Foraker has been to me. To us all." Little Mary nodded vigorous agreement. "I just don't know what we would have done without her."

"Dear Mary, it was nothing, *pas de quoi.*"

"Mrs. Foraker is our *Leader* here in Pasadena," Mary went on. "A word from her and all doors open."

"You have to have *entrée*, my dear," Mrs. Foraker murmured, "you have to have *entrée.*"

"Thanks to *you*, Mrs. Foraker."

"Your charming wife is a flatterer," Mrs. Foraker said to me, and turning to Mary she asked: "Are you happy with your tulle, my dear? I have some other very pretty things coming in from New York in the next few days. I want you to come and see them."

I looked at Mary and saw that her reaction to the Leader's casual unmasking of her millinery role—an agony of embarrassment to Mary, I should have thought—was a tenacious party smile, and I was sick with shame and pity for her and her miserable social pretensions. Poor women, poor vulnerable, defenseless women. Why do their shabby frailties, their threadbare affectations seem so much more pathetic than those no less ignoble of men? Is it because theirs, right up to the wretched moment of denouement, are more bravely worn?

"We have so much enjoyed seeing your friend Mr. Reagan, Captain," Mrs. Foraker was saying. "Such good company." She pursed her lips, popped her eyes, and nodded her head like a Mardi Gras mask. "And I expect a pret-ty bus-y man with all his war plants out here."

This revelation of Mrs. Foraker's, I was surprised to see, didn't in the least bother Mary. "He writes that he'll be back soon. Something to do with San Diego," she told the Leader.

Then I understood. Naturally Mary had been familiar with the business situation at the Tower (but not with the one at Hanes & Eckfield). Ed had told her. And naturally she was unconcerned about my knowing that Ed visited her. Now that they knew that I knew, they would be even better prepared to protect themselves. And so it all had come to a sordid stalemate.

It has been my experience that when someone has done you an injury he hates you for it; you have caused him to lose grace with himself. Ed Reagan and Mary must have hated me a great deal.

Early next morning I took Jeff out on the hotel course and we knocked some balls around until the forenoon. It was a Saturday, but I don't believe it would have made much difference whether he showed up at the Montessori shop or not. His sister was asleep, as was her mother. I left a good-by note for my niece and Jeff saw

97

me to the station where we waited for the Chief to come up from Los Angeles.

"Everything is going to work out all right, Jeff," I assured him, and suddenly realized that the last time I had used those words of optimism they had been said to Margaret Carton just before I went to Pensacola.

"Yes, George."

"Just hang on a little while longer and don't let anything or anybody get you down. I'll write you and you write me."

"Okay, George."

"If anything goes really wrong, let me know about it fast. You know how to send a telegram? Okay, telegraph me if you want to, collect." My farewell address was running down badly; when would the train come? "Now let's see. Oh. Is there anything on *your* mind, Jeff, that we ought to talk about?"

"Nope. I guess not. I write you and you write me."

"That's the ticket."

"Or telegraph."

"Right. Oh. And you begin thinking about a school for yourself. You kind of scout around, look them up, see?"

"How do I do that, George?"

"No, never mind. I'll make up a list for you and write you about it."

Still no train.

"And I'll write you back."

"You get it, Jeff. Oh, and one thing more. No cussing in front of the ladies."

The blessed eastbound whistle moaned in the distance.

Nine

In the twenties New York was a fun town; at least it was for a lot of people, a whale of a lot more people than it is now. How proud the New Yorkers were of their city. To begin with, it was a very clean city—the municipal ordinance forbidding the burning of bituminous coal saw to that—and winter and summer when the gulls flew across its bright maritime sky even the old could look up and see them. There was a fine Edwardian casino in Central Park, light and airy with trees around it, where meals and tea were served to the music of violins. Another one, fretted and octagonal like a very special wedding cake, overlooked the Hudson beside Grant's Tomb. If you had a car you might ferry across the river and dine with the opposite view at any of a dozen little restaurants on the Palisades. The vehicles of the town were a pleasure to watch and ride in. In the streets there was a scurry of small taxicabs which literally were "cabs," cabriolets whose leather tops folded back to catch the passengers a breeze, while diminutive Rolls 20-horse town cars stood jauntily with their footmen beneath the electric call boards of galleries and shops and theaters. A web of elevated railways reached all parts of the city, their cars flying between little stations like children's toys perched in the air. Air, it was a city of light and air. Foreigners spoke of the intoxication they drew from the bright Atlantic air of New York; they said it made them think and do things that they had thought and done nowhere else. New York was almost a place of enchantment. No one, it seemed, was happy until he had reached it; exile from it would be sorrow; banishment, unthinkable. At night, on gala occasions, the high street lights in the city's center were changed from silver to topaz, and here and there in the velvet dark shone twisted tubes of rose and turquoise neon, very French, amusing, and new.

In the twenties, New York was, as always, a city in a hurry, but in a quiet hurry. Unknown to most of its inhabitants it was hurrying, but almost by stealth, through another of its great transitions. A citizen who had fallen asleep in 1913 and awakened in 1923 would have aroused without undue astonishment at his surroundings. There still lingered much from the New York of James Huneker: the big newspapers on Park Row, the big palaces of Fifth Avenue, the circle of artists gathered around Mlle. Petitpas and the circle of society around Mrs. Belmont. True, the sounds of Gershwin had struck up, but they were gay sounds and not alarming.

This New York has of course passed now, leaving as little trace as have twenty other New Yorks, for it is surely the most persistently metamorphic of all the cities of history. A Parisian, in the face of a succession of national catastrophes, may spend a lifetime without changing his bookstore or his barbershop. London, smashed and torn, is nevertheless still filled with pre-Columbian buildings. Where is one Dutch wall in New York? Where, for that matter, are the elevateds? New York in its swift passage quickly covers up its footprints.

I was invited to dinner some years ago by one of the trustees of the University whose home in town I had not before visited, and naturally I recognized the address as soon as I was given it: One Beekman Place. There was no one else in the drawing room when I was shown in, so I went over to one of the windows giving on the East River and looked out, well remembering the scene. There on the opposite shore directly across the rocks at the lower tip of

100

Welfare Island stood the long concrete Pepsi-Cola warehouse, bravely reflecting on its wall surfaces and back across the water— as always on fine summer evenings—a very acceptable substitute for a painting of the Venice of Canaletto. Up to my left stuck the spikes of the Queensborough Bridge that used to take us out to Long Island and was a long illuminated moving photo mural by night. Below me, where the Franklin D. Roosevelt Drive now swept by, you would never guess that a coal wharf as grimy and alive with naked kids as any George Bellows ever painted once lived and had its raffish being. I was recalling the hot night that Bob Mayer and I climbed down the steps at the end of Fifty-first Street and refreshed ourselves with a septic dip beneath those long-gone pilings when my host entered the drawing room. He was a pleasant man who had made a lot of money in sugar I think, one of the trustees that I particularly liked.

"I've always enjoyed this view," I said. "I lived here when I first came to New York."

"At One Beekman? I didn't know that. Which apartment?"

"Right here. Right where I'm standing."

He smiled politely. "Well, not right *here*. I'm afraid we've owned this particular apartment ever since the place was built."

"No. This is the fourth floor from street level. To one side of us is where the old Number One used to be, the old Number Five to the other."

"That's right."

"And then One, Three, and Five were all torn down and the three plots thrown together to build this apartment house. It took its street number from the end plot, One. This part, Three, was my building."

"Then you lived here when it was a brownstone."

"I did. My living room was at the rear of the fourth floor and this was precisely my view. I had the third floor, too."

"Well, what do you know about that." He made a melancholy little laugh. "New Yorkers," he said. "At any time the old home place may turn out to be only a space in the air."

His wife came in followed by a maid to bring us drinks and

101

the man told her of the coincidence of our sharing the same cubage.

"I'll bet you paid a lot less when it was yours than we had to pay for it," she said with mock ruefulness.

I'll bet I didn't; I owned the whole house. But she was too nice a woman for me to disappoint her in what she obviously regarded as a delightful extravagance. She had done the place up very well. I had been pretty comfortable at that address myself.

It was Bob Mayer who found it for me. Bob and I had bumped into each other from time to time out West and my first Sunday in town he took me out to the Engineers Club at Valley Stream, where he made up a foursome and later that afternoon introduced me to some of the people whom I still see a good bit of. Bob at that time was managing editor of *Architectural Age*. He has always had a lot of friends, inside the profession and out.

Bob was then still a bachelor, it being his idea that journalism was useful as a steppingstone to a man of ability but no basis upon which to start raising a family, and to all practical purposes I was single, too. He was a hardheaded young man, Bob, but one of those people whose self-confidence and capacity came naturally enough so that he didn't require himself to keep the pressure on either his associates or acquaintances too noticeably. But he knew his business. To use a phrase of his own that he occasionally applied to people he respected, such as able jockeys or boxers or even architects, Bob never needed a nurse. After I opened my office in the Graybar Building, just around the corner from his place, we used to have lunch or dinner or a drink together two or three times a week, and he helped a good deal to set my feet on the right path in getting my New York office going. He had a solidly professional admiration for Jeff's work, but he was just as strongly opposed to my taking any kind of commission from a client who expected me to produce a copy of it. The *Age*, running an article on a couple of residences that I did in my first year in New York, went so far as to omit mention of my relationship to Jeff. "You have already given that brother of yours a long enough count," Mayer told me.

102

As I say, he was hardheaded, but there was also a romantic streak in him and it was this that persuaded him that New Yorkers, having missed creating for themselves a Thames Embankment when they crowded and vulgarized Riverside Drive, had one more chance to do so on the midtown shore of the East River. I would not say that Beekman Place was a slum when he first pointed it out to me. Respectable middle-class people lived along its two blocks, particularly in the old houses on the water side, but I would point out that as late as a decade later it was the locale of a fairly seamy play called *Dead End.*

At any rate, while Bob continued to live in a conventional apartment hotel on lower Park Avenue, leaving the James McNeill Whistler act to me, I bought my place, converting the top floor into a bedroom on the west side with a living room overlooking the river. Dining room, kitchen, and servants' quarters below. These premises I put in charge of a sainted colored man, Alfred Jones, a former Seaboard Airline dining-car cook and a lay minister of the Baptist Church.

The first and second floors went into two other apartments that I rented to a succession of tenants—musicians, actors, radio people, writers, and the like—whose only common denominator seemed to be that they chose not to sleep very much at night. This did not bother me at all because when I was not up late working I was up late having a reasonably good time of my own; either on Beekman Place or elsewhere.

Some interesting if brief companionships came my way at that period. I remember bringing home from an elaborate speakeasy one night an impromptu party which included a man whose business, he said, was raising white police dogs. He offered to give each of the girls one, was taken up, and the animals were delivered the following afternoon. Not all of these occasions turned out so happily. There was the case of the stockbroker's wife who let some of the other guests in on a speculation called the Bayano Oil Company, supposedly a concern doing prosperously in Panama. There must be people who recall the bursting of this bubble; one of the newspapers headlined its story *Yes, We Have No Bayanos.* But I shouldn't give the impression that all of the people I entertained were frivolous. Congressman Kaffey, who was brought around by Bob Mayer one evening, turned out to be a serious man indeed.

Kaffey was a young man from Massachusetts, had been an artillery officer in the war, helped found the American Legion, and was much interested in the building of veterans' hospitals. It was the one big legislative issue with him and while he was only a very junior member of the Military Affairs Committee, he was a Republican and they were carrying the ball at that time. To my surprise, he seemed to know something about hospital construction, from a layman's point of view. I had often thought the problem over as an architectural project myself.

The trouble with hospital construction, I told him since he appeared interested, was that all hospitals were built alike, as traditionally as streetcars. Whether it was to serve a hundred patients or five thousand, whether the case load was mixed or homogeneous, whether the site was urban or rural, the building always turned out to be so many boxes for service and dormitory purposes piled one on top of another until the desired volume was attained. The requirements of an institution providing isolation, surgery, or special treatment are quite different from one whose case load is largely convalescent and ambulatory such as a sanitarium, asylum, or, for that matter, a veterans' hospital. A man who has had his kidney out wants all the security and care he can get and a snug room on the twentieth floor is as good a place for him as any, but it is cruel and barbarous to hole him up in a skyscraper if fresh air, sunshine, some trees, and grass are what the doctor really ordered.

"Your veterans' hospital would be a mile long and one story high," said Bob Mayer, who usually got the point fast.

"That's about it."

"Well, wait a minute," the Congressman objected. "I'm serious about this problem."

And so was I. Bob was right; my plan would call for a huge site, but of cheap, undeveloped land, the more undeveloped the better. I got out a block of paper and spent the next half-hour or so roughing out a recuperation home in which the service areas and all communication between units would be underground; every other facility would be at ground level. All rooms would be exterior and all exterior walls would be of glass, shaded if privacy was desired, so that even the bedded patients would in effect rest in a garden. Those patients who might for psychological reasons be reluctant to go outside if they were quartered without free access to the grounds would by this plan be tempted outside or if necessary shooed outside. For the majority, the feeling of space and freedom of motion would be a kind of therapy in itself.

"It's certainly unusual," Kaffey said, "but so is everything the first time it's tried, isn't it?"

If I thought him fairly ingenuous for a tribune of the people, I had to tell myself that the former artilleryman was in fact behaving pretty decently in the face of what must have seemed to him a pretty bizarre idea. When he left he took the drawings with him, promising to show them around when he got back to Washington.

Mayer had run across Kaffey in the course of preparing some Federal construction story but he did not regard him as one of the pillars of the Republic. "Where," asked Bob, "do you suppose those other Congressmen will think he's been when he totters back from a night in New York with what looks like a map of the Hindenburg Line clutched in his arms? If he values his political future he'll keep his mouth shut about the whole thing."

The Congressman, however, sent me a letter a couple of days later telling me that he had not forgotten our evening together and that he was setting up an appointment for us to see some people at the Veterans' Bureau in the very near future. I thought at first that it was a little cool of him to assume that all he had to do was whistle and I would drop anything I might be doing and rush down there to continue what had been no more than a friendly speculative conversation. But then, it occurred to me, he was in a way speaking for the government and it's seldom enough that most of us ever inconvenience ourselves in that direction. I wrote him that I was at his service. When Kaffey replied by wire that as soon as someone or other returned to his office I could expect a telegram naming the date for our appointment, my interest picked up a little more. It amused me that the Congressman, like the man with the white police dogs, had come through, if only in a limited way, and I couldn't help anticipating what my partner Eckfield would say if by some wild chance anything really came of the meeting.

My next trip out of town was not to Washington, however, and my next telegram did not come from Kaffey. It arrived at my house early one cold morning from Mary Hanes, the elder. JEFF VANISHED COME AT ONCE.

"The child *vanished?*" asked Alfred Jones, when I showed him the wire. I could sympathize with his incredulity. The picture that Mary's communication brought to mind was that of a small boy walking across a broad hotel lawn and then, at a moment, leaving nothing in his place except some more California sunlight. It taxed the imagination.

Getting down to business I put in a call to Mary and looked up Jeff's most recent letters. It never occurred to me that any serious harm might have come to him, for this was in the days before criminal child-snatching, but boys have been running away from home for a great many generations and I wanted to see if I had missed any forewarning of his disappearance. I have the letters, along with all the others he wrote me at that time, before me now.

"Dear George:" he said in the first one that came to hand, "Mary's nerse [not his, you notice] has taken her shoping so I can have a little piece to write you." The Montessori method of orthography went on this way without betraying any other sign of mental distress on the part of the author. In the next one, however, he said that he had had to "argu and agu" with some of the children at his school after "borroing" one of their bicycles. "I guess the schol in Chacago will be all write," he continued, "better than this dreadful shole." (The Method, it seemed, not only encouraged misspelling but variations of it.) I was glad that he had no objections to the boarding school I had finally selected for him, one on the far North Shore of Chicago that had been recommended as the best "nonmilitary school" in the Midwest. After a correspondence with the headmaster, it was agreed that Jeff would enter the following September. It was now March.

Jeff's most recent letter mentioned another "argument" at his school after "borroing" candy from one of the other students, but I suppose I had not paid much attention to this repetition of his altercations over misplaced property because of his conclusion: "Chacago is where you and papa and granpapa lived. Do they have snow thir? Mr. Ragan from sant luis is back agen. Why does he always come back agen so much?" That letter from Jeff had been mailed about a week before.

The phone rang and I was connected with Mary. Naturally I expected her to be excited, which she was. Her voice came high and sharp across the long line.

"George," I heard her cry, "George, I'm frantic. He hasn't been home all night."

"Where have you looked for him, Mary?" I asked her.

"The police, everybody."

"I said where, Mary."

"He didn't come home from school, George. Oh, I don't know what I am going to do!"

"When did he leave school?"

"He didn't stay for lunch. They won't have him there any longer. He's been stealing. They won't tolerate it, George."

After putting some more of her fragmented information together I gathered that Jeff's taking things that did not belong to him had exhausted the patience of the school authorities, even those exponents of educational *laissez faire* having drawn the line at thievery, and that some time during the previous morning he had been fired. He had not since been seen by anybody who knew him.

"Let me get this straight," I said. "Do you mean to say that the school dismissed him without telling you?"

"They telephoned me. It's not the school's fault, George. They're perfectly happy with Mary. It's Jeff they can't do anything with. He even stole money out of Ed's room."

107

The poor little kid. I had banked on his being able to survive that environment for two years; he had missed the target date only by about six months. Already fairly well rejected, he couldn't have been helped much by seeing another man, or men, hanging around his mother all the time. So he had gone psychologically berserk in the midst of a posse of professional behaviorists and the best they could do for him was to run him out of town. They couldn't have known very much about the canon they professed, or worked very hard at it. I skipped the matter of Reagan's missing money for the time being: an act of aggression by Jeff against the mother's suitor, I suppose a really competent psychologist would call it.

"What did they say when they called you from school yesterday morning. I'd like to know."

There was a slight pause. "Well, you see, I wasn't here. George, you've simply got to come out here."

"I will," I said, "if he doesn't show up pretty soon. It's not daylight out there yet, is it?"

"I don't see what that's got to do with it."

"Things often look a lot different to people in the morning after they've had a night to think them over," I explained and then we rang off.

After Alfred brought me breakfast I had him call Grand Central and get me a reservation on the Century that afternoon and a connection out of Chicago on the Santa Fe. And then I began to think about the cast of characters that I had left my nephew surrounded by in California—Mrs. Foraker, the teacher Lillie and her colleagues who knew as little about when to get tough as when to go easy, one bird-brained little sister, one delinquent mother, and as an added starter, Ed Reagan, who blew the whistle on small boys when he missed his change. I called up the school in Chicago.

I am not going to name this place because it never pretended to be anything other than it was: a private boarding school for boys that had once been part of a small land-grant college that had never grown up. The circumstance of its being located in the toniest of the lakeshore suburbs was an accident; the school was

108

there long before the suburb. From his photograph in the catalogue, which was all I had seen of him, the headmaster appeared to be a rawboned, Lincolnesque type. His letters had a practical sound to them, small-town common sense from the Great Valley. He explained rather appealingly that while his school had a sound record with the College Entrance Board, his plant lacked "Eastern fluffy ruffles" because "somehow we have never found a sucker."

Mr. Richardson had been candid with me in his letters and over the phone I was candid with him. It was "way out of line," he told me, to take in a boy at the middle of the year, but he would do it if it was necessary. All he said about the stealing was "um."

I was at the office when around noon, nine o'clock Pacific Time, the second call came in from Mary. Jeff had turned up. He had spent the afternoon and evening at a movie theater and the night in the basement of the hotel, the two darkest places he knew of to hide himself in, I suppose, poor little guy.

"I've got him shut up in another room," Mary told me. "We can talk as we want. You've simply got to take him away from here, George. He's disgraced us."

"He's been shut up enough," I said. "Let him out. What I've got to propose is for both of you." So I told her about the school arrangement. Then I asked her to put Jeff on. He didn't sound at all sheepish; his voice was more like that of an old man who has survived one serious operation and foresees others, but has taken a sort of professional attitude about it. I told him that it was snowing in New York but that didn't arouse any interest, so I asked to speak to his mother again.

"Can Ed bring him East?" I asked.

"Oh, I don't think so. Oh, no," she said hurriedly.

"Well, it doesn't make any difference." Neither would miss each other's company on the train.

"Ed has to be in Texas."

"I see," I said. "Don't bother about it." Then I asked her to get a pencil and paper and after about five minutes I was satisfied that Jeff could be put on the right train to meet me in Chicago. There were just two from which to choose, but the days of the

109

week all have different names and of the month different numbers, always a source of disagreeable confusion to Mary.

Four mornings later he was the loneliest little boy whom I had ever seen, walking toward me in the crowd under that great dark barn of the Dearborn Station, not seeing me, not seeing anybody. The Pullman porter by his side spotted me waiting near the gate.

"Is you his?" he asked with that sunshine smile that used to be the registered trade-mark of the service. Then Jeff saw me and we exchanged manly embraces. From then on things picked up.

We had a couple of rooms at the Blackstone, I remember, and I also remember Jeff's order when we were seated before one of the Michigan Avenue windows in the dining room: a club sandwich and a bottle of beer. Well, why not? A sporty luncheon for a happy reunion. I expect he had picked up that menu from observing some of the gents at the hotel golf house.

Afterward we stopped by H. C. Lytton—then as now "By Appointment to His Majesty the American Boy"—to pick him up some warmer clothes and then spent the remainder of the afternoon looking over the Indian exhibits and various stuffed animals in the Field Museum. This worked us up a keen appetite for a steak the size of a saddle at the Red Star restaurant which in turn put us in just the right frame of mind to enjoy Fay Bainter in *The Dream Girl*, then showing in Louis Sullivan's beautiful old Auditorium Theater—converted to a movie house not long afterward as was ours at the Tower. The ballad which is the operetta's title song is still played occasionally on the radio, always reminding me of that afternoon and evening. Since it was Victor Herbert's last work, Jeff got in on one aspect of the end of an age.

I saw no profit in mentioning Pasadena, anybody there, or anything that ever happened there. Neither did Jeff. I still believe we were both right.

The next day was a bleak one, cold and filled with wind and shadows as Chicago often is at that time of year. We hired a car and drove out along the lake to the school.

"Lots of snow around here, eh, Jeff?" I remarked, trying to strike a cheerful note. "I believe they ski now at Onwentsia." Then I had to explain to him what skiing was and this occupied most of the rest of the trip until we drove up in front of the main building of the school. I thought the headmaster had been a little too deprecatory about the physical layout of the place. Half a dozen old brick dormitories and a gymnasium were scattered along winding walks and drives and the grounds were covered with a great many fine old oaks, bare now in winter. Richardson himself was a reliable looking man, shrewd, good-humored, that type of grass-roots educator who might have done very well for himself running a small-town bank. He asked Jeff to conjugate the verbs "lie" and "lay," which of course was a fiasco, but he carried it off in such a way that neither one seemed too disappointed in the other. Leaving for further study the task of orienting Jeff into the curriculum, the headmaster showed us Jeff's room on the second floor of one of the houses. It was clean and warm enough, with encouragingly conventional varnished pine woodwork and putty-colored walls. Then, bidding me good-by, Richardson left us alone together in the storm doorway back at the main building where the car was waiting.

"Are you going now, George?" Jeff asked.

"Yes, I guess I'd better be getting back. You'll want to unpack your stuff and they'll be having dinner pretty soon now."

"Are you going back to New York?"

"I think I'll drop down to St. Louis first, then I'll head back to New York. Pretty soon it will be spring and I'll be back out to get you. And look, if you get homesick or anything you just give me a ring on the phone. See?"

"I won't get homesick."

"Well, you might the first day or so."

"I want to go to New York with you."

There always comes that time. The time when the cord must be snapped, the plunge taken, the die cast, the curtain rung down, the chapter ended, the end made, the time for all the clichés of termination and heartbreak. It was nearly dark outside now. For one panicked moment I thought of running out to the car with him and taking him away.

"You'll be coming there soon enough, Jeff," I said.

"When, George?"

"In the spring, like I told you. Now you just brace up, Jeff. Everything's going to be all right. We got you out of that joint in California, didn't we? You just stick with it, everything's going to work out fine. You'll meet some nice kids here and the first thing you know you'll be having such a good time you'll probably even be forgetting to write me."

"No, I won't, George."

"That's the boy. That's the boy, Jeff. You go on back inside now, you'll get cold here. Better not look back, Jeff. It's bad luck."

It had begun snowing again outside. When I got into the back seat of the car I had to wipe my face.

After dinner I called the school but they told me that Jeff was in study hall and that unless there was something urgent they didn't like to disturb the boys there. Then I called Eckfield's home in St. Louis to let him know that I was in the neighborhood and thought I might as well drop down and see him. He wanted to know, of course, if there was anything he could do for me and I asked him to let the Reagans know I was coming, at which he told me he had seen Ed and the old man at lunch that day. Ed's trip to Texas must have broken all speed records. On my way to the station to take the night train I began thinking of little Jeff out there in the darkness and a sense of the intolerable loneliness of both of us fell upon me. In the station I sent a wire to the Pierces asking them to have dinner with me the next night.

As I approached the reservation desk of the Tower I saw that the reception clerk was, again, new to me. But as I bent to sign the register I heard a familiar voice saying, "Let me take care of this gentleman," and Barney came around the corner from the cashier's cubicle. I knew that he had been transferred to the manager's staff after the Rathskeller was closed; having him sign me in I considered a particularly happy omen. It's always good to see a pleasantly remembered face when you return to a place you have become uncertain about.

112

"I hope I'm the first to welcome you back, Mr. Hanes," he said.

"You are, as usual, Barney."

"Two years, isn't it?"

"Almost two."

"How have you been treating yourself? Mr. Neidlinger brought me the magazine with your picture in it." I must have looked uncertain. "Some houses you put up back East. It was a good likeness of you."

"Thank you, Barney. Do you see much of him?"

"Some of the lads drop by once in a while on their way up to the Skytop Room."

"How about Dan Pierce and his wife?" I couldn't help asking.

"I see Mr. Pierce once in a while," he said, and I let it go at that.

"Well, I'm glad to hear the room's doing a nice business."

"Most of the customers seem to have themselves a good time. A couple of shots of that squirrel whisky they carry in with them and I guess you'd be jumping up and down if you were in the morgue." Barney reached behind him for a key. "But they must feel like they've been slapped in the face with a buzzard's gut the next morning, Mr. Hanes. I'm telling you, it would kill an older man."

"Well, there's some bad whisky in New York, too, Barney. It depends on where you get it."

"Around here it all comes from one place, Mr. Hanes." He said this a little cryptically, I thought, and then he handed me the key. "Suite G," he said looking away from me. When the owners are given suites, a hotel's room business is not good. I took the key and handed it to the bellman who was waiting behind me.

"Things will pick up pretty soon, Barney," I said. "You always have a little stretch of hard times after a war. Things have to get shaken down."

"You won't want to be called for a while," he said. "I'll tell the switchboard. They wake you up in the middle of the night to get you off those Chicago trains. Why, I don't know, but they all do." I supposed that it was some kind of Celtic superstition that made

113

Barney, who had always been rather famous for his discussions of public affairs, avoid talking about the national financial situation.

His hand was gliding back and forth on the onyx counter, professionally, I thought, as it used to caress the rosewood of his section of the bar. And then I thought again; no, it was like Jeff's affectionately stroking the I-beam high on the Tower the morning long ago when we topped out the steel construction. Except that Jeff's touch had been one of love and confidence in the building. Barney's was one of love and pity.

In my room I found a note saying that the Pierces would meet me for dinner. To give the rest of the town time to get up at a decent hour and get to work, I had a long breakfast and took a long bath with the newspaper. There wasn't a great deal in it. That was a curious depression, the one of '22, although of course the word wasn't used at that time to describe the general business doldrums. It was a condition without a popular name. Hard times theretofore had been brought on by market "panics"—the Panic of 1897, the Panic of 1907, and so on. Money got tight, banks collapsed, commerce slowed, factories closed, and people were thrown out of work. There was no world-wide calamity involved, as there was in the long economic epidemic of the 1930's. But the 1922 adversity resembled neither the brief, classic, old-fashioned crash nor the later universal, all-pervading, decade-long misery that finally set off the Second World War and the calamitous chain reactions that have succeeded it.

Following the national frenzy that accompanied the 1918 war the country had undergone a period of domestic irritation—rent strikes, buyers' strikes, labor strikes, all in response to the continuing high cost of living. As the turbulence grew, some riots broke out, some bombs were thrown, some radicals deported. Then after a while the high prices did come down, not as a result of public disorder but because when the wartime money deluge really stopped, people simply couldn't pay them. A stunned economy put an end to the zest for agitation. Mr. Harding, little knowing how busy were his merrymen taking care of their own finances at the public till, had asked for normalcy; what he got was catalepsy.

There was a slump in security prices in 1922 but no stock-market disaster. Prices of equities fell largely because there was no further market for war materials or vast food production, and because the government had devised no apparatus for "reconverting" industry to peacetime purposes or supporting farm prices. But few banks failed and, since it was not then a manufacturing center, New York as a city hardly knew that times were bad.

Another novelty in the financial troubles of the early twenties was the amount of private stealing that came to light, having nothing to do with basic economic forces. Nobody lost the value of his insurance policy, but quite a few found themselves euchred out of their money by manipulators like Ponzi in Boston, and Koretz the Bayano man, in Chicago. These peculations, when brought to light as hard times called for a reckoning, had a certain element of low comedy about them—the slickers now seemed so transparent and the suckers so witless and greedy— that afforded the rest of the country a lot of amusing reading. But there was nothing funny about the general state of business. Companies went to the wall and people lost their jobs just as tragically as they always have when prosperity ceases. Barney downstairs didn't want to talk about it. Never mind, I was sure I would hear plenty on the subject before the day was over. Planning to take it by stages as easy as possible, I called Junie Neidlinger first and he told me to come at once and see him.

Junie, I knew, had taken over the Hudson agency and had a showroom out on Locust Street below Grand Avenue, automobile row. Riding there, I was entertained to remember Hudson as the make of car that got us into and then out of trouble in Pensacola at the end of the war. Times did not seem at all hard for Junie. His showroom looked more like an exhibition pavilion—vast tile floor, potted palms, long strips of green carpet laid between ranks of cars. There are not many odors, in my opinion, more exciting than the paint and upholstery smell of a new automobile. Junie's

115

place of business had a sort of sensory successfulness pervading it, and so did his offices on the floor above. A stunning girl showed me in and there was Junie, supported by more and deeper carpeting, surrounded by soft leather and glowing mahogany, the picture of the young motor magnate. The young Eastern-type motor magnate—for his shoes were seamless and by Frank Brothers, his shirt collar was buttoned down and by Brooks Brothers, and his suit had lapels rounded, not pointed, which was the odd hallmark of a famous New Haven undergraduate tailor whose name has now escaped me. Anyone could see that Junie was doing fine.

When I commented on his deep tan he told me he had just come back from Florida. "Not that deadfall where you and I were stuck in," he added with a laugh. Junie's spot was Miami Beach. I asked him if he had lost any money in real estate there. That bubble had burst, too, and helped, it was thought, bring on the business crisis.

"When I go down there," he said, "I play with the regulars, not the volunteers. Nobody I know got hurt. It was all just on the cuff. They sent it to the laundry and forgot about it."

His whole outlook was similarly optimistic and anachronous; he bubbled affirmation and assurance. And not to me alone. His phone must have rung a dozen times while I was with him. "Don't worry about a thing," I heard him say to one caller, "not a thing. And tell that other fellow not to worry either." "It was all right before," he told another, "it will be all right again." "Send him the money, he'll send you the goods, then you sell it. Nothing hard about that is there?" "Sure, use my name. We'll all get rich together." "Don't worry. That's the big thing." It was as though the whole of St. Louis could not overburden Junie with its troubles. On the contrary, it was fun for him to blow them away. I thought of the old days, and how Junie solaced his saloonkeepers. And naturally I wondered how many of these, or the successors to their affairs, were among Junie's communicants.

He asked me to have lunch with him but I couldn't; I was meeting Ed Reagan.

"Well," he said, "I have a car down in front for you."

116

"I don't need it, Junie. I can get around in cabs all right. It would just be a nuisance."

"You don't understand. It's yours. I'm giving it to you."

"Don't be nutty. I can't take a car from you."

I was amazed to see his face redden with anger. "Why the hell not from me, professor?" Then he came and held me by the shoulder, his anger controlled or gone in moments. "Look, George, they don't cost me anything, hardly. I want you to have it." He laughed. "You saved my life, don't you remember?" He began pushing me toward the door. "And anyhow, I'm kind of proud of you, professor." He said this very quickly as though he had to get it out but didn't want either of us to hear it.

The car was a very expensive dark-blue sedan; open cars were for the poor people in those days. I drove it away although I certainly had no intention of keeping it.

Expenses, living expenses, were what was on Ed Reagan's mind when we sat down to lunch in the Palm Room at the Tower. I am one of those people who feel a little uncomfortable in an enclosed space without windows, but I have never felt so in this room. Without the use of a single fish-scale lantern or a stick of bamboo, Jeff had created a strong atmosphere of the Oriental tropics in the place. Structurally the walls were solid, but indirect light shone all around through screens made of panes of abraded milk glass which gave the effect of sun coming through paper paneling. Most of the rest of the decoration consisted simply of lianas and other tropical foliage set here and there in heavy pottery shapes, which I suppose would be classified as "free forms" now, and fired with a subtle variety of greens suggesting the colors of jungle leaves. In the old days the room was reserved as a place where ladies with or without escort could have tea or a drink. Margaret and I used to come here. Now, Reagan told me, he lunched in the Palm Room almost every day to save money. I was just as satisfied to start off our projected business talk on a harmless personality, so I asked him how he saved money; it was not an inexpensive place to lunch.

117

"I put it on a due bill," he said. "Why pay money to eat at the University Club or the Noonday when I can get it here for nothing?"

"How do you happen to have a due bill, Ed?"

"Why, I'm always doing administrative jobs of one kind or the other for the management. Last year I got tired of doing it gratis so I made them give me a due bill."

Well, I suppose there was nothing wrong with that, except that none of the rest of us had ever expected free food from the Tower.

"You'd be surprised how many other guys are doing it," he went on. "The supply people and so on all make deals like that here now. It's the barter principle coming back." He chuckled. "Got to trade credit if you haven't got money."

I wondered how you could keep books on a restaurant doing business that way. The outlook for business of the hotel in general was what we had met to talk about, so over the meal we got down to it. Based on the previous year, over-all room occupancy could not be expected above sixty-eight per cent. And since the more expensive rooms were increasingly vacant, we were now in that most uncomfortable dilemma in which a hotelman can get caught: the necessity to lower rates in the face of falling occupancy, and to guess how far to reduce them and still keep the operation above the break-even point. This is known industrially as being "in the clip."

In the clip as we were, Reagan did not foresee how we were going to do much better than pay our bond interest for the next year. And here's the arithmetic of that in round figures. The Tower cost three million to build. Six per cent bonds were floated for a million and a half by the Teutonia Bank, the bank holding a million and a quarter of them. Stock certificates were issued which were sold to raise the other million and a half. The Reagans took a million and we took a half million. In addition, the Reagans received another half million shares at par value of a dollar a share for their participation and we a half million on the same basis. In other words, the bank's money was secured by the property and

118

its income fixed; the entrepreneurs and fabricators, ourselves and the Reagans, stood to make more and more money as the profits of the enterprise rose, and less and less as they fell. They were now falling.

Having at least gotten a meal out of the embattled establishment, Reagan pushed back his dishes and stroked his thin pompadour a few times. A tragic mask took possession of that notably mobile face of his.

"I'm worried about the old man," he said. "He's got me worried."

"He's not sick, is he?"

"No, no," said Ed impatiently. "They'll have to knock him in the head on Judgment Day. But he's never had a failure before. Oh, sure, he's come up from a ditch, we all hear enough about that, God knows. But it's always been *up*, see?"

"Well," I said, "at his age maybe a little adversity will be good for him. Teach him to value that ten or twenty million dollars he's got salted away." I had no use for the hysterical old scoundrel, I'll have to confess it.

"Adversity would kill him. He's running around now talking about getting old man Neidlinger down at the bank to take over our interest in the Tower. That's crazy. Old man Neidlinger would just as soon agree to jump out the window. All he's got to do is sit tight another two or three years like this one and when the Tower goes bankrupt he'll take it over all right, for the bonds."

I looked around the room, the glowing, lovely, and so vulnerable room of Jeff's, and suddenly its very loveliness, simple and disinterested as all empirically beautiful things are, made me surprised at myself for having even for a moment allowed the Reagans' pessimism to affect me. For the cool financial fact of the matter—and I am no expert at finance—was that nobody was going to be allowed to run away with a building that was worth three million in 1915, for a million and a quarter. And there were plenty of money men who knew that the Tower's stone, steel, and land were now valued at more than three times their cost.

"Another thing that gets me down is Mary," Ed said.

119

Here was surely an unexpected line of discussion. "In just what way, Ed?" I asked him.

"You'd think she was the only one in the world that had a dime's worth of investment in the Tower. I'll bet I didn't get to sleep before dawn any night last week in Pasadena with her yammering at me about the way her dividends had been cut."

In the whole chronicle of romance, I told myself, there had never been a more cockeyed situation. Except maybe in Hungarian farce. Here was—well, you conjugate it for yourself. I might as well have been a barber that he was complaining about his wife to, literally.

"Then I can't interest you in marrying her," I said with what I thought was fitting irony.

That didn't faze him in the slightest.

"You were smart to move to New York," he told me.

I got up from the table laughing—and I must have laughed most of the way up to our office—at the last line of the most outrageous dirty joke I had ever heard. I never enjoyed one so wonderfully much in my life, and of course it was my life that was the joke. But also I never felt better in my life. God cannot be sufficiently thanked for the saving perspective of humor. One obtuse sentence of Ed's and I was miraculously free and armed. Years of reflection and torturing argument with myself could not possibly have done the job for me that Ed had done by his marvelously insensitive remark.

I was just precisely ready to confront Eckfield, the stagnation of business, the Reagans, Mary, any conceivable or assorted variety of trouble. I had at last had a good big laugh at them all, and me.

Maybe it was because I was in such a remarkable state of amusement, but Eckfield made me laugh, too. No, that's not fair. Paul was a funny man. He made lots of people laugh; it wasn't the charitarian alone in him that won friends. He often showed a dry, witty point of view that was very entertaining.

"Well, well," he greeted me. "It's swell to see the New York branch back among us." This time he had my office cleared out

120

and ready for me, which was entirely needless since I was only going to be in town overnight. But it was a nice gesture, reflecting, I could not help thinking, the work that I and only three or four regular office men had been able to turn in for the firm from the East.

God had been good to the St. Louis office, literally. Even before the war the old parishes below Twelfth Street had begun to be abandoned as the residence area of the city moved farther and farther away from the river. The brief postwar housing boom accelerated the process. Now there was an actual shortage of churches in some of the newer parts of the city.

"They'll be worshiping under the trees around here pretty soon," said Eckfield delightedly. "Nature's cathedral."

And so while all other construction was at a standstill, there was a welcome flutter in ecclesiastical architecture. This was a consequence not only of the churches' desire to follow their memberships into new neighborhoods but of the acumen of their vestrymen in taking advantage of a depressed period in which to get the best building buy for their money. And they had the money, from the sale of their old downtown properties.

"But don't think these church people are easy to do business with," Eckfield said. "They're dangerous. They look at you with those baby-blue eyes of theirs and the next thing you know you've agreed to redraw the altar rail on the *maison*."

The church job that Eckfield had in the office was Lutheran. The requirements included—besides a place for divine services—kitchen facilities, a small auditorium equipped for stage and movie presentations, a bowling alley, and a large parking area. It was to be as much a community center as a house of worship and because while the Catholics may have a far greater spiritual realm, the Lutherans in the twentieth century have been much kinder to beauty, it was going to be a lot of fun to build. Paul and I spent the rest of the afternoon in the drafting room playing around with some of his ideas and some of mine. I went back to my rooms at the hotel to meet the Pierces without saying anything to Eckfield about Congressman Kaffey. The project was too nebulous and anyway if it came to anything it would be big. I wanted to start something big of my own for once. I was thirty-two and Jeff had been dead almost eight years.

Little Dan was tight when he and Margaret showed up. Barney or somebody else had had a buffet set up and flowers placed around the drawing room. "Well," said Dan, before he got his hat off, "it looks like you're doing all right," in the tone of one who was not.

"The flowers are simply lovely, George," Margaret said, letting me take her coat.

The amenities of reunion progressed from there; soon I asked them what they wanted to drink and received the plaintive counter-inquiry characteristic of the long national Ramadan: what have you got?

"This," said Dan, sampling a Scotch highball, "is more like it. Where did you get it? It's sure not any of Junie's bug juice."

"I don't know where it came from," I said. "It was sent up by somebody downstairs. So Junie's in the business, you say. How do you know?"

Little Dan gave me an outsized guffaw. "*Everybody* knows."

I wondered if that included Junie's father. It would break his scrupulous Prussian banker's heart, I would have thought.

As if she heard me, Margaret quickly put in, "Except Mr. Neidlinger. I don't think any of the family knows."

"How long that automobile agency will cover him up, nobody can tell," Dan said. "But he and the cops are like this." Dan held up his glass and peered through it at his first two fingers held side by side. "Which reminds me." He went over to the buffet to refill the glass, a movement which Margaret studiedly avoided noticing. "What I guess Junie had better look out for is competition."

"There isn't any?"

"Not yet. You know St. Louis. If Junie was in Chicago he'd be ducking lead like a clay pipe in a shooting gallery by now."

"Dan!" Margaret cried.

122

"Well, he would."

"Speaking of shooting," I said, "how is your Western painter Gottfried getting along."

Dan shrugged. "Broke like the rest of us, I guess. I haven't seen him." He came back to his chair.

"You're not broke."

"Of course not," Margaret said hurriedly. "He just talks like this."

"Me and the old man may not be broke, but we've got more foreclosed and unsalable real estate than just about anybody else in town. Don't even foreclose 'em anymore. Pays us to leave the people in 'em to keep them from burning down, falling down, whatever it is." Lying in his chair, he let his head fall back and began to laugh at the ceiling. He sat up again and shook his head as though over a good joke. "Boy, have we got real estate."

"You just wait until spring," Margaret reassured him vaguely, and then turned to me. "Isn't this the lousiest weather? Was it like this in Chicago?"

"Identically. How would you like to go upstairs and eat?"

"Lovely! We don't—we haven't been to the Skytop for weeks. It's such a nice place."

Dan got to his feet and made for the bottle of Scotch. "What do we wrap this in?" he asked himself. "Napkin, I guess."

Margaret rose and made a graceful half whirl with her arms raised as she had that night showing off the pictures in their living room. "*Such* lovely flowers, George," she said like a pleased child, "and on such a bitter winter day."

Wondering how long it had been since she had bought flowers for her house, I led them off to dinner.

On the west side of the dining room, the one opposite the windows, a low platform had been built between the two central arches for the orchestra. Nothing else had been changed in the room; I had seen to that. The tableware was as handsome as ever. Jeff had taken a lyre motif for the cutlery; the service plates were bone-white disks with a large central medallion of geometric design in strong reds and browns and blues like the glass of a

123

medieval rose window. The proper use of tradition, Jeff said, is to know everything about it and then go on from there.

Where I had last seen the spring fields of Illinois on the windows it was now cold and black, but now here inside the room glowed, the food was good, the music cheerful and up-to-date. Like our neighbors, Dan conceded to the national law by secluding the bottle on the floor beside him but he kept our glasses filled. Except for the interlude downstairs, the party had gone along merrily enough with jokes, reminiscences, and so forth. The whole day had been a good one for me, I realized, the high point being Ed Reagan's unpremeditated realignment of an important attitude of mine toward myself.

Along about ten o'clock Dan announced that we had run out of whisky and I prepared to send to my room for some more.

"A terrible waste of time," Dan declared. "Give me the key and I'll go get it myself. Save a lot of time, boy." So to save a lot of argument as well I gave him the key and we watched him very purposefully depart.

Margaret smiled at me. "I can dance," she said. "You haven't asked me to dance."

I remember that tune, too, very well. It was "Japanese Sandman." She hummed it softly in my arms for a while and then without looking up at me asked, "What were you doing in Chicago?" and I told her about putting Jeff in school.

"You didn't mind my asking?"

"Of course not."

"It's just that I think about you sometimes, what you are doing at that particular time." She looked up. "Just sometimes I do. Not all the time." She looked toward our table. "Dan's back." And then with the faintest agitation as though of surprised truancy, "I suppose we'd better stop."

Dan had the glasses filled when we returned. "I'll be sorry when you leave town, boy," he said. "Back to old Junie's prune juice and lye stirred in a gourd. When are you going?"

Margaret laughed. "Don't run him away. I was afraid to ask, myself."

124

"Tomorrow. Four o'clock."

"Well, then, you've got nothing to do all day." Dan always seemed to assume that I was perpetually idle, I remembered. "Take Margaret out to lunch."

"That's what I was planning to do."

"You were?"

"Or rather, he's coming out to the house and have lunch with me," she told him.

These wholly telepathic social appointments seemed to please Dan. "That's the stuff," he said. "Glad you had it figured out."

We stayed until the band stopped playing, then went down to have a nightcap and get their coats. I put a bottle of whisky in Dan's pocket and walked with him and Margaret to the lobby entrance. When we went outside the night had turned still. It was much less cold and there was fog and a thaw in the air.

"Do you feel very badly, George? Don't you think a whisky sour would make you feel much better?"

"I do."

"Not made out of Old Neidlinger, I mean."

It was one of those late-winter days—peculiar, I think, to St. Louis—when the air lying on the valley is heavy with a solution of cool moisture and coal smoke, a clammy vapor carrying with it a soft, spicy bituminous odor that is indigenous and curiously exciting; you are sometimes reminded of it in other cities, but the smell is never quite the same. The light is also strange. While the sun cannot be seen through the haze, a moist, sooty luminescence shimmers on the flanks of the buildings; the concrete sidewalks and the bare dirt of the turf beside them shine a little, too, beneath their grime. Winter has gone for a while, leaving behind a landscape in India ink, China white, and water, no other tone or shade added. It is a sort of mephitic spring.

The doorman at the Tower had delivered the Hudson—of which he highly approved—and I had driven it out along Lindell and through the shrouded park to the Pierces'. There, passing with a wince through the Roaring Camp of the Gottfried room, I had

125

joined Margaret on the Tudor sun porch whose rattan furniture, masonry walls, and wide windows made it architecturally and decoratively probably the least disturbing place in the house besides the kitchen.

She went away with a little dancing step to make the drinks. When she returned there was soft excitement in her dark eyes, and the generous bow of her Irish mouth turned happily upward at the corners. Going over to one of the long windows she bent a little as she looked out into the thin fog, as though inspecting something specially attractive in a shop window.

"I love this kind of a day," she said. "It's a nice, cozy, closed-in day." She came back and made a nest for herself at the other end of the couch I was sitting on. "It was a nice night last night, too. I enjoyed it."

"Dan seemed a little depressed about his business. Is it all that bad?" I thought of his optimism the last time I had been in that house. "What happened to the mazuma?"

She laughed lightly. "I don't think the mazuma's worrying him too much, really."

I expected her to go on but she didn't, so I thought it best to veer away from Dan as a subject. "How is his friend Beeman getting along? He had the mazuma problem all solved."

"Don't get me started on that," said Margaret, giving a very adequate imitation of Mr. Beeman's standard conversational peroration, as I recalled it. "He's doing fine, Dan says. Mr. Beeman is buying Liberty Bonds at eighty-two. Does that sound right? Is it legal I mean? I thought we all had to pay a hundred dollars apiece for them during the war and the government was going to give us the hundred dollars back one of these days."

"It will," I explained, "one of these days. But there are people who bought the bonds who need the money now, so they sell them to Mr. Beeman for only eighty-two dollars apiece. When the government does buy them back Mr. Beeman will be twelve dollars ahead of the game, plus the interest."

"I see." She studied me smilingly over her glass. "Oh, George, you are such a delight," she said. "You make things so interesting."

126

I tried to think if I had ever seen Margaret in a coquettishly amusing mood before. Yes, I had. Many times. It had been so long ago that I had almost forgotten.

"I'll tell you what let's do," she said gaily, suddenly jumping up from the nest. "Let's go out to Florissant Valley and build a fire and sit in front of the fireplace. There won't be anybody there."

I glanced toward the window, I suppose, apprehensively.

"Oh, don't look so grim. It will be nice out there, not sooty like here, just mist. No." She stopped herself. "Let's go out along the Meramec somewhere and have a picnic."

"What?"

"It's just the day for one. In that fine car of yours. I see it through the window. Who lent it to you?"

"Junie the Hudson man," I said.

"How nice. I'll go out and have a lunch packed." And off she went.

Left alone, waiting for her, I thought of Reagan and Mary and how much these people had cost me, and how much I had cost myself. The past is unrecapturable; to lament its loss is useless, and you had better learn to feel that way. Some people, perhaps most people, can; otherwise a great many lives would be absolutely intolerable. But to regret the future, that is bad indeed. That is to let the spark of hope go out and that is not to be endured.

Margaret, like the doorman, also approved the Hudson. There was a cigarette lighter on the dashboard that functioned from its own battery and was new to her. On the floor between us, and in the rear, pipes connected with the exhaust and covered by grilles gave off heat. She admired the dark-blue whipcord upholstery and the silk shades and vanity appointments in the tonneau.

"It's just like our own little—like a little home," she said. And then, "What is your home like, George, in New York?"

I told her about the house and Alfred Jones and the tenants. I also found myself telling her about Congressman Kaffey and the Veterans' Bureau and the hospital, this with a certain amount of ribaldry.

127

"But you'll *do* it, George," she said with sudden intensity. "I know you will. I *feel* it." She halted. "But then what, George?"

"Then what?"

"What will you do about yourself?"

"You mean about Mary."

"I could kill her."

"That may be the only thing to do about Mary," I said.

"I know it," she said in a sad little sigh.

We had come a long way out beyond Webster Groves and Kirkwood on Watson Road, carrying, it seemed, a small confine of the country with us through the fog. We had crossed the Meramec once and now we were waiting to find it again among the falsified shapes in the distance when a bridge came out of the gloom and we saw beyond and to the left a deserted store at the head of a row of summer cabins stretching down along the riverside. *Times Beach* read a sign over the store. Turning beside it, we followed the road behind the houses until we passed the last one, turning again to follow a narrow track to the shore.

"Well!" cried Margaret, recovering the earlier spirit of the expedition. "What's wrong with this? Didn't I tell you it would be nice?"

We moved to the rear seat, pulled a heavy blue baize lap robe from its silken rope hanger, spread it over our knees, and began to eat the sandwiches. She wanted to hear more about life in New York, where she had not been since her marriage, although her family had a house at Watch Hill and she and her mother used to stop off to go shopping in New York in the fall on their way home. Then we talked some more about how it had been putting little Jeff in school, how he had left Pasadena, and so forth. Suddenly she said, "Oh, God damn that marriage!"

I searched for a moment for something to say. "Well," I said, "that's just about the way I feel about it."

She took my hand swiftly and kissed it. "I know. I know, my poor George." She lowered my hand and I watched the slow, well-remembered tears filling her eyes.

"I couldn't have been more wrong, but that's what they call hindsight."

"I know. You did it because of your brother." She put a napkin to her eyes, and then, with a short bitter laugh, said, "I used to blame the war for my own mistake."

"Why, you haven't made any mistake, Margaret."

"Oh, George," she said dispiritedly, "don't try to be comforting."

I didn't know whether I wanted to hear any more of this or not.

"It's not his business troubles or anything like that, you see. It's really my fault, I know it. I don't mind these—these friends of his on the telephone. I don't mind what he does or the drinking." She had struck the rock of her agony; the painful words poured out. "I don't go near him when he's on the telephone. I knew that was what he was doing when he went downstairs to your room last night and he knew that I knew. *But it's not his fault.*" She beat her fists on her knees and cried in anguish, "*And I can't help it.*" She broke off and was quiet for a time. "I just can't help it, George, my darling."

I took her in my arms and we held each other for a long while. Then she looked up at me, quite dry-eyed and with the most amused smile on her face.

She chuckled. "What a picnic," she said. She rubbed my cheek roughly and affectionately. "And what a pair of martyrs." Then she clasped her palms together, sucked in her cheeks and raised her eyes in an outrageously funny caricature of a medieval statuary saint. Her gift was for enchantment.

Across the black, shining little river a row of poplars rose out of focus in the mist, Corot's poplars, still, like silent fans of lace come themselves to enchant eastern Missouri on a breathless winter afternoon. I kissed her and her lips were soft and wet and cool, like fruit from a cool place.

Every love affair, I suppose, is different and each scene of love in its own way strange. This one, tender and curious as the mists we had moved among all day, I shall always think of as a love affair under the sea. Twilit, shimmering, enveloping, it came to us

129

not as a happening but more as a gift—unexpected? undeserved?—
from the pale surrounding silence, from the peace, from the deep.

Along with almost everybody else I suppose, I have made some
bad judgments in my life, particularly about people, their character and conduct, and these I have regretted. Morally and ethi-
cally there have been occasions when I was blameworthy, or
thought I was, and I have regretted them, too. I have never regretted that afternoon.

Pushing and blowing up at her disordered black bangs, Margaret had struggled to get herself untangled from the lap robe.
Now she sat up, her sweet face glowing before me. "A fallen
woman," she announced merrily, digging into her bag for comb
and lipstick. "Meet Your Friends at Times Beach. *Now* what do
we do, George? Get you to your train for a starter, don't you
think?"

Ten

"You can always save yourself a lot of useless worry," Bob Mayer said to me a long time later, "if you don't take government personally. It isn't a set of rules of conduct laid down in a civics book. Government is a hell of a lot of people. Not always good people."

But government, I had found, was a hell of a lot of rules if you were trying to put up a building for it. The very first time I came back from Washington after seeing Congressman Kaffey and Dr. Muse at the Veterans' Bureau I brought with me a five-foot shelf of Army Engineer Corps construction specifications, literally. I was carrying, for instance, seventy-five different bulletins related to various kinds of plastering on government work.

The government insisted on a set of building plans that were actually construction plans. For example, I remember one concrete foundation wall on my job: one end was four feet; the other end, twenty-four. For an office building or factory I would have shown one typical section, which would have given the builder all the information he needed to estimate and construct. On the hospital project I had to present ten detailed section drawings, one for each change in elevation. Well, never mind.

My final specifications for Sheffield were as long as the Manhattan telephone book, a pretty thick volume even then. Naturally I needed extra help in the office to take care of all this. As things turned out, the fee, as they say, nearly bankrupted me.

"Nobody," Bob Mayer quoted to me one night in my studio when we were looking over the block model, "nobody ever puts up but one government hospital."

But if the government had handed me a surprise, I handed it one back: the block model. It was nothing more than a model in plywood of the site with the buildings in their proper location and scale, but at that time it was all new to Washington. Until then you made the model *after* the place was built, so that it could rest in some corridor as a decoration or memento.

Congressman Kaffey was delighted with it, a boy and a new toy. Dr. Muse, on the other hand, was disconcerted. I believe that he couldn't decide whether it was some kind of newfangled frivolity or a subtle trick. He was the direct representative of Forbes, the head of the Bureau, and he seemed very easy to disconcert. It was not true, as some said, that Dr. Muse was an osteopath; he was a dentist. He came from Ohio, as did his friend Sawyer, President Harding's personal physician, who had imported Muse, I was told. The two resembled each other. Both were small men who were never seen except in Army uniforms. They wore them in a manner which gave them the appearance of a couple of rural bellboys, this at a time when regular Army officers stationed in Washington turned out in civilian dress.

Dr. Sawyer, who in addition to being President Harding's medical advisor was Surgeon General, saw the model once or maybe twice when it was in Washington. Possibly it is only the clairvoyance of retrospection, but it seems to me that he always had a suspecting air about him, and well he might. The Veterans' Bureau was given a quarter of a billion dollars to spend—which, as the saying now wistfully goes, was a lot of money in those days—and nobody knows yet exactly how much of it the doctor's colleagues stole. Sawyer himself was never implicated in the swindle.

Dr. Muse had a sort of henchman, too, and this man, Fred Polachek, would have disconcerted anybody. He seemed to be full of secrets, for he spoke only in abbreviated whispers. In fairness to him, the impediment in his speech was due to chronic laryngitis, honorably contracted, according to some, by his being gassed in the war. Nevertheless, his susurrant tone always sounded conspiratorial to me, no matter what he said. And since he had been a power in the Republican politics of New Brunswick, New Jersey, prior to joining the contract division of the Bureau, even his general conversation tended naturally to be cabalistic and malign.

"Who made the little houses?" he had asked me hoarsely.

"You mean the model? One of the boys in my office. You like it?" I had the idea that, in his simplicity—for at that time he did not strike me as a very sophisticated man—he might want a duplicate for his children.

"How much it cost you?"

"I don't know offhand. I could look it up on the time sheets."

"Guess."

"Oh, five hundred dollars."

"You're a damn fool," he whispered.

"How do you mean?"

"I tell the highway department, Trenton, do it for nothing. Remember that next time."

Polachek's attitude toward government came out of no textbook.

He had a curious effect on his colleagues. Our conferences about Sheffield with the Building Committee of the Bureau, as the months wore on, were often long and frequently noisy. Fundamentally, none of the Committee members felt comfortable about the plan, and I could understand why. They had never seen anything quite like it before. But it was not long before I sensed that their discomfort had another cause: none of them wanted their reputations damaged if my hospital turned out to be a fiasco, and on the other hand, none of them wished to be known as having opposed it in case it turned out to be a success, for in the background, I came to realize, always loomed the vague but potential sponsorship of Congressman Kaffey and the Military Affairs Committee. The Building Committee's nervousness frequently took

133

the form of squabbling unnecessarily among themselves—as well as with me—not about the scheme itself but over details, sometimes to the point of absurdity. Dr. Muse led all the rest, his voice a continuing irritable yap. Every day was Halloween around there. You would have thought that Polachek's vocal handicap would have left him out of these rackety discussions. Not at all. When he opened his mouth, although he seldom had anything very pertinent to say, a silence fell, as when a hawk appears over a field of chattering birds.

The site of the hospital was a pretty one, fifty-four acres of rolling woods and fields along either side of the Konckapot River near the old village of Sheffield. The land was tucked right into the southwest corner of Massachusetts; a few miles to the south lay Connecticut, a few miles to the west, New York. Geographically as well as topographically it was an ideal place for a veterans' hospital, serving as it could three populous states whose case load was naturally very heavy. The first time I saw the ground was when Congressman Kaffey met me in Springfield one October morning and we drove over together. Nobody else was along.

That countryside hasn't changed much. The same scattered farmhouses, a few worth watching for a fanlight or a good door as they passed by, the same worn-down barns except for an occasional well-kept exception to remind you that the resolution and skill of the original husbandmen had not everywhere vanished. And behind them the old compassionate curve of the hills wearing now in autumn their exquisite foulard of russet and rose and yellow maple leaves.

"If a man can't get well in this scenery," I remember remarking, "he'd better apply to the Grave Registration Service."

John Kaffey smiled in a limited way. He was never much of a hand for laughter, I had found. He was a serious young man who would not have you think that he took lightly his responsibilities to his constituents, the Legion, and so forth. That was to be respected, of course, but I still felt that his mood was a little too heavy for such a bright morning. His disposition as well as his solemn good looks reminded me a bit of the movie actor Ralph Bellamy, who was young then, too.

"You must live around here some place," I went on. "Fred Polachek told me this was your district."

He was driving, but he turned to give me what I thought was a rather sharp look. "Polachek, eh?" he said. "Yes, my home's Great Barrington. I thought you knew this was my district. I wish it wasn't."

"Why in the world do you say that? What's wrong with it?"

"I mean I wish the hospital wasn't going up here. No, I don't mean that either. If you could see where some of these poor guys are now. In almshouses, by God, hundreds of them." He slapped the steering wheel angrily. "I don't care where they build the hospitals, just so they get built and built quickly."

"Well, then," I said, "I don't get you about the Sheffield location. What's the objection?"

"It's just an embarrassment, a personal embarrassment, that's all."

"You mean because it's in your district? Why, that's a compliment."

He laughed this time, a hollow laugh. "I don't want any more compliments like this one. They could have picked a site five miles in two other directions and I'd be a lot happier. There's plenty of deserving Republicans in upstate New York. Connecticut is *all* Republican. No, it just looks like Kaffey of the Military Affairs Committee couldn't wait to get his hand in the pork barrel. We've appropriated thirty-six million dollars for these hospitals, you know." He did not add that it was a lot of money. It was. "I don't want any of it sticking to any deserving hands around here. Undeserving, I guess I mean," he added, which I thought was a nice little quip for Congressman Kaffey.

I still didn't follow him, however. Who, if not he, had chosen Sheffield as a location? I put the question to him.

"The Bureau, of course," he said.

"But the Military Affairs Committee could have disapproved it. You're on the Committee."

135

He turned to me from the wheel again; this time, I gathered, in incredulity. "You don't imagine I'd lift a finger to impede any part of this program, do you? What would the Legion think? What would the country think?" He faced the road again. "All the same, it's most embarrassing to me, most embarrassing."

Americans, I have often thought, do not have the acute sense of one another that Europeans do, who have had the advantage of living for centuries in practically the same bed. Even those Americans who write books about other Americans are, compared to European writers, markedly unanalytical. Americans are strangers to most of their neighbors' less obvious workings. I, for example, couldn't make up my mind whether John Kaffey was a Boy Scout or a very smooth operator. Contract day, September first of next year—one month after my presentation was up for final approval and the competitive bids for construction would be turned in—was still nine months away. Plenty could happen in that time, I told myself, to form my lasting judgment of the Congressman.

"Is there anything *I* can do?" Paul Eckfield wanted to know. He came East every three or four weeks to see how things were going on the project and he really was a lot of help. I turned over almost all of the plumbing and wiring problems of Sheffield to him, for instance. But what I didn't want him to do was monkey around Washington. I felt that he saw enough of the Bureau crowd when they met with us in New York to satisfy the gregarious side of him.

"Is there anything *I* can do?"

We were over at my house on Beekman Place, I remember, where I spent most of my working time all that winter and spring, and I had told him that the plan had struck a large and unexpected snag. About half of the two thousand cases at Sheffield were to be custodial or continued treatment patients, who would work around the farm or in the shops without supervision. There was no reason that Dr. Muse's medical staff could see why these men should not use the same dining quarters that the rest of the

136

patients did. But now the word had come that the Bureau wanted a separate dining hall for the custodial patients.

"Maybe there's something *I* could do," Paul repeated.

"What, for instance, Paul?" I asked him impatiently.

"I could tell Polachek that you would settle for two dining halls if they shared central kitchen facilities."

"For God's sake, why waste that money?"

Paul didn't reply at once. Instead, he wandered over to the window and stood looking reflectively at the river, as though seeking the right set of words to explain himself to me.

"I think there's something you don't realize yet, George," he turned and said. "These guys *want* to spend money." He made a broad gesticulation. "It's the spirit of the times. We're spending more on veterans than for any other part of the government. I don't say *wasting money, but,*" here he gave me a smiling wink, "nothing's too good for the soldier boys, you know. That's what Polachek says."

And that's what Dr. Muse said, too, when the issue of the divided dining halls was ultimately settled the way the Bureau chose.

"Mr. Forbes will have nothing but the best for the boys at Sheffield or at any of the rest of the hospitals he is building," Muse told me.

"It isn't a question of the best, it's a question of the least practical," I said. "And you know it."

That started his medals jingling. "Don't talk that way to me, Hanes. As long as you're working for us, you'll do what we tell you. And we're telling you we don't want those boys herded together like hogs around a swill trough. Out in Ohio where I come from we don't feed humans that way."

So, as Bob Mayer said when I let him know about the interview, Ohio won that game. In fact, Ohio went undefeated right up to the end of the season. My partner Eckfield was never sunnier; it was pretty plain by now that he was betting on them. He was betting on the Reagans, too. In a perfectly routine manner, Ed's firm had written in to request specifications for Sheffield on the date

137

available, notifying us that the government had approved their application to bid on the construction. When I expressed surprise that the Reagans were interested in a job so far from home, Eckfield pointed out that Thompson & Black, another St. Louis contracting outfit, were in on the Northampton, Massachusetts, hospital and another at Livermore, California. "If you want to land a big piece of business, you've got to reach out for it no matter where it is," Eckfield explained. He could not then have foreseen that reaching out for that piece of business landed Jack Thompson in Leavenworth about three years later.

It gives me a curious feeling to read some of these names in the history books now. Not in the pages of newspapers where for a few weeks or months they appeared often and prominently enough, but on the pages of books, very authoritative books, with hard covers, and photographs on coated stock. It doesn't make you feel very old; it just makes you feel very detached. If that's all that history is. . . .

I remember the afternoon that Bob Mayer called me up about Cramer.

"How well did you know this fellow Cramer?" he asked.

"What Cramer?"

"Charles Cramer, Chief Counsel of the Veterans' Bureau. Forbes' right-hand man."

Well, I had heard the name but that was all. My dealings with Forbes' office went through Dr. Muse.

"Cramer shot himself," Bob said. "You better send Alfred out for a paper."

That I did. There was quite a story about it. The fact that Cramer had killed himself in the home in Washington that he had bought from Harding when Harding moved from the Senate to the White House added another odd note to the affair.

About the first week in June I received a visit from Fred Polachek. I fix the date at that time because the history books show that Cramer's suicide occurred in the middle of March, and Jess Smith's on Decoration Day. Smith was described as Attorney

General Daugherty's right-hand man, giving rise to Bob Mayer's remark, "They'll have to start calling in the southpaws pretty soon. The right-handers are knocking themselves off like flies." I remember thinking it proper to offer Polachek my condolences on the recent death of a second colleague of his in the public service within so short a time.

"Both nice guys," he said in his husky, uninflected voice. "But sick." He patted himself low on the vest. "Here. Indigestion. Let's talk about something happy," he whispered. "You got a lot of money coming to you."

I knew I hadn't. My firm would just about break even on our two years' work on the job.

"You were a good boy about the dining rooms, George. Now I want you to be a good boy about the bedrooms."

"How do you mean?"

"You got them fixed up way too cheap."

"I see. You're talking about the over-all room cost at Sheffield. Well, that's about what the Public Health Service hospitals figure out at."

He made an impatient and scornful gesture. "What do I care about P.H.S.? This is different, George."

"Why?"

"Why?" the hoarse voice repeated. "Because that's what it's going to be at Northampton, Livermore, Excelsior Springs. Because that's how you get the bonus."

"What bonus, Fred?"

"One hundred fifty thousand dollars split three ways. Fifty to you, fifty to the contractor. And maybe you like to pick the contractor. Maybe your business partner Reagan."

Involuntarily I shot a look at the door, as though I might catch someone listening to us. This was my first experience at being suborned to embezzle the United States Government. I didn't even think to ask him where the third fifty thousand of the boodle was to go.

"What if we just let the specifications stay as they are, Fred?"

He looked at me with pity. "Why are you so foolish? We just want you to make some improvements. Like the land up there at Sheffield. Some damn fool was going to sell it for buttons."

"What improvements did they make on the site?"

"I don't know. How should I know, way up there in Massachusetts? Enough, anyhow."

"Well, I don't see why you don't make the improvements on the specification costs yourself. I don't have to have anything to do with it."

"But of course you do, George. You are the expert. You have a reputation in the business."

"I wouldn't have one very long, Fred."

Again he gave me the pitying look. "Poor George," he muttered. "You don't want all your work for nothing, do you?" And he got up and made ready to leave. "I don't want the changes sent through for two, three weeks."

I remember that several days passed before I found a plausible reason for going down to Washington. It was late afternoon when I called at Kaffey's office, but his secretary said that the House would be in session another half-hour or so. He showed me into Kaffey's own room, where I was to wait. The marble Capitol dome was already illuminated. Through the window, against the pale blue of the early evening sky, it looked like a design in Wedgwood. It is a handsome structure; so many of our nineteenth-century government buildings have great style and pride. And then I began to think about men like John Russell Pope, and Aldrich, and Clarence Wunder, giants in their time of our architecture and indeed of our culture, seated at their ease in the Lincoln study, the piqué piping elegant on their broadcloth waistcoats, the long coronas and bourbon comfortably at hand, speaking to the President—Mr. Roosevelt or Mr. Taft, men of the same tastes, associates—of what edifices might next be required by the Republic.

Congressman Kaffey, the friend of the veterans, came in.

"Well," he said as we shook hands, "it's good to talk to someone who is doing something *for* the government rather than doing the government *out* of something." That was another pretty good one, coming from Congressman Kaffey.

I didn't have much that I wanted to talk to him about. I just wanted to take another good look into that All-American face of his and see if it told me anything. I did ask him if it was true that the tract at Sheffield had been altered. He seemed puzzled.

"No," he said, "I don't see how it could be. Oh yes, there's a couple of farmhouses on the place, you remember. Somebody brought in electricity and a phone line. But don't worry about it. The land's ours all right. Tear them out or make use of them as you wish."

"I see," I said, and wondered if I did.

Over the East River the sun shone hot and bright on the morning of the Fourth of July. The city lay still, its heavy holiday quiet broken only from time to time by the distant crackle of fireworks. So was the river quiet; only now and then did a pleasure boat, scurrying upstream lest it be late for the day's fun on the Sound, make its determined little chevron on the water below us while Margaret and I were having breakfast by the windows of my sitting room. In Egypt the bones of a king of the eighteenth dynasty, Tutankhamen, had not long before been rifled from their tomb, and in consequence Margaret fashionably wore a dress of soft white cotton printed horizontally with small hieroglyphs in ocher and lemon and black. I remember that its neckline was wide and square and that her lovely shoulders were tanned to a light bronze from the summer weeks at Watch Hill, and that the light from the river came up to dance along the curve of her fawn cheek and make tiny white stars twinkle in her short dark hair.

She pushed her plate purposefully from her, rose, and came around to my side of the table where she stood scratching my head. "My mother," she said, "asked me as I was leaving what I might find to do in New York on the Fourth of July and I told her that, naturally, you would take me to Coney Island, just like everybody else. I've never been."

"And I certainly will."

"Oh ho," she said doubtfully. "That's the sort of thing that a man promises in the night. In the morning it means little, as every woman knows."

We went, just the same. We went in a sturdy Dodge touring car that I had at the time, over the great clanging Queensborough Bridge and then across Prospect Park, where the wide lawns were freshly clipped and on a tall white flagstaff the national colors, flying high in the sun-whitened sky, looked happy and fearless as especially they do when you see them unexpectedly in a foreign country or anywhere on the Fourth of July. And then, after a long ride out on a broad avenue lined on either side with interminable rows of small apartment houses, came the smell and feel of the ocean, and suddenly there before us beneath the spires and minarets massed the enormous crowd, always gently in motion, like the ocean itself. Leaving the car, happily and hand in hand we hurried into it as bathers to the sea.

First we tried the Thunderbolt for a few rides, during which my hat blew away; then some looping swings where all the change fell out of my pocket; then we made our way to a barroom whose whole front was open to the boardwalk, for Coney so far as Prohibition was concerned had arrogated to itself extraterritorial rights.

Margaret, who had lost nothing since she wore no hat and carried no bag, sat sipping her highball entranced. "I had no idea," she said, "no idea at all it was so exciting and lovely. So many people, look, little ones and big ones and black ones and white ones. Isn't it simply lovely? All our fellow citizens. What a wonderful place to celebrate Independence Day!"

I think my face must have changed at the word "independence"; there were certainly bonds that I was not free of. She covered my hands with hers. "Drink up, Citizen Hanes," she said. "Where are we going for lunch?"

We went to Feltman's and it, too, delighted her with its airy pergolas, little fountains on bits of lawn shaded with old maples, and space after wide space divided at random by trellises where innumerable people sat at innumerable tables. Sometimes at night I dream of a charming and absolutely inarticulated plan, and then

142

realize just before waking that I am somewhere in the green and shady labyrinth of Feltman's. Feltman's as it was then.

We had a long lunch of steamed clams and lobster, with frosty glass seidels of beer and then, agreeing that because of the Fourth of July and our own special circumstances even the laws of pathology were temporarily rescinded, we went immediately in swimming. Meeting each other on the beach side of our bathhouse in our gray wool one-piece bathing suits with our room keys strung from our necks, we stopped and smiled at each other, for a moment almost strangers. Now we had even put off the clothes that had trailed us from the world we had left.

"Yes," she said, with that old mind-reading trick of hers as we crossed the sand through the recumbent crowd, "wouldn't it be nice if we never had to go back?"

In the late afternoon we were photographed on the observation platform of a railway car, kissed a number of times while floating through the Tunnel of Love, and stopped at various booths for frankfurters and sauerkraut, spun sugar, pineapple juice, and other regional delicacies. This we topped off with a session at a shooting gallery, where Margaret gave the doll we won to a little girl who accepted it without surprise at anything that might happen in this wonderland, and made a return visit to the open-front saloon.

The fireworks we saw in the evening from a car on the Ferris wheel, great streaks and bursts of the most incongruously innocent colors—the simple, limited colors of schoolroom chalk, on a blackboard of night sky—while below us on one side streamed the golden lights of the midway and boardwalk and on the other the long silver combers that gleamed and faded on the dark sea.

We stayed in our car on the wheel for ride after ride and spoke to a number of our transient fellow passengers. One, I remember, was a sparse man in cowboy boots and a Stetson who told us that he was a rope artist with tricks that surpassed those of Will Rogers, but that he had no patter. Another was a small boy who possessed an inexhaustible supply of dimes and was not lost. When there was no one else in the car she rested her head on my shoulder, and it lay on my shoulder all the way as we drove back into the quiet city. We had dinner in the garden of an almost deserted French restaurant in the East Fifties; cold lamb and a salad, I remember, and, just because no rules applied, champagne.

She asked me for the photograph and sat gloating over it. "Just think," she said, "my fellow took me to Coney Island on the Fourth of July. Wasn't it lovely?"

How lovely, I thought, how lovely if life could be lived as though it were a perpetual musical comedy, in which an orchestra played unendingly at one's feet and happy crowds danced beneath colored lights, in which nothing more serious befell than the hero's losing his hat and the resolution, sure from the beginning, found the beautiful girl in his arms. And I thought of the resolution that many months ago I had tried to force on Margaret by letter and telephone. "I understand," she had said. "You want to come out here and go through the man-to-man ceremony with Dan. It's a matter of etiquette to you, like your marrying Mary. I won't be the pawn in a Pinero drawing-room drama. This is between me and Dan, not you and Dan. Anyhow, what would you say to him? Offer to make an honest woman of me? You can't you know, George. You're married."

Now she looked up and turned the photograph to me. "Isn't it wonderful? A couple of demented shoplifters?"

I heard myself saying, "It will look well on your bedroom table back in St. Louis."

Her large dark eyes widened in complete surprise, and then remained wide open from shocked anger. "Why did you say that? Why?"

"Well," I began, tentatively.

"Do you think—? Is that what's been going on in your mind? Do you think I would let anybody else touch me?"

So that, I thought bitterly, is how I make an end to our day of happiness. And then as suddenly as her anger had come, she leaned across the table to me, all tenderness. "Dear George, my dearest George."

"I am so God-damned sorry," I said.

144

"I know," she said, "I know. Please, it's all right. It was my fault."

"In God's name, how?"

"I should have given you your going-away present before."

"What do you mean?"

"I was saving the going-away present to give you just before I had to go back to Watch Hill. I mean it's all right, George. Dan and I are getting a divorce. He *wants* a divorce."

For a few moments I found nothing to say. Here was I, struggling numbly with my tangled difficulties, while she, so small and dear and vulnerable, had dealt with her part of the problem clearly, bravely, and definitely. I was filled with love for her, and compassion.

"Well," Margaret said brightly, leaning back in her chair and holding up her empty glass, "shouldn't we have some more champagne? A lot more?"

The only unresolved element in the proposition I had decided to make to Ed Reagan was where I wanted the talk to take place. Writing him or phoning him was of course out of the question. If I went to see him in St. Louis without any other reason for the trip, it might later arouse suspicion. If I asked him to come to New York he might become wary and cautious, and I could not wait until we met in the normal course of business. I had been deliberating this phase of the intrigue during the day or so after Margaret left town when I received a wire from Eckfield saying that he thought I would want to be advised that Junie Neidlinger had been badly injured in an automobile smash. That was what made up my mind to go to St. Louis. I think I would have gone to see Junie under any circumstances; as you live into your thirties a few college or war associations have a way of growing more valuable to you. I suppose their intrinsic quality is there all the while, but they tend to call themselves to your attention as the passage of time disposes of less emotional relationships, and also the nostalgia that the years bring can ripen your affection toward certain people, even though you do not see or think about them

145

very often. And I expect, in addition, that in some obscure way my guilt craved the company of the only out-and-out criminal of my acquaintance.

So the first thing that I did when I got to St. Louis was phone Reagan and ask him to join me in my room at the Tower for a drink after work, and the second was to go out to Barnes Hospital to call on Junie. I found him lying uncovered in a bed which his bulk seemed to make about a size too small for him, and attended by a young woman in a pale-blue dress punctured with many eyelets. Her face reminded me of the face of the doll that Margaret had won at Coney Island. Junie's face was cut in several places; his head wore a heavy cap of bandages. A cast reached from his waist down each leg to his feet; among other injuries he had a fractured pelvis. Electric fans on either side of the room blew but did not cool the air around him—in good St. Louis style it was hot enough outside to break the bricks—but he wore a derisive grin in spite of what must have been considerable discomfort.

"Well, George," he said, "you catch me on the deck again. Meet Olive. Olive, this is Mr. Hanes. We were in the Navy together."

Olive turned her head to me very slowly as though she were not too confident of its connection with her neck and shoulders, and I saw that, beneath its wig of springy lifeless silver hair, the girl's face was not so much blank as stunned.

"Olive has a compound hangover," Junie explained. "She hasn't learned that this isn't drinking weather."

"Jesus," said Olive.

"Never you mind," Junie said. "You just wait until Daddy can get out of this crank case. Daddy knows how to bring the roses back to his little girl's cheeks."

"You shut up," Olive said.

"Now go out and play somewhere for a while," continued Junie paternally, "and when you come back I'll give you a nice big bottle of gin."

"Oh, shut up," Olive said. She rose slowly and walked herself on little careful steps out of the room.

"A swell kid," said Junie.

146

"How did all this happen?" I asked.

Junie stopped smiling and looked at me thoughtfully. "It was an accident, George. A kind of an accident."

"What do you mean, a kind of an accident."

He reached down and scratched at his stomach under the cast. "Did you ever hear of an accident going someplace to happen, George? Well, I went someplace and it happened." He scratched some more, his lips drawn back from the pain and pleasure that it gave him. "Only the car didn't catch fire."

"Well, that was lucky, anyhow."

"Some people think so, George, and some people don't." He chuckled. "It all depends on the point of view." He reached overhead for the button to signal a nurse. "Sit down where I can look at you. We'll have a drink."

I took Olive's torture chair.

"Was anybody with you?"

"No, George. I was going someplace by myself."

"How about the other car?"

"They were going in my direction, you see. More or less. They weren't hurt, I don't think. Just me."

"What were they, drunk?"

"They were strangers in town, George."

The nurse came in and Junie ordered two Tom Collinses as though he were in a barroom, and such evidently was Junie's standing with the staff that presently the order was filled as though he were indeed in a barroom. I drank some of mine, thinking of what Dan Pierce had said about Junie having no competition in the liquor business, but that was some time ago. I gathered from what Junie had chosen to tell me that an era of free enterprise had dawned on bootlegging in St. Louis, as elsewhere.

We talked through the hot afternoon: about people we had been with in the Navy and people in St. Louis, friends, my family and his. I wanted to ask him about his father, but thought that their relationship might have become too sensitive a matter by now. As it was, Junie finally brought him into the conversation, saying that he would drop in at the hospital a little later and asking me to stay to see him.

147

"I want him to see that I have friends outside the automobile business," he said lightly.

"He must have been pretty upset by your accident," I remarked.

Junie's face darkened suddenly and angrily as it had the time when I refused the car. "He doesn't know a thing about it. Not a damned thing! And he's not going to!"

"You mean about how it happened."

"Not a damned thing!" he repeated.

I wondered how long a man of Mr. Neidlinger's connections—after all, he was an important industrial and business financier in the town, not a monk—could remain or be kept uninformed about his youngest son's affairs. It was not long afterward that he joined us. Stubbornly, Teutonically impervious to the temperature, he had on a single-breasted blue serge suit and a high hard collar. His only concession to the season was that he wore a hard straw hat and had left off his vest. I would not have been surprised to see him with gloves and an umbrella. As Junie had predicted, it pleased him to find me there.

"So you are building a great hospital in the East, George. I am very glad. Here we are much the same. Our old hotel—" He shrugged. "We have new competition, as you know."

The Chase had just been built a few blocks down Kingshighway from Barnes, at the corner of Lindell and the park. It had grounds around it and a large roof garden. It was not so cool inside in the summer as the Tower, but it looked cooler; most of the cream of the transient business now stopped there.

"So what do you think of my boy?" he asked. "An automobile man, he gets himself wrecked in one of his own cars." He chuckled at the little joke he was going to make. "Edward," he said, recalling to me their common first name, "you must do as we used to say in the olden days, get a horse." He turned to me and mirthfully explained, "The new ways are too dangerous for him."

I noticed that the nap on the carpet near the door in my sitting room at the hotel was beginning to hint at the weave beneath; Barney's flowers and buffet only gave the place a slightly more pathetic air, like a lady, who has come down a bit in the world,

148

wearing a good hat and her jewelry to spruce up last year's frock. But it was still fundamentally a very fine frock. The architect of the Chase would never see the day when he could design a room of this grace of proportion. Reagan's presence, of course, did not in my view add to the decoration, but I had to disregard him as an old and unpleasant acquaintance. I must deal with him as a problem in ethics.

The problem was simple as I saw it: I was going to match the opportunity for him to make a killing against his wife's religious scruples. I was convinced that when the really big chips were down he himself had no scruples, and I also believed that he was ruthless or cunning enough to circumvent hers.

My own moral dialectic ran this way: if I did not submit to the fraud of needlessly adding to the hospital's expense, I would surely be kicked off the job, certainly lose my and my firm's commission, and inevitably delay—if not indeed prevent, were an investigation aroused—the hospital's construction. I had at my command no evidence beyond Polachek's conversation that any dirty work was afoot; denunciation at this time by me would be absurd. On the other hand, by diverting a comparatively tiny trickle of the public funds to Reagan, I would collect my fee, the hospital would be built, and, for a price, Reagan would get himself free to marry Mary and me to marry Margaret. If this begins to sound like the synopsis of a Shakespearean comedy, let me tell you that it was not comic to me. I asked myself if I would have been prepared for larceny if only my life with Margaret were at stake, if only my job on the hospital were at stake? But the questions were academic, it seemed to me. And anyway, I told myself, we are all constantly expecting more of each other, more of ourselves, than we should. In other words, I went crooked.

"Ed," I said, "how would you like to make a great deal of money?"

Ed looked around him derisively. "You mean by selling this old flea-bag?"

"I mean by your getting the contract to build Sheffield. No ifs, ands, or buts."

"No ifs, ands, or buts, eh?"

149

"And a fifty thousand dollar bonus. Just for your good kind face," I couldn't help adding.

"For my good kind face," he repeated. I wondered at the unruffled smoothness with which he received the proposition. "Who says that I could have it?"

"I do and Fred Polachek."

"Polachek. A very powerful man. And what, as my old father would say, would you be wantin' in return?"

"For you to get a divorce and marry Mary."

"But would she be havin' me?" He was up to his ears in the mocking Hibernian dialect act now.

"She'll marry you the hour you get your divorce. She can have one from me in twenty-eight days."

"But my own poor wife. What will she be sayin', and her a very religious woman."

"Let's cut the comedy, Ed. This is damned serious, to me at least."

He got up and went over to the buffet and poured himself a drink; after all, it was as much his as mine. And when he turned and raised the glass he was the picture of contented amusement. He had also dropped the Irish cross-talk act.

"The job's already ours, George," he told me. "Quite a while ago, in fact. Eckfield fixed it up."

I felt like an old whore who has not only been cheated out of her price but in addition made the victim of a monstrous practical joke. What a lesson.

"You're the one who led with your chin this time, George," Ed said. He put his drink down, waved me a friendly salute, and walked out of the door. So that was that, and how right he was.

And Paul Eckfield—"Is there anything I can do?" He had done plenty. He was a funny man all right, I thought; way too funny for me. First he had nudged me out of my office, now he had beat me out of my deal with Ed Reagan. But of course that was neither just, fair, nor true. Paul had done exactly what I had tried to do. Possibly he planned for the firm to profit in the way that Polachek

150

had suggested it to me. I certainly had been in no position to explore that part of the arrangement with Ed.

After dinner I made a reservation on the morning train East and went out to the hospital again to say good-by to Junie.

He studied me for a moment or so when I came into his room. Olive was back on duty but revived; I expect she had gotten her present from Junie when she came in from play. "You all right?" he asked me.

"Sure. Fine. Me, I've got both of *my* feet. See?"

"Make Mr. Hanes a drink, Olive. Is that hospital of yours really going up?"

"It sure is, Junie."

"No troubles there, then."

"It's going up."

"But the hotel, that worries you."

Olive gave me a drink and fixed her glass doll's eyes on me.

"A little."

"I want to do something about that one of these days," Junie said. "It ought to be all yours. Those Reagans aren't any good, are they? I have an idea they skate pretty close to the edge of the law once in a while. Putting bum material into their jobs and so forth, I mean."

"I don't know everything about them, Junie. None of the downtown hotels are turning the customers away nowadays. I can't blame that on the Reagans."

"Anyhow, you couldn't just leave the hotel in my garage like you did the sedan." He laughed. "Olive, you could read a different Bible in a different room every night. I've always had a soft spot in my heart for the old Tower."

"Oh, shut up," she said.

"Which one of the boys is downstairs?" he asked her.

"Julie."

"Well, you go and play with him for a while." Again she obeyed his dismissal automatically; it must have been a familiar order to Olive. "But not too rough," he cheerily called after her. He shifted what he could of the upper part of his body but there could have been very little relief for him to find, half covered in plaster in that torrid bed.

"A great little girl, Olive," he said. "Good company."

"She's not garrulous," I conceded.

"It's good to have company around," he went on, unresponsive as ever to any observation off the track of his thought. He looked at me for a few moments as though searching my face for some further clue that might resolve his problem of what to do for my good, and it occurred to me that one of the main reasons for my fondness for him was his stubborn, almost monotonous concern about me. "You must be lonely a good deal of the time, professor. That wife of yours isn't any wife at all, is she? Her out in California, you in New York. And you can't shake her, can you?"

"You quit worrying about me and the hotel and the Reagans," I said. "You're only about half alive right now. Just keep your mind on getting well and getting out of here."

"Did you ever think of knocking her off? Not you, but I mean it could be done simply enough."

He was dead serious, so help me.

"Well," I said in my best sick-room manner, "I don't want to stay here and tire you. I'd better be going now."

"It was nice of you to come all the way out here to see me, professor," he said, and I swear that to look at him you would have sworn yourself that homicide had never in his life entered his mind. "Don't think I don't appreciate it."

I had known all along that I would have to face that embarrassment, although I had made it clear enough that I had also come for a meeting with Ed Reagan.

"I told you it was a business trip," I said.

"And don't think I'll forget it," he continued, as though I had said nothing at all.

When I got back to the hotel Barney told me that the switchboard had been holding a long-distance call for me and I went up to my room to take it. The call came from Washington; Congressman Kaffey was on the line. For a wild moment I had the sense of being not a character in a Shakespearean comedy but the pro-

152

tagonist of a Greek drama of retribution. And what swift retribution. Had the eye of Kaffey been upon me all the time I was trying to bribe Ed that afternoon? As quickly as had come the feeling of guilt came a sense of suspicion. Was the Congressman, aware that I had gone to St. Louis, about to declare himself in on the building graft, assuming that he had already diddled the government on the Sheffield land deal?

"George," he said, rather ominously I thought, "I tried to get you in New York. When will you be back?" I told him. "Well, this is something I can't talk to you about over the phone." So we arranged a meeting, at my house as he stipulated, the morning after next.

All the way East I couldn't quite reject the idea that Kaffey had in some way gotten onto my perfidy. I knew that there was nothing conceivable to incriminate me in the way of documentary evidence. But I have the bad conscience of the almost habitually honest man, or at least the nervousness in these matters of a man with neither inherited nor acquired skills in dishonesty. When Congressman Kaffey arrived at the studio the next morning I searched his face and found a troubled look upon it. He closed the door carefully behind him.

"George," he asked, almost in the hollow tone of Fred Polachek, "how much have you at stake in the Sheffield hospital? I mean, are your draftsmen, office expenses, and all that paid up to date?"

I told him they were. He nodded and bit his lips in earnest reflection.

"But the money that represents the profit to you, the balance of the fee, that hasn't been paid?" he asked.

"It's not due until the finished plan is accepted. Not until August fifteenth."

"George, old man," said the Congressman, coming over to put a pastoral hand on my shoulder, "I've got some bad news for you. The Sheffield hospital will probably never be built."

By now I hardly knew whether to laugh or cry. "What's the trouble, John?" I asked him. That seemed a safe question.

"Crookery. Crookery from the top to the bottom of the Bureau.

The whole organization will have to be cleaned out from Forbes down. The hospital program will be investigated, the surplus sales at Perryville, everything. I tell you this in confidence. In a sense I'm breaking my oath of office to divulge the information prematurely outside Congress. But I didn't want to see you suffer further financial loss by continuing work on the plans."

"Well," I said, "thanks a lot for telling me, John."

Life can get moving pretty fast sometimes, I reflected. Within the short span of a fortnight I had successively been on the point of achieving a considerable professional success, then willing to make a dishonorable compromise of it, and now as relieved as the most contemptible of green-horn gamblers to get out of the whole affair with my skin.

Kaffey went over and began fiddling with a pair of dividers on the drawing board. "I don't know," he said, "I just don't know what the Legion will say to all this. We all had our hearts so set on the program." He suddenly turned to me. "By golly, *you* were the first one to put your finger on this mess. Days before the committee's investigators began making their reports."

"Oh, I don't think so, John," I said hurriedly. "How do you mean?"

"Don't you remember mentioning those so-called improvements on the site at Sheffield? If I'd only paid more attention I would have smelled a rat."

"Oh."

"But you don't have any idea, no idea at all, the amount of detail that piles up every day, day after day, when you're in public life." He laid aside the dividers with one of the few genuinely tired sighs that I have ever heard. "It's no bed of roses. Representing the people is no bed of roses."

"I'm sure it's not."

He got ready to leave. "The best that I can say, George, is thank God these birds didn't get *you* involved in any of their sorry machinations."

I have never had any sense of, much less aptitude for, politics, whether on the social, professional, national, or international level.

154

Immaturity, timidity, laziness, call it what you like—the social sciences leave me cold. I am convinced that the world is dying of too much of all kinds of government. The intricacies, manipulation, and the apparently inescapable corruption of that phase of human activity—from what I have read of it and what I have personally seen—only make me feel uncomfortable, like a slightly effeminate schoolboy adrift in a mining camp. For this lacuna in my personality I offer no excuse. I was not meant to play on that team, or even to watch that team play. But Kaffey was. And for all his staggering self-preoccupation and his solemn absurdities, he was a good man for the job of tribune of the people. He was not too absurd to cherish ideals and to abominate those who did not. And he was not too preoccupied to be thoughtful of others; he had gone to some pains in the midst of what must have been a very sensitive moment in his own career to consider my welfare. It should be surprising only to the cynical that John Kaffey's constituents have continued him in office year after year and that he was elected by a substantial majority to a year as state commander of the American Legion, which is all that you can serve.

Nobody ever builds but one government hospital, Bob Mayer had said. I never built any. And so ended what we might call My Life with Warren Harding—except for a slight sequel.

Some years later in McCormick Hall I was giving my opening lecture in an introductory course on Art and Archeology to a group of sophomores—Architecture 20. The chief purpose is to accustom the boys to the use of slides and give them a brief rundown on the kind of antiquities they may expect to encounter as the term proceeds. There is often a little diffidence at these opening sessions, so I have always found it best to humanize the proceedings with a joke or two. For example, you flash on a picture of the Porch of the Maidens on the Acropolis, showing the dear old battered caryatids holding up the western entablature. You explain what it is all about and then add: "This is, of course, not the first time that an architect has used the female form for support." It is a wheeze that has never failed to click with any undergraduate group in my experience, nor did it fail this time. A few of the students thawed out sufficiently to come up and chat at the end of the lecture. Then one of them introduced himself as Tom Polachek.

"You and my father were in Washington together," he said. "Fred Polachek."

"Indeed we were," I said. "Where is he now? I've often wondered what he was doing."

"Oh, he's still in New Brunswick. He has a contracting business."

I thought I knew most of the contracting firms in the state, but the name of Polachek had not turned up among them. I asked the boy what his father's firm was called, and he said it was the Acme Building Company, which was one of the largest in central Jersey.

"You probably don't connect him with the company. Dad's not one to shout much about his business." He laughed. "Even if he could, I mean."

"No," I said. "That's true."

"Dad told me to be sure to look you up. He said you were a square shooter."

Eleven

WHEN my mother and father were alive and we all lived in Chicago I was sent to the Latin School and in due course was graduated from it. It was then an old, adequate and respected local institution, and as far as I know it still is. From there I went to Princeton—as had my brother Jeff, my father, and his father—where I had a most congenial time. No one else in my college class happened to be from Chicago. But from the moment I alighted from the "dinky"—which in those days puffed right up to the steps of Blair—and was received with the rest of the newcomers by a mob of waiting sophomores, I felt completely at home.

The well-known enchantment of the setting—which by some magic insoluble to me still visually grows in scope and beauty with the years—could have had little to do with my feeling of ease and security. I had visited my brother on several occasions while he was there. The ivied towers and the green fountains of elm, always just missing theatricality and therefore always achieving, I suppose, great theater, were not new to me. What was it then that said that this was sanctuary, the ever loving and ever to be beloved place? It was surely not the immediate appearance and deportment of the upperclassmen. On the contrary. This was a period of transition in the fashion of dress among the young men at the college, so that some of them still affected the greasy corduroys and huge coarse sweaters of an earlier time when the thing to do was to look like yeggs or safe-crackers. Others in the crowd, however, had adorned themselves—with their narrow white canvas shoes, sparse flannels, hard collars, and the rest of it—in the manner of Newport dudes. The effect created by these youngsters was therefore not unlike that of a contemporary prize-fight mob, and their rowdyism toward us incoming freshmen was in character. But it was not really disturbing. It was violence of the good-natured sort that swallowed you up in it instead of buffeting or rejecting you. I at once felt jovially accepted, as I am sure was the case with all the rest of the new class. And for four years I never had a lonely moment. In fact, from that first afternoon I can't recall ever having had a moment entirely to myself. We must have even done our studying curled up around one another in the manner of those nests of Laocoöns to be seen in the group photographs of the period.

To none of my college generation—or those of my father, brother, and grandfather—did it make the slightest difference to your social acceptability what part of the country you came from or where you had gone to school. We indeed had heroes and leaders of one sort and another among us, but the classes themselves were small and extremely egalitarian. That is probably to say that financially everybody was about equally well to do, although I am sure that I never considered that aspect of it at the time.

One's native geography, as I say, did not matter. My grandfather recalled that when, as a freshman, it became known that his family's place was outside Rock Island, in western Illinois, he received a certain amount of chaff about living among the Indians. He feigned indignation. But, he said, even if he had revealed—as he certainly did not—that in point of fact a permanent encampment of Pawnee horse dealers was located in the river meadow behind his home, he was sure that it would not have affected his standing in the coterie.

In the years that Jeff and I were at Princeton the same spirit

158

prevailed; everybody had about the same amount of money to spend, which in those far more uniform times meant that everybody came from about the same kind of family, no matter what its address. There are many comforts to be had from a frozen society, provided you are not among those in the deeper freeze. It was assumed, I suppose, that everybody had previously gone to school in some decent sort of way, if it were ever thought of at all.

Looking back over what I have written, as the customary autobiographical phrase goes, I have indicated that I married Mary (in Margaret's well-chosen words) out of a sense of etiquette. I badly overdrew on the affectionate understanding between Margaret and myself when I chose to be secretive with her about my marriage. In the wake of that mistake, scandal took me by surprise, as did the course of history when it began the wreckage of the Tower. Those were all matters of bad judgment, in fact damned bad judgment. The sensible man deplores such errors, resolves to use his head more to capacity should ever (God forbid) similar situations arise, and gets on with the ever continuing business of living. But carelessness, too, can turn the events of our lives, and that really is infuriating. What I am trying to say is that I mishandled an important element in young Jeff's education due to a lack of current information which I might easily have come by through hearsay, and surely at the cost of only a little investigation.

When, a decade after the upheavals of the First World War, young Jeff went to college, the size of the undergraduate body had enormously increased, and so of course had the number of its social stratifications. Every kind of person you could imagine went to Princeton. The old sense of universal homogeneity—of belonging—had almost passed away, surviving now only among the cadres of boys from the large and long established Eastern private preparatory schools. From the very beginning of their freshman year these boys, by their numbers and mutual influence, formed the heart of the undergraduate society, fabricating a sort of college within a college. They achieved the leadership of the various organizations, dominated whatever there was of youthful politics, made the top four or five clubs and in general had the best of it. Most

159

distressing to those not admitted to their sphere, they gave the distinct impression that they were going to have the best of it for the rest of their lives. If you had missed out now, the mien of these golden careerists seemed to say, you had missed out forever. It was a surprising maverick who could wallow himself a comfortable corner in the well-managed pastures of this blooded herd. A few originals, of course, did not want to belong to the herd or even to live near its fence lines. But everybody else, simple social animals that they were, certainly did. Failure to do so made many of them in one way or another lonely, uncomfortable, and very unhappy.

Jeff, coming from a faraway hick school—his family consisting of a mother and younger sister moving by then from one resort hotel to another, and me, a bachelor—was, on the basis of his background, not much of a prospect for acceptance among the elite. And since he wasn't an accomplished athlete, that side door to the companionship of the elect was closed to him too. Jeff settled for literature and alcohol.

I don't know what my brother, that disciplined, creative man with few peers and fewer competitors, would have made out of all this so far as it concerned his son. Yes, as a matter of fact, I think I do. The social complications he would have considered—if he could have comprehended them at all—as frivolous, absurd, although perhaps momentarily a little amusing. He would have deplored his son's drinking as a pathetic sort of aberration in anyone not hopelessly defeated or ill, and an unbelievable waste of time for a young man with the world before him. But he would have approved the reading and writing part of it.

The company that young Jeff kept at this time—boys like himself distracted and more reckless than they need have been—would have dismayed if not his father, certainly his grandfather. For a while they even dismayed me. I had been living in Princeton for several years when Jeff came to school there and I shall never forget the first member of his clique that he brought around to my house for a drink—Peter Maben. What a raffish type he was, with well-cut unpressed clothes plus the usual guarded, challenging air

160

about him of a square peg defying the round hole. In the course of the conversation I am sure that he ventured any number of strong opinions, but one has stuck with me ever since. "The only two things in life that are worth a damn," Peter said, "are sleep and gin." My nephew chuckling in agreement, I made a note to reserve the Scotch for more sophisticated tastes in future. I couldn't afford an unlimited supply of it even for myself. But Maben's was by and large a harmless election, I thought—anodyne and repose—for a scholar of his age and without many demands upon his time.

Peter was not to be much longer among us, as it turned out, but we were to see him from time to time as the years passed and even to read his name in the newspapers for he joined the foreign service and went on to make a record for himself as a career man in troubled posts. It wasn't very long ago that I ran across him at one of those parties in New York where the young and old of wider views are brought together—to start a ballet, end an injustice, or something of the sort—and it occurred to me to ask him if he were still getting his share of sleep and gin. "Brandy now, George," he said. "Sleep, of course, whenever possible." He smiled in recollection. "We were special cases, weren't we?" And I said I believed that was so.

Ah, the torture of a human being who is a Special Case. Particularly a young human being. Even more particularly, a sensitive one.

Young Jeff's mother had grown restless, I suppose, from waiting for Ed Reagan to take her permanently in his arms. At any rate she no longer spent all her time at the hotel in Pasadena. She began going to other hotels—in Maine, Florida, the West Indies. She never stopped very long anywhere and she never went very far away from the United States, possibly because she was nervous about leaving Ed at much distance or for much time. Often she went alone. But there were times when she took little Mary along—to the delight, I am sure, of that Sybaritic young Bedouin, for there was a child far more suited to oasis life than home life. "In an hotel," she airily explained to me at the age of thirteen, "one

161

gets whatever one wishes. One always selects an establishment *de grande luxe*, of course."

With young Jeff it was different. His career with his mother was a jerky succession of glimpses of places where he would have loved to have settled into, like the other people. How he must have yearned to belong to the young crowd so obviously established for the season around the casinos and beaches, the corrals and chuck shops of a dozen resorts where Mary and he paused for a few afternoons. He was the little boy with the lady and the little girl who did not have any regular table in the dining room, or cabana, or saddle horse; they were just going to be here three or four days. Too bad he wasn't around for the costume dance the Saturday before, or wasn't staying for the one next Saturday. You hadn't been to Jackson's Hole? Well, of course that was a six-day trip, there and back. Sorry, those bikes were for the guests remaining all season. There were special ones rented by the day (not very good ones), like the special catboats (not very new ones), and the special lockers (over on the other corridor somewhere) for the transients. He was a special case, a fleeting spectator, at all the established national pleasure domes. And of course he was a special case in school: the boy whose mother and father were married to each other but didn't live together, the boy who had no home town.

In the spring that had ended his first session of boarding school I had flown out to get him and had brought him back to New York. It was his first trip in an airplane. I remember how intelligent his responses and reactions to the experience had been. Keeping his nose flattened on the window most of the time, he was surprised, he told me, that the contour of the Appalachians appeared from aloft so modulated and that the long-settled East should still present such vast areas of forest land; and, stamping on the deck a few times, he said that he had somehow not expected flooring to have so substantial a feeling when suspended seven thousand feet in the air. His comments showed a searching kind of curiosity and a propensity toward fundamental reflection rare for a kid, it seemed to me.

162

Little Jeff and Alfred Jones accepted each other without prejudice and at affectionate face value within a very few hours after having been introduced. There followed several days of my showing Jeff around the town—a visit to the Statue of Liberty, a matinee at the Hippodrome (he figured out how those girls must have invisibly emerged after disappearing in the swimming tank), a tour of Chinatown by night (bed was not reached until eleven o'clock *that* evening), a look-in on the Stock Exchange, and an ascent to the pinnacle of the Woolworth Building (far below us the *Leviathan* was sailing for Europe). But it was obvious to me that a child should not be shut up in a flat on the East River all summer and, with the Sheffield job on my boards, I couldn't remain chairman of the entertainment committee indefinitely. So at the end of about a week I told him, after dinner one night, that I had in mind taking a house for the summer out in Locust Valley where he and Alfred could batch it together.

"It's near the Sound and there's a yacht club not far away where they see that the kids have a lot of fun, swimming and sailing and all that," I told him.

"Where will you be, George?" he asked.

"Don't worry about that. I'll be able to get out three or four nights a week."

His face sank, and my heart right along with it.

"Some of the kids at school go to camp with a lot of other kids. Could I go off to a camp, George?"

It was a little late to get him into a good one, but we made it. As a matter of fact, I became a pretty discriminating patron of a cycle of camps and ranches as the years went by. There was nothing I could do in that line for little Mary, my niece, of course; her mother controlled the child's recreational program as well as everything else concerning her. And even my summer programs for little Jeff were subject to change without notice, I was soon to learn to my sorrow.

I would settle him in some Northern camp or Western kids' ranch after he had come to see me for a while when the school term was over, but I don't think that Mary ever allowed him to

163

stay put in any one of them for a full summer. He was again the special case, the boy whose mother incredibly showed up on the eve of the pack trip to take him off traveling with her. The continual threat of her embarrassment to him must have hung over his head like a sword. Poor resourceless woman, I believe she needed him for an escort as much as anything. And perhaps that was forgivable. What was unforgivable was the way she touted him along the veranda circuit to anyone in whose opinion she wished to attain importance, in the same way that she had pushed me several thousand positions up the Navy list to gain Mrs. Foraker's esteem years before. He was wearing on one occasion a blazer, the sort that many of the boys at his school had bought from a visiting haberdasher who had invented them with no other purpose or authority than that given him by his own mercantile acuity. This garment Jeff heard to his horror described as the "colors" he had won in some varsity sport. By his mother's account, on another occasion, he was about to be admitted to college, this being two years before he had finished boarding school. She read aloud in public his little poems from the school magazine. I don't think she ever made him feel sorry for himself. I think she made him despise himself. He felt sorry for her—and miserably ashamed.

And I suppose what I principally felt for her at this time was sorrow, too. You only live once, according to most of the people I know, so that if you are dealt a bad hand to begin with, and can't improve it, you are in a hell of a shape. And so she was. But I resented her raids on Jeff's established routine, poor facsimile though it was of home and family and the other conventional symbols of security for a child. Nevertheless, his life at camps and ranches, combined with school, did represent a kind of domestic regularity. It galled me when, to spare the three of us humiliation, I had to stand by while she smashed its routine with some further planless exploit of her own. For a generation now our family had put down no roots in any community. I expect that in the ecology of human nature there are a number of successful air plants—in fact I have known a few—but young Jeff was not

164

one of them. I'm sure that he would have been a much happier man for a little more soil growth.

In the course of Mary's willful abductions, she finally yanked Jeff out of school in the winter of his last year and took him on a two-week cruise to Jamaica. "Everybody here knew about it before I did," Richardson, the headmaster, wrote me—more in resignation than ill-humor. "If the kid comes back with a sunburn in February," he continued, with what I understood to be rustic jocularity, "I guess it will give us some class. Mrs. Hanes is certainly a high flyer."

Jeff was never a notable scholar; when he came back he was hopelessly behind in his studies. The next news I had from Richardson was that the boy had been caught during a French examination with a page on his desk closely penciled with some irregular French verbs. I flew out to Chicago.

Richardson was as much the country banker as ever, and I felt more of a valued special customer of his institution than I cared to.

"I think Jeff's a gambler," he said. "He kind of likes to take a chance."

"What explanation did he give for the paper he was found with?" I asked.

"He said he had written the verbs out by heart just before the examination to sort of refresh his memory. He forgot to destroy them."

"Did you ask him to write them out again from memory?"

"Well, as a matter of fact, as it turned out there was no occasion in the examination for him to have used those particular verbs."

"But if he had been able to rewrite them anyhow, that would have cleared the question up one way or the other."

Richardson gave me a shrewd rural smile. "Well, Mr. Hanes," he said, "I didn't want to take a chance."

I wonder which of us felt more ashamed of the school. I knew then that I had made a mistake sending Jeff there, no matter what my geographical theory had been and no matter how much more another school would have taken out of the cash register.

There was only a half-hour or so remaining for me to spend with Jeff before I had to leave. He was a slim, nice-looking boy with a shock of the family's blond hair and I remember thinking for the first time that he was always going to be one of those men who kept themselves neat under every condition. He seemed fairly undisturbed by the French verbs affair, neither injured nor repentant.

"I guess that jam is behind us," I told him. "Just try to keep out of trouble pitching this last inning."

"Don't worry," he said. "I'll make my next one a fast curve."

No, a hard straight one, I checked myself from saying. What could you do? We talk about how a character is toughened by the blows upon it. But you knock any character around hard enough and it's going to crack somewhere. Nobody's nature is indestructible.

Jeff was graduated that spring, winning an award or two, as a matter of fact, for writing and dramatics. This pleased us all— particularly his mother, who, although unable for some reason or other to attend the ceremony, chose to regard the citations as equivalent to Phi Beta Kappa and the Pyne Prize. Under the portico of the main building, where I had first taken leave of Jeff that miserable autumn evening long ago and gone on down to St. Louis to see Dan and Margaret, Richardson came up to shake hands.

"Well," he said, "we got him through, didn't we?"

"Yes, he seems to have made it. Won a prize, too."

Richardson nodded and then gave me an astonishing conspiratorial smile, the headmaster whose school had finally found a sucker. "But don't think you and I have seen the last of each other," he warned.

But, poor fellow, we had.

It was not, I am sorry to say, the last time I was to see in uncomfortable circumstances the countenance of other of Jeff's scholastic authorities.

Washington's Birthday is always the occasion for a small gala at Princeton because of the General's association with the place,

166

the battle, the Congressional seating, and so on. A full holiday is observed, alumni meetings and other celebrations are held, followed by a hockey game with Yale. In that February of Jeff's freshman year I had just taken a two-story house out on Nassau Street in the old Queenston section of the Borough. The house was quaint enough, not only as to appearance but as to plumbing. A century or more before it had been a smithy, so that the first floor was divided by an arched driveway giving access from the street to where the forge and works in the rear had surrounded a small cobbled courtyard. All trace of the manufactory had long since vanished, but the plan worked out quite suitably for my purposes. The archway had been pierced on either side by opposite doors. One gave entrance to rooms that I used for my office (reception and library downstairs, drafting room above) as had the smith. Across the way was a sitting room with dining room and kitchen to rear and sleeping quarters above. Here Alfred Jones and I were settled in, as had been the smith's family. It was cheerful to think that the old premises were still employed as before in the business of construction, although now not very briskly. This was the winter of 1930.

I had asked Jeff to join Margaret and me for dinner on the evening of the holiday, since he of course had as yet no club to go to, and then we would go on down to see the hockey game. We had a strong forward line that year. We won all but one game. It wasn't a cold night but one of our cool damp ones. I lit a fire when it grew dark and did some reading for a little lecture course that I had taken on that term for fun and, I must admit, remuneration. When the clock on the mantelpiece rang once for six-thirty I looked up, saw that the dining room was dark and the table unlaid, went over to the coaching table to make myself a drink, and set off to the kitchen. There I found Alfred seated at his table staring down at a copy of that morning's New York *Graphic* but, it appeared to me, not seeing very much of it. He was given to moods of reflection, I knew, but not at mealtime.

"Alfred," I asked, "what's going on?"

167

He came to life in a flash, far overcompensating for the stimulus of my question, it seemed to me.

"Not a thing, Mr. Hanes," he said in a voice a little loud for the occasion, "not a thing."

"That's the way it struck me," I said. "Why isn't the table set and where is everybody? Where's Mrs. Pierce?"

"Mrs. *Pierce*?"

For some years now Margaret had had her shop in Princeton. She dealt in English and American cabinet work of the eighteenth century. I expect that she owed something to her mother's taste and interest in antiquarianism. But Margaret's quite unusual sense of form and line and texture could not have been wholly inherited, and certainly not her feeling for historic environment about a piece, her gift of seeing it in its time and place and of letting others see it so. I believe that she was one of the first dealers of any authority to take an interest in good Regency pieces. "They have all the grace of Georgian, I think," she once said to me, "with all the sturdiness of industrial England—the beginning of industrial England." And I looked again at a mahogany drum table and some side chairs that she was showing me, and which I had thought a little coarse, and saw what she meant.

That may be an attitude toward artifacts too academic, too literary. But I don't think so. Form and time, understood in certain examples of fine furniture as well as in certain buildings, may have a glowing and inseparable unity, either the poorer without the other. If you don't believe me, see the copy of the Parthenon at Nashville or visit Williamsburg. At any rate, Margaret's sense of what I call presence in art turned out to be worth money to her. That winter she had moved her showroom to the new building at 20 Nassau and taken an apartment above it. Her customers came from all over the country, many of them alumni and their families, so when this evening she was late in appearing at my place I supposed that the holiday had brought some of them into town and she was therefore delayed.

"Did Miss Margaret call this afternoon?" I now asked Alfred, rephrasing my last inquiry to him.

"Call where, Mr. George?"

"Call here. She didn't call the office."

"Nossuh. I don't think she did." He appeared to concentrate his mind on the problem. "I don't believe she did. On the telephone, you mean."

"On the telephone, yes. Did Mr. Jeff call, on the telephone?"

"Nossuh! *He* didn't call on any telephone. I know *he* didn't."

So I went back in the sitting room and waited some more. Alfred set the table for two, retired for a while, then came back and hurriedly set a third place, a curious afterthought it seemed to me. I recalled that I hadn't seen anything cooking while I was in the kitchen. At seven-thirty I telephoned Margaret's shop and then her apartment. Nobody answered at either place. It was almost eight when I heard a car pull up outside. Margaret came in wearing a burberry and a small round brown felt hat that I always associated with happy outings and looking very sweet to me in it, as usual, but very intense. Jeff followed her, his face as white as his shirt. Whiter, for he had slept in his shirt as it turned out.

"Darling," she said, pulling off her things, "don't say anything for just a minute or two, will you?"

"Very well."

"Not for a minute or two."

"Okay. What's the matter?"

"Well, you see," she said, "Jeff has been in jail."

The information at least cleared up some of the early evening's hocus-pocus.

"What's he charged with and where?" I asked.

"Now don't *you* start that Bulldog Drummond business, George," she said. "Let's sit down and have a drink." She saw Alfred hovering in the dining room. "He's all right, Alfred," she called to him.

Alfred came in and took Jeff's arms in his hands. Moist-eyed, without saying anything he released the boy and went back to the kitchen. I was glad that Jeff had these two good friends but it hurt me—to tell the truth it made me angry—that something had happened to Jeff, something evidently quite serious, and I had

169

been left out of it. Kept out of it, apparently. You think you know people, and then you don't.

"Well," I said, looking perhaps for something new in Margaret and Jeff, something I had missed in their two faces, "you'd better tell me the story."

The plot was not very involved. Peter Maben and Jeff had decided to spend the eve of the holiday by going to Trenton to see a prize fight. To do so they had hired a car, which was a violation of the University regulations. After the fight they made a visit to a bar—a speakeasy—and on the way home they had begun to sing. It was an open car, so that their voices carried strongly into the night, and it was their misfortune that a couple of troopers parked in a side road saw as well as heard them pass. Maben, who was at the wheel, was arrested for drunken driving; Jeff was locked up for disorderly conduct after referring to the officers as "myrmidons." The New Jersey State Police do not take anything lightly. Not from uninfluential students, at any rate. Early the next morning, this morning, Jeff had managed to get to a telephone to raise bail for himself and his friend, his own family being the nearest at hand. He had called Margaret, not me.

I heard all this, and all at once I felt an absolutely new experience. For one sharp moment I felt a breath of disaster in the air.

When Jeff had reached the point in his account at which he had telephoned Margaret, he fell silent and lay back in his chair, his pale face faintly moist with nervous fatigue, as though that were the end of the affair.

My voice came to me from a throat that surprised me by its dryness.

"Why," I asked him, "did you call Margaret instead of me?"

He smiled tiredly. "Maben and I wanted to get out of there as fast as we could, you see. I knew she would act quickly—we'd get action without words from Margaret." He turned his head languidly toward her. "Besides, she's the best heeled." Seeing my expression, he added, "Always money at the shop, I mean."

Margaret rose and, going over to him, ran her hand across his forehead and then over the brush of his straw-colored hair. "Why

170

don't you go upstairs to the dressing room and get in bed, dear?" she said to him, and turning to me, "He's had a hard day." Her eyes lit up a bit in amusement. "I think he still has something of a hangover, too. Go ahead now, Jeff." He went toward the stairway which ascended the wall east from the sitting room to the upper quarters.

"What," I asked, "is the University going to do about this?" All but Jeff's trousers were out of sight on the stairs.

"Nothing, George," he said, and then the trousers went out of sight. Margaret moved to the settee between the street windows where I was and sat down beside me.

Although I knew I shouldn't, I found myself feeling very tired about the whole thing. "What did he mean, nothing?" I asked.

"The policeman dropped the charge against him. The myrmidon did."

"I suppose you had something to do with that."

"I was there, of course. And since the police took no action, the University takes no action. Mike the proctor has already told us that."

"How about renting the car?"

"They were stopped well outside the Borough. Oh, please don't be so gloomy, George. Don't you see? We beat the rap."

"How about Maben?"

"Well, of course, that's not so good."

"I'll bet it isn't. Drunken driving is a mandatory offense in New Jersey."

"But Jeff wasn't driving, thank God."

"Lucky Jeff."

She squeezed my hand and shook it playfully. "You're just pouting because you weren't in on the excitement. It was much better this way."

"Alfred knew about it. How was that?"

"I called here to make sure you weren't being worried about it. I didn't want you disturbed at business."

At another time I might have laughed at that. Margaret would have been a lot busier that day than I was.

171

"I think," I said, "he was too yellow to call me."

And I did. But more terribly than that, I thought of my own miserable case, a half-defeated, middle-aged man, instinctively eased of his responsibility by the kindness of a goodhearted servant and an affectionate woman, the custodian softly relieved of his custody. Jeff was quite right about one thing. Margaret could lay her hand on quicker assets than I could. But he had said that what he wanted was action without words. When had I ever berated him for anything? No, he was a liar by implication and a coward in fact. And he was my brother's son, and my brother was long dead. This was not a very good moment for me, I don't mind telling you.

"You'll feel a lot better about it all in the morning, dearest," Margaret said softly, and then her dear buoyancy left her. She leaned her elbows on her knees and hugged her shoulders, the picture of a small woman's melancholy. "Late on a February night is a very depressing time," she said. "I know."

I drew her out of her position and into my arms and we were quiet for a long time while the fire made tired rustling sounds. My poor darling, I knew that February was not the only month of her own bad nights. . . .

But Margaret was right in a way. There are usually other things to do besides think about your troubles when it comes daytime. I had lunch next day at the Nassau Club with a man who wanted his boxwood garden relaid. I wondered how it was that some people had kept their money while that of the rest of us had largely vanished. Had this man put his in a post office, perhaps? After we'd had our talk and I saw him off I started home myself and at the bottom of the front steps of the club I ran into Christian Gauss, who at that time and for some years after was dean of the college. Looking at him I always thought of him as the chief justice of a supreme court of small owls, but a small owl that knew a couple of good jokes.

"Your nephew was in my office just now," he said, his large shadowed eyes hooded against the daylight.

"Yes, I imagined so."

172

"I asked him how much liquor he usually drank." The dean paused, solemnly waiting for me to put the appropriate legal cross-query.

"And what did he say?" I asked.

"He said that he never touched it except once a year on my birthday, when you and he toasted my health in a glass of watered sherry."

Keeping the hooded eyes on mine, the dean moved past me; when his head was almost staring over his back, it slowly turned toward the front of him again as he mounted the steps of the club.

I don't know why this levity of Jeff's lightened the day for me so. Yes, of course I do. The essence of humor is a sensible attitude toward life. I felt much better about Jeff by the time I got home and began relocating on paper the rich man's box trees. I was of course glad to have the work.

I remember some ironist saying in 1931—Bob Mayer I guess it was—that he knew at last that we were in a depression; the Brooks polo shirt was now selling under five dollars. "It's the collapse of what I always considered an unshakable empiricism, like the verst in Russia." But the Depression was no joke to architects.

As a matter of fact, not many people knew what the Depression meant to architects because there are really not very many of them, only about thirteen thousand in the A.I.A. today. By the time the Depression ended, the great construction companies, out of savage self-protection I suppose, had killed off most of the smaller firms by employing only their own "captive" architects and engineers. Meanwhile, there was almost no work to be had in a drafting room for the young men who had completed their training. They did whatever they could lay their hands on: a little remodeling for the family's friends; shop decoration; and that curse of the profession, the submission of plans drawn on spec with the outcome, like as not, that the client would either decide not to build, or build later on using a few carpenters and the heisted plan. There are more ways to cheat an architect than a woman. I often wonder if the first architect—the one who set up the original tent pole—was ever paid for his work. If times were hard, the chances are against it. Architecture is in some ways the bravest profession.

I think it was Margaret, with her sense of the living present as well as the living past, who was most responsible for giving me the idea of the little houses. Depressions can be times of great mercantile inventiveness; cheap and useful gadgets appear to lure whatever money there is left around. The American kitchen came in for a great deal of venture capital's attention in the early thirties, with the result that all sorts of appliances to cook, freeze, clean, and so forth, were put on the market. With plenty of time on their hands to stay home, people seemed to gravitate around the hearth, as it were. Just, Margaret pointed out, as it had been two centuries before in our country. And two or three graduate students whom I had hanging around my office, because neither they nor I could figure out any other place for them to go, and I began to work out some low-cost housing schemes in which the core of the home—the assembly space, the heating and plumbing units— were in effect consolidated around the kitchen. To be sure, we ran some cabinets and bookshelves here and there to give the illusion of separated areas, for prejudices in dwelling habits die harder than a society's theology, but the fact was that we had built a big kitchen with nothing much else of a house around it. And we did very well for those times. I still pass those houses scattered along old U.S. 1, the back road now from New Brunswick to Trenton, and they stand up very well. They should. They had put into them the last decent materials that we have seen in this century, wars and their inevitably attendant building booms having left us stuck largely with shoddy. Outside they had a proper little air of elegance, too—brick veneer painted white. Is there anything that looks more expensive than white-painted brick?

Margaret helped a great deal to make the interior decorative effects agreeable though economical. It worked out fine, and why not? The decorator and the architect were in bed together, a happy situation for the client.

And so, professionally, that's the way one architect survived the onset of the bad times. There wasn't a great deal of "money in the cash register," as Jeff himself had occasionally to admit about his own enterprises, but there was reasonable happiness at both ends of Nassau Street.

Young Jeff had managed to survive into his upperclass years in his own way, becoming a sort of rural François Villon, stalking around with a book in hand or pocket, given to late hours in his solitary room over a few bottles of the local needled beer, reading or writing. But he was obviously fulfilling some dream of himself and I was far from disappointed in him. He kept himself neat as always, had some stories and verse printed in the *Lit*, joined a club filled with minor letter men and roughneck *littérateurs*, and was once in a while invited away for dances or house parties. It was at one of the latter in Wilmington, given by a perfectly good Du Pont, that he met Carol Beeman. He had left St. Louis, of course, before either of them had developed much of a social sense. She had served out her twelve-year stretch at Mary Institute and had somehow managed to get that xenophobic father of hers to let her go East to college, at Smith. Her mother had meantime died, perhaps causing Beeman to relax his principles of the West for Westerners and the minimum of educational advantages for women—so clearly expressed long ago that night at Dan and Margaret's house—in some reckless moment of remorse. At any rate, Carol and Jeff met, and met again. He took her to the club-house parties in his junior year and she had him to visit her at Beeman's place in Charlevoix that summer. They were to return to St. Louis together the first week in September and I would see him there because on the first of September the lease on the architectural offices in the Tower—first T. J. Hanes, then Hanes & Hanes, then Hanes & Eckfield, and finally Paul Eckfield Associates —was after sixteen years to expire. Eckfield had cleared out months before and was now practicing in Minneapolis, I heard, or some place around there. There were some papers and things of mine— unimportant before and probably unimportant still—that I nevertheless wanted to take away, make a neat dustpan finish of a part of my life perhaps. And so the scene shifts to St. Louis again.

175

There is something that happens together to poor ill-tended people and poor ill-tended buildings. The literal threadbareness, of course, the run-down shoes and worn-down flooring; but something more than these, something beyond the mere appearance of abjection. The poor have their own odor, like the frightened. You can smell it in a down-at-heels movie theater or office building or hotel, and in the buildings it's not entirely the aroma of their own aged dirt or uncleaned drapery; it is the odor of personal poverty itself, for poor people are found in poor buildings.

The lobby of the Tower as I passed through it was held by only a half dozen lifeless transients sitting or standing in attitudes that might have been taken an hour before and kept an hour hence. Above them in the evening gloom winked the gilt in Jeff's glorious frescoes and around them shone the massive tawny onyx of the dado, the mosaics of the piers; but dully somehow, as though seen through the film of tired old eyes. The huge room was in neglected slumber. I thought of the engravings by Piranesi of the ruins of Rome where the figures stand about in torpid ignorance beneath the wreckage of vast magnificence. And yet there was a great quiet joyousness in the room to me; it was still home to my heart. It was still a beautiful place.

The odor was more noticeable in the hall upstairs. I remember how, when I was here last, the carpeting near the doors in the rooms had begun to show the shadow of use, like the faint trace of some furtive animal before its den. Down the middle of the halls now, and turning in to the door of each chamber, lay a path as well-beaten as a muskrat slide.

The bellhop put my bag on the baggage rest, shook the curtains a few times, and slapped the key down on the dresser while I was looking around the room. The shades on the wall brackets, once crepe de Chine and now parchment, showed a few raddled edges and scorched spots; the mattress would soon be seriously on its way toward concavity; the linen was very clean.

"You all by yourself?" the bellhop asked.

"Yes."

"Lonesome?"

176

I looked at him for the first time and saw that he had a face of unusual impurity.

"Have you got a line of hookers in here now?" I asked him.

"Could be," he said.

"Does Mr. Walsh know about it?"

"Mr. Walsh? Who's he?"

"He's the manager."

"Oh. Barney."

"Well?"

"Maybe he does, maybe he doesn't. How should I know?"

"My name is Hanes. What's yours?"

His face broke into a surprised grin and then he made for the door. "You'll never know, bud," I heard him say as the door closed.

I looked at the bed again and I remembered what Jeff had specified when I bought the first mattresses for the hotel—"see that they're soft enough to sleep on, hard enough to make love on." The bellhop had certainly grasped one of the essential functions of the design anyhow.

I must have still been amused at the idea when I got Junie on the line—he had recently sent me his unlisted number; the mail address was a post-office box in Clayton—because he asked me what I had been laughing about.

"Just about form following function, and vice versa. An old joke of my brother's about beds."

We talked along for a few moments arranging to see each other the next afternoon. Young Jeff was not due in town until the following day. I told Junie that I would drive out after lunch and asked him for his address.

"I'll have you picked up," he said. "What time? Three o'clock?"

"Don't bother, Junie—"

"Three o'clock where?"

"You don't have to worry about my finding your place, Junie."

"The hell I don't, professor," he said, and he said it very sharply.

When I hung up after settling it about the pickup, I'm sure I wasn't smiling any more.

177

I called Mrs. Adams to see about making an appointment in the morning at our old office to take away the last of my things.

"I don't know why I didn't have the place cleaned up," Sylvia Adams said as we glanced around us at the grimy, wild moraine of sixteen years of professional debris. "Well, yes, as a matter of fact I do. The people coming in here don't deserve any better."

I thought she was looking extremely attractive; her face was wrinkled like an apricot as always and she'd always had more nose than she needed, but she was wearing a trim, expensive gray tailored suit which properly showed her to be a very small but very well-designed little woman, and there were always those eyes, bright, concentrating, intelligent button eyes like the eyes of a cherished toy animal in one's childhood.

I knew about the new tenants, too: a fly-by-night casualty company, the heirs in a very indirect line of succession indeed to an insurance firm that had really gotten into trouble with the state examiners. When we leased them the space we were aware that they were looking for an address which would not cost them much but might impress people who didn't keep very up to date on things. What we didn't know was that they were going to use a view of the Tower as their symbol and trade-mark, in the manner of the Prudential Life Insurance Company. Whores in the bedrooms, swindlers in the campanile. It might have amused Jeff, at that. He was a tough nut.

But it did not amuse Mrs. Adams, who, we used to say, if the firm's records should have been incinerated, would have been put to no great inconvenience, who knew everything that had ever gone on, everything. And now nothing would go on any more. It was not funny to her to leave her long and well-fixed post to contemptible intruders.

"Here are the things I believe you wanted to have," said Mrs. Adams, leading me into my old office, ankle-deep in trash and with that inevitably sad sight, the lighter rectangles on the walls where the pictures and photographs and designs that one thought worth hanging used to hang. One corner was neatly cleared and

178

there my stuff was packed. With the whitest of gloves she tapped a stout freshly made case bolted and riveted as though it might contain the "Mona Lisa."

"You know what's in this?" she asked me. I was astonished to see that the black button eyes could contain such a swimming expression of nostalgia.

I nodded. I remembered the size of the glassed frame it must hold.

"The willow branches from the topped steel," she said. "They would only be dust now, but I had them waxed before framing them. I don't believe Mr. Hanes ever knew."

Oh, handmaiden, I thought.

"And there," she indicated a stack of uniform new fiber containers, "the drawings, *esquisses*, his day books, and some other material like that. I think you'll find them all clearly labeled."

I was very sure I would.

"Is there anything more you might think of that I could do, Mr. Hanes?"

No more, you devotedly good, good little woman, I thought, no more from you is to be expected now. I could feel two rims of liquid start behind each eye.

"You have as usual left nothing to be thought about, Mrs. Adams," I said. "I'll have somebody come up from the hotel to get the boxes. You wrote me that you had found something very interesting that you were going to do now."

A smile broke beneath her generous nose. "I'm going to take charge of the women's end of things for my husband."

"What does that mean, Mrs. Adams? I'm afraid I don't know."

Whereupon she swung a little on one heel and tilted her head to one side, coquettish and delightful. "We're in politics now, Mr. Hanes. Didn't you know my husband was a councilman? No, of course not. You never read the St. Louis papers."

"Well, that's great. How did it all happen?"

"Well, he's a lawyer of course, and he's always been interested in the progressive side." She paused. "I know you don't, but Mr. Adams thinks a great deal of Mr. Roosevelt, Mr. Hanes."

179

"Well, that's great," I said again. So there *was* a Mr. Adams after all, quite a Mr. Adams.

"Now, you don't have to say that—I know you've always been a Republican, Mr. Hanes. But your *brother* would have been a Democrat, if he had ever taken time to vote."

And I expect she was right. We moved out into the old reception room and then to the elevator foyer. She didn't bother to close or lock the office door, but stood looking back for a long time. The black eyes were clouded when she turned to me again, and the woman and the councilman forgotten.

"It wouldn't have helped if I had come to New York, would it?"

"Not a bit."

"He wasn't really such a bad man, Mr. Eckfield. He just wasn't—" she stopped.

"He wasn't like Jeff," I agreed.

The elevator door opened and we went down in silence. Outside on the pavement we involuntarily moved into a corner of the arched entrance, protected from the passing crowd. Her small face looked up to mine.

"It *means* so much, Mr. Hanes. Why does it *mean* so much?" Her expression was one of greatest bewilderment and loss and distress.

Because there is so much love everywhere, I thought; all over us, all around us, everywhere, and all of us have many kinds of it. Love of home, of family, love of another man's wife, love of money and dogs, love of your country, almost terrifying love for very small parts of it, love of reputation, of beauty, of ease, intense love for someone known only to you by his work, love of God, the world is up to its bottom in love.

I leaned over and we kissed, and she turned and went away.

The movies, I think, have taken quite a lot of the edge off the realities of life. When I was young and had just been made a member of the firm, I used to travel a bit on vacation, once by cruise boat getting as far south as Valparaiso. Two or three of us hired a car to motor up into the foothills to the east for a look at the highest of the Andes, and after a while suddenly there they were in all their shattering grandeur, snow peaks and all, just exactly as they were in the travelogue on the screen of the Fox Theater, St. Louis, Missouri.

The two men in the black sedan that Junie sent to pick me up were just exactly like the gangsters I had so often seen before in the movies. One of them was even a colored man, a twist of casting that M-G-M used to employ now and then. We drove through the park and out past the university, along Forsyth Boulevard and the neighborhood where Margaret and Dan used to live, then beyond the town of Clayton and onto the Ladue road. I remember the conversation among the three of us; it concerned shaving: the merits of stick soap versus cream, which of us had to shave oftenest, and so on. And all of us had heard, and were willing to believe, that the Gillette people could produce a blade which would hold its edge for a lifetime, but through venality refrained from putting it on the market. Both the white man and his partner were obviously armed. They wore shoulder holsters that showed through their summer suits, as they slumped in the car seat, like carelessly hitched pack saddles.

The place I was taken to was a modest beer garden of the kind that the breweries had spotted here and there about the county in the generation before Prohibition, and had been restored to usefulness in the years afterward under other management. You entered from the road through a high wooden gate decorated with intricate carpentry such as used to stand before small amusement parks, and then you were inside a tall hedge of wild-growing privet that enclosed a closely planted grove of maples. These were whitewashed to halfway up their trunks, making, I have always thought, the trees look old-fashioned and indecent, as though they had pulled up their foliage to expose their underclothing. There were tables and chairs scattered everywhere over the pebbled ground and a small wooden platform for dancing was hung round with colored light bulbs which were also strung among the trees. No one was there. In the hot midafternoon stillness our feet whispered in the pebbles as we made our way around the one-story

181

building at the far side of the grove that housed the dining room, bar and kitchen, and came to a bungalow behind it which had been built, I suppose, to accommodate the proprietor and his family.

As we reached the bottom of the porch steps the door was opened by Junie.

"Hi, George," he said, grinning. "Welcome to our city." He nodded without speaking to the two men with me, at which they started back toward the grove. "Come into the parlor," he said to me.

He was dressed in a beautiful suit of blue raw silk and he still had the Uhlan good looks of his youth, loose black curls now a little flecked with gray, face only a bit heavier set; he was a most attractive man. Then he turned to lead me into his living room with a slow, deliberate walk that showed the tortured movement of his hips beneath the light material, like a hoist swinging unsteadily on a shaky fulcrum, which, I supposed, was just about how the injury had left his central skeleton.

A cobbled monstrosity of a fireplace was all that remained of the former décor; the room was furnished in expensive chintz, carpeting, upholstered pieces, and reproductions—Trorlicht-Dunker's very best, I guessed, and not installed by any of the store's regular delivery men. The drapes were not drawn but the windows were down; at two of them air-cooling units hummed softly. From a sofa behind a wide Chinoiserie coffee table—littered with a few bottles and some cards where he and Junie had apparently been passing time—a man arose, another M-G-M character, this one the neat, spare, pinch-cheeked, silver-haired type with small clipped mustache. We were introduced by our first names only and then he went off somewhere in the back of the house. At no time during the afternoon did Junie make any reference to his companions, the location or appearance of the place, or why he was there.

"Well, George," he said heartily, lowering his big frame carefully onto a solid-looking leather chair and waving me toward the couch, "sit down and tell me all about yourself."

And somehow, in that most unlikely of all places to be, and in

182

the presence of a man whose life was so utterly remote from mine and everyone else's around me—somehow I knew that sometime during that afternoon I would indeed tell him about myself; a good deal anyhow. And, as I think back, it was not so unreasonable a premonition. If an atmosphere of soothing detachment encourages the giving of confidences, what more fitting place and company than the underworld hide-out of an old and affectionate friend? And I was very fond of Junie.

I looked at him now more carefully and thought of him when he was a bustling, aggressive, enormously good-humored young man with a cigar that he manipulated expertly and the self-confidence of a heavyweight champion. He was not youthful any more but there was still the spring of youth somewhere within him in spite of his crippling injury. Now he reminded me more of a hard-working corporation executive, a little tense, a little tired from keeping a roaring business under control; but it was under control.

He had been making a couple of tall gin drinks—did you suppose he remembered my choice from my visit to the hospital, or did he by now simply give anyone else what he was drinking? He handed me mine.

"*Wie geht's*," he said, and then I knew that Junie the beer agent still lived. "How's Margaret?"

"Fine. We're an old unmarried couple now."

"Me, too," he said, smiling. "Olive's okay. I send her up to Michigan when it's hot like this, but when she's gone I miss her. She's awfully good company."

I recalled the blistering day that I had met the almost wordless Olive, and the impacted hangover from which she was suffering. Where had she gone to in Michigan, I wondered; to Charlevoix, where so many nice St. Louis families went to escape the summer heat? She might have even passed young Jeff and Carol at a beach or in a roadhouse, neither she nor they knowing of each other.

"Have you seen the old man since you've been in town?" Junie asked.

I told him I had not.

183

"Neither have I. I mean, we haven't seen each other very much lately."

I tried to imagine where old Mr. Neidlinger and Junie might meet at all in the course of Junie's well-protected mode of living. At the Hudson sales office perhaps. I couldn't imagine what they would have to say to each other. As to Junie's relations with the rest of his family, his brothers and sisters, they must not exist at all. What must it mean to an important German family, tight-knit, interdependent as they usually were, to have one member living in the same city but never seen? What whisperings, what sorrow.

"How are you fixed for money now, professor?" he asked, sudden with any inquiry that came to his mind, as always.

"What money? I own a house in New York that I rent."

"I told you about those Reagans, didn't I? Strictly larcenous, that pair. Eckfield, too."

"They didn't have much to do with starting the Depression, Junie," I said.

"I put all my money in money. The old Tower's a real flea-bag by now, isn't it?"

His habit of apparently paying no attention to response in conversation was still with him, I observed. Perhaps, as befitted the busy executive, it had even been accentuated, but I don't mind other people occasionally carrying the chitchat. The truth was, I was content for a while to feel my way around in the spell of this strange afternoon.

"You could have sold out your part years ago and put the money into a good business."

"You mean like an automobile dealership?" I asked, but he didn't seem to hear that. "No, I would never sell out the Tower. As a matter of fact, it can't be sold unless your father—the bank, that is—and the Reagans agree. Or unless we go into bankruptcy. We're not in yet, but we're thinking about scaring up somebody to take out a second mortgage."

"What about Mary and the two kids?"

"I'm trustee for their shares, which equal mine."

184

"Couldn't they go to court and shake up the trusteeship?"

"I don't think we're that bad off yet," I told him, probably not convincing myself too strongly.

"*You* don't. Jesus," he said. He stretched over toward the table stiffly and got himself a cigar, lit it, rolled the end of it around in his mouth a few times, leaned back, and here came Junie the judicial man of business, I could see. "Well," he said, "it doesn't look like anything more serious to me than a good fire wouldn't fix up. Have you thought of that? I'm serious."

Once Junie had suggested murder to me as a solution for one of my difficulties. Now arson. He was quite a boy. But a bad boy, nevertheless, and suddenly I had had enough of the movies. Maybe it was the sickness I felt in my heart at the thought of the Tower's destruction, and maybe it was a surfeit of cheap hoodlumism, the beer garden, the bungalow, the sleazy hiddenness of it all.

"I don't think you understand about my brother," I said as evenly as I could. "He was a very famous man. I was very fond of him."

"Sure, George, I get that. But lots of guys had big brothers they looked up to. I was crazy about Augie when I was a kid."

Well, the hell with him and Augie. I was going to tell him about Jeff and the police dog in Danville. I hadn't thought about it, from start to finish, scenery and all, for years and probably had never said anything at all about it to anyone else. No, I must have told my mother and father, for they were still alive then. Anyhow, I told my bootlegger friend now. Jeff was putting up the new Vermilion County courthouse in Danville. I suppose I was nine, maybe ten. Almost every month he would have me down from Chicago to stay with him over the weekend. It was only a couple of hours on the train, I explained to Junie, so I could come by myself. One Saturday evening in early winter Jeff and I were taking a walk after dinner. The scene came back brilliantly clear now. There were no leaves on the trees, I remembered, but the grass was still green on the lawns in front of the houses out north along the river in the part of the town where we were walking, and on

185

the strip between the sidewalk and the street under the pale-blue arc lights the turf lay in pools of arsenic green. Jeff never sauntered or strolled; when he walked he walked for exercise, at a fast, surging pace. As we hurried along I saw that we were quickly approaching a dog lying, crouching I suppose now, on the arsenical grass close to the base of one of the light poles. I could soon see that it was a police dog, a great big one with a wiry crest of hair on the back of its neck. I leaned forward to pat its head as we passed and with one great roar it came up into the air at me, a hideous grimace and fangs for a face. At the same moment I heard a wild guttural shout. *Aaaah!* I saw, I could still see, that picture of Jeff and the dog in the night under the arc light as though it were caught and instantly held forever stationary like a single frame from a motion-picture reel.

"I don't know which was the more terrifying to me," I told Junie, "the ferocity of the man or the ferocity of the beast. The dog found its feet and turned and ran. 'That son of a bitch,' Jeff said, 'he must be crazy,' and we kept right on walking. I knew then that he loved me as much as his own life. Every single moment he must love me, or how could he have sprung to save me at almost the instant the dog sprang? Do you see what I mean? Can you?"

Junie had put the cigar aside; his thick black eyebrows had come together in a harsh expression of concentration. What had he ever had to think about before like this? Why did I imagine that the story would have any significance to him?

"I think I see what you mean," he said at last.

I wasn't convinced, but I went on anyway; I wanted to hear the rest of it myself—out loud for once.

"Nothing in the world," I said, "would make me let go of that building." I heard the disconsolate voice of Mrs. Adams that morning. *It means so much. Why does it mean so much?* "It means two things to me, one as important as the other. It means Jeff, everything about Jeff, everything he loved and everything *he* meant. And side by side, the Tower is an object of beauty. Believe me, that is very important. It may be a flea-bag now to most peo-

186

ple, but to a few thousand others in the world it happens to be, no, it was made to be, it *is* one of the fine pieces of architecture in America. It is a work of art and it shall not be destroyed. The Alhambra is full of bums now, too, but it is a great work of art. When you grow older you find that there are fewer rather than more things you must be true to. The Tower is one of those few things to me."

Junie shifted his hips to relieve his pain. "There's a lot of you in it, too, professor," he said.

Yes, that, too. My first youth.

"It's a matter of love, I guess," Junie said. He must have caught the look of complete surprise on my face; by God, he had understood after all. "What's the matter?" he asked.

"Nothing, just something I was thinking about this morning."

"I surprised you, didn't I?"

"A little."

"Stick around and you'll get a lot of surprises. You know what I think? I think you're a fighter, George, but I don't think you're a hungry fighter. I guess your brother was the hungry fighter."

It is extraordinary the credence you will put in even the most random observation you come across in reading or in conversation if it is at all applicable to you. I had never thought of myself or Jeff in Junie's terms, but I filed his remarks away for further consideration nevertheless.

"I'll get a little peckish pretty soon," I said, "if things keep going the way they are."

"Then, too, it's like the hopelessly sick child the parents are so crazy about," he said.

"What?"

"The Tower. It never had a chance, built at the wrong time, wrong place."

"Maybe a sick child," I said, "but a beautiful sick child."

He looked at his wristwatch. I don't believe he had heard me.

"You say you may be seeing the old man?"

This, I understood, was not only where I came in but where I went out.

187

"I may be. I hadn't planned to. Is there something you want me to tell him?"

"Oh, no. Well, yes. I just thought he might be glad to know we spent the afternoon talking."

"I'll see him."

He hobbled with me to the door.

"It was nice of you to come all the way out here to see me, professor. By the way, you *are* a professor now, aren't you?"

"Not exactly."

"Well," he said, broadly confident as always, "you'll get there. And it was swell of you to come out to see me."

This time I didn't question whether he meant all the way out to Clayton or all the way out to St. Louis. He might have meant either.

On the drive into town the colored man and the white man were discussing the relative merits of various members of the Cardinals baseball team, a strong club at that time, but I didn't join the conversation. Fond as I was of Junie, that was enough gangsters for one afternoon.

"Now tell me all about the afternoon at Mr. Beeman's. Was Mrs. Cox there?"

Margaret had driven over to meet my train that evening at Trenton; we were going on to have dinner at the old roadhouse by the bridge at Washington's Crossing. I remember that she wore no hat—she and a few others had started to go hatless now—her short black hair tumbling in the breeze of the open car. We were very happy, as always, to see each other after a separation and her eager teasing interest touched my heart as it always did.

"Mrs. Cox was there," I said, "carrying her years very gracefully. She reminds me of some very well-preserved and well-respected night-club hostess, like Eva Tanguay, only not noisy."

"Then she has the freedom of the house now."

"Well, limited freedom. I'm sure she doesn't live there and I don't believe she and Mr. Beeman will ever get married." We had begun calling Beeman *Mr.* Beeman long ago out of mockery at his self-importance, and I supposed we always would.

188

"Who will?" said Margaret, a parody of wistfulness. "Well, so you had a family Sunday dinner—you, Mr. Beeman, Mrs. Cox, and Carol and Jeff. What was it like?"

"It was like," I said, "that farcical short story by Chekhov, I think. The one where the old couple catch the two kids necking—"

"Oh *no*! And run in on them holding up an icon so that they are *engaged*?"

"That's the one."

"Oh, no! Well, hurry up and tell me all about it, right from the beginning." She impulsively accelerated the car, taking us up the river road at a faster clip.

Right from the beginning, I told her, it was fairly gummy and it didn't get any better as the occasion progressed. The wind that brushed past us smelled sweet from the fully ripened grasses of the ended summer; everywhere the twilit foliage hung its heaviest; the year was shattering voluptuously like a great repleted rose. Unless you have lived in St. Louis County, where I had been only the afternoon before, you can't know how bleak and lifeless the hills can get when summer there has finished with them. Beeman's house—a sort of miniature Rhenish castle of brick and limestone, with its front door at the base of a small round watchtower—sat on top of a burned-out dome of lawn spotted here and there at the corners of the building with parched ornamental pines. I believe the place had been constructed to harmonize with the neighboring restaurant and golf club that the Busch people had put up some years before to advertise Bevo, a near-beer. So there, in the hall of the hardware king, we sat down to a delicatessen of cold cuts, cole slaw with carrots, salted hard rolls, and iced tea.

"I'll bet Mr. Beeman had the floor," Margaret said.

"He did, and he doesn't like Mr. Roosevelt any more than he liked Mr. Wilson. He refers to Mr. Roosevelt as 'that crippled egomaniac in the White House.' And he doesn't call him Roosevelt. It's Rosenfelt. He commiserated with me about my taxes."

"How about the Americanos?"

The Americanos, as usual, had everything, but for some reason

189

that only made Beeman furiously contemptuous of the rest of the people in the world—"niggers, yellow-bellies, and what-not" he called them. "With nine per cent of the world's population and six per cent of the earth's surface, we have eighty-nine per cent of the world's automobiles, ninety-one per cent of the world's telephones—and now wait a minute—*ninety-four per cent of the bath tubs in the world, by damn!*" Having to listen to this sort of backwoods xenophobia, which is also nothing more than a form of conversational aggression, has always seemed to me the absolute bottom of tedium. The Arabs have *all* the camels.

"How does poor Carol seem to take it?" Margaret asked.

"She winced."

She winced at her father's noise, if nothing else. He was a loud-talking bird. He talked like an ash can being closed, I always thought.

"Then after they brought in the ice cream," I said, "Beeman banged the table and yelled over to Jeff to ask him if he hadn't anything to say. 'To say about what?' Jeff asked him. 'To say about you and Carol,' he said."

That was what had happened. What a family to be invited to marry into.

"*Ooh!*" Margaret breathed a long compassionate sigh. "*Poor Carol.* What could anybody do?"

"Mrs. Cox somehow grabbed the ball and we all scattered out toward the living room. Jeff and Carol drove off in a car somewhere. Beeman guffawed and said, 'I guess I kind of embarrassed them.' Then he said he always took forty winks after lunch and I asked Mrs. Cox to drive me to Clayton so I could catch a cab into town."

"Didn't she offer to drive you in?"

I said that a cab was what I needed more than anything else right then and that I had resolved on oath never again to be caught in hostile territory without a horse.

"How did Mrs. Cox seem to take all this?"

"Very calmly and very decently, I thought. I guess Beeman can't do anything wrong as far as she's concerned."

190

After a few thoughtful moments Margaret said, "He's strong. And she loves him."

Late in the afternoon, I went on, Jeff came back to the Tower. "What did you say to him?"

"I didn't have time to say anything to him at first. He opened up by telling me he and Carol were going to get married when he finishes school next year. Then I guess I made a mistake. I said that I thought they were just a couple of lonely kids, and that was a hell of a poor basis for marriage. I also told him I thought he was simply sorry for her. He said, 'Well, that's why you married mother, wasn't it?' and of course he had me there. Then he gave me hell."

We had made a turn toward the river and at that moment the car began to set up a great bang and rattle crossing the old iron bridge to the Pennsylvania side; at the end of the bridge Margaret whipped the car into the parking lot behind the inn and switched off the ignition.

"He gave you hell about what?" she asked fiercely.

"About us. I told you it was a fairly lousy afternoon."

"What about us?"

"He said I was a poor choice for marriage counselor, or something like that."

"What did he mean?"

"Never mind, darling."

"Tell me what else he said."

"Well, he said, just referring to me of course, that I was the joke of Princeton the way I hung around you year after year, married myself and never doing anything one way or the other about you. He was very defensive about you."

I got out of the car and went around to open the door on her side.

"He made you feel miserable, didn't he?" she said to me.

"He certainly did."

"Why do you keep on taking responsibility for these people? Why? They're *grown* now, all of them—those that aren't dead."

"I know that."

"*I'm* your responsibility. Don't you ever think of that?"

"Yes," I said miserably. "All the time. That, too."

"That, hell!" she cried. "You've made my life wonderful, you damned fool." She took me by the shoulders from where she sat in the car and gave me a fierce little shake. "Just love *me* and let the rest of them go. For a while at least?" she added softly.

I ran my hands into her hair, at which the moon-shaped mouth made a lovely smile.

"Come on," she said. "Let's have dinner."

And so, it seemed to me, you lost and lost; but then every once in a while you won, too; something good happened. Quite often, in fact. Look around you almost anywhere and you would find a prevalence of love: even in the hopeless fondness between Junie and his father; the pitiable attachment, or so I thought it, of Jeff for Carol; Mrs. Adams and her poignant longing after the memory of my brother. I supposed you could add Reagan's veneration for his father, too, and whatever passion it was between Reagan and Mary. Mrs. Cox and Beeman. On it flowed, a slow unending river of sympathies and affections moving through our hearts. So much love, so much more love than hate when you stopped and thought about it.

Twelve

This was the impossible party, the one to which Mary had once long ago ironically alluded as never likely to take place, the convention in full of the Tower's owners and inheritors. But here we all were. We were all on hand with the exception of young Jeff and his sister; they, however, were well and truly represented. The Supreme Court itself couldn't fault Jeff's representation; he had seen to that.

There is this to be said about differences that arise between kinsmen: they don't have to be ineradicable. Unlike professional or business disagreements, they are generally part of a relationship where the rough and the smooth have been taken together over so long a period of time that no one mat-burn need be the last. And then, blood is not only thicker, it is more precious than water. At any rate, Jeff and I had never revived our discussion of his intention to marry Carol. In due course the banns had in a manner been published among the society notes of the *Post-Dispatch* and things went along between us in our warm, familiar, and uncritical association pretty much as before.

Between Jeff and me, that is. But not between Jeff and the rest of the world. In the few months since his engagement Jeff had—mellowed, I suppose you would call it in an older character. In his Bohemian phase he had affected an expectably disillusioned cast of mind; now he was almost somber under the gravity of his new conventionality. He had Carol down for all the proper functions, as was to be foreseen. But he also assumed a large part of the social responsibility for his sister Mary, who that winter had settled into the quasi-nunnery of the Barbizon Hotel in New York, ostensibly to study painting.

I thought I understood the reason for the change in Jeff's behavior, and it made me sad: he was determined to bring order to his own domestic arrangements, not as a protest against, I think, but rather in alarm over the long-standing lack of it in his family. He had also gotten hold of a writers' directory, and was busy sending off book reviews, jokes, essays, any kind of hack work he thought to be purchasable by house organs, trade magazines, and other small undiscriminating publications of the sort. He received a meager check once in a while from these sources and I suppose he felt that in so doing he was practicing industry and thrift. I myself regretted his turning his back at this time on gin and pure literature. Most young men agree at last to a decent armistice with convention; Jeff's capitulation had more the look of headlong unconditional surrender. It was painful to see him taking onto himself burdens, unnecessary perhaps, so early in life—much as I had.

So matters stood on the evening he drove me up to Newark in my car to catch the plane West. I had weighed my bag in and was chatting about this and that when he reached into his pocket and handed me what appeared to be the torn-out fly leaf of a book on which he had written and signed a sentence: "I name George W. Hanes to act for me in any matter concerning Tower Real-estate Co."

I looked at the document and was touched. The penciled script, the casual stationery were so like my old informal Jeff.

"It's all correct," he said. "That's a perfect power of attorney."

Now the new Jeff, of the shrewd shopkeeper's mind.

"I'm sure it is, Jeff," I said, "but why give it to me? I'm trustee for you and your mother and Mary in the building until you kids come of age."

194

His young face regarded me solemnly. "I don't want there to be any doubt about it, George," he said.

"This may be an embarrassment to your mother, a needless one. It could look like—well, a vote against her."

"I'm voting with my father," he said. "I'm voting with you."

I don't know which moved me more, the expression of his loyalty to his father—we hadn't spoken of him, I suppose, for years—or his associating his father and me in the same approval. At any rate, I knew I had Jeff's earnest young support when I went into the Reagans' offices next morning to join the party that had never been expected to occur.

I had been getting myself prepared to see Mary and Ed Reagan together before me for the first time since—when? Before the war; no, since the day she and I were married. *There* had been a fairly unusual get-together. What would we three now do when we met? Grin foolishly? Talk rapidly in embarrassment about nothing? Behave very formally? I was all braced for just about anything, I believed, except to find that the only two people in the Reagans' reception room were Nat Pierce and Donald Beeman. That did take me by surprise and it undoubtedly showed in my expression because Beeman—just the man to get a great laugh out of another's obvious discomfiture—gave a monstrous bray.

"Did I discombobulate you, Hanes?" he said when his mirth had run its course. "Well, you never can tell from the wart on a pickle which way the juice will squirt." I remember that aphorism of his from long ago, the night we had met at the Pierces'. It was a favorite, however, that he had failed to bring out for us at the pre-engagement luncheon, I found myself recalling. One came to employ this kind of whimsical scholarship when considering Beeman.

Beside my nephew's craggy father-in-law-designate, little Nat Pierce looked like a jockey. All the Pierces were small men, but the briefcase which Nat carried seemed almost too big for him to lift. I had never had any close acquaintance with him and knew him only as Dan's uncle and a lawyer who could get you out of

195

trouble if anybody could. He was the one, I recalled Dan's telling me, who rescued another of Dan's uncles when that uncle's wife's death by shooting caused the family some embarrassment. We nodded and Beeman told me that the rest of them were already in old man Reagan's office. I left Beeman and Pierce with as much surprise as I had found them; the Tower meeting was not due to begin for another half-hour.

I must have interrupted a general discussion when I entered, for when they saw me a total silence fell. In that attitude they presented a sort of living tableau or panorama as I followed their faces around the room. Ed and Mary were seated together on the couch to the right under the huge old oak-framed architectural rendering of the Tower. Ed looked about the same as when I'd seen him last. The expanse of his blue serge suit was a bit more liberal perhaps; the rosy, well-barbered jowls were caught a little more snugly by his broker's hard collar; the fixed hachure marks of his hair were sketched on a trifle more widely. But he was the same Irishman inevitably in search of the best of it for himself. Mary's face had been quite classic as a young woman. Easy life had later filled and relaxed it. Now it had pulled itself together again, leaving lines of webbing at the corners of her eyes and mouth, but a short veil from a smart little black silk cloche was kind to her, giving her if not an appearance of attractiveness, then one of considerable seasoned chic. She and Ed smiled and nodded to me faintly, as though we were recognizing each other at a distance across a large party. I needn't have disturbed myself about that encounter.

Mr. Neidlinger had a chair between the windows and the harsh light from outside did him no favors. He reminded me of those photographs we were now seeing, long after the war, of the Kaiser's ancient generals. Hitler had put them back in uniform again but the lower lids of their eyes—although the eyes themselves were still steadfast and indomitable—had fallen to pieces. Mr. Neidlinger's own uniform, the dark suit with the fobs across the vest and the high black kid shoes, was as correct as ever and so was the exact white bristle that covered his head. To the left, clumped crookedly

196

in his seat behind the desk, old man Reagan looked as old and hard as anybody will ever look. He looked like an old tree.

The Reagans, I knew, had not retained their offices in the Tower out of sentiment. As managers of the building they had been forced to reduce all the office rentals—their own reduction the only one made cheerfully, I'm sure. There had been no receptionist on duty in the outer rooms and it was my guess that the typing for Reagan & Son was handled nowadays by the public stenographer in the hotel.

So there they all sat in that faded room where a brisk provincial construction business had once been carried on, seeming not a little like a family gathered around for the reading of a will from which there were small expectations. And evidently the reading had started without anyone's bothering about whether I was there or not.

"We were just going over the brief preliminaries, George," Mr. Neidlinger said as if in explanation. "Have a chair." I took the nearest one, by the door where I had entered.

"None of it's going to take very long," Ed said. "Don't get too relaxed."

Old man Reagan went through one of his minor convulsions. "To the business," he grumbled, "to the business." Thinking of Mr. Neidlinger I wondered if old man Reagan's sentiments toward Germans were any less homicidal than they were the last time I had seen him writhing in that chair. There were, of course, no English among us.

"It seems to be some tiresome matter of Mr. Neidlinger's bonds," Mary told me. "Did *you* know about them?" The implication of her tone was that the Teutonia Bank's financial interest in the building was some parlor jugglery suddenly produced to astonish the other owners.

I knew about the bonds. They were once worth a million; the bank would sell them now for two hundred thousand dollars. I also knew, through Bob Mayer and others, that an amendment to the Bankruptcy Act, a sort of tonic for sick companies whose immediate values had gone way down but whose long-range prospects

197

were not hopeless, had a good chance of passing the next Congress. I hoped we could hang on long enough to avoid by that means foreclosure, if by no other.

"Not my bonds please, Mrs. Hanes," I heard Mr. Neidlinger saying. "The bank's bonds."

"Oh, come now, Mr. Neidlinger. *You* are the *bank*, you know you are."

"Pipe down, Mary, for God's sake," said Ed, the oldest husband to the oldest wife in the world. Only it was my wife, I had to realize.

"Well, are you going to just sit there and let him sell us all out?"

"Listen," Ed said, "how often do I have to explain it to you?" He made a waving gesture of exhausted patience. "Never mind, I'm not going to explain it to you any more."

"Well," I said, "why doesn't somebody explain something to me? I'll listen." I tried to sound amiable about it.

"Why can't everybody—" old man Reagan querulously began.

"Please," said Mr. Neidlinger, and he made the word very authoritative. We all shut up.

"George," he said, "it was as I was saying when you came in. Since last year—when I think it was that you and I had a pleasant little talk together about some other affair—the bonds are in default. By law," he said, "by law," he repeated almost pleadingly, "the bonds should be foreclosed." A ghost of relief then passed over his haggard face. "But since last week we have a much more agreeable proposition. The bank's price for the bonds has been met."

"You may say that," old man Reagan said.

"A party has come forward who is in a position to purchase the bonds from the bank, although somewhat under par, and to pay a very fair price it seems to me to the stockholders for their equity in the building and the property also."

"Of course," Mary said in amused self-reproof. "Now I remember what it's all about."

"Who is the party?" I asked.

"It is Mr. Donald Beeman," Mr. Neidlinger said.

198

Before I could say anything else old man Reagan had uncoiled himself from his chair with surprising spryness and hopped over to the door, pulling it open with a gnomish demonstration of welcome. "Come in, Donald," he called, "come in!" And, "Coming! Coming right up, Papa!" cried a voice outside. The gathering had suddenly taken on the aspect to me of some sort of Halloween surprise affair arranged by superannuated children. Beeman plunged in with a grin and a wave for everybody and, amid grunts and giggles, squeezed himself onto the couch beside Ed and Mary.

"Say," he said, looking over to see if the door had been closed, "what's Nat Pierce doing out there?"

Now that Beeman's presence in the office was clarified, that question was the one that I myself had next begun to wonder about. Mr. Neidlinger looked at old man Reagan in inquiry and old man Reagan passed the look along to his son.

"Don't ask me," said Ed, "but we can sure use a client. Don't anybody chase him away." When his remark drew laughter, he tried another. "Maybe Nat wants to buy the building, too." That one got a laugh as well.

"Well," said Beeman when the amusement had subsided, "have you settled it all among you?"

"Settled what?" I asked.

Everyone looked at me with his own expression of weary toleration except Mr. Neidlinger.

"The price for the building is very fair, George, believe me."

"What is he going to do with it?"

"Why scrap it of course!" came the ash-can voice. "We'll put up a one-story taxpayer on the property until times get better."

"Don't even have to do that," Ed said, yawning. "Parking lot'll pay about as well."

"Who's going to buy the scrap?" I heard myself saying over the thunder in my ears.

"Why, the Japs," Beeman said. "They're in the scrap market up to their necks!" He turned to Mary. "Don't let me get started on the Japs. Boy, they may be yellow-bellies but they're a wonderfully industrious little people."

199

"Believe me, George," said Mr. Neidlinger, "it is the only possible way out of this situation."

"Of course it is," Beeman said. "What's he thinking about anyway?"

"I was thinking about my brother, I guess," I said. The sound of their voices was small and distant but still very clear to me.

"Oh, for Christ's sake." This from Mary.

"Well, Hanes," Beeman said, "I'm thinking about my daughter. I've got to see that she and young Jeff get something out of this wreck."

That was something else I hadn't thought about—like the Japs buying and carrying away the steel that my brother and I and Baken (or Dakin), the Czech foreman, and his crew had put up in the winter of 1915. Would young Jeff, whose so carefully drawn proxy was to be used if necessary against his mother, approve its use against his prospective father-in-law and bride-to-be? There comes a time in a fight when, punched silly, you know you are bound to lose, that you just swing a few more for the hell of it.

"There is no majority that can beat my vote and my trusteeships," I said. My own voice sounded clear but far away, too.

Mr. Neidlinger gave me a long glance of pity. "There is not a court in the country today that wouldn't approve this liquidation, George," he said. And of course he was right. And Junie had been right that afternoon back of the beer garden.

"For God's sake, yes!" shouted Beeman.

For God's sake, for God's sake, the voice went aimlessly echoing around the room, it seemed to me.

Then there came that knock on the door. It came very sharp and very near me. All the rest I heard quite normally and very well. Nat Pierce, his bag hanging down by his side, pushed the door open and came a few steps into the room.

Ed spoke first. "Hi, Nat," he said. "What's on your mind? We'll be through here in a couple of minutes."

"I want to bring in a client of mine," Nat said.

Old man Reagan, who was looking beyond my back, gave another of his contortions and said, "What the hell?"

200

When I turned to see what he was looking at I saw Junie. Instinctively I turned back to look at Mr. Neidlinger. He was erect and tense but absolutely undismayed at what must have been a shocking surprise.

"Please come in, my boy," he said. "We have just been concluding a negotiation."

I watched Junie begin to hobble forward and got up and moved him into my chair.

"Thanks, professor," he said, grinning up at me. "This is a funny way to do this, isn't it?"

"Do what?" asked Ed sharply.

"Oh, buy a piece of a hotel, and," he waved his hand gracefully around the room, "all the rest that goes with it. *Nicht wahr?*"

"Mr. Neidlinger," said Nat, "Mr. Neidlinger, Junior, wants to offer to buy the Teutonia bonds."

"Yes?" said Junie's father with nothing more, it seemed to me, than curiosity and deep interest.

"What the hell with?" asked Beeman who, inexplicably to me, had remained silent so long.

"Money," Junie said. I must say he cut a very admirable and composed figure there, surrounded by the disorder he had caused. This was the man of affairs in his most attractive phase, the harassments of operations put aside, the competent negotiator to the fore. I wondered if he got away with it very often in his own business circles.

"Yes?" his father repeated.

"He wants to buy the bonds for the going price, of course, Mr. Neidlinger," Pierce said.

"Of course," said Mr. Neidlinger, and he turned to look on his son with complete fascination. Fascination with what? I should have thought it would have been horror that showed from his face. Or the despair of ruin, for where else could Junie have gotten his money except from the source that everybody knew it came—even his father now could put no other face on it. For Junie, too, this was the end of whatever masquerade he might have hoped to comfort or appease his father with. And all at once I knew

201

that I myself was the cause of their utter and irrevocable misfortune.

Beeman of course broke the spell. "Oh," he said savagely, "get the hell out of here, you two! We're not talking about buying the bonds. That's only part of the deal. These people are selling the whole damned building. What are you guys doing here anyhow?"

I thought I could have told him what one of them had been doing. Nat Pierce had been listening at the door.

"It is perfectly proper, Mr. Beeman," Mr. Neidlinger said quietly. "The stockholders are entitled to entertain further offers. It would be your intention to continue the Tower in operation, Junior?"

"Yes, Father." Their eyes met in an intense glow of affection, the brighter, I thought, for having been so long denied. I think all of us watched it, except perhaps old man Reagan, and for a moment the room and its refuse of old emotions was swept by a gust of tragedy.

Mr. Neidlinger looked at Nat Pierce's bag. "And the currency is there?"

"Yes." In Junie's business you kept your money in money; his father had accepted that, too.

"Well," said his father, moving toward the door a little stiffly, eyes forward, the cropped white head very straight on his shoulders, "I'm sure that will suit Mr. Hanes's purposes, and I have always wanted to do business with my son."

"Would you like us to send some people over with this, Mr. Neidlinger?" Nat asked as the old man passed him.

Mr. Neidlinger stopped. He shook his head and frowned. "Oh, no," he said. "No, nothing like that. If you will please remain here for a few minutes I will have the bank messengers take charge." And with that he left us.

"A God-damned bootlegger!" Mary wailed, at last finding tongue. "I don't want this terrible place run a day longer. I want it torn down! I want my money!"

And all the rest of them started raising hell, too. But they hadn't while Mr. Neidlinger was there.

202

In the elevator hall the colored man with whom I had discussed the perpetually honed razor was waiting, but not the white man of that earlier afternoon going out to Junie's headquarters. In his place there was a different one. He was large, plump, with fat hands and almond eyes and an olive sheen to his skin; this one looked more like the proprietor of a cigar store or, I thought, a mill-end house, than a man-at-arms.

"I want you to meet a guy," Junie said.

"Another one?" I looked toward the colored gunman and his companion.

"I'm talking about my new manager. For the hotel."

We went down to the Chestnut Street entrance and then north a few blocks—our attendants close before and behind us, Nat having been left behind—to the alley beside the Boatman's Bank where there used to be a place that was a saloon and business-man's café which was now a saloon and businessman's café and horse parlor.

I didn't know exactly what I was to meet there in the way of a solution for the Tower's future but I was sure that it would be unpleasant. Salvage is never what my friend Mayer would call a Cadillac operation. There is great style to a vessel when it sets out, clean-lined, paint bright, brand-new, and flags flying, on its maiden voyage. But when it wallows wrecked and dishonored behind the weedy hawser and the smoke-smeared tug that drags it to the hacker's yard, there is no style. Depressions bring out a class of unstylish people whose skill it is to make a last cheap profit from converting to a baser use the vestige of a handsome venture. It is a pinchbeck and unenviable business, the conversionist's, the sal-vager's. It is certainly not a custodian's job, although I suppose nobody makes much money from either.

The agent of our salvation at the Tower, to whom Junie intro-duced me, was named Samstag, Chick Samstag. I had been wrong; he was not what I might have called stylish, but he was surely not unpleasant. He was a stocky young man in his early thirties with hyperthyroid eyes that stuck out in a constant parody of eager surprise. The truth was that the failure of tomorrow's sunrise

203

would not have astonished him. Most of his business experience, I learned, had been acquired around carnivals.

"We're going to make the old Tower a straw house, George," he assured me within the first five minutes of our acquaintance. If you live long enough and circulate with a little attention and curiosity, the vernaculars of our rich tongue can be a source of much interest and entertainment. The Tower might indeed have been characterized as a house of straw by the classicist or student of nursery tales; financially it was quite impermanent. But when Chick Samstag used the term "straw house" he meant a great popular success, a sellout, the allusion being to the situation in which traveling circuses find themselves so overwhelmed with patronage that they must seat the overflow at the ends of the arena on bales of straw. His sanguineness encouraged me.

What we all wanted, he went on to say, was a good score (prosperity) in the Red Wagon (the front office or treasury of a circus or carnival), no ding among the coolies (stealing by the staff), plenty of butchers (concessionaires), and of course a world of marks (customers). Who could ask for anything more?

"How about grift?" Chick asked Junie.

"We'll see," Junie said. "The joint's already full of hustlers. Games, I don't know."

They looked at me together.

"Yeah," Chick then said. "We'll see."

Well, he was Junie's man and it was Junie's show, but I did want to know what their plans might be about keeping on Barney Walsh.

"Don't worry about Barney," Junie said. After all, they were old friends, too.

"The manager? Oh, sure, I'll need him to help me dig the business," Chick told me.

Don't crawl, walk! Jeff used to say. I had an idea that Chick might have met with my brother's approval. The Lord knew he was hard and enthusiastic. I doubted that he would need a nurse, not poor Barney at any rate. At all events the Tower was not on its way to Japan, as it had been just about an hour and a half before.

204

When Junie started to follow me to the cut-glass street door of the café the colored man rose from another table and arranged to stand between the door and him. Between the door and me, I observed, was clear air.

"He was great, wasn't he?" Junie said, and of course I knew whom he meant.

"Yes, I thought he was magnificent."

"You did have a chance to go and see him that time last year, didn't you, professor?"

"Of course. I told you I would. I had to anyhow on business."

"Don't kid me, professor," he said, laughing. "You didn't have much business left." He gave me a push toward the door. "But you have now. This Chick's a killer. He really is. He'll make the old joint sing."

I looked in on Barney in the manager's office on my way upstairs to my room. It was not necessary to tell him a great deal about what had gone on; he would have been an incredibly limited hotel man not to have sensitive communications with every corner of his building. There wasn't much bounce left in him, I could see. I don't think that he was hurt or frightened by the change of management. It was just that he, like the Tower, had had it; they were both on their last legs. He leaned back from his desk—I wondered if I had ever seen Barney behind a library desk before, or sitting down, for that matter—and rubbed his hand around on his thin bartender's hair.

"You try to hold things together but they keep falling apart, don't they, Mr. Hanes?" he said.

When I got up to my room Mary was there.

This was the third time in our lives that my wife and I had been in a bedroom together. She was leaning with her hips resting on the end of the bed, her head tilted provocatively as I came in. Her little veiled hat, I noticed now, had a bow that sort of dashed off one side of it and her dress—a good black one, I believe the ladies call it—had a bow of the same material that flared away from her flank on the opposite side. Like her face her figure had been pulled together, too, doubtless by someone else's exercise. Her hair, a

205

long bob, was of no human color but nevertheless attractive; it was the color of light gun metal—no, dove-colored—and I supposed that the same brush that had tinted it had also supplied its softness and sheen. Altogether, a good-looking, modern middle-aged woman.

"Surprised?" she asked me.

"Not after this morning," I said. "I'm never going to be surprised at anything any more."

"It was quite a party."

"The one you said would never happen—you and I and all the Reagans and Mr. Neidlinger gathered under one tent."

"Oh, did I? When?"

"A long time ago."

She smiled and moved over on the bed. "I didn't know you ever paid any attention to anything I said, George."

"Oh, yes, I do," I replied warmly.

She looked me over for a moment or so. "You know, George," she said, "you could be a very attractive-looking man. With a mustache, I think."

"And a Homburg hat."

"No, seriously, George. You've kept your figger, you have nice regular features, the family pile of blond hair. Does Margaret adore you madly?"

"What did you come here for, Mary?" I asked.

"Now, George, don't be cross, but you see I need money."

"Who doesn't?"

"And since you have always managed to ball up my affairs so beautifully," she continued, "you'll simply have to find some for me." A spasm of vindictiveness flashed under the veil. "If you had let them go ahead and sell this cathouse this morning I wouldn't have to have bothered myself coming to you."

Well, she was right about that.

"Tell me something, George."

"Go ahead."

"Why are you such an insane jerk on the subject of your brother?"

206

She knew she could always hurt me that way and the only explanation for her behavior that I could think of was that the venting of hatred and giving of pain to chosen partners, you might say, must give certain people, Mary for example, some sort of orgiastic satisfaction. There could be no other reason for her seeking me out to slander Jeff and me. Her being angry about the sale of the building—or rather our not selling it—I could of course understand, and once again I resolved not to let her make me lose my temper.

"What were you two, queer for each other?"

And once again I lost it.

"Maybe you'll tell me," I said, "why you've gone panting around after Reagan all these years. Do you two do something odd with each other that you can't get anyone else to do for you?"

Well, that was a filthy thing to say, wasn't it? If I had intended to get her goat—and I am afraid I most certainly had—I succeeded. She spent the better part of the next five minutes calling me all the worst words in the lexicon of the construction business and wound up by shouting: "You couldn't possibly understand Ed Reagan and me. You bet I love him. I've always loved him. I love him because he's big and strong and when he takes me in his arms I feel like no other woman in the world!"

An echo there. Hadn't Margaret said that Mrs. Cox loved the implausible Mr. Beeman because he was strong? I would never have thought of Reagan as either big or strong—heavy, perhaps—but Mary's declaration cleared up one thing for me: when I had inadvertently got my foot caught in the collision between those two it had not been a matter of puppy love. In an odd way I felt better about them. I was thinking over this when she suddenly flung herself down on the bed and began shaking convulsively with sobbing. Same woman, same scene, it might as well have been the same bed and bedroom as in Pasadena, God knew how many years ago.

She turned her stricken face toward me, the mascara smearing the poor wrinkled eyes and the veil sticking to her cheeks. "Oh, God," she cried, "I am so damned unhappy!" A woman weeping in distress is hard enough to take; a woman weeping in her best clothes is unbearable.

After a while I got her some water and washed her up and she pulled herself more or less together.

"Now about this money business," I said. "You've got enough to live on."

"Oh, George," she sighed wearily. "Don't be tiresome, dear."

"Well, if you need more can't Ed help you out?"

"Ed? He hasn't anything any more. You and your bootlegger friend have seen to that. What little he has goes to that juvenile mob of his at Georgetown and Fordham and the Sacred Heart, et cetera, et cetera. Ed hasn't anything."

I was thinking of the school bills I had been paying for some years myself when she said: "You must have some money, George. You've no dependents." That should have made me angry. But poor, foolish Mary, I thought.

"I don't have much besides a house in New York."

"*Well.*"

So I heard myself telling her that she could have the rentals from it. "I'll give you the name of the agent, you tell him what you want done with it." Pity, as Jeff said, is never an inexpensive emotion. But it was surely true that I had helped cut her out of a lot of money that morning.

"You mean I own it?"

She had stopped crying now, and some saving sense of self-preservation came to my rescue.

"No, Mary, you don't own it. You just get the rent from it." I could already foresee enough trouble in store for me when I got home.

"Oh, George, why not be nice and give the building to me?"

"I've been too nice as it is, Mary," I said ruefully. "Don't be like Andrew Mellon. Leave a little for the rest of us."

She then looked up at me with a small naughty smile.

"Are you going to tell Margaret about this?" she asked.

"This calls for a party, I think," Margaret said. "Don't you? A small one?"

"Sure."

"What's the matter, dearest? Cheer up. Mafeking has been relieved."

But had Mafeking? Yes, relieved maybe. But not rehabilitated. I had told her about Samstag the carnival man and his interesting factional English and she had been bright enough to suggest that while he might not be the ideal hotel or office-building operator as yet, he would certainly have some ideas about what to do with the Tower's moldering theater. The truth was that I was suffering perhaps a natural reaction to Junie's rescue of the building; what he had done was really only to produce a palliative, a jury-rig, a stopgap; it was as though you had come to a quack doctor suffering from cancer and he had given you a whisk broom to brush yourself off with. Had the Tower been sold, we all surely could have used the money. Money could buy a great deal in those days. You could get a pretty good new automobile, for example, for seven or eight hundred dollars. I wonder why people don't cheer in an era of low-priced living as loudly as they complain when the cost of living is high; certainly not out of sensitivity, for there is suffering under both conditions. Yes, there would indeed have been a pleasant amount of money in the cash register if we had scrapped the building. And I would not have awakened in the night any more thinking of it standing out there so far away and so sick and so alone.

"You think about the Tower in the night, don't you, George?"

"How's that?" The old trick of her sensing a thought of mine never failed to shock me, although it must not be too difficult for a person, very close, very much together with another, to follow the other's mood or line of reverie, particularly when the signposts of expression are so familiar.

"You think about the Tower, lonely out there in the night," she said.

"How do you know?"

"Oh, I know." She laid her hand on my shoulder. "It would really be frightful for you if it weren't there at all. But it is there. It's there still. Cheer up."

"Why do you suppose Junie did it?" I asked. "That's been puzzling me. I know he did it for me but I don't understand quite why."

"Because you're a very cultivated and romantic man." She cocked her head and smiled. "And you bring out the romantic in other people, such as me."

"Who will we have for the party?" I asked.

It was the weekend of the Navy boat race, and we had Jeff and Carol and young Mary already coming to be with us anyhow, so the party only meant asking Bob Mayer over from Rumson. I remember thinking that it wouldn't be much of a function to attract Bob. He was quite a man of affairs now. Journalism, he had once told me, was merely a steppingstone for a man of purpose. In his case he had picked up the stone and put it in his pocket as he had stepped along. He owned *Architectural Age* now, as well as two or three drive-in movies, a piece of a cheap clothing-store chain, and some other enterprises of the sort that he had spied flourishing in the rock garden of hard times. The house at Rumson he bought at a very low figure from the estate of a stockbroker who had jumped out of his office window a year or so before. Bob never needed a nurse. Or so I thought.

"The secret of living in this old world is no secret at all, George," he said to me. "You've just got to be contemporary, that's all." We had remained sitting around the table where we had been having lunch, in the courtyard behind my house. He indicated the out-buildings about us. "This used to be a farrier's yard," he said. "Well, you've brought its usefulness up to date. You've made a dwelling and an architect's office of it. You've made it contemporary. The same thing's being done for the Tower and I'll bet your brother would be the first to approve. God knows he was contemporary."

"On the ball—in there—*au courant*," my niece murmured.

Bob beamed a wink at her. "You've got the right idea," he said.

I wondered, however, if he had the right idea about her. The shadow line between childhood and youth is crossed much more suddenly by girls than boys. A boy seems to shuffle along into maturity by fits and false starts and accident, but in a matter of a

210

very few weeks or months a girl can be a woman, with all a woman's fears and powers. It is a shocking experience and no wonder some of them never get over it.

My niece Mary had just crossed that shadow line, so that to me there were still smoky, unrecognizable corners in her personality. She had always been a pretty child; she was now a slim and quite beautiful young woman. Compared to Carol's clouded little face, Mary's was a hard sunburst. Her years on the hotel circuit had taught her many subtleties in presenting her person to the world's best view that poor Carol had not found in any part of the curriculum at Smith. Like her mother's on my last inspection, Mary's hair was also long, lustrous, and dove gray, which, in combination with diamond-blue eyes beneath a pair of dark strangely arched brows, made her a girl you would please yourself by glancing twice at. Bob Mayer had thus pleased himself a number of times that forenoon. But I doubted if he had gotten the correct idea about her; I was just learning myself.

"On the ball," he repeated vigorously.

"This house of yours in Rumson," Mary said, "is it contemporary, too?"

"No, no. It's one of a number that Stanford White designed, or his office designed."

"You mean, with lots of paneling and pilasters and Georgian mantelpieces so intricately decorated by those celebrated Italian wood-carvers—my God, were there any left at home in Italy?—that no union painter can recoat them without hopelessly filling in all the prettiest little details?"

Bob laughed. "That's right, and you're your father's daughter. You must come over and see the place."

"I have," she said. "A thousand times—counting photographs."

There so often comes a time and a place when a man of forty-odd mistakes snappish bad manners in a young woman for a lively mind. This evidently was that time and place for my friend in the case of my niece.

"You've got a point there," he said. "It isn't a Hanes job."

"I've only seen it twice," Carol said, widely missing the fairly

211

blunt edge of Mary's remark, "but, oh, Mary, it's quite beautiful. Margaret's put some lovely things in it. Have you been there since then?"

Jeff, I think it was, at this juncture suggested that we all should be getting down to the lake. Then Mary, to Bob's clear disappointment, announced that she was going to take a nap. The party thus thinned of its glamour from the start, the rest of us piled into a car and drove down the hill to the public boathouse, where, under the sturdy young leaves of oak and hickory and maple, spring was coming quick and strong out of the Jersey mud.

I've almost always kept a canoe on Carnegie for the bass fishing over on the other side of the canal on the Millstone River, in late summer, and for just such occasions as this one. The weather was fine, lots of youngsters and their girls were about—just the day for messing about in boats. It was my idea that Jeff would take Margaret and Carol down near the finish line and Bob and I would wander around on the shore. So I hauled the boat out of the shed and Jeff and I put it in the water, holding it near the stringpiece for the others to get in, glancing up at Carol as I did so. She was looking down into the canoe, bobbling and slithering a little while we held it, as though she were looking into an abyss. Her lips were pulled back from her teeth and her eyes were wide and glassy.

"Oh, no!" she said. "I don't think—I couldn't!"

"What's the matter, dear?" Jeff asked her.

"There's a hole," she said chokingly.

"Oh, no, Carol," I said. "A patch or two, but no hole. She's tight as a drum."

"I couldn't!" she cried, and put her hands to her face, miserably shaking her head. "There's a big hole!"

By this time, of course, a few bystanders had begun watching us.

"I don't think she's ever been in a canoe," Jeff said.

"Well, then there's certainly no reason to begin now," Margaret said. "They're really mainly for Indians."

So the party began to dissolve again, everybody offering every possible rearrangement unfavorable to himself but favorable to poor Carol's comfort or convenience. In the end Bob and I took the canoe ("Bob has something he wants to talk to you about," Margaret had whispered sharply) and the others went back home. I'm sure Bob didn't care about the races one way or the other; he went to the Armour Institute.

As he faced me in the thwarts and I paddled we ambled upstream, past the old dyspeptic swans and the groups happily picnicking along the muddy banks, so that we could watch the freshmen boat their shells for the first race. Naturally we spoke of poor Carol's curious seizure; Bob, the contemporary, attempted to place some kind of clinical Freudian significance to the child's repetition of the word "hole," while I, as I recall, suggested that she might be subject to vertigo from looking down on moving water. We got nowhere. Then—at his instance, I'm sure—we discussed Mary for a while: with whom she was studying (it was Raphael Soyer at the time), where she was living, and so forth. He said that he thought her extremely attractive and went on to pay her a characteristically cockeyed compliment. "She's going to make some man a damned bad wife," Bob said.

We had turned around after the freshman race and were drifting downstream with the breeze at our back when Bob brought up the something he wanted to talk to me about.

"I want you to do me a favor," he said.

I have never been in a position to do many favors in my life, so naturally I asked him to name it.

"You think *Architectural Age* is a pretty good magazine, don't you?" he asked.

Well, of course I did, in its way. Occasionally it digested professional papers that those who did not keep up too closely with their reading might find worthwhile, and by presenting a man's work, as it had on gratifying occasions in the past shown mine, it might help an architect attract a client. But the principal purpose of such a publication is to make money for the owner. That I knew, too.

"We need circulation, like everybody else," Bob went on, "and you have to scramble around pretty hard nowadays to get it. One way to attract attention—in the daily press, among building groups, and so on—is to put out a big special issue, like the *Forum* did on Wright, see what I mean?"

I said I saw. The device was also calculated to attract a heavy volume of special advertising. Far away a gun went off and I turned to watch the jayvee crews begin to bear down on us. Crew must be the most restricted of sports outside weight-lifting and I have never been able to identify myself with a man in a shell, but I nevertheless like to watch it close up, the grunt and thrust and creak of it when all the sweeps reach frantically together into the stream. The whole idea is such a parody of propulsive engineering, getting someplace across water by the hardest but most sporting way.

"Only I'm going to make the *Forum* stunt look like a tired issue of *Godey's Lady's Book*," Bob said. "I'm going to throw a festival."

I returned him my attention. "Yes?" I said. "What kind of a festival?"

"A T. J. Hanes festival, and I need your help."

Naturally I was pleased. I told him he could count on me for any assistance he might feel I could offer; I mentioned the unpublished drawings, notebooks, and so forth, that I had at home.

"Great," said Bob. "I want to throw a big shindig in the ballroom of the Tower on the twentieth anniversary of ground-breaking for the building more or less, and I want you to make the principal address."

Something about the nervous way he lit a cigarette at this moment, some evasive look in his eye, raised a warning flag. "What," I asked him, "is this really about? You always respected Jeff but you never wanted to build a shrine to him."

He scowled up at me through a cloud of cigarette smoke. "I'm trying to make some money. I'm asking you to help me out."

"No," I said. "You're the one who wants to help *me* out." Good Lord—my cold-blooded, opportunistic friend Bob, going about this thing with all the subtlety of a man making an anonymous conscience-gift to the Treasury. "You'd get me up there in front of all the directors in the A.I.A. to make a speech on the glories of architecture, and no matter how you looked at it I'd be taking a free ride on my brother's reputation. I'll bet you even had it rigged to get me some kind of medal. The answer is no, Bob. In fact, nix."

He threw his cigarette overboard with the violence he might have used had he been sitting in a swivel chair, and the canoe nearly capsized us. When we got to rights again, I would have thought the ridiculousness of the situation would have cooled him off, but it hadn't.

"Now you listen to me, George. I'm not kidding. What do you think is happening to you professionally? You weren't young when this depression began, and when we get out of it—because we will and only a damned suicide would think of anything else—when we get out of it you're not going to be any chicken. The kids that come out of this one are going to be hungry kids ["hungry," I recognized as Junie's key word], and the competition for men like you is going to be brutal. I want your name up there big—the hell with your brother—when the building business opens up again." He must have seen no responsive spark in my face. "Well, what are you going to do? Haven't you even any sense of self-preservation?"

I suppose that it takes just such a moment of pressure, when you're most unprepared for it, to force out of you something, some fundamental assertion, that you haven't even made to yourself. "I know that I will now never be the head of a large firm of my own," I said, "and I know that when this is over I will be past the age when I will be wanted by a large firm in any important capacity, nor would I want to go into one under any circumstances. Tough as times are for the kids now, they will be a good, case-hardened bunch and the right age to carry on when we turn the corner. They will be a hard crowd to beat."

"Are you kidding me or quoting me?" he asked. "This all leaves you pretty much out in the cold. As I said."

"No. Just about where I should have been anyhow. I'll keep on building a little, and I want to teach."

"Teach what?"

"Teach what I know best, a man's capacity for reverence. Teach the best half-educated people in the world a capacity for respect that follows on well-grounded instruction."

Upstream the starting gun went off again.

"You know I won't let you get away with this," Bob said.

"What do you mean?"

"I mean that if you won't make this speech I'll have the festival anyhow."

"Not in the Tower."

"No, not in the Tower. But I'll have it in Carnegie Hall, and everybody will wonder where the hell his brother is, the one who kept the flame lighted all these years. They'll say you either turned sour or pooped out. Quit laughing. And I'll get Eckfield to make the memorial address—he used to work in that office—and if I can't find him I'll get fairies from the Museum of Modern Art. If you think I'm kidding, you don't know me very well yet."

But I knew him, God bless him.

"Listen," he said. "Wouldn't any important faculty you wanted to teach in be impressed with this kind of publicity—I mean, recognition?"

And here came the varsities, creaking and grunting along, the little coxswains shouting, and I suddenly thought, looking across the bright afternoon wide on the water, of an easy way of doing something very hard, although a sort of a dirty trick on Bob Mayer. On the far shore the blue Navy flag went up at the half mile and I expected that it would go up all the way down the lake.

"Okay," I said, "you win."

You should have seen the way his expression changed. These tycoons become unlike the rest of us in this respect: they do not feel that they have to dissemble when they are losing, and when they win they permit themselves to show almost fatuous happiness. They are not, you might say, sportsmen. Nor is there any reason that they should be.

Walking homeward up the hill in the crowd Bob told me that he really had no plans for the A.I.A. to give me a medal.

216

When we got home the four of them were sitting around the trestle table under the old crab-apple tree that grew out of the flagstones in the courtyard, a tranquil family scene *champêtre* in the lime-colored twilight. Mary was fixing Carol a new hair-do, with Margaret and Jeff interested spectators. The party had pulled itself together again.

"This way, don't you think, George?" Mary called to me, sweeping Carol's stiff dark curls over one side of her forehead. "She has lovely eyes. See what it does to them."

"Oh, Mary," Carol protested, but obviously loving every moment of the younger, much prettier girl's attention. If she needed any therapy after her convulsive experience of the afternoon, this was it; she looked serene and quite pretty herself. I wondered, however, what satisfaction my niece derived from this scene. What did she get out of it? Was it merely an attractive girl's offhand attention to one who could not possibly be competitive? Why should a young woman so almost wholly absorbed in herself—the normal status of the belle—bother with Carol's hair or anything else about Carol or anyone else? And then, as I was checking my own propensity to analyze too sharply the details of Mary's new personality, impulsively she embraced Carol's head and face, crying happily: "It's so nice that Jeff hasn't picked a bitch for a wife!" The eyes of the three of them met for a moment in a youthful embrace. It was a sweet picture, one that I have carried around with me for a good many years now. For of course I should have known that Jeff's children would reach out to each other, even across childhoods as tattered as those that had been given them. If only for this flying hour, if only in illusion, they were happy in each other. And of course I was happy. Then Carol reached up her arms to caress Mary's. I remember, and of this I am certain: from that hour Carol loved Mary all her life.

Why must perfection speed so fast? Alfred's dinner was a good one as I remember it, it usually was; Margaret had hung some gesso lanterns in the waxen-leaved branches we dined beneath; the night was spring. But the spell had passed. No one was to blame.

217

We naturally talked about the festival, in which Jeff and Mary showed—I must credit them this—all the polite interest that could be expected of them. But they were no more than infants when their father died; they had never come under his magic. We might as well have been discussing a celebration of Christopher Wren. Jeff and Carol went away early so that he could put her on a train.

That left Margaret and me to watch a performance of that old classic, the rich man amusing himself by trying to impress a beautiful, indifferent girl. I remember that Bob said that he wanted to get some paddle boats for the lake on his place at Rumson. He'd seen them on the Lido, and would probably put someone in his office to the task of importing two or three for him.

"You mean you haven't seen the Abercrombie ads in *The New Yorker?*" asked Mary. There, I thought, was truly a key to my niece's character. There are several ways to call a person's attention to the whereabouts of merchandise without implying that anyone who does not follow the advertising pages of *The New Yorker* is scarcely qualified for human companionship—as she did.

"No!" he said. "Really? When?"

Oh, Bob, Bob, I wanted to tell him, you're a grown man; you surely must know better than to ask for this humiliation.

"Every spring," she said.

He might have put up with any amount of this erotic counter-punching at that time, I suppose, but before long she became restless, and not much after ten o'clock said that she thought she would go upstairs to bed and read *Rasselas*. Under those conditions he made his first date to have dinner with her in New York.

And now he and his infernal improvement project for the house at Rumson got *me* into trouble, or at least hastened trouble's inevitable arrival. Mind you, I had only been back from St. Louis a day.

This time it was the matter of an English break-front cabinet and a pair of gilt sconces of the same period that had come on the market when some people named Cryder had sold their collection. I don't know why I should remember the name Cryder after all these years, except that things like that are likely to stick with you under certain circumstances, as you may see.

"You bought them, didn't you?" Bob asked Margaret.

"Yes," she said, "and I paid a great deal for them. More than I should."

"Well," he said, "that's all right. They're what we wanted. When will you send them over? They don't need any work done on them, do they?"

She lit a cigarette and put on a very pleased smile. "Bob," she said, "I'm not going to sell them to you."

"Somebody must have offered you a lot more money."

This was all playful, I thought. They enjoyed buying things together.

"No. I want to put them along the north wall of George's old sitting room in New York. You remember the room. View of the river?" And here was where it began to hurt; she laid her hand in mine. "I have a warm spot in my heart for that room." She turned to me, her eyes very soft in the lantern light. "I had breakfast there one morning before going to Coney Island."

Bob laughed. "I can't bid against that kind of sentiment, Margaret."

"Oh," she said, very businesslike again, "we'll ask the next tenant twice the rent. It's a good investment."

The Gift of the Magi. I know I could very well have ducked the issue until the next morning, but you never want to do anything like that.

"You'd better let Bob have the furniture, Margaret," I said.

"What do you mean?"

"I turned the house over to Mary yesterday." The quicker said the better, I thought.

She looked straight ahead of her for several long, terrible moments, as though letting my statement sink in, permanently sink in. Then she arose and walked around to the other side of the trestle table and looked at me. She was the image of ultimately disillusioned, completely outraged womanhood—as she surely had a right to be. I thought she picked the precise epithet for me.

219

"George Hanes," she said, "you are a cluck." And she added, "I'll never see you again."

She turned and ran quickly out through the arched passageway to the street. I went after her of course, calling to her that I had not given Mary the building, only the rental of it, but she was in her car and gone before I reached the street.

When I came back I mixed myself a drink and one for Bob. He said something about all the Hanes girls presenting problems, and we probably tried to talk about other matters, but the heart had for good and all gone out of that party, and presently he, too, left. I sat there alone under my lanterns and crab-apple tree from one chime from the Nassau Hall tower to the next. It was very late, but still dark when the phone rang inside. I answered it in the kitchen. It was Margaret.

"George," she asked, "do you want to hear a very funny dirty joke?"

Well, of course I said yes, and she told me to come over. This I did very quickly.

I found her sitting up in bed in her bedroom looking appealing as always, and of course I began to try to explain to her about still retaining ownership of the house on Beekman Place, but she cut me short, bidding me to sit beside her and keep quiet.

"I don't know who told me this one," she said, "but I have been holding it in for a long time, partly from maidenly modesty but chiefly because it's too damned close to home. It seems there was this old Southern colonel who lived in a mansion on his plantation long before the war. One morning he woke up in his great four-poster bed and rang for his body servant whose name was Mose, of course. 'Mose,' he said, 'that was a lovely little dinner party last night. Miss Amanda never looked lovelier.' 'Nossuh,' Mose says. 'Mose,' says the colonel, 'Miss Amanda expressly noticed the flavor of our peanut-fed, sassafras-smoked, Smithfield ham. I think it would be nice if you went out to the smokehouse and took down three or four of them and carried them over to her.'"

Well, we've all heard this one, although poor dear Margaret did

220

not think so, so I let her go on with the story about how the colonel now thought of sending the Paul Storr platter the ham was on over to Miss Amanda by Mose, then the Duncan Phyfe sideboard, and so forth. Margaret was having a very good time telling it.

"About that time Mose said, 'Boss, may I make a suggestion?' and the colonel said, 'Why, of course, Mose.' And Mose said, 'Boss, maybe you better get up and go to the bathroom before you gives away the whole plantation!' "

I laughed as hard as I have ever laughed in my life. Then I reached over and mussed her wiry black hair and she reached over and pulled mine a little harder than was necessary.

A long while later when the windows were electric blue from the dawn she whispered, "What was it that Mary said you would never know anything about?" and our laughter was soft but very real indeed this time.

Thirteen

THE whole thing was grotesque, from the beginning.

When I got into the cab that evening at the station and told the driver that I wanted to go to the Tower, he asked me if I wanted the "hotel side" or the "terminal side." He was very brisk about it and that cheered me up; on one occasion when I had last been in town it had been necessary for me to give the hotel's street address. Now the old place seemed to be spoken of as though it were some great public installation, like an airport. And, when I arrived—at the hotel side—I ceased to wonder. In the nine months since the carnival man had taken over, the atmosphere around Eighth and Chestnut had livened up considerably. I paid off the cab, sent my bag in by a porter who wore a sort of shako, and backed off to the opposite corner to see what had happened to our famous façade.

Strong the Tower stood like a strong man's arm, but around its wrist, just below the parapet, was strapped a vast neon sign the color of cheap filled gold and bearing the burning device of the INTERNATIONAL WORLD CASUALTY CO. So the swindlers were still in the campanile, and surely making no secret of it.

The International World Casualty display, however, paled into quiet good taste when one looked at the rest of the electrical pyrotechnics with which the building was loaded. A great vertical sign that would have pulled the walls out of a lesser structure plunged down the Chestnut Street side above the theater, which was still called, but now with multiwatt stridency, the TOWER. There was nothing left to be seen of the beautiful old arches of the theater entrance; all that had vanished behind an inferno of a marquee which might blind a man before he had read its complete announcement of four movies and a burlesque bill. If you shopped shrewdly you could get a lot of distraction for your money during the Depression. From the theater to the Eighth Street corner the buses took over, for the old Rathskeller entrance was now the portal of the Terminal, the bus terminal.

The three arches of the hotel entrance had also gone out of sight behind an acre of sheet metal, a forest of incandescent globes and leagues of illuminated gas tubing. But the real triumphs of imagination to be observed in the Tower's nighttime décor had been left to the owners of the street-level and second-floor shops and offices. I liked best the streaks of baby-blue lightning that flashed their way up to a tooth-extraction headquarters, and the lime-green giraffe that winked his neck up and down over the door to Jerry the Furrier's. All in all, you wouldn't know the old place.

But if you wouldn't, it then occurred to me, would it make any difference to you? Who at all had ever cared as I cared about what I thought of as "the old place"? How many had ever truly seen or known how to see Tower in the West the day it was first completed and stood risen on the corner of Eighth and Chestnut, all its plain greatness completed? Few indeed. Who, then, among the million-footed who for a generation had passed beneath it night and day would cast up a knowledgeable look at it this night to wince at its deformity? To how many—to put the question in possibly its proper form—did the appearance, even the existence of the Tower, make the slightest difference in a personal lifetime? The Acropolis had long ago been blown half apart because it was used as a gun hide-out in a small Mediterranean war. Wright's office building in Buffalo, the only one he had ever done, had been cleared away for warehouse space. Who cared? Who cared what defacement, what fate at all came to my brother's beautiful building? And why should they care?

Chick Samstag, the monarch of this hell on earth, was waiting for me in the lobby. I judged it either painstakingly courteous or alarmingly adventitious of him, this making it a point of being there to greet me. In point of fact, as I later learned, he was all over the place all the time—or almost all the time.

"Well, George," he said, smacking his hands together, "how do you like it?"

It was hard to deny those popeyes and that jack-o'-lantern grin. "You've certainly got action, Chick," I said.

"You said it!"

We turned to look about us. Abraham Lincoln would have felt right at home; the place was filled with more common people then I had seen together in a long time: men, women, and children, not spread out as in a railway depot, but all clustered very close. This was the kind of place where you saw soldiers in peacetime.

The old mosaics no longer blinked in the shadows above: they were blinded from the wild glow of a hundred vending machines that bubbled and flashed and blared music. What had been the Palm Room where Margaret and I had sipped tea—and later where businessmen like Ed Reagan had taken lunch—was now, I was touched to see, a women's preserve again. The Travelers Aid had set up its post there to succor women and their children.

"Barney thought of that," Chick told me. "It doesn't make a dime, but—what the hell?"

Where Barney himself had once held forth, half a floor down in the old corner Rathskeller, dimes at least were being made. That former cave of shadowy repose was lit up now with long batteries of cold-light fixtures that gave it the ghostly appearance of a sandhog's bore-head. Nothing of the old furnishings or appointments remained except one section of the bar, and here masonite had replaced mahogany on the counter tops. Food was being feverishly passed across it to customers banked three deep who grabbed for it as though it were the last on earth. The attendants worked as

224

if they were bailing out a sinking boat. The place rang with the names of cities far and near as microphones adenoidally called arrivals and departures over the heads of the straining crowd.

"As soon as Frankie-boy lets us have that three-oh-two beer we're going to be doing ourselves a lot more good in here," Chick yelled to me. "And when we get the booze back it'll be murder."

I remember his saying it that way.

What could I have been thinking of, I asked myself, to have agreed to a serious architectural function in a place like this? And in honor of my own brother. I looked around the two rooms they had given me. I knew that they looked not much shabbier than they had last year, but now I was thinking of how they would seem to the other visitors at the anniversary celebration. This tribute to Jeff—the dinner, the speeches, the publicity—was going to be something monstrous, something unholy, like high mass on a midway. I went into the bathroom to get a drink of water and found that there was a coin-operated perfume dispenser over the washstand. Oh, my brother. . . .

I had breakfast in my rooms the next morning. The toast came in some sort of glazed paper envelope instead of folded napery, I noticed, but then I realized that the napery had been gone for a long time now. When the boy had taken the things away Barney arrived to pay me a visit, properly advised that I had finished my meal, no doubt. I took a fresh, or rather a reappraising, look at him, too. He, too, had crossed the shadow line into a kind of personal shamefulness. Perhaps it had happened a long time ago but I hadn't seen it before so clearly. The knowing Irish bartender of my youth, the sharp reporter on local, national, and international affairs, had—what shall we say?—sagged. He was on the editorial page now, it seemed to me. He was out of the reportorial contest. His clean formless double-breasted gray suit, his formless expression—on a face that used to seem to me so tight and wise—told the story of a man who would cling to the job, some job, any job, with the old firm no matter how much less and less the old firm needed him. I asked him to sit down.

225

"Well," I said as brightly as seemed decent, on the theory that the cheerleader rather than the crepe-hanger is usually the more welcome company in most circumstances, "tonight's the night, eh?"

"Yes, sir."

He didn't carry the ball any farther than that, so I tried another conversational tack. "Samstag seems to have the old joint jumping. You wouldn't know it, would you? Four-feature movies, pinball games, bus station, and so on. By the way, I'm glad to see you turned the old palm garden into a nook for the women and kids. That was a swell idea."

He smiled wanly. "We wanted to keep the airplane passengers here," he said, "but they leave from the Chase now." Then he added, a little more cheerfully, "My boy's at the Chase."

This, I am sorry to say, was the first time that I had ever known that Barney had a son, or even thought of him as a family man. So there was not only a Mr. Adams, there was a Mrs. Walsh. It can make you feel awfully cheap to find that you have bothered to learn so little about people who have for years concerned themselves so much about you. On my questioning, Barney went on to tell me that his wife had passed away only the winter before and that his other son was with a natural-gas company in Louisiana; Barney now lived with the son who was at the Chase and that son's wife. He thought very highly of his daughter-in-law, who had been educated at the City House of the Sacred Heart. The phone rang and it was Junie.

"I hear you're making a speech down there tonight," he said. "It better be good, I'm going to be there watching you."

It hadn't occurred to me that Junie might come to the dinner. For such a long time now I hadn't seen him without being made well aware of his exile. I was slow in gathering myself for a response.

"What's the matter, professor?" he asked sharply. "Don't you want to see me?"

"I want to see you more than anybody else in the world," I told him honestly.

"Well, that's better."

226

"Will you come to my room for a drink before dinner? It's Five-seventeen."

"No," he said, "I'll see you in mine. Ten-twenty. Make it at a quarter to seven."

"Can I bring my friend Bob Mayer? He's putting on the show."

"Why not?"

"Ten-twenty," I repeated, and he said good-by and we hung up.

"That's their rooms," Barney said softly, almost as in a spell. "Ten-twenty, Ten-twenty-four."

I didn't question him further as to whom "their" referred to; I was sure it wasn't to Junie and Olive themselves. "Junie Neidlinger's throwing a little cocktail party before the dinner," was all I said.

"I'm sorry we're not having the dinner in the ballroom," Barney said.

"What do you mean?"

"We had the poultry show booked into the ballroom, Mr. Hanes, some months ago. But you'll be nice and comfortable in the dining room. And I knew you'd feel like Mr. Samstag did. Those rubes' money is as good as anybody's The hotel is making a nice score off of them." The prospect of profiting from the chicken people actually seemed to give him pulse, sending a little blood through the old man's gray face; I needn't have worried about how he and Samstag would get along. And I didn't worry about not having the dinner in the ballroom. I've always preferred the dining room's concentric vaulting; the whole arch structure sweeps down to the floor level on either side, giving a wonderful sense of personal shelter for so large an enclosure. It's the room you usually see photographed.

"Do you want to go over the arrangements, Mr. Hanes?" Barney asked. "The magazine people seem satisfied, but maybe there was something you'd like to speak about."

As a matter of fact, there was. I looked at my watch and saw that it was close to noon; Bob Mayer was due shortly, but there was time for what I had in mind. It was only sentimental.

"What are you going to feed us off of, Barney?" I asked. He

didn't understand me. "I mean, do you suppose there is any of the old china service left? The old rose-window pattern, the plates that Jeff designed?"

"Oh, Mr. Hanes," Barney said, with a deprecatory smile.

"Let's take a look anyhow," I said. "It's Jeff's party, let's see if any of Jeff's plates are left."

So we went below. Nobody has laid out a kitchen since Nineveh that anybody else has ever approved of, but I had always thought that the Tower's were fairly sensibly arranged. We at least had half a dozen coffee urns spotted right next to the service exit so that there could never be a legitimate excuse for not giving a man a pot of it at the same moment you set his food before him, if he wanted it. My brother could never abide the procedure by which it was no trouble at all to go all the way down to the cellar to whip up a bottle of any kind of booze to serve along with a meal, but an industrial cataclysm occurred if the patron wanted instead to drink a cup of coffee with what he ate.

The coffee urns were still there, I noticed, but not much else looked the way I remembered it. I don't suppose that half the old kitchen area was now being used. No institutional kitchen that I had ever seen has ever been that sunlit garden spot that the management would like the customer to think it is; the best one on earth is a place of naked light bulbs and sour steam, a region of the lower depths like the dismal working parts of a battleship. But the Tower's kitchen was now more like the working part of a battleship that had been sunk. In an island of light among the shadows we found the checker on duty, a startlingly pale plump woman in a beaded black dress who gave us a huge ring of keys, and we made our way through one greasy latticed partition after another, poking around the dark old bins and barrels and shelves. I remember that we unearthed in the gloom a couple of cases of split pints of porter, and I found myself thinking of the vanished sporting men who must have called for it to be laced into their shells of champagne on what long-forgotten noons following what irretrievable revelries. We found two dozen or so of the chinaware we were looking for and debated whether to put them on the

228

speakers' dais, but decided against it. It was Jeff's party, but very few of Jeff's plates were left.

"I think," said Barney, as we left these melancholy catacombs, "I'll just have what's left packed up and sent to your home."

I wished again that I had known something to say to him about Mrs. Walsh.

What do you do with an idle February afternoon in St. Louis? Bob Mayer was waiting for us when we came back upstairs, and the problem instantly posed itself. There are some people—busy, important types—whom one somehow fears are even more vulnerable to boredom than oneself. We all had a drink. We had two drinks. Then Barney, recalling himself to other duties, asked if there was anything he might take care of for me at the moment. There was, although I regretted that I had not thought of it before Bob Mayer arrived. I got the manuscript of my speech out of my suitcase and gave it to Barney, asking him to have it mimeographed and distributed to the newspaper boys when they showed up for the dinner.

"Wait a minute," Bob said. "I've been trying to get my hands on that thing for weeks."

"You won't have to wait much longer now," I said. "Go ahead and get it run off, Barney," I said, shoving him out the door.

Mayer looked at me curiously. "What's all the hassle about this speech? We should have had it set up in type ten days ago."

"Yes, but you're indulging me," I reminded him. "You know— the artist. You've got all the rest of your circus in the bag, tied down, copper-riveted. What are you worried about? Let's have a drink." And we did.

"That fellow Barney," he said after a while. "It doesn't take much to get you by in this world, does it?"

"Not on the ball?"

"Millions of them. They don't even know where the batter's box is. But they all have a vote."

I thought it was time for lunch, so we went out to that place on De Bolivar where they used to cut such good sandwiches— what was the name of it? It was a Busch place, too—and after that we went over into the park to the Art Museum on top of the hill where little Jeff and I used to sled in the wintertime. They were holding their first W.P.A. exhibit, and of course Joe Jones, the local find, was featured.

"I approve of this soup-line art completely," Bob pronounced. "If they'd set these guys to painting houses it would have cost us all a hundred times as much money. Did you ever think of that?"

The old Gottfried collection he really savored. "Full of action and quite lifeless," he declared with delight. "Like Penrod Schofield's novel—*Harold Ramirez, the Road Agent*." After that it was time for us to go back to the hotel.

"This bootlegger friend of yours," said Bob when we had changed our clothes for the dinner, "he's the real Tabasco, is he?"

"Just like mother used to make. A Yale man, too."

"Why should that surprise you?" Bob asked. "It's only an accident. Like me being in the two-pants-suit business. He's contemporary, see?"

"Like the Tower is now?" I couldn't help saying.

And then, tough baby though he was, he said a very kind and characteristic thing. "Sure, like the Tower. Like Joe Jones. You mustn't be ashamed of the Tower, George. This is just a cheap phase of our national life that we're going through. These are tough times. Let's go see the New Haven Capone."

On the tenth floor it was almost like Old Home Week. The older one, the one with the little gray mustache who had been playing cards with Junie that summer afternoon at the bungalow, was standing against the wall across from the elevator and we nodded amiably to each other. Up the corridor, seated on a chair beside the door to suite 1020-24, I recognized the Levantine one with almond eyes who I thought might have operated a mill-end store.

"Oh, brother," whispered Bob appreciatively, "this is the stuff, isn't it? Like getting in to see Hitler at Berchtesgaden. The hall of the mountain king."

"*Achtung!*" he called playfully as we reached the man guarding the door. "*Presentiert das Gewehr!*" The man looked at him carefully for a moment and then gave him a good-natured understanding smile, both of them being Jews of course.

Bob and Junie got along very well from the start. Seeing them together for the first time I couldn't help thinking, as a matter of fact, how much my two friends were alike; there, but for the grace of, and so forth—in either case. For example, although they had both in quite different circumstances been acquainted with Jeff—one as a trade-press reporter and the other as a friend of the kid brother—they held rather similar impressions of him, and these they began exchanging almost as soon as they had been introduced.

"He was a champion," Bob said, "but a laughing champion."

"Smiling, anyhow," Junie said.

"Like Ace Hudkins."

"Only Ace was never a champ," Junie pointed out, but not as though Bob could have been mistaken about Hudkins' record; they both knew what they were talking about.

"Maybe we better shift divisions," Bob said. "Like Frank Roosevelt?"

"That's better," Junie agreed, and they laughed.

Some drinks had been served by Junie's colored man, whom I also recalled from the trip out to the bungalow behind the beer garden. Besides Junie, he and Olive were the only other members of the party that we found in suite 1020-24. She was a little heavier than I remembered her from that smothering afternoon at the hospital and, as they say—but often dishonestly—her fullness became her, I thought. Her evening dress was of black lace, and lots of it. To me it looked expensive and very becoming. Silvered hair, young woman, plump shoulders, black lace dress—very nice.

"That Roosevelt," she said, in a tone of resignation that was making the phrase a kind of national shibboleth. Recognizing its familiarity, we all laughed.

In his chair Junie shifted his great handsome body to a position of less discomfort. "That's the man who's going to put me out of business," he said, "and, brother, I'm not sad about it." His dinner jacket had been loosely draped to conceal the gun and the shoulder holster beneath it, but there were limits to obscurantism,

231

I realized, beyond which even the skill of Phil Goldstein, the best West End (of St. Louis) tailor, could not go. Observing that what he had said had brought about a conversational impasse, Junie smiled and continued.

"I mean it. I can't even go to the can by myself. I'm sick of it."

"Baby!" protested Olive, but whether out of shocked modesty or from tender concern I could not tell.

"I mean it. Not even to the can without Jimmy or Herb or somebody on duty outside. Olive maybe."

"Baby, *dear*," she said, and this time I for one didn't have any doubt about the sound of her words, for it was the sound of anguish.

"You think I'm kidding?" Junie turned to Bob Mayer when he asked the question.

"No," Bob said, "I don't think you're kidding."

"You, George?" Junie asked.

"Well," I said, "the hotel entrance is crawling with cops tonight, getting everybody out of their cars for the banquet. I guess we don't have to worry too much about the safety of our movements." I meant this for a simple pleasantry, and then realized that it might sound like an impromptu dirty joke, but neither effect had registered on Junie. Nor was I surprised.

"A lot of cops down there, eh? What a waste of public money," was what he said.

"We've had to become a nation of many men in little jobs—like France," Bob Mayer said. But that irony sailed by Junie's consideration, too.

"*Well.*" Junie slapped the arm of his chair, the committee chief ending—no, not ending, but steering the meeting toward its close. "The government can take over this racket of mine from me from now on. They can have it. Frankie-boy's going to get me off the hook, see?" He gave us the good-looking uhlan's smile. "If I'm lucky, that is," he added.

That last emendation also stopped us again. Then he saw that I was looking at the blue glint of the gun butt under his coat.

232

Glancing down at it himself he pulled the thing out, weighing it up and down in the flat of his hand. I suppose I should say that we all regarded it with fixed horror, as though it were a cobra. But we didn't. It was just a gun and it belonged there, along with Junie and Olive and the men guarding the hall. This was 1933 and we were in a suite of rooms in a second-rate downtown hotel in a big city in the Middle West which our host was in the business of supplying with whisky.

He spoke to me. "What a laugh, eh, George?" he said. "Remember how we almost didn't get out of the Navy because I couldn't find one of these things to give back to them?"

I remembered, I said. I also remembered that he had said that he would never have any use for one of those things for the rest of his life, but I didn't remind him of that, of course.

"George and I have lived dangerously, too," Bob said. "We once took a swim in the East River off Fifty-second Street—naked."

That put the conversational ball in motion again. Junie restored the gun to its well-tailored hiding place and we all had another drink. Current events seemed a safe subject and I remember that we discussed the Germans and the English and even the Arab world, those being some of the people around whose orbit hell, about as usual, was being raised at the time.

"The Arab world," Bob said, musingly. "Why does everybody always get so alarmed about the Arab world? The police of Passaic, New Jersey, could take care of the Arab world any afternoon." Bob, as I knew, was also a contributing Zionist. Junie, the good German, said that he couldn't agree with him more. They got along very well.

"At home here," Junie asked, "how do we get out of the economic jam? Spend ourselves out, like Franklin says?"

"We spend ourselves out with a building boom," Bob said. "At any rate, that's what my publishing house is betting on."

"Well," Junie said, "we sure can't drink ourselves out of it. We've tried that."

And so it went, these liberal exchanges of opinion on national and world affairs, until Chick Samstag dropped in for a drink himself, and pretty soon it was time for Bob and me to go upstairs and join the other celebrants before moving on to the speakers' table. Junie said that he and Olive would occupy Table 17, but not before they had been told that it was time for me to make my remarks, the closing act of the show. "We'll eat here—cozy as usual," he said.

"Baby," Olive said.

So here we were. Arranged in ranks along the dais to my left and to my right sat the faculty of personages whom *Architectural Age* had persuaded—well, invited—to appear at the twentieth anniversary of the ground-breaking—well, plan-approval—of Tower in the West, the largest edifice to which the hand of Thomas Jefferson Hanes had set itself, he dead an inconvenient seventeen years before and born a previous sixty-three. We Americans do so love our properly decennial anniversaries; it was a pity that the clock of time had actually proved so awkward for Bob and his magazine. There was a bank building of Jeff's at Mason City, Iowa—a quite beautiful little one in which a local brick had been used for facing inside and out and which for the first time so far as I knew had eliminated prison bars from the cash-transaction area—that had been opened for business a good even forty years before, and, by an accident of course, on one of Jeff's actual birthdays. But never mind. Here we were.

The invocation was spoken by the Rev. John Henry O'Hara, S.J.—I have all the memoranda before me, a grayed menu and a very few newspaper cuttings browned at the edges—and the bare words of his text are all that are left: "Remember Ye Them." Mayor Kiel, one finds, sent a telegram of felicitation. The dean of the Rolla School of Mines is represented by the subject "Steel: An Anniversary." I personally recall a young man from Columbia who put in a plea for some money for his institution's architectural library. The M.I.T. man who spoke concerned himself with the function of "ergs," a fad of the time which had something to do with supplanting capital with measured public energy. Never mind. Bob Mayer's managing editor, the one who preceded me in the

234

speechmaking, said some things about the Tower that only a Beaux Arts boy *and* Bauhaus boy (he was both; you could be both in those yeasty times) could have known how to say. This young man—Dix was his name, and long since migrated into the aircraft industry—called the Tower a rational projection of the Heaven Mountain outside Charlottesville and made the appropriate allusions to Jeff's given names. He was a romantic and he also knew what he was talking about. Some boy, I thought.

Prior to young Mr. Dix's address, there had been plenty of time for me to look over the audience, gathered at tables seating ten or so and each bearing on its central standard a numeral. Contractors and bankers and insurance people were liberally represented, one saw by the printed key to the table arrangements, and also the museum people, local architects (what was left of them), teachers of our craft, and assorted moral spokesmen of the town. There was also the press table, conveniently located by the door to my left, and, empty, Table 17 by the door toward my right. Mary and Ed Reagan were sitting under the dais below the dean of Rolla. I wondered how long she had been in St. Louis—perhaps ever since the sale of the building had not taken place the year before?—or had she, like the rest of our family, never been able to free herself of the spell of the building? Had she come back simply to be in on this shabby memorial, the widow of the great man returned to receive her due of acclaim? God knows, she could have had a dozen motives inexplicable to me; I am no scab psychologist. Old Mr. Reagan was not there, however, nor was old Mr. Neidlinger. But Barney I saw, hovering occasionally with Samstag about the service entrances. It was a pretty good meal, by the way, no matter about the service ware. The catacombs had come through creditably.

So then it became my turn to speak. As I pulled my manuscript out of my pocket and smiled my appreciation to Bob Mayer for his introductory remarks (he had called me my brother's "surging standard-bearer"; God forgive him, for I know he was sober) there was the usual rustle of polite recognition that the anchorman of any relay of speechmaking is entitled to. And then, a little different noise. The hitherto lethargic press table was suddenly heard from. And no wonder. Led by Barney, here came the occupants of Table 17: Junie hobbling along on the arm of Olive, then the man with the small clipped mustache, then the almond-eyed character and the white man who had driven me out to Junie's country place (but not the colored man; there seemed to be some sort of Jim Crowism even among unofficial armed guards), and two or three other companions of Junie's that I had not before seen. This must have been the first chance that the press of St. Louis—and what a break for the kind of reporters sent to cover a mere anniversary banquet—had been afforded to view Junie in public with his entourage. How they must have wished that I might never have been born (and Jeff, too) so that they could rush the Neidlinger table. Convention, however, makes cowards of us all; even, at times, of newspaper people. The other diners, of course, had no reason to take any interest in Table 17. They just wished that they were home.

Across the seated and assembled heads Junie winked at me (and so, bless her heart, seeing him do it, did Olive). Thus encouraged, I laid out my papers on the rostrum and went about my part in the night's work—and the inescapable, so far as I was concerned, dirty trick on Bob Mayer. The scant newspaper clippings of the evening's events in the Tower dining room are not to be depended upon for what I had to say. In fact, except for some cut-caption material carried six weeks later in *Architectural Age*, there was no journalistic coverage whatever of any of the oratory that took place on that evening. But I still have the manuscript of what I read to those people. It began this way:

"Gentlemen of architecture—and its allied practices, propagandas, and conspiracies:"

Amused or slightly shocked chuckles.

"I speak to you tonight under a roof hallowed—perhaps too hallowed—by its association with the hand of an eminent designer. Forget it, if you wish, and him. I should like to talk a little not of the past, noble though it may be, but of the future. For, in spite of many of the—mature, shall we say?—faces that I see around me,

236

we are a young and vigorous people who may look forward to a vast natural increase from the loins of our Republic."

A few ribald guffaws.

"For make no mistake. Our coming generations shall have the freedom to assimilate their impressions and to nurture their emotions in a fruitfulness commensurate with the energy of an unexhausted soil and in the bright air of an unconquered country."

Here there was a relieved lift of brave applause.

My speech then proceeded to examine some of the other American arts, not flatteringly: a docile and timid literature, a sentimental sculpture and painting, and the continuing threat of charlatanism in building. "A building," I read from the pages before me, "is an organic conception with an organic purpose. It is not a screen for men to hide behind. Nevertheless, within this withering period architects as a professional class have grown to follow the financier and businessman, and at the same time to have sought to lead the public—when it was often more wise for the architect to have led the financier and followed the public. Thus, the architect is gravely in danger of exhausting himself from the exertions of mistaken expediency."

This part had become unpleasant for most of the audience and also a little puzzling, as I had expected it would be. Junie's dark face, however, I saw to be lit with rebellious amusement. Then I read on into an appraisal of architectural schools, winding up with what I thought of as several nicely balanced paradoxical interrogations.

"Why do we find in our curricula courses in accounting, but none in accountability? Why are our young men taught the arts of reproduction, but as to the lessons of the past so little true understanding and respect? The use of mechanics is daily drill; where is there paramount study of the uses of the mind?"

Here and there the pedagogues fidgeted in their chairs, twiddled with their crumpled napkins, and lost interest completely. Bob Mayer, I saw by glancing down to my side, wore a frown. It deepened as the minutes lengthened, for it was becoming more and more apparent that I was not talking about Jeff at all. I was

237

simply delivering to my listeners a lot of home truths, and an old-fashioned scolding.

"Do we ask our architects for leadership? They give us fear. For style? Excuses of the times. For youth? Old age."

Now almost nobody was happy except Junie on one side of me and the boys at the press table on the other. As for Junie, he was amused at the general discomfiture. As for the reporters, the speech would soon be over; they would not have to wait much longer for their plunge to Table 17.

"This is not the time in any phase of our national endeavor for the gravedigger and the ghoul, take my word for it. This, of all times, is the moment for great building, great achievement. An army follows its banners, a civilization its towers. Do not be vanquished by the cash register and the coward. The dimensions of American architecture are the dimensions of American life."

The lads at the press table had followed me to the ends of the mimeographed sheets with which Barney had provided them. These they began to shove into their pockets, with an eye to livelier business as soon as the conventional applause should begin. As you see, I had not been very long at my talking, but I had not quite finished. When the press table sensed this they registered surprise and irritation, but not to the degree that, though unaware, Bob was on the point of. I, too, folded my papers and put them in my pocket.

"You have been good to come here tonight to honor my brother, Thomas Jefferson Hanes, and I think I would have been most derelict in honoring the spirit of the occasion, as well as his genius, had I in the principal address presented you with anything less than the genuine article." Bob looked up at me now with astonishment kindling to anger. "The remarks that you have heard were made by my brother before a dinner—a much smaller dinner—at the T-Square Club in Chicago on the evening of October fifth, 1903."

I don't believe that everybody heard the last couple of sentences which followed. I simply said that 1903 to 1933 made a properly decennial anniversary, too, and that the roof Jeff spoke of was of

238

course designed by Stanford White. Everything else in the talk had seemed to me applicable enough, I said. And of course it still is.

There was a small sensation, as I am afraid I had anticipated. In the buzz of voices around me, Bob Mayer stood up. "You son of a bitch," he said quietly and intensely, "who did you expect that performance to do any good for? Yourself? Your brother? The magazine? And quit grinning!"

"Why, Bob," I said, as seriously as I could, "the whole country ought to benefit. You yourself said we'd shake off the Depression with a building boom. Out of the past, you might say, Jeff sounded a kind of clarion call, or so it seemed to me."

"You son—"

"Well, squirt," said a woman's drunken voice behind me, "you did it again." It was Mary, of course, and she appeared to be in that enigmatic state, indicated by a frowning smile (or is it a smiling frown?), of a drinker whose spirit has not decided whether to stay contented or turn mean.

"I don't believe you've ever met my wife," I said to Bob Mayer. For a country boy—well, surely not a courtier—I thought this rather suave and quick-witted of me, for once. Two opposing forces coming at you from opposite sides, and you simply switch them into a head-on collision. Not exactly a head-on collision, I promptly saw: on her part Mary gathered herself together with quite a flair, looking Bob up and down with the slowly lifting eyebrows of a soubrette's dawning approval; and Bob, truculence at me draining from his countenance, gave her an approving look, too.

"I've met your daughter," he said. "You must have been a child bride when she was born. India?"

"Rather more like Arkansas," breathed Mary, "but you're a dear man." So those two were off my hands for the time being at any rate and I turned my attention to the rest of the room.

I will try to give as coherent and consecutive account as I can of what happened next.

Pushing away from their own table, the members of the press split off in two directions. The larger posse was trying to shoulder its way through the confusion of rising diners and toward Table 17, where Junie and Olive had sat with their party. But when I from my elevation on the dais looked in that direction I saw that while the almond-eyed man and the man with the clipped mustache and the others of the group were still in the neighborhood of their dinner places—although obviously struggling against their neighbors with objectionable vigor to achieve an exit—neither Junie nor Olive were to be seen.

When I say that the group from the press table split off in two directions, I mean that three of their number, the very youngest as I could see, were trying to make their way not to Table 17 but to where I still stood—with Bob and Mary now hobnobbing gaily at my side—at the center of the speakers' table. The spearhead of this minority of reporters was a girl of perhaps twenty years or so with red hair and horn-rimmed glasses, and she reached the lower side of our table before her colleagues.

"Mr. Hanes," she began, "I would like to check my notes on the addendum which you made to your remarks."

I have no idea what publication she represented and had no time to inquire, because at that moment there was Barney grabbing my shoulder from the side opposite to that occupied by Bob and Mary, who were paying no attention to anyone else and so missed what briefly took place across my back in the next few moments. Barney was weeping.

"Mr. Hanes," he said.

Here he was interrupted by Chick Samstag coming up behind him and grabbing *him* by the shoulder. Samstag snapped at him very quietly and yet quite audibly, like a kidnaper's voice on a telephone.

"I told you to get Doc Hartzfeld," he said.

"But *he* told me to get Mr. Hanes."

"Get Hartzfeld. If he ain't in his room he's over at Abe's. Get him quick!"

Samstag whipped the older man around as you might spin a packet of matches between your fingers and sent him on his way. Then he turned to me, his popeyes looking with a curious expression of milky abstraction—like an alligator's eyes—into mine. He jolted my chest briefly with his index finger.

"You follow me."

I followed him immediately and implicitly down the line of now almost vacated chairs behind the speakers' table, turning right and into a pantry entrance, then right again to where one of the two service elevators—on the bank behind the passenger cars—lay with an open waiting door. He banged the door closed and we started down the twenty stories to the main floor. Not many things except automobile tires have notably improved in function since 1915— the year that I bought this Otis system—and so there couldn't have been more than thirty or forty seconds taken up by our brief downward journey. And still there was plenty of time, plenty of time, for the whisper to swing around and around and around again in the echo chamber of one's mind: *Junie finally went to the toilet by himself.* Samstag had only said, when he banged the elevator door to, and only looking at the padded side of the elevator wall in front of him, "He's down in the men's can."

I came around from the service side of the shaft to the corridor in front of the passenger banks on the main floor with Samstag beside me. Then he went quickly off into the crowd in the lobby and I turned left toward where the white marble stairs, hollowed gently by a generation's footprints, began their broad descent into the men's lavatory. Somebody had placed in the middle of the upper entrance (Barney? Samstag?) an old brass standard from the elevator hall bearing the notice OUT OF ORDER. There was no one on the stairs.

Nobody was in the long wide white marble washroom below except Junie and Olive. His voice made a rich echo in the empty resonant room as I approached him.

"Did you ever hear a forty-five go off in a marble crapper, George?"

"No," I said. "Where the hell's the doctor?"

"It's the biggest noise in the world. Did you ever hear a forty-five go off in a crapper?"

Halfway down the left side of the room Junie was sitting on

241

the white marble floor, his back straight against the marble wall in an open space between a long row of marble toilet stalls to the left of him and, on my side as I came toward him, a long marble shoeshine stand, its worn brass foot-holders glimmering in the vast steady light. Olive in her black lace evening gown was kneeling close beside him frozen in the classic pose of hopeless anxiety proffering help that can be neither of the least assistance nor of the least need, like the wrong Mary at the foot of the Cross. Junie was now staring and smiling at some invisible point between his knees.

"You really told 'em, professor, didn't you?" he said softly. "Lotsa guts."

I knelt down on the other side of him.

Junie chuckled. "Always on the deck, aren't we, George?"

Ed Reagan came up from somewhere behind me.

"Come on, George," he said, "you'd better get the hell out of here. The cops and the reporters will be all over the place in a minute."

"Please go get the God-damned doctor," I said.

Then he went away. As a matter of fact, I didn't remember his being there at all or what we had said to each other until much later in the night. But I'm trying to keep the story as straight as I can.

Junie's shining black hair had fallen in fingers over his forehead and I saw that his face was sweating. He looked as though he might have just been interrupted while playing some very hard game and his expression was thoughtful, as though it were a game whose issue was still in doubt. The single dark spot on his white shirt front was quite small but blood had begun to wet one corner of his mouth. Now he reached to his breast pocket and pulled out a handkerchief, and in wiping at the blood from his mouth his hand and the handkerchief got the first really noticeable smears of blood on his shirt front.

"Jesus," he said disgustedly, "what a mess."

There were footfalls on the stairs, I remember, from a long way off. That must have been Barney and the doctor coming. They

242

were the first of the crowd. Olive's eyes had followed the tracings of blood on Junie's shirt front, and then I saw her look at the floor beneath and behind him. It was all moving dark blood.

Her face turned to mine.

"He was crazy about you," she said. "He used to talk about you all the time lots of times."

She was speaking of Junie as though he had been dead for months, but I didn't realize that either until later.

"What a God-damned mess," Junie said. He threw the bloody handkerchief away and put his hand inside his coat searching for another one. His hand instead came out with his gun and this he angrily flung across the marble floor toward the line of urinals along the far wall. It made enough noise in the washroom even without going off.

"*That* frigging thing," he said.

Then the doctor and the others were there and all at once the whole low wide empty white place was black with people.

The wide floor of the Great Valley, so designedly uniform in its passing fields and farms and towns, so almost absurdly explicit in the sameness of its plan—the fences and phone lines rigidly following the artificial boundaries squarely vectored around the 360-acre units now for a century laid down on the limitless old sea bed since its horse-high reeds and house-deep humus had been sod-busted—all this vast artificial ordering went, as it seemed, slowly past the eyes, a stately arc turning very slowly at the horizon; but beside the tracks, as one looked down from the Pullman window, it slipped by at a blur of a mile a minute, the remote of the horizon and the immediate rail-side having so little apparent relevancy.

Bob Mayer sitting beside me in our stateroom with a cigar in his mouth and a pile of mail before him on the slap-up table in front of us, looked out the window and then, more closely, at me. Under the table he punched my knee, once.

"Yeah," he said. "That was a tough one to lose."

No one can say that he was an insensitive man. There was no

243

reason in the world that he should have stayed around St. Louis that three days with me. I certainly hadn't needed him. There was nothing he could do. I'd hardly seen him. But there he had been and here he now was, bound back East with me after it was all over.

"I liked him so damn much," he said. "Just the little I saw him. Just that once." He reached across to the couch along the inboard wall of the stateroom where on an aluminum tray a bowl of ice and a bottle of whisky and a bottle of Apollinaris were jingling with two glasses. With one hand alone he skillfully made two drinks and gave me one. He raised a token of salute with his own glass. Then he went back to the mail that his man, who was up forward in our car, had brought him after we had left the terminal.

A tough one to lose. That comment was relevant enough, immediate, and sharp. The afternoon before, old Mr. Neidlinger had said it in another way. I had gone to call on him, after arranging the appointment by telephone, at his office in the Teutonia Bank. It was a corner room overlooking through two high, deep windows along each street wall both south Broadway and Lafayette Avenue. This was the heart of the old German enclave, so German in its shops and signs and the lingering appearance of the people even at that date that one felt a slight embarrassment at being there, as one might in a ghetto. Mr. Neidlinger's office had been built when the bank itself had been built and neither had changed. He sat behind a huge pear-wood secrétaire topped in black morocco leather and elaborately bound and ornamented in brass. The gray room itself was high, square, and heavily corniced; the floor was of the blackest shining oak, where it appeared in narrow margins beyond a great Kirman rug. His youngest son, I thought, in his own business premises behind the beer garden on the other side of Clayton, must often have remembered this room; it was filled with ancient, deep, Middle European money-wisdom.

"It was good of you to come. You were always very kind to old people, George," Mr. Neidlinger said. "Did you know that this was in my day an example of great principle in a man?"

244

"Of affection, Mr. Neidlinger," I said.

"Mrs. Carton always spoke most highly of you, George."

Here was a moment of European delicacy indeed, I thought. Margaret's mother, so far as I knew, had never been aware of my relationship with Margaret. Mrs. Carton had died a year or more before her daughter had come East to live. But there must have been very few relationships of any kind that had begun in that city, and of which Mr. Neidlinger had wished to know about, of which he was wholly ignorant. He was a banker.

"Time," Mr. Neidlinger went on, making a thought connective that I was not even expected, I realized, to follow, "time is always going back and forward, also. Like history." And then he said something so astonishingly akin to what Bob Mayer had said in the Tower only a few hours before Junie was killed there that I could hardly believe my ears. "My son," he said, "had never any business to be associated in this kind of enterprise." He made a grimace of utter repugnance and swept his old hand across the black morocco desk top as if to sweep away the blood and corruption of an entire Constitutional amendment. "With him it was only an accident of history."

Embarrassed, of course, at Mr. Neidlinger's speaking of Junie's bootlegging business, I found myself wondering how long he had known about it. For a good long time, I was now sure; for years, for much longer, very probably, than any of us had realized. It was quiet in the room and in the bank itself for it was well after business hours. An ashen light came through the high old windows, the late afternoon light of the end of winter in the streets outside. The traffic noise could scarcely be heard, only the occasional sound of a streetcar bell from far away.

Mr. Neidlinger sighed. "The years play tricks, George," he went on. "Who would have thought that a boy of Edward's advantages and upbringing—his mother, his brothers. . . ." The sentence trailed off helplessly. Then a wintry smile crossed his stern old face. "Who would have thought, for that matter, the day that you and your brother and the Reagans made the financial arrangements for the Tower here in this room, that my youngest son

245

would obtain possession of the bonds? He was a small employee of Anheuser-Busch at the time."

"That's what I came to talk about, Mr. Neidlinger," I said.

"It has provided a great surprise to the newspapers, has it not?" he said.

It certainly had. And when it was revealed to them—by whom, I wondered; Ed Reagan? Mary?—when it at any rate came out in the papers, the story of the gang killing became an even "better" one for the reporters, prolonging its reader interest at least another day. No, that's not true; I'm being shortsighted and bitter. The story of the bank president's son's execution in a bootlegging war was obviously a great and natural sensation and people would talk about it for years, no matter how the newspapers handled it. And talk about it they did, to my later sorrow, not in St. Louis alone. But Junie's disposition of the bonds, coming on top of the tragedy, had been one more staggering punch for me, personally.

"I don't know what I ought to do with them," I said.

The frosty old eyebrows rose above the ruined old eyes. "You wish me to locate a purchaser?"

"No, no. I don't think I ought to keep them at all. I don't think they belong to me. I don't think Junie should have left them to me."

"To whom do you think they should have been left, George?"

To either his family or, even, to Olive, was my thought. But I didn't know how much, if anything, Mr. Neidlinger knew about Olive, so I said, "To his family."

He looked at me quietly for a few moments. "My son chose you for the legatee, George. Neither I nor, so far as I know, any member of my family desires any arrangement to any other effect." He rose and slowly, heavily, for he was an old man now and badly buffeted with sorrows, came around the desk to where I sat and, when I arose, too, he clasped my hand.

"You must please get some rest, George," he said. "This has been a most burdensome time for you, I know."

Burdensome? Well, yes, that's one way to describe what happens to you when the reporters and the cops and photographers

246

catch you at your best friend's side after he has been shot to death in a gang war, he having been a notable gangster himself as it turns out.

The first thing that happened to me was that I was taken from the washroom in the company of three or four policemen whom I only remember as seeming as stunned and distracted as myself, with all the noise and flashlights, and rushed up to Twelfth Street to the central police station. It was, of course, the same place I had been taken to that night long ago after I had clipped Ed Reagan in the University Club, and it had changed very little. I was not given a cell in the old section set apart for the more permanent residents, as I had been that other time, but the surroundings were familiar enough. Chiefly I recalled the vast darkness and the endless oily winking cylinders of the bars, a nightmare which seems to characterize jails at night in spite of their almost brutal illumination. A hallucination of the sickened spirit, I expect. At any rate, I thought, I'd come full circle, and there was no Junie to make things a little easier for me this time.

But in that I was wrong. There was Junie's lawyer, little Nat Pierce. I don't believe the bars had clanged behind me for more than the time it takes to smoke a cigarette than they clanged open again.

"Well," I said, surprised but appreciative, "that was quick."

"It doesn't take long to spring a property owner," Nat said. "And, brother," he added, "you are a property owner."

He led me with his swift little steps along a couple of corridors and then out a side entrance. From there we hurried up Twelfth Street to the Jefferson, where he already had reserved a room, or maybe he kept a room there permanently to conceal clients for a little while when he had to. I had never, I think, been in a private room at that hotel or any other in the city besides the Tower. Having already thoughtfully provided a bottle of whisky and a pitcher of ice, he left me for a few minutes to get the papers. Since both the *Globe* and the *Post* are published within a few hundred feet of the Jefferson, he was not long away. Together and silently we read the first stories of the crime.

247

The *Globe*, which is the only morning newspaper in town, has never felt itself required to show much enterprise. The *Post* has always had enough enterprise for five newspapers, and it was from the first extra edition of the *Post* that I got most of my news. It was also there that I saw the first pictures of myself—leaving the washroom, leaving the Tower, and entering the police headquarters—in connection with the case. I was described as "slain gang chief's pal" as well as associated with the Tower's construction and ownership. In that edition no mention of the dinner or of my speech appeared. So far, just the more pertinent facts, and harsh facts they were.

At that time there were two other mobs operating in St. Louis, bearing the bravura titles, believe it or not, of the Jelly Roll Hogan Gang and Eagan's Rats. Junie's cabala, I found, was simply called the Clayton Mob. It appeared from the lead story that Junie's command of the Clayton Mob had been well known to the *Post-Dispatch* crime reporters for years but until now no occasion had arisen to make the news public. This I suspect of being a feat of the most transparent hindsight; Junie had been extremely painstaking to conceal his activities, as I surely well knew, and very probably was successful at it until, so far as the press was concerned, not more than about an hour and a half ago. The *Globe* laid his death to the Eagan Rats. The *Post*, with more knowledgeability I thought, said that either the Rats or the Hogan Gang could have shot him down, competition in the local liquor traffic being as keen as it was. Nobody could be found who would say he had seen the shooting in the washroom, and no one ever was. Olive, it was established by both Barney and Chick Samstag, had only arrived in the washroom after the shooting, and in their company. They had seen her leave the main-floor elevator hall, where they had happened to be at the same time, and her disturbed manner had led them to accompany her on her way to the washroom. When Junie had abruptly left the dining room, the story said, she had followed him. As to the men-at-arms whom I had seen at Table 17, there was no account.

"You want to call anybody?" Nat asked me after we had finished with the papers. "The switchboard downstairs is fixed to keep quiet about where you are for another hour or so."

Naturally I wanted to call Margaret. She was still awake, reading, she said, and I told her what I could of what had happened.

"My poor darling," she said. And then she asked, "Who gets the bonds?" Well, somebody has to be practical about these things.

"What bonds?" I asked, stupidly, I suppose.

And Nat Pierce, who had very little trouble construing that kind of a phone conversation, said, "You do." That was the first I knew about it.

I don't think there is a great deal more to tell about in this part of the story. I met the press, by Pierce's arrangement, later on in the morning. Nobody asked me about my speech, let alone about the banquet to Jeff's memory. The reporters wanted to know when I had first met Junie, and when I said that we had been in Naval air together they fell oddly silent and ill at ease, all having been too young to get into that war. Then I had to go with Pierce to the coroner's inquiry and there was some talk about the district attorney's taking me and Olive before the grand jury for questioning, but in those days the authorities were more relieved than anything else when bootleggers killed each other off; nothing came of it. Junie was cremated in the complete privacy of his immediate family; Nat Pierce and the Teutonia Bank saw to that. The ashes were held for later disposition.

So there I was on the train on my way back home the third afternoon following the murder.

Bob Mayer finished with his *Wall Street Journal* and pushed it under the seat beneath us.

"Let's have another one of these, what do you say?" he suggested, motioning toward the tray on the couch in the stateroom.

I nodded and he made another couple of drinks.

"I have never been able to accept loss agreeably," he said with a kind of studied equanimity for my benefit, I believe. "You can take it, but you don't have to like it." He looked over his shoulder at me. "You agree?"

I agreed.

"My father and mother believed that in this life you were—what did they say?—just passing through. Well, no argument about that. They believed that life was a jewel that was merely loaned to you, and that sooner or later you had to return the loan and that you must do it without protest. I don't know about that lack of protest. Have you ever been to an orthodox funeral? Very noisy. Well, why not? I kick like hell when I lose something I love or want. In other words, you can lose but you don't have to like it." He leaned over and turned the lights on because now the windows barely drew enough afterglow from the plain for us to see each other by.

The new yellow light in the stateroom made it more cheerful, but my own sense of loss felt no different, no easier either to bear or understand.

There he had lain, my friend, an end suddenly put to all the little skills of his arms and legs and fingers, to all the myriad little things he had been told or seen or read, few of which he had ever thought of more than once, but some—tunes, rhymes, useful combinations of numbers—which he knew wholly and by heart, and all of it preciously accumulated whether he knew it or not hour after hour since the very start of his life. All this haphazard treasure had now disappeared. All useless to anyone's else collection. The wrist trick of the backswing, vanished. The own true habit of caress, gone. The attitude of mind, as hardly won as his alphabet, incommunicable. None of these unbelievably complicated personal acquisitions—so deeply, so personally different to all—none ever to be added to another's vast and intricate store. All quite useless now and absolutely lost to the sum of life, now he had left it.

And his curious and long fondness for me, that, too, had come to its absolute stop with the rest of him? Bled out on the tile of the lavatory floor?

And then I thought: no. That of course would continue until the moment of my own death.

250

Fourteen

THOSE bonds, those Tower bonds: what a worry and mischief they were to me from time to time through the years that followed. There is a description—in *The Golden Bough*, I think— of a legendary priest who, having won it, must protect with his very life night and day some sort of prize against all comers. He was in charge of the grove at the temple of Nemi. If he was like me, once he won the prize I'll bet he must have gotten very sick of it. No, that's not a fair remark. I was grateful for Junie's legacy to me, and for a long while it kept the custodianship of the grove, you might say, safe in my hands. But plenty of people in one way or another concerned themselves with my owning the bonds and some, like the fabled antagonists at Nemi, would have been glad to get them away from me. The first bad time I had about them was, as a matter of fact, in a grove, the locust grove below Bob Mayer's house beside the Shrewsbury River in Rumson. That is probably the reason that I associate the control of the bonds with the classical reference to Nemi, now I think of it.

The occasion was the wedding reception that Bob gave in honor of young Jeff's marriage to Carol Beeman. This would be at the end of the last week in June of 1933. Jeff was just graduated from the University.

There had been a certain amount of discussion back and forth regarding the locale of the ceremony itself. As I understand it, the marriage rites, if you wish them conventional, are supposed to take place either in a church or at the bride's house. In this case, since none of us were church people, that would have meant Beeman's Rhenish keep out in Clayton, and that would certainly have been agreeable to me; I would have made sure to be present if Jeff were to have been married in a mushroom cave. Late in May, however, I was told by Margaret that the Beeman site had been ruled out. Margaret was getting her information from young Mary, who was speaking not for poor Carol but for her mother, old Mary, and the latter had balked at going to the Beeman place because Mrs. Cox would be there. On her part, the elder Mary, my wife and the groom's mother, had proposed to stage the ceremony in some hotel in New York, she having settled herself that spring at the Barbizon, where her daughter was staying. When that plan was reported to me it seemed as sensible as any; one more trip to St. Louis avoided. Then young Jeff balked; this was now toward the beginning of June. He wasn't going to start out his married life in front of a lot of busboys, he said.

"Why," was my suggestion, "don't you and Carol buzz over to Doylestown after graduation and get the job done quietly and with no fuss? In Pennsylvania they don't even bother about the three-day waiting rule for marriage licenses."

He wouldn't hear of that either. "I want one marriage in this family to be decent," he said, "with a real ceremony and people around."

I don't know what other marriages in the family he was criticizing. I'd married his mother with people around, and decently. He'd even been there. He'd not seen his father's marriage of course, but that had been, while not ornamental, decent enough. But I could sympathize with his impression of the casualness of his family's attitude toward matrimony. When you came to think of it, not one of the older people immediately concerned in his affairs was married to the person with whom he or she was living. U.S. upper-middle-class society, 1933 style; or at least our little

252

accidental sector of it. Nobody had deliberately or viciously planned it that way. It had just happened that way. And yet, as I thought of young Jeff—and me, too—it didn't have a very good feeling to it. I could see what he meant.

In the end I got the assistant dean of the Chapel to do the job in my back yard under the crab-apple tree. Mary had consented to the arrangement, preferring the irregularity of my household to that of Beeman's, I suppose, because Mrs. Cox was Mrs. Cox but Margaret was a Carton. At no time, at any rate, was there any mention of Ed Reagan's joining the group. I don't think, either, that anybody ever asked Carol about her preference before the final order of battle was drawn, although I telephoned her toward the middle of June and in the course of a general conversation about the affair she—so sweetly and timidly that it made my heart sore for the neglect we had all shown her—made one suggestion: that somewhere in the service the ring lines from *The Merchant of Venice* be read. At Smith she was an English major.

I was touched. That judge who had sent me to the can in St. Louis all those years ago had also married me to Mary with the same well-chosen wedding lines. And so the ever-tightening paths of our civilization press on.

At this point Bob Mayer and young Mary put themselves into the picture—in which order I am not sure because by this time when it came to the disposition of the amenities of his house at Rumson one spoke about as authoritatively as the other. She had evidently some months before made her peace with Stanford White and entered into her own kind of unilateral trade agreement with Bob Mayer. Well, that was none of my business any more. If you start worrying about the night-to-night fate of all the beautiful girls among your relations or acquaintanceship who are above the age of consent, you might as well get packed up for the laughing academy. If I had worried about either of them at the time, it would as a matter of fact have been about Bob. At any rate, they said that they wanted the wedding reception to be held at his place, which was only a twenty-mile drive away from mine, and on this point, thank heaven, there was no objection

253

or reservation offered by anyone concerned. It promised to be a good party.

The minister at first had a little difficulty in getting some of the names and roles straight. For a few moments before we all moved out of my sitting room into the courtyard I believe that he assumed that Bob Mayer, a powerful but somewhat reserved type, was the father of the bride and that Beeman, a powerful and noisy type, was either a rich Western uncle of the bride's or Mary's husband. He had Margaret for a time erroneously spotted as Carol's mother, since they were both dark and rather clung together. He knew that the groom was my nephew since I had told him so when asking him to officiate, and had so introduced them as soon as I could get them together. Yet how was he to know that I was also Mary's husband? But it was at last straightened out with him that Beeman was the one to give the bride away and I stand up for Jeff; that part of the function must have appeared to the minister conventional enough. And so, with Alfred murmuring and smiling through the little gathering, we got ourselves out into the sunshine under the old gray elephant-hided tree and fairly well organized, Jeff scowling around at anyone's clumsiness and Carol a wide star in each eye.

> ... *But when this ring*
> *Parts from this finger, then parts life from hence....*

The assistant dean of the Chapel, a cheerful young Christian in a tan Palm Beach suit, had said it as Carol had wished him to. Then with a prayer he made them man and wife.

Jeff and I turned and started to shake hands—again, conventional enough—when like a cataclysm in a bucket factory a voice beside us began yelling, "Boy! if you don't make my little girl—" and then there was a sudden rush of violet taffeta among the three of us. "Oh, go away, you stupid clown!" young Mary cried, and fell upon her brother's cheek, the tears running down her own. "Be happy, my dearest! Please be happy!" Roaring with indulgent mirth, Beeman caromed off to some other group. Young Mary was the only one who wept that day.

254

"Keep smilin'," Alfred whispered with a grin to me as he passed me a glass of wine from a well-loaded salver. I could certainly use it, and the pause gave me a few moments to look about at some of the other wedding guests. For the first time I observed that old Mary and Margaret were wearing hats of the same design. I don't know if you recall the hat, but it was later widely copied. No matter who wore it, it was one that I always liked: essentially a dozen or more wide equilateral concentric disks of stiffened tulle ("dressed" tulle Margaret tells me it was called), and topping it off a small flat planting of variegated cloth French flowers. I remember very well that Margaret set great store by hers, because she had told me that she had bought it for the occasion from Lilly Daché, who had just opened her New York shop that year. Evidently Mary had been to the same place, although the colors of the two hats were quite different. Margaret's tulle was black and the flowers generally jonquil and primrose; Mary's was smoke with lilacs. You would think that this coincidence, coming on top of all the other smashing antagonisms that the years had piled up between them, would have set off the flames; but not at all. Not now.

"Such a lovely bride," said Mary.

"Such a handsome groom," said Margaret, "and no wonder."

That exchange seemed safe enough, so I went over to where Jeff was now standing with Carol.

"Did the minister say your piece properly?" I asked her.

"Yes. Oh, yes. Thank you, George. Thank you, dearest George."

I looked at her more closely. "Are you feeling okay, baby?"

"I'll never feel so gloriously again in all my life," she said.

"Well," I said, giving her a pat and wishing to keep things on the up-beat, "we'll see about that later."

That is all that I remember about that conversation; Bob Mayer and his chauffeur had begun milling about the courtyard, the chauffeur efficiently taking care of out-of-town baggage and Bob urging us all to get going so as to arrive at his place before the other invited guests, mostly young friends of Jeff's and a few older people living round about Rumson. So we embarked: Bob taking

255

both the Marys in a Rolls-Royce cabriolet that he had acquired reasonably from a couple in Tuxedo who had decided the year before that it would be cheaper to live in Majorca; Jeff and Carol in an Oakland coupé that Beeman had given them; Margaret at the wheel of a LaSalle phaeton which she thought a great deal of. I remember that its top was down but that she kept her hat on. And I certainly remember that we had Beeman between us on the front seat. Margaret usually drives just about as fast as she can, but Beeman's normal conversational tone suffered no loss of carrying power in the noise of the slip-stream. We heard him perfectly.

"That's going to be a great team," he told us. "Carol and the boy."

We nodded; Mr. Beeman took the floor, and he kept it all the way to Rumson.

"I'm not crazy about these college educations. We've got more people in college, of course, than all the balance of the world. Don't get me started on that. But the business of America is business; Cal Coolidge said that and the little old redhead was right. So I want the boy in business, by God, and in *my* business! And don't think I can't line him up some nice franchises of his own. The abrasives field! It's crying for distributors!"

Margaret and I swiveled our heads to him, eyes opened a little wider, then saw each other and looked back at the road stretching across the smiling fields of Mercer County.

"Now when I was a boy the three things that a boy needed to have were character, capital, and opportunity. Luck, you might say for the latter, because you never can tell from the wart on a pickle which way the juice will squirt!" Here he let loose a baboon laugh which challenged the wind-roar.

"Now I tell you frankly that I don't know about this boy Jeff's *character*. I've got to take my chance on that. Carol, of course—well, she's just a girl, she wouldn't know. But I'm willing to take my chance. Opportunity, that's what a dad is there to give a son-in-law. Of course there's drawbacks in this boy Jeff's case. I don't know if you know about St. Louis, but it's a pretty straightlaced old town—the French, the Irish, the Germans; pretty straight-laced old-fashioned people—the best of them, I mean. You got to watch your step in St. Louis. But, as I say, I'm willing to take the chance, even considering this kid Jeff's background."

Now we were in Monmouth County; no less green but not, to me, so smiling.

"Capital, so far as I see it, may be all the boy really needs. That I'm not going to give him. I don't believe in doing *everything* for a kid. But what has he really got of his own? A few common shares in that building of his father's. He couldn't raise much on that. Nothing, is my guess. And, my God, the reputation of the place. Oh, I know it may have been cleaned up for a while now. But that Neidlinger killing there. Jesus. That stink would be enough to queer a kid businesswise in St. Louis for life."

The breath of the shore, the old melon-rind breath, reached us. Among the sand-shouldered drives Margaret began turning her way down the low slope toward Bob's house along the river.

"So for God's sake, Hanes, let's sell the dump and tear it down and give the kid his money and a real chance to make a name for himself in the town. I've thought about it—I don't mind telling you—deeply and with a sore heart. But I'm willing to take the plunge."

Up the gravel we were now, curving through the ancient spice smell of box and onto the parking plain before the high white portico of Mayer's place. We were the first ones there. Margaret got out on her side and started briskly for the doorsteps. Beeman and I got out on mine.

"So there's the deal," he said, and now in the late afternoon quiet his voice clanged as authoritatively as the gates of hell. "Hey! Where's she going?" he barked, looking toward Margaret's departing back.

"I think she's going inside," I said.

"Oh," he said, "I thought she was going to be sick, or something."

That was how the party began.

There was a portico, too, on the back of Bob's house, of course. From it fell another sweep of steps to his lawn which, descending

257

among plantings of honey locusts, reached at last the tidal river. After the milky-blue June twilight came to its end the river lay as still and black as India ink; tree frogs began to vibrate on a note just beneath the human middle C, and the river frogs began to grunt and groan just beneath the sound of human love-making; now that the light was out of the sky the soft air seemed to come down and suppress an almost embarrassingly aphrodisiacal odor from the locust blossoms. There were lanterns in the trees.

"What a night for romance," said Bob Mayer, standing in the middle of his two-story Palladian back porch—his bar to the left of him; to the right his band, picked up from a nearby roadhouse and well amplified from a loud-speaker—and looking down with great good will upon his guests scattered like lively moths under the lanterns.

"It was nice of you to do this," I told him.

"The pleasure is mine," he said, a little more formally than I might have expected of a friend so very well known. And he continued the vein. "What a most attractive pair of women, Mary and her mother," he said. "Great style. They both have it."

Moving away I mixed with the company. The largest complement was made up of Jeff's classmates and clubmates and their girls, extremely agreeable nursery characters who, whether they were standing or actually prone on the grass, gave the impression of tumbling around on top of one another. Then there was a contingent of horse-loving friends of Bob's from Rumson and Red Bank, and of course the inevitable lovers of horse-lovers: for instance, a thin, sad stockbroker named Wane and Wane's possibly blonde wife and Wane's wife's authentically rich lover and Wane's wife's lover's authentically brunette and horse-loving wife. People like that.

There were also, I was glad to see, Peter Maben and his sister Eileen—she so very golden and beautiful that your instinct was to credit the lanterns and the night for her effect—and her husband who was just out of Yale. They were casually brushing out of an exchange of felicitations with Jeff and Carol as I came upon them.

258

"My, my!" I said when they had folded gracefully into another group.

"Oh, yes," Carol said. "Isn't she lovely!"

"What do you mean?" Jeff asked, a little shortly I thought.

"That Peter's sister is lovely," I said.

"Let's dance," Jeff said to Carol.

Well, you put the recollection of these little episodes away somewhere in the back of your skull, I suppose, and some of them pop up later in the file and most of the rest of them vanish. I put this one away, at any rate, and joined the crowd at the bar, where the father of the bride was telling an anecdote about colored people which did the race no credit and telling it within six feet of Alfred Jones, who had come over to help out with the party. The classic line of old-fashioned retributive drama would be followed if I could record that Beeman became in the course of the evening disgracefully drunk. The fact is that, without ever bringing up again his proposal voiced on the ride over from Princeton, he left early in a hired car for New York. What alcohol he consumed had no apparent effect on that granite metabolism and it was the Hanes family, not Beeman, that made the scene. Or what scene there was.

Fortunately the bride and groom had left before that. We all saw them out onto the drive and into their new Oakland, all of us: the nursery characters, the lovers of horses, Alfred Jones, Bob, both Marys, Margaret, I, everybody now except Mr. Beeman. Rice of course was thrown, and as it sprinkled down in silvery sprays between the porch lights and the black of the night beyond the boxwoods, one saw before the Oakland coupé's door a small grouping of great charm and elegance. Bob Mayer and Mary, the mother, were embracing and speeding the newlyweds. Carol was then closed into the car by Jeff. Suddenly he seemed to have lost or forgotten something. He looked about him helplessly for a moment, and eyes began to observe his perplexity. He then perceived in the darkness of the crowd what he was looking for and came quickly to where I was standing with Margaret. Seizing her in both arms he gave her a sound whack on the back and kissed her not once but several times on the cheek—a little desperately, I thought.

"Good girl," he said quickly. "Good, good old girl!"

Then he whipped around to the other side of the coupé, slammed its door, and he and Carol were gone, a ritual shoe or two skipping from the rear bumper. The crowd laughed and coagulated and I was left not with Margaret at my side but with Peter and Eileen Maben.

"So sweet," Eileen, the so very fair, was murmuring, "so very sweet."

"A cute couple, you're right," Peter said.

"No, I meant Jeff and Mrs.—" she faltered, appealing with cornflower-blue eyes to me.

"Mrs. Pierce," I said.

"Oh," she said, and then she and Peter were lost in the group that was making its way back up the portico steps and into the house again.

Looking for Margaret I found her in a group seated around a rustic table backed by some arborvitae down along the edge of the lawn. The others with her were both Marys and their admirer Bob Mayer.

"Well, here he comes," said my wife with a stridency that I heard with a certain foreboding, "the big real-estate man from St. Louis! When are you going to divvy up, George?"

I sat down and the others exchanged nervous pleasantries with me.

"When do we cut the melon, George?" Mary continued.

"How about a dance?" Bob asked her.

"We can dance later, darling," she said. "Now's the time to cut the melon."

"Let's cut a rug first," Bob said.

Young Mary thought that was quite funny.

"I'm sick of starving," her mother said, "while George and Margaret there roll in my husband's wealth."

"Which husband?" Margaret asked. She had sand in her voice.

Mary paused a moment. "Well, now," she said, "I guess you've

260

got something there. The dead one, Margaret. The old dead one. You want the live one, don't you?"

"Yes," Margaret said, and the night itself seemed to fall silent.

I suppose that when two human females really go after each other the proper costume that the scene calls for is something primitive like a sarong. These two women, eyes full of the hottest hate, assaulted each other with vicious pecking motions of their almost identical tulle hats, more like the agitated combs of fighting roosters. And I suppose that it might have been absurd, the sight of them, except that one was so absolutely right and the other so absolutely wrong.

"Yes, you would, wouldn't you?" mocked Mary.

"Yes, I would," Margaret stubbornly repeated.

"Why?"

"Because I want children! I've always wanted children! What does any woman want?"

So help me God, I thought, this is the first time she has ever said it. And for her to have to say it here and now.

"What do you mean? You've always had mine!"

"Jeff? The little bit of Jeff we've had?"

"Yes! I never had him!"

"Oh, for God's sake. That's not having—"

"Let's quit this," young Mary said.

"Yeah," Bob agreed.

"No, I won't quit it!" her mother cried. "If she's so damned hungry for marriage and kids, let her make George sell the damned Tower and I'll see what I can do to help her."

Margaret turned a face to me quite blank, it was so erased by emotion.

"Would you?" she asked.

"You bet I will," I said.

The conquering smile of Helen of Troy incredibly took place on her countenance as she turned it back across the table to Mary. Her voice was very low and she spoke very slowly.

"But I wouldn't let him," she said.

Even before this, other people on the lawn had begun to look

261

in our direction, I realized, for none of us had at all times kept our voices down.

"Then you're a God-damned fool!" Mary shouted. "Every Carton was a God-damned fool! A bunch of keelboat people!"

Now we had the undivided attention of practically the entire party. Bob jumped up and for a moment I did not know what he was going to do until I saw him striding as quickly as he decently could without actually running to the orchestra microphone on the porch. He looked the picture of aplomb, I must say, under the porch lights as he raised a hand to stop the murmuring music and began to speak into the silvered microphone disk. "Friends," he said, and his voice came out from the loudspeaker with all the balmy appeal of Graham McNamee, "we've all toasted the bride, the groom, their happiness and so on. Now how about coming up here to the bar and joining in a toast to ourselves? How about that, eh? Let's all drink a toast to the future!"

To the future.

About the only foreseeable event in the future, as it turned out, was that my nephew Jeff would decline his father-in-law's invitation to place him advantageously in the abrasives field. After a few summer weeks at the Beeman place in Charlevoix, Jeff and Carol came back East for good and in New York he went into the magazine field, where Bob Mayer of course had a great many connections.

I know nothing about the periodical publishing business at first hand, of course. Almost all that I know is from half a lifetime's casual association with Bob and, more recently, from my nephew's later contact—I think that's the occupational word: the noun also made into the verb—with it. That's about all, except for a sampling of the general product from time to time as anyone is likely to make: in barbershops, dentists' offices, club lounges, during long journeys on trains and planes where they also come free, and even occasionally from direct purchase from the newsstands or occasional trial subscriptions. From these only casual connections, however, I have formed a few lasting, indeed, in a way architectonic—to wit, basic—impressions and for what they are worth I shall gladly put them down here, for they have some bearing on part of the narrative that follows:

1) Side by side with a few responsible and even great ones, there are a number of American publications in the general field that apparently don't have to be of any real worth successfully to survive year after year. There exist, you might say, many nettles among the corn; many Tom Swifts among the Gutenbergs. Choose your own examples of either.

2) But this quality of worthlessness is not one that you can really blame on the worthless publication itself. It is rather the fault of a bone-headed section of the public which is that publication's readership. The worthless publication is not really culpable; it is not vicious. It is simply cheap and without pride or style.

3) The real villains of this kind of American publishing are not the people who put the stuff out, but the hopelessly ignorant ones who read it, advertise in it, and otherwise support it. Those hundreds of thousands of the best half-educated population on earth— so marvelously undiscriminating—are the ones ultimately responsible for what there is of our thriving jerk periodical press.

I only set these impressions down to show how an intelligent young man entering the magazine publishing business may be playing in very bad luck indeed if he has succeeded in joining one of the Tom Swifts of the business rather than one of the Gutenbergs. Young Jeff joined one of the former his first time out.

Well, that's not quite true. He'd had a few months of radio work before that. In those days the radio networks themselves still had control of their programs, which their salesmen then went and sold to this client or that. The National Broadcasting Company then still functioned at 711 Fifth Avenue, and that was where its total product originated. Jeff was set to work on a show called "Eight Bells," a weekly program concerning the cod-fishing industry. When he told me that he had contributed the idea of reinforcing the program with a mixed octet consisting of four men (the four Bells) and of four women (the four Belles), I had to congratulate him. A client or sponsor had been discovered who actually packed codfish and would send them to you on ice, no matter where in the United States you lived. And all might have gone well except that the codfish that very autumn moved away from the banks where this particular client's boats could most advantageously net them.

"Can't you just see them?" Jeff said gloomily to me one early winter afternoon as we sat at one of those semi-official drugstore counters where radio, and now even television people seem to conduct so large a part of their business and social affairs.

"See who?" I asked.

"Those cod. Way down there in the icy lime-green waters. One cod comes up and bumps his nose gently in another's. 'Let's blow out of here,' he says, and then another cod whispers it to another until the whole sea bottom is quietly a disappearing mass of codfish, going someplace else. The men in the boats tell each other, 'We haven't got any more fish.' The men in Boston phone NBC, 'We haven't got any more fish!' 'Why not?' 'Don't know. Anyhow, they've gone so we cancel. The movements of cod are inscrutable.'"

"I see," I said.

"And they are, too, you know," Jeff said. "We've all looked that up and it's true. Codfish can cool on you anytime."

"So no more Eight Bells?" I asked.

"No more."

I expect that these curious experiences, so indicative of the tenuousness of the literary career, are often amusing to reflect upon much later. They may even be genuinely humorous at the time to a young writer, provided he is in easy circumstances. But Jeff was not and by now he had a little apartment on upper Madison over a grocery store and he and Carol were expecting, in minimum time, a baby. That was when a friend opportunely found Jeff a job on his first publication, a weekly magazine—one of the Tom Swifts.

You can become very unhappy doing something day after day

264

that you have no respect for and don't want to do, and if in addition are paid badly for it. When you are paid rather well for the same kind of job and advanced quickly in it, I imagine that you simply become stunned not only with security but with self-contempt. I don't know about this firsthand, of course. But I do know that when Margaret and I went to see Jeff and Carol in their little apartment every month or so it became each time a little more apparent that this was not a happy ship. Even after the little girl came. Often Jeff would be quite late, so that Carol and we would be waiting dinner for him when he came in, he trying so very hard, acrobatically you might even say, to raise the scowl from his face as he opened the door into the small foyer that immediately faced the not much larger living room.

"What's the matter, darling?" Carol would ask.

"Nothing." He would try as hard as he could to smile. "I'm just fresh from the swine pen. How's everybody?"

His boss would have made him write or edit something that was a small lie to please an advertiser; or even a small truth; something like that. Well, if you're not working for yourself, if you're taking an employer's money, I suppose you must expect to put up with that kind of thing in almost any kind of business. I once recall reading that Mr. Gerard Swope's father, a scientist, told Mr. Gerard Swope, when he, the son, became head of General Electric, that anybody could make a success by merely sticking with a corporation. But I'll bet that the sticking can on occasion take some bitter fortitude. And if you don't conceal it, it can take a lot out of the wife at home, too. Certainly if she isn't an iron woman to begin with. That I do know. And I told Jeff so. Carol was looking like a dark little death's head. I began to think about seeing what Bob Mayer could do toward finding Jeff a decent job.

All that late winter and spring I was fiddling with some household radiator designs. The idea was that you distributed most heat by making the louvers as thin as possible so as to provide the optimum air contact (no great feat of the imagination; *vide* any automobile radiator). Anyhow, I was communing with this important bunch of plumbers in their skyscraper on Park Avenue every week or so and I tried to see my niece and nephew as often as it was convenient for them, and me.

On this occasion I had gotten a call from young Mary, a day or so before, asking me when I would be in town and if I then could see her. I said I could indeed. And then, thinking to make a little family gathering of it, since I had seen neither of them for almost a month, I phoned her brother and arranged for him to show up at the same place, same time.

The place was Shor's restaurant, opened only a little while previously, and one that I liked not only for its convenient mid-town location but also for its interesting (at that time) arrangement of traffic circulation. You came in from a central entrance and then moved in either of two directions which brought you around a circular bar and thence to a spacious refectory foyer. "Well designed," observed F. L. Wright, whanging that great dog-killing Malacca stick of his around him, the only time I ever took him there. I must confess that I don't know the name of the designing architect. It's all changed now anyway, possibly by a different man.

On this late-spring afternoon, a fine violet light all over the top of the city, I came into the place and took a seat in one of the lung-shaped cubicles near the bar. My niece arrived soon after, and the appearance of her beautiful young face gave me surprise and concern. Over the diamond-blue eyes, over the bright blond flesh of her cheeks some sort of a shade seemed to have fallen—much like, I now recalled, her mother's face had appeared to me long ago when she was for a time stricken by her affairs and her bright blondeness had seemed to repose in shadow. I have said that I hadn't seen young Mary for the better part of a month.

"How's the painting going?" I asked, as soon as I had gotten her settled in our cubicle and a drink ordered for her. That seemed a neutral enough subject to begin with. As a matter of fact, young Mary had done one or two very interesting little things early that winter, it had seemed to me, under Soyer's teaching. They were Soyeresque, of course—intense, low-key, and with his trick of

266

bringing to bear the eye and the palette of the cinquecento masters upon the Brooklyn gasworks—but Mary's Soyerism had a little flair of its own. She had done a small canvas of only a poor city doorway with a mourning wreath hung on it that struck the heart, I thought, with its tiny pretense and pathos. Then later there were some other things of hers that I couldn't understand at all. These were canvases frankly copied from news photographs (Hitler reoccupying the Rhineland, and so forth) which I thought better left undiscussed. I now believe myself that she had artistically run out of gas quite early in the game. It can happen. Anyhow, I asked, "How's the painting going?"

"That was about enough of that," she said.

"All through?"

"All through."

"Well, I wouldn't worry too much about it. I still like the little funeral wreath."

"So symbolic," she said, with a smile at me that was supposed to convey enigma and disillusion, and did.

Then young Jeff came up to us and it was all too apparent that neither of the children had expected the other to be there, which in turn made me see that each had been anticipating this as a private audience with me: to wit, some sort of trouble session. I felt clumsy not to have foreseen it; at least not to have made it clear that both were expected. And yet, why? Neither had overburdened me with his or her problems at any time in their lives. Nevertheless, I was sorry. I had not even handled the appointment schedule properly, you might say, when the time for their need had arrived.

"How's Carol?" I asked, having gotten Jeff seated and served.

"Well. . . ." He turned to Mary. "What would you say?"

"I think she's going cuckoo," Mary said.

"For God's sake, why?" I asked, it being the first sentence that came to my mind, I suppose.

"I don't know," Jeff said.

"The pressures of metropolitan life," Mary said. "And young motherhood." Her tone was very light, but she was quite serious

267

nevertheless. "Motherhood, or being denied it—either one can get a young girl down sometimes."

"Shut up," Jeff said, I thought with surprising rudeness.

Mary laughed at him, a laugh whose source I was obviously not expected to comprehend.

Then Mr. James Reilley came up, or rather wobbled up, to our table. This, you understand, was no later than five-thirty in the afternoon, but he was clearly drunk. It was getting to be quite a vesper-time.

He was a little man, a Fenian type by the looks of him with his angry fringe of black bangs over a bitter round white face, and he began by saying, "Bran for everybody? Bran to stop up your guts?"

Jeff looked up almost lifelessly. "Hello, Jim," he said.

"How about some of that good old bran, Jeff? To stop up the old guts."

"Excuse me, Mary," I said, rising. "I'll lead this one away."

"No. Never mind," Jeff said, also getting up. "I'll take him. Come on, Jim." And so he did, the two of them moving slowly together around to the far side of the bar and seeming to fall head to head into a morose colloquy.

"What in the world do you suppose that was all about?" I asked Mary, sitting down.

"I know," she said tiredly.

"You do? Then what?"

"Jim Reilley was the man who wrote Jeff's medicine department for him. Two or three weeks ago they reprinted a piece from a medical journal that said that far from being a laxative, bran simply chocked up your stomach—like sawdust."

"Naturally. Old stuff. So what?"

"So the bran people who make and advertise the product jumped on poor Mr. McCallister, Jeff's publisher. Well, he's only a poor old Scotch thief so they made him promise to print the findings of a hired professor out of the State University of Somewhere saying that studies that were continuing continued to show that bran was an O.K. laxative. So Jim said he wouldn't write the story, and Jeff said he understood. So Jeff wrote it and it was printed last week and Jim resigned. And Jeff said he understood. I guess everybody," Mary ended, "understood."

"Well," I said, "it's nice that you and Jeff have each other to talk over your troubles with."

"Yes," she said, "isn't it? Reilley called it Cuban journalism."

"Excuse me for a moment," I said, rising again. I thought that I might with a little effort try to put an end to the coruscating effect of Tom Swift—or Cuban—journalism at least on my nephew and his immediate family.

"Where are you going?"

"I'm going to call Bob Mayer," I said.

"Oh, please!"

"What's the matter, Mary?"

"Oh, please don't ask him any favors!" The young body was strained across the table toward me.

"Why not, Mary? I don't understand. Bob's always been a good friend to all of us."

The young body sank back onto the banquette. "Never mind, then," she said.

So I went to the phone booth by the entrance and called Mayer's office. When I got him on the line I said, "Bob, I want to talk to you about one of my kids."

"Oh?" he said, rather strangely I thought. "Then I guess you better come over here, George. There won't be anybody around."

Well, that seemed odd. "No," I said, "it's just that you've got to get a decent job for young Jeff." This seemed to relieve him. After I'd told him what was on my mind, the whole thing became simple as pie. Bob said that, even as he had predicted, building—principally building for armaments plants—was closer than right around the corner and that he was putting a new department into *Architectural Age* to watch its developments. It was a good spot for a young editor. It had a future.

On the strength of this perhaps equivocal good news we fell to talking about when we might next see each other. We settled that

269

he should come down to visit us commencement week. There was always a lot going on at that time, I told him.

When I went back to the table, young Mary and Jeff were talking and joking together (Reilley was nowhere in sight), so that it really did end up as a sort of family get-together as I had planned it. How quickly does a family sometimes close ranks.

Alfred had lashed together front-to-front two upholstered arm-chairs in the guest room upstairs for the little girl's *crèche,* and there, with suitable improvised bedclothing, he and Carol had laid her to rest without, so far as I could discern, any sound other than a gurgling acquiescence on the part of my two-month-old grandniece. Alfred had the widest, kindest mouth of any man, black or white, that I ever knew, and two eyes to match. "Now you just don't worry," I heard him croon to the young mother and the young baby, simultaneously. "You just leave it to me, and keep smilin'." So Carol was persuaded to come back downstairs to the sitting room and join the rest of us. This was the first anniversary of her marriage to Jeff and all the original wedding party had been gathered, with the exception of my niece Mary. On this late June afternoon, however, it had chosen to rain, great warm globules of it spattering the windows and running in the half-sunshine down to the gutters and along the streets and sidewalks. With the same salver of the wedding day in hand Alfred passed among us in a crisp white cotton coat, offering the wine.

"To the only absent one," I proposed, lifting my glass. "To young Mary."

"Oh, well," her mother said, sitting comfortably on the window settee beside Bob Mayer, now her son's employer, and looking, in her more recent varieties of tulle—and in the low light of a rainy afternoon—about thirty years old. "Oh, well, we've got a new member of the group upstairs to make up for the absence."

"Well said," agreed Bob Mayer. He, too, was looking agreeably handsome for his years—black kinky hair, straight long nose, square dark jaw; quite Grecian, in fact, I remember thinking, as some of them often do. Phidian.

270

"But why isn't she here?" Carol, the little darkling, asked, tensed on the edge of a straight chair, her glass of champagne held straight in front of her, the portrait by Manet of a little girl at a family party to which she had barely been admitted.

"She called to say that she had been ill, dearest," Margaret told her. "But we'll miss her, won't we?"

"Yes," Carol said, "and Bob must miss her more than anyone. The wedding will be soon now, won't it, Bob?"

"I don't know what you mean, Carol," Bob said. "I'm much, much too old to marry a lovely young girl of Mary's age."

"I should certainly think so," Mary's mother said, with her old hotel veranda trill and smile. "Really, Carol dear."

Carol looked at her with the deepest complexity. "But, Mrs. Hanes, I don't understand."

"Understand what, dear?"

"When you and Jeff and Bob brought her up to our apartment —when she was sick and stayed on our couch and I took care of her and watched her temperature for three days—she told me often, often—"

"What the hell is this all about?" I asked, beginning at last quite well to know.

"She had simply lost a baby, Carol dear," Mary said, so help me, as coolly as a hustler slipping a rube a pair of fixed dice. "Didn't you understand?"

"Sit still, George," Margaret said.

"*You* knew about this?" I turned and asked Jeff.

"Well—"

"You weren't too hot at this kind of a thing when you were a girl, were you?" I said to Mary.

"Don't be tiresome, George."

"Keep your seat, I tell you, George," Margaret said.

"Let me get into this," said Mayer, rising from the settee.

When he got up I got up.

"*They killed a baby! They killed Mary's baby!*" The poor little black moth of a girl arose and literally began to make a frantic flight around the room, bumping into me as I was moving on

271

Mayer, then against him, then into the outstretched arms of Margaret and Jeff. But she eluded them and started fluttering crazily up the stairs toward the rooms overhead. "They killed a baby!" she cried. "A baby!"

Margaret and I were on her heels as she reached the guest room where her own little girl was lying deep within the cradle made of chairs. She sprang to it with arms extended like wings, and then stood frozen as she gave a terrifying cry. It was like the time she had stared down into my boat.

"*Holes!* All the little children have holes and are down in holes! Oh, my God, they are all dead and down in the holes!"

It took the better part of an hour for us to get her out of the room and downstairs and into a car and to a room with attendants at the Infirmary.

"She's mighty pretty, Mr. Hanes, Miss Margaret," Alfred said softly, clutching his good bony black hands over the sleeping baby. "Yes, she is." He turned that incredibly believing great smile of his toward us where Margaret and I sat beside each other on the twin bed in the guest room nearest the crib that Alfred had made of the two chairs. "What her name, Miss Margaret?"

"It's Eileen, Alfred," Margaret said.

"That's a pretty name," Alfred said, and then, looking down into the crib he had made, "and it certainly is a mighty pretty child."

"Yes," Margaret said. "We'll look after her now, Alfred. You've had a long night."

"Yes," he said, "but you know I don't mind," and went away softly, leaving us alone.

"You were quite right, not getting into a steam-up about Bob Mayer after the hospital. I was very proud of you."

"It wasn't his fault, I suppose. For all I know, the kid may have tricked him—or them—into it. A terrible thing to say, isn't it?" And it was indeed a terrible thing to say, for surely my own implication in her affairs was deep enough. And yet what chance had I ever had to take serious responsibility for her? She was not

272

really any part mine except that she was my brother's daughter. Mary was, in the end, her mother's child, a hotel child. There are some losses which you have to take that it is simply irrational to torture yourself about.

"Well, Bob surely never had any idea of marrying her—before or after," Margaret said. "Anyhow, the mother seems to have taken care of everything."

Then she went over to where the baby slept and from the intensity of her leaning posture and the yearning of her expression I thought that she might pick up and waken the child; but she restrained herself. Instead she sat on the edge of the chair crib.

"But not of this one," Margaret said.

"She made it pretty clear that she could hardly set up a nursery at the Barbizon," I reminded her.

"It will be a long time until Jeff can take care of the baby," Margaret went on, looking toward the future as she seemed to try to see it somewhere in the air above my head. "We can't know about poor Carol. Not for a long time either, I should imagine."

"No."

"This is my own custodianship," she said with a sudden firmness. "Do you understand that? This baby."

"Ours," I said.

"No, George. You've always had something to take care of, even though it wasn't yours, all your life. This one is mine."

"Very well," I said.

She came over and kissed me on my forehead—always a reliable sign, I expect, that you are now being shortchanged a bit of another's whole love.

"You see, you've taught me this for such a long time," she said. "For such a long, long time, my dearest."

Fifteen

WHENEVER the Republic finds itself in trouble everybody seems to want to hurry to Washington, and this has always struck me as an appealing and heart-warming impulse. I know that under similar circumstances the British also descend on London from the ends of the earth and I believe the same thing is true of the Germans and Berlin; as to what the French and Italians do upon such occasions I have no impression; the Russians, I suppose, have always done pretty much what they were told, although I recall that there are scenes in *War and Peace* of individuals offering disinterested voluntary service to St. Petersburg in a time of national crisis. But everybody and his brother has always headed for Washington when the country was in a jam, and such was the case even months before the Second World War was actually upon us.

Naturally there were opportunists in the crowd looking for more money than they could make at home, adventurers looking for more prestige than they could find at home, and fellows who just wanted to escape home itself for a while. However, I don't think that either chiselers, phonies, or bums were present in the national capital in greater proportion than they existed in the national population. Plenty of good people showed up, plenty.

Nobody in Washington, of course, was very young. The young people had their work to do, but it was not done as a rule in Wash-

274

ington. They were off at their camps and cantonments—bases, they called them in this war—as our old bunch had ourselves been in the other one. I could have saved myself some burdensome hours had I earlier in the game acquiesced to this immemorial division of labor.

The first draft registration came, if you remember, in September, 1940, and included men from eighteen to forty. Wide as it was, the top figure in this range still undershot me by six full years. Mr. Hoover's economies, and much needed I am sure they were, had many years before flunked our old crowd out of the Naval Reserve. Just as a rich man lays up his yacht when times are hard, so the democracies had during the Depression laid up their navies; for the part-time veteran volunteer there was not only no money to pay for a cruise or a refresher course—there hadn't been the price of a smoker or a beer. All that was long past; still, they were now waving the flag again and I wanted to get into the show. When the boy perishes, the man dies. I had some momentary wild idea of trying to register for the draft by falsifying my age—like the drummer lads of '61, only in reverse—but you couldn't get away with a thing like that in a little town like ours. Everybody knows how old you are. And in any case I should certainly not in the end have been so quixotic as to let my colleagues in the department down and run out on the courses that had been assigned me to conduct through the following June.

The students themselves began to drift away during the winter months, however—the best of them I, perhaps unjustly, thought—and by the time that spring arrived I became fairly restless myself. Many of the faculty were restless.

Late one afternoon a day or so after final examinations I had a quarter of an hour to kill before calling at Margaret's shop to walk her home to dinner, so I stepped across the street to the Nassau Club, expecting to join the little group which at this season of the year gathers on the back porch at this time of day to moisten the clay. As a rule a robin or two jumps around with a lonely piping on the evening grass and, except for the small rustle of good-fellowship, the world is as hushed as it might be in an en-

275

chanted village. The trees and their new foliage make an acoustical baffle, I suppose. Anyhow, not so this evening. On the back porch there were to be heard the high voices of citizens in the know determined to make other citizens privy to their information.

"If you will just listen to me," said a man named Stevens whom I recognized as from the Department of Oriental Studies, "anybody who has a dime's worth of Mandarin can learn Japanese in a month. And if you've got Japanese, the Navy—"

"Same thing for Old English and German," someone with a pipe from the English Department interrupted.

"Well then, how about French *vis-à-vis* Italian?" asked a young man with a small waxed mustache from the Department of Romance Languages who also translated current American novels for the overseas trade. "Or Spanish to Italian for that matter. A breeze."

"What I'm trying to tell you," Stevens said, regaining the floor, "is that there is this man from Brown—and by an odd coincidence his *own* name is Brown; perhaps you've heard him do his stunt locating American accents on the radio—at any rate, this man Brown is looking for language teachers for the Navy. They'll be doing their stuff up at Columbia."

"Oh, *Columbia*," somebody said dispiritedly.

"No, no. It's a very good deal." (How quaint, it seemed, for the old ones already to have undertaken the current speech of the young; philologists they surely were.) "They commission you fast and if you get sharp they may send you out with the fleet."

"Like the translators they sent out with Columbus to communicate with the savages?" a sanguine type from the History Department inquired, so bitterly and sarcastically that it was not hard to guess the depths of his own hopeless desire to be with the fleet.

"How about the case of somebody," I asked in the unhappy pause that followed, "who would just settle for the ground force auxiliary of the Air Force?"

"Oh, hell," said Stevens, "that's *really* a breeze. There's a young fellow down in Washington—Cap and Gown boy from the class of 'thirty-three-or-four; young personnel vice president of the Chase Bank—and as far as the Air Force goes he can fix you up any way you want. That's another fast commission deal."

I moved over to Stevens' side as soon as I could and got the boy's name, which was Stapleton, as well as his Washington address, which was in one of the old temporary military buildings, 243-A, Constitution Avenue. This bit of inside information folded in my wallet, I proceeded out into the violet light of Nassau Street and with a heart lighter than it had been for some months joined Margaret.

"You look as though you had won the bingo prize, George," she said, turning to me after she had locked up the front door of the shop.

"Who can say?" I answered as enigmatically as I could. And so we went down the long old street toward my house. The boys we saw were mostly graduated seniors in their beer suits now, for the rest of the college had gone home and the alumni were not due to arrive for their ceremonies for a day or so. But here and there along the street was a kid in Navy white or Air Force tan, back to pick up the last of his stuff before leaving the place for good. For good? Well, for a time. I hoped, looking at each of their faces, so indistinguishable yet from the rest, that it would be only for a time.

Margaret and I had the duty that evening, Alfred being about due for relief and a trip to the movies. Not that taking care of little Eileen was ever what you would call a duty. She was the dearest little thing. She had curly sand-colored hair and four buttons for a face: button eyes, button nose, button mouth. And she was the most energetic little child I think I have ever seen. I have seen them when they lie on their backs and kick all the time; this one did that for the first nine months of her life. I have also seen them when they get so that they can grab hold of the top of the play-pen and jump up and down all the time. What I had never seen before was one who when it began to walk, not only constantly jumped up and down on its feet but jumped up and down on its knees. Never a dull moment, you might say.

I have always believed in spoiling little children if they are interesting. Few of us have many years in store that are really made free and happy for us. You can always whack the bright ones a time or two and they will learn soon enough not to pull the Lowestoft off the coffee-table. From then on they can be as agreeable company in your drawing room as people of any other age whom you might want to see there. Provided, as I say, that they are bright, that they have something of interest to communicate to you and (of course) you have something of interest to communicate to them. God pity you, I have always felt, if you are stuck with a dumb one. In that case your only salvation is in having been born a professional child-lover. I am not one; nor, fortunately, was Eileen dumb. Discovering, as she had by herself, that it was possible to jump from the knees is not what I would call the mark of an unintelligent child. She always instantly recognized her father, who came down to see her about every week, and I am fairly sure that she identified her mother whenever Jeff or Margaret and I took her down to Baltimore so that Carol could see her. She was surely always most affectionate with Carol, I know, although of course the little thing was never other than affectionate with anyone. She had a warm group of back-yard acquaintances: dogs, children, the electric-meter man, and so forth. Margaret, the antiquarian, called her The Publick Universal Friend, generally shortened simply to The Friend. A great favorite, Eileen, as I am afraid I have already made too clear.

Margaret, in Alfred's absence having prepared our supper that evening and tucked the baby away upstairs, came back down to the sitting room.

"The last time you went away to a war," she said, absolutely without preamble, "I got married. Doesn't it bother you to think about that?"

"Well, wait a minute—"

Then she started laughing, and hers is much more of an Irish laugh than a French one so that you are invited—no, pretty much compelled—to laugh yourself. I did.

"Let's hear about the bingo prize you won this afternoon," she said, and I told her about what Stevens had said about this boy Stapleton's job of getting people commissioned in the Army air service for ground work. There are, as I have heard and read, a lot of women who in similar circumstances are moved to sarcasm and ridicule toward the superannuated incipient volunteer. Not Margaret. But then, of course not Margaret.

"So you'll go away," she said, and already I could see in her dark eyes a look of distance—and also of planning.

"Maybe it won't be too far," I said.

"At any rate you'll be away."

"Yes."

"Then don't you think I'd better move down here? The Friend, I mean."

"I guess you should—unless you think it would be embarrassing for you, living in my house." I honestly hadn't thought that far ahead; that's how selfishly, or at least inattentively, these ancient impulses can make you behave.

She smiled. "Our house. It surely must be known as our house by now. What's Jeff going to do?"

"How do you mean?"

"Well, he's young and able. Doesn't he hear the bugle call, too?"

"He's a journalist. He's in it up to his neck reporting on what the war plants are doing and all that kind of thing."

"But not a Boy Volunteer. Not one of the Ivy League Rifles."

"Stop it, Margaret," I said.

"I know, my dearest," she said.

It couldn't have been more than a day or so later that I presented myself at 243-A on Constitution Avenue, one of those imperishably temporary two-floor buildings that serve to house the efforts of war after war, and was most courteously shown to the cubicle occupied by Mr. Stapleton, the patriot's friend.

He seemed a nice enough young fellow: dandruff and closely bitten fingernails, to be sure, but I expect his life in the bank had been a nervous one. He had a mimeographed pamphlet of about

279

sixteen pages before him, and he reversed it across the desk for a moment so that I could see it. From my brief perusal it seemed to be simply a long series of categories of civilian help that the Air Force might make use of. He then switched the brochure back to himself so that he could read the categories and proceeded to interrogate me, following, as I understood it, the requirements as they were outlined in the pamphlet before him.

"The first heading here," he said, peering down at the pamphlet, "is called Security." He looked up. "That means people who can protect an air base. Have you ever," he looked down to the booklet again, "have you ever had any police experience?"

"No."

"Detective?"

"No."

"Well, how about a lawyer? Were you ever—I mean, are you a lawyer, Mr. Hanes?"

"No. An architect."

"Oh." He turned a page. "Well, the lawyer business comes up here again. Under Interrogation. That is, interrogating pilots after they have returned from their missions. They need lawyers for that. You can understand: lawyers are able to put the information together properly for the intelligence people. But you're not a lawyer."

"No," I said. "Just an architect."

"Well, then," he said, flipping another page. "Journalism. They need newspapermen to interrogate pilots, too. How about journalism?"

"I was a pilot once," I said.

"Yeah?" he said doubtfully, and flipped a few more pages. "Nothing under P except Pastor. That's more for morale work around the bases, pastors. Or, of course, other clergymen."

"How about T for Teacher?" I asked. "You know—like Mr. Chips."

That fired him. "Mr. Chips is just who we're looking for! Somebody to keep the kids' morale bucked up. You play the piano?"

"No, but I've often wished I could."

"How about baseball? Could you get up a team and coach it?"

"Just golf," I said. "And a little shooting and fishing."

He looked at me and shook his head.

"No golf or fishing on bases like ours, Mr. Hanes," he said.

"And no place for old pilots? Observation pilots?"

He must have started looking under P once more, below Pastor, where we already knew no other walk of life existed.

"Navy observation pilots," I suggested. "N."

This relieved him, for he stopped his search with an indulgent smile. "Not in the Army Air Force, Mr. Hanes," he said.

So I got up; but he was going to be conscientious about the interview, I could see, to the very end. He motioned me into my seat again.

"How about restaurant and hotel experience?" he asked. "Had any of that?"

"I've built some," I said.

"It says here you have to have run one."

So that whole trip was clearly a miscue. It has been my experience that you never get a job from anybody that you don't know, or at least through mutual friends. I could hardly hold this absurd interview against Stapleton; I have never known but one or two people in Cap and Gown and I have banked all my life at the Hanover. However, fiascoes like this can irritate you if you let them, and as I got on the Pennsylvania at five o'clock to go back home I told myself that anybody could take America—even the Americans. That feeling simply arose from the anger of disappointment, of course.

Margaret had already moved into the Queenston house, fixing me up very snugly indeed with quarters across the archway off the office reception room. It wasn't much later than ten o'clock when I got home, and she was in the sitting room sewing away at something of little Eileen's when I arrived. Her expression was a nice balance of welcome with just enough surprise when I came in. What a tactful woman.

"How did it go?" she asked.

"It didn't go well at all," I said.

281

"Well, I'm glad. Sit down and take your shoes off and I'll get you a drink."

When she came back with the drink, I asked her, "How do you mean you're glad?"

"Bigger things are in train. Do you know a Congressman named Kafer? Kaffer?"

"Kaffey? Of course."

"The Military Affairs Committee?"

"He used to be."

"Well, that's the man who wants you to call him at once. Naturally I didn't know where to get you this afternoon while you were running around all over Washington. To think your paths might have crossed."

"Now, settle down here and quit kidding."

"All right. Operator 24 is your girl. In your knapsack is the baton of a marshal of France. I hope the marshal doesn't want it back—but isn't it *exciting*, George? I told you I was glad."

A dear funny woman, too.

Kaffey wasn't too hard to reach. Over the wires he sounded about as I remembered his voice—once, notably, when he called me in St. Louis toward the close of the Sheffield hospital debacle—a good twenty years ago. His manner of address I recognized as part of that kind of timeless familiarity found in police officers, priests, and politicians: he might have last spoken to me the day before. "George," he said, "is that you?"

"This is me, John, old boy," I said. Well, why not? Social lubricant costs so little.

"I want to see you in New York tomorrow, George. You've got a duty to do by your country."

"Any old time, John," I said, grinning now and winking the acknowledgment of good news at Margaret.

"Where can we meet? I've got to take the six o'clock to Springfield out of Grand Central."

Well, that wasn't hard to figure. "How about the Princeton Club, Thirty-ninth and Park. Right close by."

"Splendid, George!" The Congressional voice called across two hundred miles. "Splendid!"

282

"Four o'clock?"

"Make it five, George. This won't take much time. Just a paper or two for you to sign. Good night and God bless you, George, old boy."

Placing the instrument in its cradle, I gave Margaret another wink.

"Baton?" she asked eagerly.

"What else, baby?" I said. And I think I snapped my fingers.

At five o'clock sharp the following afternoon—the Congressman was prompt—we sat ourselves down across the long table in the center of the Woodrow Wilson Room. I had chosen this site for our meeting out of martial sentiment, and also because it is the only place I know of in that club where you can be alone without going to bed or holding a private dinner. I have said earlier that the Congressman had reminded me in his youth of the young Ralph Bellamy, a movie actor of the time. Kaffey and his stage prototype still ran parallel in manner and appearance: both were still equally pompous and sincere and, alas, each was now a little overblown. Kaffey burst open a briefcase upon the table. I waited upon his words.

"George," he said, "you know and I know that we can get every resort hotel in the nation that we need to house our tactical troops while in training. Anybody who has a resort hotel—and I don't care whether it's in the White Mountains or Miami Beach—they all know that the tourist business falls on its fanny the moment war is declared. Gas rationing, food rationing, travel restriction, and so forth. You get me?"

Only up to a point, I had to tell him. Where in this preamble, I wondered, might lie the baton?

"Now—what we're having a devil of a time leasing is hotels for training programs in the big cities, where technical pedagogy and all that kind of thing are most immediately available. You see?"

"Not quite," I said.

"There is where the sacrifice of ownership lies. A man with a hotel in a city can make a mint of money in wartime—civilians

283

and even military personnel coming and going from hither and yon. But we need such hotels very badly, George. We need them very badly."

"Who does?" I asked.

"Army Air Force. We want to take over your own Tower for a navigators' school. And right now." He began to spew a few papers from his briefcase in my direction; he also produced a fountain pen from among the other writing instruments clipped within his breast pocket and proffered it to me. I took it.

"Who else's hotel have you got in our area?" was about all I felt able to ask.

"In Chicago we've got the Stevens and also—let's see—yes, the old Auditorium."

That did it. If he'd got Louis' building, he might as well have Jeff's. How could I have held out against a national emergency anyhow? Who would?

"Okay, John," I said.

"I knew that you and I wouldn't have any trouble, George," the Congressman said. "I knew it."

"What do we do now?" I asked.

He looked at his watch, a wristwatch, and I found myself wondering if he had ever really gotten used to the effeminacy with which he must have regarded it when first he put one on in the artillery in 1917. He didn't seem too at home with one yet. "We must make this fast, George, if I'm to catch my train to Springfield. Do you have any legal experience, George?"

No—I thought in my disappointment and dismay—and I can't play the piano or baseball either. "No," I said. "Is it required at this stage of the game? There's a lawyer I've used in St. Louis on building matters. Pierce is his name."

"Never mind. Just put your name here as the owner *in supra*."

I wrote down my name with Kaffey's pen on the blank that he had slid toward me.

"Now." He slid that sheet back and shoved another under my hands. "This one's the quit-claim."

"What's that?"

284

"You just turn over your title *pro tem* to the War Department. There'll be a lot more of these things to sign later, but this will get the ball rolling."

"Rolling right now?"

"As of this moment," said the Congressman, rising with a forty-eight-star smile. "You'd better notify your people to start getting out of there tonight. We don't take an elevator down, do we? No. The stairs here will do."

"John," I said.

"Yes?"

"I'd like to get in on this thing myself. Retread and all that, you know."

"But you're in it up to your neck, George! You've made a great patriotic gesture. No, not a gesture, an act of faith. Not to be compared with those resort hotel men."

"I mean I want a job in the war. A uniform."

By now we were down at the Thirty-ninth Street entrance, and the girl doorman—there were girls on duty by that time, the boys having started to go away—was looking apathetically once more upon the spectacle of one who was hurried to go held by one who wished him but for another moment to stay. Pausing then between the steel-bound glass doors, his treasure—and my building—clasped in the briefcase beneath his arm, Congressman Kaffey said, "That? Oh, that, yes, George. Army Engineers Corps. You write me when I get back to Washington." And then he was gone.

I felt as though I were once again carrying the Engineers Corps' old hospital specification material on my back—the whole hundred pounds of it—as I went down the half flight of stairs to the telephone booths next to the cigar stand. I called Chick Samstag in St. Louis. He said he was happy to hear from me.

"We've got it now, George!" he said. "We've made it. You couldn't poke another midget into the old joint now. And I mean I've tried."

"Lots of suckers?"

"Straw, George. Nothing but straw. Haven't you heard about the draft, man?"

285

"Yes, of course."

"Close the doors, they're coming through the windows!"

"Close the doors anyhow," I said. And then I told him that the War Department was taking over our building on behalf of the Army Air Force. Chick made quite a lot of noise. He said that I couldn't do this to him. All I could say was that I already had. He said that I had put him in the position of a bug-man in Texas, by which he meant that I had ruined him. In a carnival a bug-man sells chameleons, and when one finds himself in the Southwest, where chameleons naturally abound, he is faced with sure misfortune. Who, in this case, wasn't? Notwithstanding the sneaking fondness that I had for Samstag—let alone my gratitude for his having made some money from the Tower for the first time in its last fifteen years—I at last grew tired of his high, protesting carnival voice. There comes a point at which you cannot longer take on everyone's distress and your own as well. At any rate, that time —for the moment at least—had come to me.

"Cheer up, Chick," I said, and this I know was dirty of me, "there's a war job begging for you. Commission and all. You've not only run a restaurant but a hotel."

"What's this about?"

"You just go to see a man named Stapleton at 243-A Constitution Avenue, Washington, D.C. He'll fix you up!"

"George!"

"Good night, Chick," I said.

"George!"

"Yes?"

"At least tell me what kind of a score you made off Whiskers for the rent."

"I don't know," I said. "Good night, Chick," I said again and hung up.

There was an evening paper on the table in the bar at which I took my seat. I must have looked at it for about as long a time as it took the people to write what was in it but I certainly don't remember what I read. My brother's building was all that I really could think of. They didn't want me, they wanted Jeff's Tower

286

for the war. Well, of course it was only by luck—that is, by the accident of Junie's death—that the Tower was mine to give them. But it was always something of someone else's—Jeff's art, Junie's money—that I had to give. Or lease, I suppose you would put it in this present case. Something that I hadn't made, something that I was merely the trustee of, the custodian. I'd never really made or had anything for myself or by myself in my life. *Just sign here. This one's the quit-claim. . . . Write me when I get back to Washington.*

There was a man named Fred Gebaur who used to officiate at that bar in those days, and had for many years past. He had a head of vigorous silver hair parted in the middle and a mustache to match, and he looked very much like a man who must have been his contemporary, Henry Cabot Lodge. Both also were serious men, I would assume. Fred was something of a horticulturalist; at any season there were always flowers of his growing to be seen in vases on the back bar. Multiple-blossomed jonquils they were, I believe, on this evening.

The cocktail crowd had come and gone; the after-dinner crowd had come and gone. I expect I must have drunk as many as eight Scotch highballs, staring at that newspaper. When Fred appeared with another drink, which I must have asked for, and when he presented me with two venerable white heads and two mustaches, I figured that I should go and get something to eat. The dining room was of course by now closed, so I went outside and started down Murray Hill toward Thompson's in Grand Central. I crossed Forty-second Street and just beneath the overpass, where there was a Navy recruiting booth, I saw before me the biggest petty officer I had ever seen in my life. The hash marks and ratings on his sleeve ran from cuff to shoulder. I stood, I suppose, in wonder.

"What," he asked me, "are you staring at?"

"That's more garbage," I said, pointing to his sleeve, "than I ever saw in my life before."

"Were you ever in the Navy?" he asked.

"I sure was," I said.

"Were you ever in the construction business?"

"I sure was."

"What kind?"

"Steel."

"Well," he said, "you look big enough and old enough and tough enough."

"I sure am," I said.

"What did you ever put up?"

"I put up the prettiest piece of steel," I told him, "in the United States. Tower in the West."

"Who was your foreman on that job?" he asked.

"Bakin," I said, "Daken. Anyhow, a Czech."

"I know him," the petty officer said. "I worked with him in Buffalo."

"This was in St. Louis," I said.

"St. Louis, Buffalo, what's the difference? You want to get back in the service?"

"I sure do," I said.

"You're not feeling very well, are you, Mac?"

"Kind of tired."

"You come along with me," he said, and he took me inside the Grand Central and laid me out as comfortably as he could on one of the benches in the front waiting room. A long time later, it must have been, two other sailors helped me up and into a car of some kind. In the morning I awakened in a little white-plastered room with the refraction of water-light dancing on the ceiling. I have never been happier in my life. This was the wonderfully traditional way to get back into the Navy. Shanghaied, by God! I didn't even have a hangover.

These people, it turned out, were being formed up for Naval construction battalions, the Seabees. This was City Island.

They couldn't have treated me better. By nine o'clock I had not only had the best breakfast I had ever eaten in my life—ham, bacon, sausage, any kind of eggs, waffles *and* wheat cakes—but had been fitted with the finest piece of serge I will ever wear. All on the Navy. A fine, gray warrant officer signed me up. All he wanted from me, he said, was my union card, but when all that I had to

288

give him was my A.I.A. card that satisfied him. He rated me a machinist's mate first class and they had the full embroidery right there to put on you! Nobody that I saw around the place rated below that. It was a petty officers' paradise. If there were seamen, they kept them out of sight.

After lunch—another feast: fresh pork, sweet potatoes, candied apples, kale, rolls, the works—the dozen or so of us who had joined up that morning were asked to step over to the master-at-arms' quarters where we found our warrant officer again. He was standing behind one of those steel service desks and holding in his hand a copy of the old blue-bound U.S. Navy Regulations which I had not seen since that long-ago time when I was cadet in Pensacola.

When we were seated, the warrant officer cleared his throat and said, "What the Navy wants from you men is for you to build whatever it is that they want to have built." And he added, "Wherever they want to have it built." He held up the blue-bound book. "This here is the old Rocks and Shoals which you are acquainted with. It says you don't horseshit the officers, and vice versa." He tossed the volume on the desk. "I guess that's about got it," he concluded, and we were indoctrinated.

I wasn't outside long enough to smoke half a cigarette when who should come up but a man named Ed Cole, one of the finest window-men I ever knew and whom I had not seen for years. After trading reminiscences of old jobs he suggested that we go down to one of the cafés that lie along the dockyard, and there we spent a most agreeable afternoon in the company of some other people from the battalion drinking canned beer and shooting crap. As I say, I never felt better in my life. Someone I once knew who had been having a lot of trouble told me that he would like to get t.b. so that he could just crawl into bed and let somebody else worry about things for a while. That was exactly the way I felt. Let somebody else worry for a while. This is of course not a very courageous attitude to take, nor a very realistic one.

When the game broke up about suppertime, and the old nagging twilight began to come down, the telephone booth dragged me over to it and I put in a call to Margaret. Maybe they will never graduate all the undergraduates, but the shadow of the proctor always hangs around.

"Well," she said, and sweetly, not angrily or anything like that, "I was wondering when I would hear from you. How big a baton did you get?"

"No baton, baby," I said. "I'm in the Navy."

"The Navy?"

"A jack-tar again. Do you remember when I once told you the same thing back on Westminster Place?"

"Yes, dearest," she said. "But Congressman Kaffey was the Army, wasn't he?"

"That's the big difference," I said, "between us. Except that he made off with the hotel to train flyers in."

"Are you sober, George dear?"

"Just about. I'm a Seabee."

"A what?"

"Look. I'm in the Navy and I'm making twice as much as I did the last time out. Two hundred and thirty dollars a month. And I just picked up another forty dollars shooting crap."

"Can The Friend and I always depend on that additional income?" she asked. "Where are you calling from, George?"

"City Island, but I'll be moving out of here in a day or so," I told her.

"I know you will, dearest," she said. "And I think you're adorable."

So we hung up and I went back to the base where, after another delicious meal, we were shown a Betty Grable movie and so to bed.

After breakfast the next morning the warrant officer came over to me and said, "I think the captain wants to see you about something."

"About what?" I asked. I didn't know that there were any officers on the station.

"I don't know."

"Well, I guess I better go see him."

"I think so," the w.o. agreed, and pointed out how to get there.

It was a small house on the grounds to which I had paid no attention before. There was a young woman in Naval uniform on duty in a sort of anteroom on the first floor and she quickly admitted me to where the captain had his office.

There he sat behind another one of those green steel desks, the U.S. flag on a standard at one side of him and the blue Naval captain's ensign drooping on the other—Fred Polachek.

"Sit down here beside me, George," he whispered. "Sit down here, my old friend."

I sat down.

"Well, George," the well-remembered susurrant voice came, "long time no see."

"That's right," I said.

"My boy who studied under you," hissed the voice that used to be so full of secrets, "he thinks you're a star, George. A star."

"He was a very good student," I replied. "He told me you were in the contracting business in New Brunswick."

Polachek smiled an old, knowing European smile. "With a war going on? Not any more, George. The Navy needs constructors. So what in the hell," he asked, "are you doing here in this place?"

"I'm a constructor, Fred," I said.

His expression suddenly turned to one of menacing fury, as it had so often in the long-remembered past when he was bullying the sycophants of Dr. Muse while we were trying to get the Sheffield veterans' hospital built—and which I well recalled that Polachek had scuttled almost singlehanded by his attempted thievery.

"You are a *designer*, George!" he croaked. "You get the hell out of here!"

"Who says so, Fred?"

"Your wife, for one! That nice lady from Princeton!" (Here he obviously was talking about Margaret, the girl who, I now remembered, had predicted only the night before that it would not be long before I would be leaving City Island.) "And Kaffey that she got hold of. Don't you remember Kaffey—your old friend? The Congressman? You certainly ought to remember him."

"Yes," I said, "I do indeed. All the old Sheffield bunch seem to be getting in touch again."

But this wonderful brigand had no shame. He made no acknowledgment at all of our former sinful association. That was all right with me; I didn't see how he could steal very much in his job under the present Administration as a mere captain in the Seabees. I believed, and I still believe, that Fred Polachek had finally made enough money for himself to go square. In other words, he could now afford to be a patriot, and I was pleased to know it.

"Kaffey had no idea that a man of your abilities would sink to enlisting in the construction battalions," he hissed. "And I didn't either!"

"I didn't sink. I like it fine."

"You *liked* it fine, George. Since before you woke up this morning you were commissioned to the Bureau of Ships. That's on Constitution Avenue and Sixteenth Street in Washington."

"I don't quite see how you can do that, Fred. I'm enlisted."

"You're enlisted, but you can be promoted. You can be commissioned. You don't seem to understand that this Kaffey is now a very influential man in Washington. Not like you and I knew him when he was a kid."

Laryngitis may have kept him in its thrall for most of his life, but he still had plenty of energy. He came around from behind that Navy desk and literally shoved me out of his door.

"Please, George, please!" he groaned hoarsely. "Get the hell out of here! At once!"

And so I went. Paradise, in a way, lost. . . .

I have two overpowering impressions of Washington during the war years: the winters were filled with nothing but chill rain, the kind that would take the heart out of an eider duck; the summers would melt the brains in your skull. Spring in Washington is notoriously lovely, I know, but not in a war year. Maybe they don't have spring in Washington during war years.

Don't misunderstand me: I'm not kicking about the job I was given to do, which was to help co-ordinate construction plans for

292

shore installations as they came in to us from private firms as well as from our own people. Somebody had to do the work, and there were mountains of it to be done. Of red tape, on the other hand, there was very little. I know this may not sound like the Navy or, from what I have heard, the Army to many who were in service, but in our case it was true. I sometimes had to smile, thinking back on my old strangulating experience with Army Engineer Corps specifications when I was working on the Sheffield project. In the BuShips Building we took whatever we could get that worked and wherever we could find it quickest, which is why for example the aviation barracks at San Juan, Puerto Rico, got gold-plated knobs and fittings on all interior doors. The boys had to get the doors open and shut; that was all Crane had where and when we needed it. And here's the paradox, when you come to think of it: for all the iron-bound rigmarole that surrounded its buildings, the old veterans' hospital program turned out to be a tremendous steal; but while money was thrown away hysterically during the war, I don't believe that a great deal of stealing went on. War and peace, so different. In peacetime you hate to see a man in uniform; in wartime you hate to see one out of it. I'm now speaking, I realize, of a former period in which there was a real dissimilarity between the two conditions.

If Washington was somewhat uncomfortable during the war years—and it really was not; nobody went hungry and certainly nobody got shot, at least, not by enemy action—it was almost unbearably pathetic in the last few weeks before the war began: the pictures in the newspapers of the draftees on autumn maneuvers down South with their wooden mock-up fieldpieces; the large men from the industrial West in their sharkskin suits, huddled in whispered anxious conference in the lobbies of the Carlton and the Mayflower; so many of us poking around with our rainbow ribbons and feeling a little foolish, like chaperons at a fraternity party, among the so very much younger ones in uniform; the whole sense of the great Republic getting muscled up to do something that it didn't really want to do, that it didn't even know if it could do, but knew that it probably had to do. And all the time the Japanese

293

delegation in their little silk hats and morning dress, come all the way around the world from Tokyo and calling every day at the State Department to talk nobody could say what queer business to old Mr. Hull.

Everyone of us who is not a very young child must have the clearest recollective picture of what he or she was doing the afternoon that the talks ceased.

The Metropolitan Club on H Street, which—with its collection of huge oil portraits of admirals and generals in tiny caps and blue uniform coats hanging down to their knees—had always given me the impression of having gone to sleep right after the war with Spain, had on the contrary already mobilized, and touchingly, too, I thought, for this war. The Turkish bath on the third floor had been divided into half a dozen or so cubicles to accommodate members on business in the city, for even then the capital was crowded to the point of coming apart at the seams. I had upon arriving in Washington been lucky enough to get one of these snuggeries for myself.

Jeff was in town that Sunday on some business in connection with the defense-plant survey job he was doing for Bob Mayer's magazine, and after lunch downstairs we came up to my place to have a chat. I well remember that the man next door had his radio on—softly enough, for the partitions were so fragile that you could wake up everybody in the place with a sneeze—and this neighbor was listening to some sort of a concert. As Jeff had recently passed through St. Louis, I asked him if he had looked in on the Tower.

"All I got to do was look *at* the Tower," he said. "The inside is full of soldiers."

"Aviation cadets, you mean."

"Well, they were noisy enough for soldiers. It sounded like they were tearing the old joint apart."

I think I remember saying something to him to the effect that the Air Force was pretty strict with cadets, and that anyhow if anything was broken Uncle Sam had agreed to pay for it, for by now I had a valise full of documents from the government covering every conceivable angle of the deal. I asked him how Carol

294

was the last time he had seen her in Baltimore. For a few moments he didn't answer—lighting a cigarette, looking at the ceiling, or making some stall of that kind—and I was a little sorry I'd asked him. The radio concert beyond the plank partition went softly on.

"Isn't she feeling any better?" I ventured. "She's not too unhappy in that home, or whatever it is, is she?"

"No, no," he then said. "Carol's a sick girl, of course." He paused.

Well, I knew she was a sick girl, of course, myself. Again, I say, I have absolutely no clinical information about the misfortunes of the spirit. Once or twice, when Margaret and I had been to see her, one doctor or another would be kind enough to talk to me about Carol's case. To me she seemed to live in a kind of soft, cloudy dream. She was pleased to see her baby when it was brought to visit her, but she was not particularly sorry or upset when the baby was taken away. "She had a shock, maybe many shocks," one of the doctors told me (and I could well understand the psychic beating the poor kid might have taken living around Beeman), "so she has in self-defense withdrawn from the world. It is an affliction we call schizophrenia." It was also an affliction that cost—although most certainly I did not grudge it—a lot of money. Nurses' care, medical help, and so on. I suppose poor people just die of it in public madhouses. But, the hell with that. I had the largest share of the Army's rent from our building, and money that you get when your family is in a jam is the luckiest kind of money. No financial problem there at all.

"I expect they're doing the best they can to make her well," I told Jeff. "Don't you still feel it was the best place for her that we could find?"

"Oh, sure, George. It's not that."

"Then what is it, Jeff?"

"It's the baby. I worry about what's going to happen to her in the next couple of years."

Ah, now I thought I had the pitch.

"Don't you worry about that at all, boy," I said. "That part of it's all taped." (I had begun, as you see, to use the language of a new military generation myself.) "All taped. The Friend has day and night service, white and colored, and of the very best. So you can go away feeling happy about that at least, old boy. What branch have you got in mind?"

"What do you mean what branch? You mean like the Army or the Navy?" He looked at me, sitting there with my blue pants on and my blue jacket and greatcoat hanging from the wall, as though I might have been an Ojibway trying to enlist a Quaker for a frontier raid. "Uh-uh," he said, negatively. "I've seen what they're going to have to fight with. The first ones out, as usual, will get their ears shot off."

That's the December-seventh scene that I remember. They say you're crazy if you mentally photograph pictures in color. But I still see this one in color: the color of his corn-colored hair, his rather pale good-looking face, even the pale geranium of his downcast, nonconformist (poor kid) smile. And the picture has sound, too, because it was then—in the pause of my pity and surprise—that the radio concert in the cubicle next door abruptly shut off and we all got the bad news.

Not at that time the worst, the true news, of course. My God, how could they have given us that? All seven of the big ones down and the whole island, until the maneuvering task force came in that forenoon, absolutely defenseless. Nevertheless, what we were told was bad enough.

The man next door said: "Jesus!"

Then up and down the wide old stairs of the club you could hear the murmurs growing into calls and then people shouting.

"Well," I think I said to Jeff, "I guess the balloon's gone up." I know that I got off the bed where we had been sitting and put on my jacket.

"Sure," Jeff said, also rising. "The coldest news of the year. We knew that one was coming."

"Well," I conceded, "I guess we could all have guessed it."

"What I meant to say about the baby," he went on, as though the world had not taken a belly-flop, "was that it may be an embarrassment having her there in your house with Margaret."

296

"Cut it out," I said, getting into the greatcoat. "She's our chaperon."

"No," he said, "I mean an embarrassment to the baby when she gets a little older."

"Wait a minute. You mean we'd compromise the kid?"

"You and Margaret have got to get married, George! I mean it."

"For Christ's sake," I said, "I've got to go to work." I don't believe that I had ever been short with him before, but what did he think we'd been trying to do all these years? He knew.

I certainly didn't bother waiting for the elevator and of course there was no cab in the streets that wasn't filled and going like hell. You could see all ranks running down Seventeenth Street and across the Ellipse and I didn't think that a lieutenant commander needed to walk either.

There were many who got to the BuShips Building before I did.

Everybody came to Washington.

I had a girl who helped me, a girl named Mackenzie from Evanston, Illinois. And where do you guess she went to college? Northwestern; her home town as well as the University's. She had pale-red hair and freckles even in the wintertime and she was a swell kid. She had joined the Waves in a burst of patriotism and by the time she became my secretary or stenographer or whatever you might call it, she had taken on not one but two wars: (1) against her country's enemies and (2) against the Navy. She did her Navy job well, and there was plenty of it to do. But she was also a born scrounger. When everybody else in the building was reduced to smoking cigarettes of a brand you had never heard of— Milady Something-or-other, with a taste so bitter that you knew that they had been made out of a blend of poison ivy and anonymous letters—Mac always had the deck of Chesterfields on my desk every morning until I had to tell her that I didn't want them any more because I had given up smoking. Which I had; it isn't hard to do. All over the earth there must have been many guys who needed Chesterfields more than I did. Or any kind of cigarettes.

Then there was the motor-pool business. Mac had cards for me that Nimitz might have envied. When I told her that I only had to go up to H Street to hit my sack—and walked it—she looked at me with rebellion in her eyes. I got the pitch, of course. All these wonderful kids in the building were competing to see who could do the most for their boss—and in every way. Mac had a hard time in my office that winter in respect to unclaimed luxuries. She made all the touchdowns, but they were always recalled.

Then one evening when I was working a little later than I usually did there came a knock at my door and somebody walked in. I suppose I was surprised because it was rather late at night. I leaned back in my really wonderfully functional chair that the Navy gave us—it supported the skeleton at every part that the poor old skeleton needed it—and I rubbed my eyes to see above the gooseneck service lamp—another triumph of optics, believe you me—and there I saw Joe Priam. I hadn't seen Priam (I know that it's an unbelievable name, but he was a Virginian and one of the students of whom I was fondest in the middle thirties) since we had built the little white-painted brick houses on Route 1 together. I recognized him at once.

"Joe," I said gladly.

"George," he said, "you old rascal."

Now I saw from his uniform that he was a yeoman second class. And, on further inspection, that he was attached to the Construction Battalions. Old acquaintance, I then realized, was not his only pass key to barging in on me and giving me my Christian name.

"How," I asked with some acerbity, "did you get here?"

"We're all in the Navy, George. You and me and the guy down there on the deck."

"Well," I said, "that's for sure. Where have you been? Have you been where there was any trouble?"

"No trouble, George. Johnson's Island. Your friend Ed Cole was there and he told me you were here. What a great guy!"

Ed Cole, of course—my old friend from City Island, the window-worker of my youth.

298

"Do you still have your same old girl friend, George? Margaret, that killer?"

"I think you're drunk, Joe," I said. "You better slide out before I call the patrol."

"Don't do it yet, George." He then produced from his pea-jacket two very large and very embossed tickets. "These," he said, "are for you and your girl." He handed them to me across my gooseneck desk lamp and I looked at them. They purported to be some sort of credentials entitling the bearers to a free dinner at the Occidental Restaurant and later admission to a U.S.O. concert by Glenn Miller and his band at the National Theater the following Saturday night.

I laid them on my desk.

"You Seabee bastards forge these things," I said. "Like samurai swords."

"Not for Margaret, we don't," he said. "I won that pair of ducats in a raffle. At a saloon on Fourteenth Street. It's square. Where is she, George?"

"Same old place."

"I hope she's well. Will you give her my love?"

"I will, Joe. How did you do when you left us and went back home to Virginia?"

"I went into the automobile business."

"That was a very rough time."

"It sure was, George. Well, good night. They got a smoker going on over at the Australian Embassy."

And I bid this wonderful scrounger, too, good night; two masters of arts—the teacher and the taught—once more taking leave of each other under the pressure of unusual historical circumstances.

Next day I gave a colored man a bonus of ten dollars and so I got a room at the Washington Hotel for Margaret for Saturday night. Since it was Saturday, I didn't work later than five o'clock, by which time she was settled down in the place when I got there. It was, of course, raining, but that made it snugger inside. She always made me send my torn clothes home, and was finishing some little patching and darning on a small pile of them when I

299

came in. It was a very domestic scene, with her in the one chair in the room under the one standing lamp in the room and the mending on her lap. There was, of course, also a bed.

When we came downstairs to the Treasury side of the hotel it was pouring buckets. You try to find a taxicab at that place and at that moment in our history.

"I honestly don't want to be a bitch, George," she said, "but these shoes cost me my last ration stamps and they're made out of paper of about the same thickness. Doesn't your work entitle you to anything, darling?"

Well, the Occidental is just down the hill and around the corner and Margaret is such a little thing anyhow, so, as I was myself wearing one of those really good storm coats that they gave us, I picked her up in my arms and started us off for the free lottery dinner, telling her, "Close your eyes, my darling, so you won't get raindrops in them." She got a great chuckle out of that.

The prize of the Seabee raffle, or whatever it was, turned out to be quite on the level. There were, of course, people standing around who had been waiting to eat at the Occidental—and every other place in town—all afternoon. We were given a nice reserved table underneath an autographed photograph of Will Hays and we had Chincoteague oysters, sweetbreads on real Virginia ham, asparagus vinaigrette—the works. Oh, and a liberal amount of bourbon whisky, too.

"Tell me, George," Margaret said when we had our dessert of peach cobbler and another shot of the Virginia Gentleman, "are you really going to win the war by conserving the gas that you might have used tonight by calling out a Navy car? I'm serious." She fixed her eyes on my left shoulder.

And serious she was. But, I'm afraid, at that point I wasn't.

"You bet," I said. "I'm always going to be able to say to my grandchildren that in the Second World War I always did my part. I not only conserved gas but I also made it a point to put the caps back on the beer bottles, like they asked us to."

Her lovely eyes started to cloud. The grandchildren business I should never have brought up; I knew it. She and I would now never even have children, let alone grandchildren. We were too old now, by about ten years, to start that kind of life.

"Please don't cry about the grandchildren crack. I'm so sorry, my darling."

But she didn't weep, as I had expected her to. She just kept looking at my left shoulder.

"Why don't you wear your wings?" she asked.

Well, how do you explain a thing like that? Should I have said: Because I work at a desk? Because I've got a shield on my sleeve instead of a star? Because I'm not now an officer of the line? Because it would be absurd? The only reason I wore the rainbow ribbon was to keep me from looking like a doorman; would that have sounded right?

"I had them but I lost them," I said. "Let's not be late for Glenn Miller."

Outside the Occidental there was now occurring a cloudburst. The marquee was banging around under the buffeting of the rain and there was no cab or car for anyone of any rank in sight until two feeble little lights poked up along the Willard side and the wettest Navy jeep in the world opened its sopping canvas door. The always freckled face of Mac from Northwestern showed itself in the left high corner.

"Come aboard, Commander," she called. "And the Commander's lady," she added. Mac had made some arrangements of her own about the motor pool. At the wheel was one of those Greek gods that they occasionally acquire in the Navy—maybe in the Army, too, for all I know.

What a nice evening. Everybody knows the kind of a show Miller could put on—fifty stands of music that made the hackles rise on the back of your head and rhythm that raised you a little out of your seat. Architectonic. Mac and the god and the jeep were waiting for us when the concert was over. First we went to one of those shrimp palaces on Maine Avenue on the Channel and then we went to a delightful joint at the far corner of Farragut Square, where there was a piano player who could play everything

301

good—Youmans, Rodgers, Gershwin, all the great stuff and no kidding about the harder chord work. He knew the songs and, better still, loved to play them. He knew, notably for Margaret and me, "our" song. It had been our musical signature, you might say, for years and a melody by which we always assayed a piano player's recollection and ability. "Bye and Bye," from *Dearest Enemy*, the first Rodgers and Hart musical comedy:

> *Bye and bye*
> *Not now but bye and bye . . .*
> *Ev'ry cloud just flies on,*
> *Love is on the far horizon,*
> *You'll be my sweetheart*
> *Bye and bye.*

Big night. This man had it cold. The Greek god, another yeoman, liked the song too. Mac adored it. It really is a quite simple but also a quite lovely tune, recommendable particularly for people who are having a hard time getting together.

> *Our happy days will come*
> *Though slight delays will come*
> *The bright sun's rays will come*
> *From out of the sky.*

We were singing it over the shining streets as we began to take each other home. I dropped off for a few moments at the Washington to see Margaret to her room.

"How do you like the war?" I asked her.

"It's lovely, darling. A little like Coney Island on the Fourth of July, don't you think?"

As I kissed her good night at her door she dipped into her handbag and brought out a pair of wings.

"See that you don't lose these, George," she said.

What do you do about a dear, kind woman like that?

In the office next morning Mac had the funniest expression on her face—like a ground hog peeping out of its hole and suffering from a terrible hangover. But a ground hog with a sense of humor, nevertheless.

And so we marched onward to beat the Germans and the Japs.

Bob Mayer came to Washington often, and quite often he got in touch with me and we had lunch or dinner or a drink together.

As a rule, when his call came through I would hear something like this from Mac's end of the line, she sitting at the other end of the room behind a smaller copy of my steel desk: "Yes, this is she. . . . Well, I hardly know you do I? No, not any *particular* Marine. . . . They're so *rough* and so *young.* . . . Myself, I rather go for a more mature type, like a capitalist. Preferably one with journalistic connections." He knew her weakness: great big boxes of illicit candy; and she knew his: a great big forty-five-second telephonic love affair. They got along fine. "Commander," she would then say, "Mr. Mayer is on the wire—Mr. Mayer *from New York City.*"

This particular afternoon, however, there was no persiflage between them. It was the beginning of the second winter of the war, I remember. And raining.

"Mr. Mayer," Mac said, "wants to come over and see you here, right away."

"Why not?"

"Alone."

"Well, sure, why not?"

Not long after, my Phidian friend came in, a Weatherill long-staple Egyptian-cotton raincoat sopping about his shoulders. He blew a kiss to Mac, who promptly disappeared, and held up two fingers toward me.

"Two fast points," he said. This I understood to be part of the feverish argot of the periodical publishing business. "One: Jeff is going overseas for us."

"Good," I said.

"He's spent two years reporting on how the stuff is made; now he goes out to report on how it works in the field. You agree?"

303

"Certainly."

"Point Two: Mary and I are going to get married. That's okay with you, too, isn't it?"

"Which one?"

"Don't be a damned fool, George. Your wife."

"Great," I said.

"For some reason or another I didn't tell Jeff about it. But you'll be hearing from him before he shoves off."

"Oke," I said. We can all be speedy and laconic at times, tycoons and commoners alike.

I heard from Jeff, in fact, before the long wet afternoon was over. It happened to be a bad telephone connection so that we had to do a lot of shouting at each other; the effect was as though he had already left the shore and we had to call very loudly to each other to make the last words between us heard.

"Do you like the idea?" I asked.

"What?"

"Do you like it? Going overseas?"

"No! It's just business!"

"I see. Have you got a soldier suit on?"

"A what?"

"Where are you going?"

"For Christ's sake, George, you know I can't tell you that! You and Margaret take care of my kid, now!"

"Yes, of course! Carol, too!"

"Have you heard from Reagan, George?"

"Who?"

"Ed Reagan!"

"No!"

"Well, you probably will. But my kid—take care of her, George! I've got to go now! The plane's ready!"

"Good-by, boy! Take care!"

"Good-by, George!"

Why would you expect that a boy raised as he was—no roots, no family, no real home—would have the same feeling that we, so much more innocent and so much better cared for, had felt about going to our own war a generation ago?

He was right about hearing from Reagan. It must have been less than a week later when Mac put him on to me.

"George? Ed."

"Yes, Ed."

"I'm in town. I'd like to see you tonight."

"Any time, Ed."

"Well, then, let's combine business with pleasure. Meet me at five o'clock at the F Street Club. Aviation Associates are throwing a party."

"That would have to be more like six-thirty, Ed."

"Why?"

"Because I won't be out of work until then."

"Well—okay."

Aviation Associates was selling small training planes to the Navy and its head man, a plump, good-natured fellow named Eastman, knew very well how to make the little jobs and also how to keep aviators of all ages happy when he gave parties in Washington or New York or elsewhere. He made the place look like recess in heaven; you have never seen such beautiful girls as he was famous for producing for these occasions. He even had English ones, sly and sweet and very amusing with their little proper accents that contrasted so provocatively with their décolletage. I found Ed and after some cordial words with our host and some cheerful gab with the girls, Ed and I made our way to a settee at the back of the entrance hall.

"I was sorry to hear about your father," I told him.

Ed sighed. "He was a fine old man, but we all have to go some day."

"Too bad he didn't live to see us lay it on the Germans the second time. He never liked the Germans very much, did he?"

"No. But what about you, George? I spoke with your nephew Jeff only a month or so ago when he came to visit me at my little factory out in St. Charles. We make a few parts for Eastman there."

305

"Yes, I heard."

"George," he said. "You can't go on like this."

"Like what? What are you talking about?"

"You and Margaret Carton have got to get married. It's not fair to that poor little baby of your nephew's. He told me about how the little thing is living. And Margaret Carton! I knew her well when we were young. It's not fair to a girl like that, George. You must surely see that."

Well, you live long enough and you've heard everything. I thought I'd heard all the real-life Hungarian farce that was coming to me on the afternoon in the old Palm Room of the Tower when Ed had taxed me about how my wife had kept him awake nagging him at night in Pasadena. Somehow, however, I now saw that the transit of his dear old Irish Catholic father's recent death crossing Jeff's conventional protest about his daughter's environment had brought up a new conception in Ed's skull. Margaret, personally, had never so far as I knew ever seen any of the Reagans except on the street.

"I'm making Mary give you a divorce," he said, "and no two ways about it. She does what I say."

"Then what, Ed?"

"Naturally, she and I shall be married."

"And your wife, Ed?"

"The kids are all grown now, and the poor old father is in his grave."

How could I tell him that fifteen or even ten years ago his words and his decision would have made a great difference in the lives of Margaret and myself—when I had asked him for them? How could I tell him that a medieval man would indignantly have slapped his face and maybe run him through with a sword, a Renaissance man would have laughed at him, but a man like myself from the age—I suppose you would call it from the Age of Freud—now felt only numbness and sorrow? It was not because it was too late, this decision of his, to do me any good. No, no; that is only the reaction of pessimism and defeat. And I certainly felt no final elation of victory over him or revenge. Revenge must be the least satisfactory of emotions, after so long a time as Ed and I had locked horns. And I certainly had no will to say to him that this time he had led with his own chin. Why do it?

"Have you seen Mary recently, Ed?" I asked him.

"No. This is the first time I've been able to get East in a couple of months."

"Have you talked with her?"

"Maybe a week or so ago. Why?"

"Well, I expect you will be talking to her soon."

"Naturally. But the point is, are you going to do what I'm telling you to do about Margaret Carton—and for the good of the little baby?"

"Yes," I said. "After Mary divorces me, Margaret and I shall be married."

"I'm glad to hear you take it that way, George, very glad. Will you now have another drink with me?"

"I don't think so, Ed," I said.

"Well, suit yourself."

And so I made my way out through the garden of Mr. Eastman's girls and their young men in uniform and down the steps into F Street, wondering how many hours or even perhaps, now, days ago Mary had been to Guadalajara or wherever it might be to dissolve the ties that had bound her matrimonially to me for so long. And how long she would take to tell Ed Reagan about it.

In those months and years, as I say, everybody came to Washington. I saw Paul Eckfield once in the bar at the Carlton. He was, he told me, connected with the contract division of the Air Force, but he wasn't in uniform. Before we made our good-bys he related a most outrageously long and funny routine about a K Street whore who was saddened by seeing a revival of *Uncle Tom's Cabin.* He was really a quite humorous man. And Beeman I saw more than once, for somehow he, too, belonged to the Metropolitan Club. He was in uniform and he had a job with Strategic Materials and a home out near Arlington he told me, although I was never invited there. He never said anything funny to me, but blasted off quite a lot when we ran into each other about Jeff and Carol.

"I don't know what's wrong with her do you?" he would bellow at me. "She's up there in Baltimore. They tell me I can't see her. Well, that's all right with me. Nut stuff, isn't it?"

"I don't know."

"Well, I'm damned if I'm going to pay for any of it. What do you know about it? Have you any idea what it's all about?"

"Not very much."

"Well, I'm damned if I have, either. For Christ sake, my only daughter. Well, as they say, you never can tell from the wart. . . ." And so forth. "You let the Air Force take your building, didn't you?"

"Yes, they have it."

"Jesus," he said, shaking his head pityingly.

Documents can represent people, too, and here are a couple from the Washington of that period that I came across not long ago among some papers of mine that I had kept from that time. The first one is a fragment from a stenographic report of a conference that I attended which, as I recall it, had to do with an advertising program calculated primarily to call attention to some construction firm's service to the nation but also to salute the institution of awarding Navy "E" flags to particularly enterprising industrial operations concerned in the war effort:

He stated further he would have the 8½ x 11's in four days, but that the flop-over easel presentation would not jell mediawise for two weeks. Of course, the 8½ x 11's are an outline in detail, and as soon as they are buttoned together, he can fancy it up and erect a façade. He wants to kick off with two knowledgeable shirtsleeve men to organize a seed-money group and get the operation into skeleton-scale being, over and above and including the grass-roots conception. If he is asked to firing-pin the spot kickoff figures, his guess-estimate would be $5,000. Without this much, the project would go over like a wet washrag, but $5,000 would sock hardheaded men right between the eyes.

308

I remember the afternoon that Mac laid this curiosity of English speech on my desk. "A souvenir of your visit to Washington, Commander," she said. "I thought you might like to have it." Bright young people can be very harshly critical, not to say fresh. But it takes all kinds of people to fight a war, not the least among them, I suppose, ad men. After all, we were totally mobilized.

And then I have here a letter from Jeff which I must have received at about the same time; it's in the same fiber-board file box. He had been gone for quite a long while and, as you may see, didn't expect to come home very soon. The theater to which he had been accredited was China-Burma-India, and since it was not a very popular one with all war correspondents, he found himself helping publications other than Mayer's with coverage, and Mayer was generous about letting him do the work. It's a rather long letter.

I don't know whether these letters get to you very often and you may have wondered where I have been the last couple of months since I wrote from Delhi. You ask if I am with the foot soldiery. I'm attached to the Mars Force which you may have read about, and am playing the atabrine and vitamin-pill circuit between them, the Kachin resistance army, and the 10th A/F close-support boys. After cleaning up in the area, I hope to go on the first land caravan to China (reopening the Burma Road, as per Uncle Joe Stillwell's plan).

I don't know whether any of my recent stuff has appeared. One story was about the India-China Rescue Squadron, one about the supply droppers, and one on an evacuation hospital. The Chinese patients are right interesting guys and some of them have some amazingly large holes in the old mortal envelope, yet seem to be making out o.k. They use the Orr cast treatment quite a bit and the docs around the hosp. swear by it. I've watched a number of operations—wearing gown, mask and cap, and staring at the bossman's left hand. (That's the one you've got to look out for.) These boys have set up their hospital in bamboo huts and it is right interesting. I saw them take a piece of iron out of a guy's center of musical appreciation so when he feels better they will ask him to sing a tune to see how much damage was done. Pretty hard to tell in a Chinese. I have heard them singing in their wards and it doesn't sound quite as well as the March of Time radio chorus giving out with Chi-Lai.

It's really true about the Chinese people. They're swell. It would take a hundred pages to write just what I've observed—I've drawn no conclusions, merely wish to affirm that you become aware of the value of the common Chinese almost immediately and almost instinctively. All they need is birth control, health officers in the cities, a fresh deck, and a reasonably honest cut. I know that it has been said that they, like the Indians, "don't even get along among themselves"—Commie v. Kuomintang, warlords, etc. That is like saying, while robbing a man's house, that he doesn't get along with his wife and hasn't spoken to his son-in-law for six months.

The saddest thing to see, though, is an American grave. They come from so far—farther than any American has ever come to fight (if he came any farther he would be back on his way around the world toward home again)—and when they die you feel that they have had so much more to lose than the others.

I spent my 32nd birthday carrying a 75 lb. pack up 4,000 ft. to visit a detachment of Kachin partisans whose leaders proved to be two Princeton guys of the classes of 39 and 34. If you haven't got a family, or I mean much of a family, then I guess people like these are your family. I see what you mean. We got drunk on the local grog, called Lak'hu, and joined in a impressive war dance around the bones of an L-1 which had made an unsuccessful attempt to land in this eyrie. It was sort of like Carver Doone's hideaway, except that on one side you could see the smoke rising from the ruins of Bhamo and on the other, China.

I wouldn't say that I'm a Christian yet, George, but maybe half a Christian. And you were always right in not worrying too much about "what was in the cash register," as you said my father used to say. I haven't heard much from Carol, of course. Nor, of course, from my kid. Do you ever hear anything of Peter Maben or his sister Eileen what's-her-name? I sent a Jap .25 rifle to Margaret but I doubt if she ever got it. They steal that sort of thing fast in the A.P.O.

When, my Commander, will this cruel war be over? After we've lowered the boom on the Nips I know what I'm going to insist on: 5,000 Chinese drivers turned loose in the streets of Tokyo. What a holocaust.

Yr's aff'ly,

MACARTHUR

Just as we all remember the afternoon of Pearl Harbor I'm sure all of us have our own very personal recollections of the early September afternoon, a Saturday, when it was announced by President Truman that the Japanese had surrendered. There was excited noise all over the BuShips Building and when Mac came back, having verified the announcement, she prepared to set off for the nearest liquor store, because all military personnel were being given the afternoon off as well as the Sunday which was coming up. "Everybody in the world," she said, "will have his tongue hanging down to his knees. First come, et cetera. I'm putting you a call through to Mrs. Pierce: you take it from there. Gas rationing's over, too—get it?"

I don't know what many of the other Americans did on that memorable Saturday, of course, but I know what Margaret and I did. She filled up the tank of the old LaSalle and I climbed on a well-loaded train and we met at Elkton, Maryland, and got married. Here's a funny, or maybe a pathetic, recollection. We were so confused—or perhaps so stunned or beat-up after waiting all those years—that the short-order j.p. who married us had to tell us to kiss each other after he had performed the ceremony.

We lit out for Cape May after the knot was tied and arrived well after midnight in that paradise of Victorian rooming houses whose white paint on carpenter gothic was so plastered coat-on-coat that behind the scattered street lights they gave the appearance, appropriately I thought, of a whole village of softly glowing wedding cakes. It was a wonderful shining morning next day. We surfed until noon on the finest, widest, flattest beach in America, then had two or three drinks and some Maine lobsters for lunch, after which we went around to the telegraph station in the little old railroad depot to let interested parties in on our news.

V-J Day plus one; one day after the titular end, if you count them properly, of the sixteenth American war.

Sixteen

Two American wars had been enough for the Tower; the second one put an end to it as a commercial enterprise. The premonition of my nephew Jeff and the baleful foresight of Mr. Beeman had proved correct. When it was turned back to me the interior of the building was ruined.

I could understand this; it's not hard to understand. The kids that were trained there were bomber navigators. Naturally they were nervous; no, frightened, terrified. No American fighting man has ever been prepared for action with such a cold, certain, actuarial knowledge of his chance of survival: if you went twenty missions the chances were three against five that you would be killed. As deathly simple as that. And of course the longer the course of missions the shorter your chance of survival. Who wouldn't be nervous, with that kind of foreknowledge? And of course they all knew it.

The doomed men of Sparta upset the sacred statues in despair the night before they had to sail against Troy. The men of the Air Force, these navigation cadets, class after class tore the old Tower's insides apart.

Barney took me over the abandoned classrooms and dormitory areas. There wasn't a door that had not been shattered, apparently at the beginning by thrown case knives. "Toward the end they went after them with bottle ends," Barney said. "No more panels left to whang the knives at."

The last class had wrenched the old standing bathtubs away from their plumbing connections, as a sort of celebration of freedom I suppose, and dragged them up and down the halls as though they were sleighs. That put an end for good and all to the poor old furrowed carpets. Why the boys twisted the electrical fixtures and elevator gratings away from their hangings I couldn't quite see. That kind of savagery must have required so far much more muscle power and malice than the mere breaking of the walls and paneling and the kicking apart of the furniture. Oh, my brother. . . .

But they had even smashed the tables and chairs of their own canteen, the old Rathskeller. That I couldn't quite understand.

"What kind of a commanding officer did they have here, Barney?"

"The boys used to date his wife," Barney said.

Well, many and many a man has been chewed up in the defense of the Republic. And of course much, much matériel. I guess the Tower got banged up in a good cause. No, I mean in the best of causes.

Paul Eckfield, of course, was the man who represented the War Department in the matter of the claim that I made for the damage that had been done to the Tower. I say "of course" because the longer you live the more resigned you become to the inescapability of the wheels-within-wheels relationships in life. I had a Leica full of photographs to show him of the interior wreckage of the building, but he didn't want to see any of it.

"You think that I'm a jerk, don't you?" he said.

"No, Paul, I don't," I said, and honestly didn't.

"Well, you sure will now."

"What do you mean?"

"What's your claim?" he asked.

And I told him.

"You couldn't get fifteen per cent of it, George. Honest to God, I'm telling you the truth."

"Why not, Paul? Don't the indemnity clauses I've got here from the government mean anything? They've wrecked my building. I'm out of business."

"Not a chance. And you know that if there was anything I could do for you I would."

I winced at the now negative subjunctive which had taken the place of that age-old philanthropic offer of Paul's. But he was not a really bad man and I hope that I have never given a bad impression of him.

"Well, then, what-ho, Paul?"

"We can't have a scandal. This joint of yours was run scandalously."

"Not by me, Paul."

"Did you ever hear"—and then he told me the name of a hotel out at the end of Long Island and another one in Florida where the installations had also been taken apart and for which the government was simply not going to pay indemnity. Both resort hotels, I reflected: not one of those hard-to-get city places that Kaffey wanted to acquire, like the Tower. But never mind.

"So, no dice?" I said.

"No dice, George," he said. "You might have had a better chance if any of the owners had been on active service, that's the policy of the War Department."

"I see," I said.

Then, with Nat Pierce at my sleeve, I tried another tack. I called Congressman Kaffey.

"John," I said, "the Air Force boys wrecked my building and they won't pay me for it."

"Why, that's terrible, George, but what can I do?"

"I don't want any money from Uncle Sam, John. I just want a lot of surplus carpets and furniture so I can get back in business. And fast. And cheap. You guys must have warehouses full of it."

"Oh, golly, George, I wouldn't know where any of that stuff is. Why don't you let me put you on to my secretary?"

"Why don't you go—?" Nat Pierce slapped me on the arm and I shut up.

314

"This is an election year, George, and I'm busier than a one-armed paperhanger."

"This is the first year after the war, John, and I'm trying to get my hotel and office building back in business."

"George—now listen to me, George." Here it came, antiphonally, Ralph Bellamy of Great Barrington, the tribune of the people, the former American Legion State Commander. "Suppose you had irreplacably lost a loved one, a dear one, in the war. You didn't though, did you, George?"

"No, we all got through all right."

"Then if you had lost a brother, a son, a father—do you know how much compensation you would have coming to you from the United States Government, at the maximum?"

"I lost my family's building. It's got to be torn down because of what some of your crazy people did to it."

"Ten thousand dollars, George," the Congressman equably continued.

And of course in his way the Congressman had a very good point.

"Okay, John."

"About those carpets, I honestly don't know."

"Sign off," Nat Pierce said.

The wound tends to anneal, the skin to cover the surface; often it is a sounder skin than before. Certainly that was true of the University after the war. What a congress of bright young undergraduate minds they were, how serious, how many, and how married. And in its well-ordered way the organization of the foundation itself had to flex its wings a bit so as to mother its larger brood of new young. There were expansions—always within reason (for we at Princeton do not unhealthily proliferate)—in train for certain departments, and one of them was Art and Archeology. This is what the University used to say when it really meant the Department of Architecture—much as Yale, so self-consciously unassuming, prefers to refer to itself as New Haven. Anyhow, having done my service in the building Navy, I thought I had something rather good coming to me. In fact, I was damned sure of it. Well, let's not kid around with mechanical suspense. Here's how it worked out. There is nothing in the world that, for me, I would ever want to be more than a professor of Architecture at Princeton University. It is a small school but there are those who love it. So many good men: Baldy Smith, Franny Comstock, Labatut, all the rest, never mind. Anyhow, I got this summons, you might say, to come and see my favorite trustee, the one who lived in my old air-space over the East River at Beekman Place. And of course I went.

There were just the three of us at dinner: the trustee, his wife, and myself. She, one of those good-looking, slim-figured, and now silver-haired types from Long Island, kept up a long banter about a grandson of theirs who was a freshman at Dartmouth. It seemed that the boy's father had gone to Dartmouth, and one of the things that tickled her, since it was blowing a gale of snow outside, was what the weather must be like in Hanover that night. Her grandson, who had up to that year attended school at Lawrenceville, must be getting his first taste of the New Hampshire winter climate, as contrasted with that of New Jersey. We all smiled as she developed this thought.

But I was thinking all the while of other, much older images.

Here, almost exactly here, was where the man had given away the white police dogs one night so long ago when I had owned Number Three Beekman Place. This was almost the same room, before my old brownstone had been torn down and the site rebuilt, where the call had come through to tell me that young Jeff had deserted school in Pasadena, and where the headmaster of his boarding school had later called to tell me that the boy had been caught cheating. Here was where the design of the Sheffield hospital had been made, after Bob Mayer had brought Congressman Kaffey up to see me. Margaret and I had looked out of windows, placed almost exactly where these were now placed, on the Fourth of July morning before we set out for Coney Island. Polachek had attempted to suborn me—no, as it turned out he *had* suborned me —on the floor that was now the floor of his apartment.

316

We moved into the trustee's study, his wife excusing herself on the grounds of wishing to put in a phone call for Teddy, the grandson in Hanover, to ask him if he now did not wish he had gone to the other shop. The trustee was a man of considerable civilization and taste. His study, almost exactly where my old sitting room had been, was hung with small Audubon oils. The Audubon elephant folios were kept in a case against the south wall. On the north wall hung one of Audubon's tiny little specimen shotguns, where Margaret had wanted to put the break-front cabinet that she had bought on the eve of my giving the use and rental of my old house to my former wife Mary. When the house was sold as part of the land parcel that was to make place for the present apartment dwelling, I had put the proceeds at the disposal of Jeff for Carol's medical care.

I had been a guest in the trustee's apartment on several occasions since my first visit there, but not since the war. Perhaps that was why this procession of ghost scenes had come to haunt me tonight.

"George, I must tell you something right at the beginning," the trustee said. "There is nothing we would rather have than a member of your family on the faculty of the School of Architecture. In fact, I for one think that the school should be named after your brother. We all ought to get down on our knees and thank God that he was a student there. Your brother surely has been its most distinguished graduate up to now."

I murmured some sort of appreciation.

"But—now. . . ."

But now what, I wondered. He was looking about on the ceiling for help to his words; much, I found myself thinking, as Paul Eckfield had once done the same thing, trying to find the words that would tell me some unwelcome but important news.

"Let's put it this way," the trustee continued with that kind of a tight smile that a civilized man wears when he knows that he is going to hurt someone whom he bitterly does not want to hurt. "In the high empyrean of a trustees' meeting we even discuss full professorships, even potential heads of departments. Your name has come up, and I might say for full discussion."

317

I had nothing to say.

"George, there were two men to whom this job was open. You and another." He stopped looking at the ceiling and turned his eyes, which I believe were slightly moist, to mine.

"I see," I said.

"No, I don't think you do see. But I'm the one who was told off to do this bloody job, so I'm going to try to make you see."

"Go ahead," I said.

"Between the two of you—you and this other man—there is absolutely nothing to choose professionally. As architects, and teachers of architecture, you both possess what I would call truth and poetry, the art of harmonizing the useful and the agreeable, the necessary and the beautiful. I'm cribbing somebody else's words, of course."

"Why go on?" I asked him. "This is painful to you."

"No. This has to be done."

"Why?"

"What tipped the balance against you, George, and a small tipping it was because we fought it out among ourselves for some time—for an hour or so, anyhow—was your personal record."

"My what?"

"Look, George: that strange God-damned marriage in St. Louis. Having to leave town." He now began to tick off my old transgressions on his fingers as I suppose they must have been ticked off in the trustees' room in Nassau Hall the last time the body of our governorship had met there. "That business of the Sheffield hospital—oh, I know it was long ago. Then of course your friendship with the man who—the man who left you the ownership of your building out there."

"Wouldn't you like to add my living with my present wife in the Borough all these years before I could get a divorce and marry her?"

"How about a drink?" he asked.

"No," I said. "I guess I see how the scales were tipped." I got up.

"Where are you going?"

"I've got to catch the train back," I said.

318

"I hope you understand, George."

"I sure do," I said.

Black night. Black luck. Black fate. And noise, the clanging inexorable noise of the steel wheels of the coach crashing away at seventy miles an hour along hundred-and-twenty-pound steel rails. What a seething black turbulence of mind and memory this scene recalls to me.

Was it that I had never believed that I—as an individual, as George Hanes—had ever had any particular importance? Was that why they felt that they could fault me for a job that I wanted very badly, the job which I had thought for these long last years I might be best fitted? The scales, the trustee had said, had been tipped against me. By whom, for the love of God? In my anger, the answer came back: by everyone in your life except you. You are nothing. You are a man without importance.

But no, that wasn't true. I had always felt pretty good about myself, my values, and my value. I had learned for myself and then taught others the order and discipline of the art of architecture, and a stern discipline it is, and a thing of value. "Truth and poetry," in the trustee's borrowed words. Nothing was of more importance, it seemed to me.

But it was as obvious to me now as the slanting sleet across the flying black-sooted windowpane at my side that in certain circumstances one's importance might be stolen away, even flung away by oneself. By bad luck? In that case the train of my misfortune would go all the way back to my brother Jeff's first meeting the Kansas City banker's daughter whom he married. And yet could you blame all of your ill luck on another, I wondered. Perhaps it came from the displeasure of God himself, were he really an old-fashioned, half-pagan, capricious or vengeful God. Genes; maybe some twentieth-century fate of metabolism hadn't given me the right collection or galaxy or whatever it was of these intricate personal cells to make my way successfully in the world. Or was it some unlucky tragic complex of all these alien befallen circumstances? I didn't know.

But this, I told myself, I did know. It was my own sense of

319

order—a pattern raked, as it were, neatly together; kept together out of all this trash of life—that had compelled me to the doom of preserving a work of art, the Tower. It was the teacher's, the curator's talent, his compulsion. It had made me, at considerable cost, conserve the memory and the reputation of a great artist like Jeff to the brink—and beyond, I now realized—of self-immolation. And so, because one might not be important as an artist, then one gladly threw one's life away as a conservator? Or, more particularly, because your artist brother died leaving you an almost insoluble domestic scandal behind him? No, damn it, no. Believe me, I was now not glad to have thrown my life away.

The train banged on, jerking and plunging crazily into the night.

Now, at last, I knew that it *did* matter what became of me, now that it was too late. Of course I had importance—to me and to those whom I loved, at any rate. The wounds given an idealist hurt deep. The wounds, self-inflicted or not, to a romantic hurt even deeper. What good to me, in the end, were either of these tattered roles of mine? The cost to me had been too high for what I had lost that night. Far too high. Jeff was long since dead under my chaste tombstone above his head in Bellefontaine Cemetery. And the ashes of Junie, too, were somewhere cold. And yet all their old mischievous circumstances still curled around me. Rebellion seized me. You can take it, as Bob Mayer once said, but you don't have to like it. It occurred to me on that crashing journey to Princeton Junction that at long sweet last I had had about all the self-immolation that was coming to me. I was sore.

At the Junction and in the sleet I got off and took a cab home.

I didn't go into the sitting room where the light was on and where I knew that Margaret was waiting with a fire going. I went into the office on the other side of the archway and I pulled out from the files Jeff's old sketches of his unbuilt masterpieces, and from the wall I tore off the glass-framed willow branches that had flown from the topped-out steel of the Tower.

Then I went across the archway and into the sitting room, carrying the stuff with me.

320

Margaret looked up, startled of course, as I barged in.

"Here it goes!" I said, moving on the blazing fireplace.

"George!"

"Every God-damned bit of it!"

She saw now what I had in my arms and where I was heading for, and she ran in front of me. I certainly didn't push her but as she ran into me she fell backward. I grabbed at her as well as I could with my arms filled as they were but she had already started to go backward. There was a splintering of wood and a crash of glass as the lamp behind her fell and a spurt of blue light as the lamp smashed and went out. Then we were down on the floor together, the glass of the framed willow branches cracked but the pile of Jeff's drawings safe on the carpet beside us.

She got her breath first.

"Do you know what you were doing?"

"Yes," I said.

She raised herself up from the floor and with her fingers brushed the moisture from my cheeks.

Looking then around her at the cracked glass of the willows' frame and at the wreckage of what she had gone over against, she said in the gentlest of reproof, "The Phyfe candlestand, George. The Troy astral lamp."

"Yes," I said, "I know."

Then she stood up.

"Never you mind, dearest," she said. "It can all be mended. It can all be kept."

Part III

Seventeen

A GOOD day has to begin, as all days do, at the end of the day before. "Unsettled" had been the official word that the Weather Bureau had used for the day before. For this present one the Bureau had chosen "fair." And yet who among us, even the far-flung Weather Bureau, can with confidence put a name on tomorrow?

Down from the Upper Appalachians and the Blue Ridge, as they often do in this part of the East and at this time of the year, came mean and ghostlike swirling shrouds of rain. They gave the almost colorless autumn hillsides of Alexandria a thorough and depressing soaking. That was what was holding up the funeral and making all of us devilishly bored and nervous. And that was what was the last and most galling delay, I knew, to what was keeping Jeff from getting to Eileen Maben—Eileen George had been her married name—the pathetically apparent "Eileen what's-her-name" of his war letters. For, whatever long days had been bad for them in the past, this one was to be the beginning of many long perfect ones. The old long bad ones must have been by now, and at considerable pain, pushed aside at last, expiated. This was the one that was to be their good day, and how I wished them the happiness of it.

325

I, myself, was a witness at these watery obsequies largely for the reason that I had been in Washington for the purpose of winding up at last the almost interminable paper work by which the government finally and officially returned to me my ruined building. When I had heard about the funeral I had telephoned Jeff and met him with a cab at the Union Station. That had been some hours before.

And now, about three o'clock, the low flat flying clouds that had been angrily feinting back and forth beneath and above each other all afternoon suddenly dispersed without either side winning a victory, and the rain ceased to fall. In front of the gray stucco portico of the headquarters of the Arlington National Cemetery our little cortege began to form.

From the parking lot a few yards to the right three span of patient old drenched and faintly steaming white horses mounted by three enlisted men in waterproof gear, equally and quite as obviously enduring, brought up the caisson. Then from behind us where we stood under the short Ionic columns came the chaplain, from whose expression I got the notion that he preferred the full-panoplied service in the Fort Meyer chapel rather than one of these short-order ones for those merely shipped into the rear of the mortuary for interment. Following behind the Army chaplain, six more enlisted men wearing very white gloves stoically brought out the flag-draped casket and placed it upon the caisson. A lieutenant in Peel boots, who obviously disliked getting too much of the soles wet on the slopping pavement and whose rank was so junior on the post that he had yet to receive a really top-grade formation with an escort and a band, tiptoed to his position at the rear wheel of the still rain-glistened olive-drab funeral car. The order of procession was now established this way: chaplain in command car, horses and riders, lieutenant, three pallbearers on either side of the caisson, and of course the corpse.

There followed a small period of hesitation among the five of us civilians still on the steps of the portico. The lieutenant tiptoed back to us and murmured: "Okay, folks. Let's go."

"Who goes first?" my niece Mary asked, a little sharply it seemed to the lieutenant, and to me, too. This was a bit of a stumper.

You could be very sure that the officer had memorized the regulations, and so, indeed, had an old crock like me: *All wishes of the next of kin are to be considered as paramount considerations, so long as they are in keeping with basic military usage and the principles of good taste—Section II, 4a. Conduct of a Military Funeral, War Department Pamphlet No. 21-39, September 1947.*

By a slight perplexed gesture the lieutenant moved his hat a little toward the rear of his head and by some impulse not foreseen in Pamphlet No. 21-39, said: "Jeez, I don't know, Mrs. Houghton."

My niece thereupon gave her husband an impatient push. "All right, Jeff," she then said to her brother, "you and Uncle George go ahead in your ghastly green taxicab. After all, he was *your* father-in-law. Edward and I will follow you." Edward, her husband, was a man named Edward Houghton, not a bad little fellow at all.

Edward was what you might describe as a stock character in old-time fiction—a dude. His family, or perhaps it was his family's family, had made fortunate investments. The Solvay process or something like that. Anyway, Ed had inherited a lot of money and he now raised some sort of rare and fancy cattle—Devons, I think, to be really snobbish toward the neighboring Angus people —and hunted foxes on horses around Warrenton in the Valley of Virginia. A stock character, as I say. The kind of a man who doesn't want any trouble but I expect that my niece Mary gave him quite a bit of it. Her manners were formed in California, poor child.

Jeff tried quietly and diffidently to protest about the order of his father-in-law's funeral procession. I think it was some idea of ladies first, God knows why.

"Come on," I said. I put two fingers to my mouth and whistled for our cab. The effect was to send the lieutenant hurrying back to his solemn post and to bring a radiant green hack whizzing and splashing out of its parking space. Jeff and I embarked.

Next due to depart were of course Mr. and Mrs. Edward Houghton, but there was a slight hitch. Mr. Houghton attempted to escort Mrs. Houghton down the few steps to the driveway by touching her under one karakuled arm. This attention she shrugged off, commanding him instead: "Go and get it and hurry up."

327

"It will take a moment to get the tarp off."

"Just for God's sake go and get it," requested Mrs. Houghton steadily.

In a few moments a two-seater, tomato-colored Allard with an exhaust sound like the rip of the most enormous piece of canvas in the world cut up in front of the portico and Mrs. Houghton climbed in beside Mr. Houghton. How could I help recalling Ed Reagan's striking red Winton at my brother Jeff's funeral so many years ago?

Then, with the tired resignation of an overweight old character actress knowing that this was her final tour with this company, the last of us five mourners pulled her Lenten purple satins inside her Cadillac limousine with no assistance from her chauffeur, who looked to be a very recent honor graduate of Howard University. "Just trail along behind Mr. Beeman's funeral, Erskine," she wearily directed, settling herself on the silken upholstery. This I heard, for none of us in our cars could have been ten yards apart.

"Yessum, Mrs. Cox," he agreed. "Any way you want it."

And so, curving along Wilson Drive, Memorial Drive (here the entrance to the Cenotaph), Porter Drive, past MacArthur Circle (named for the earlier MacArthur), down the curling wet dark roads and under the old leafless despairing trees went the funeral procession of young Jeff's father-in-law, who was also playing *his* final show in this company. Cast across every tired curve of the long rolling hillside were scattered the uncountable small gravestones. Whatever Cadmus had sowed these square dragon's teeth, he would not raise warriors again. For that kind of crop this was the last and most barren field.

"Plot Four," I said with amazement when we had come to the open grave under the hill a few yards back from Jessup Drive. "How in the hell do you suppose he ever managed it? Boy, I don't know about you, but I'm going to find me a different burying ground." My nephew rebuffed me with a sharp sibilant.

"Sh-h-h!"

We had arrived at the site. The firing squad, which had been waiting for us, shuffled for a moment and then formed two smart lines at the far end of the yellow clay hole. We dismounted, Jeff and I. The others followed. I pointed my stick up to that ghastly little black obelisk that old Dewey lies under. And I said to my nephew: "What do you want to bet he isn't spinning like a pinwheel?" A commonplace remark, it seemed to me.

"You've really got to behave yourself," Jeff told me.

Whether or not we wanted the short-order service, the chaplain gave it to us. About all that I recall of the ceremony was "I am the resurrection and the life" and the three volleys, so muted in the wet steel-gray air that they did not reverberate even from the closest bare slopes. Then like professional gymnasts the Army pallbearers lifted the flag from the top of the casket and with half a dozen intricate well-practiced gyrations in only a few moments reduced the whole great national standard to a mere triangle of three stars. This the lieutenant received and handed to Jeff. And taking this, Jeff, looking across the lowered casket at Mrs. Cox standing alone in her lavender and expensive and unbecoming clothes—clothing in which most people who saw her would, I expect, heartlessly assay as worth many times the poor gross old body which wore it—Jeff took this triangle of fine bunting and walked around the grave and put the flag into the arms of Mrs. Cox.

I took that very kind of him.

He didn't wait—or wish, I suppose—to see her face. Instead he returned to express the family's—well, the in-laws'—thanks to the lieutenant, who by this time must have believed that he had seen about everything unstylish that an Arlington funeral could offer. But the lieutenant was wrong, for only a moment later Mrs. Edward Houghton approached her brother and asked: "How is Eileen?"

"Just fine thanks. I'm going to see her in New York tonight. Little later than I thought but—"

"I was not speaking of that tramp that you say you are going to marry," she said in a subdued but strictly cadenced voice. This is sister talking to brother, you understand. "I was speaking of my *niece* Eileen. Poor Carol's little daughter. Come on, Edward."

"Let's go, boy," I said to my nephew. "We've missed two trains already."

The obsequies were definitely over.

329

As Jeff and I climbed into our colorful cab, down again came the rain. It pursued us up Dewey Drive, along Patton Drive, beyond some impressive masonry that through the slanting fall could be seen as called Treasury Gate and on and on until the distant sprawl of the Pentagon on the far right vanished and the Memorial Bridge with its turns and crowding cars full of straying and dismayed strangers from elsewhere in the Union began to haunt our fenders, and then we navigated in a long round swish of street water the front of the Lincoln Memorial.

Well, you always like to think of something cheerful to say at the end of a funeral, particularly on a rainy day, so I observed: "Old what's-his-name didn't do too badly on that thing, you know."

"I thought you always said it even loused up the postage stamp, George," Jeff absently said. He was more interested in observing the circling and neighboring fenders.

"Changed my mind. Not badly design-ed."

Design-ed. The three-syllabled pronunciation of the word by Sullivan—handed to Jeff's father and to Wright, and thence of course to me, the self-appointed last custodian. Jeff didn't listen.

"Not badly design-ed at all," I repeated, to get his attention. "But why didn't what's-his-name do the truly and magnificently obvious?" I was only trying to convey the light touch.

"Okay. What would that have been, George?"

"Even a fool could have seen it. Or at least revised it correctly. Place those nice big Doric columns not vertically but lay them horizontally, one along top of the other all around the joint as the four walls. Make a kind of a mammoth Hellenic log cabin—you get it? Much more appropriate for Lincoln, although it might have comprised a somewhat smaller edifice of course. They could probably have saved all of the marble roof; keeping it flat, as though it were sad," I said. "You must agree."

"Oh, sure," Jeff said, but with preoccupation. He was worrying about the death of his father-in-law, I could understand. And also about the death of his wife.

330

Now we had long since passed the shrine of the Emancipator and were six deep in the early-evening traffic of Constitution Avenue. We were in my old terrain. The rain made a close gray backdrop behind. As usual, I thought. The foreground was an equally interminable line of rain-beaded, green, and aluminum Capital Transit buses. And lifelessly, block after block of Naval officers with briefcases and civilian women with newspapers over their heads stood absolutely motionless in the rain in front of the interminable, imperishable old "temporary buildings."

Why? It was not possible now that the veriest Molly Pitcher or Nathan Hale of them all could abide their present situations, I thought, nor indeed their miserable jobs. Why had they taken them? Not for joy or love or patriotism surely. For three thousand four hundred (tax deductible) dollars a year? What for? To stand that way—after sitting in line precisely eight hours behind our old green steel desks—to stand now in the rain in line? On your two hands could you no doubt number them, the people who truly and knowingly loved their country. For the rest, contempt of themselves and what they did must be hideous. Not anything like pushing that long-ago frail implement of war of mine out of a tent and into a slough, I thought. Nor even, with Mac from Northwestern, trying to win a war in this same place. But then, those emotions came from a dream so long distant.

"Damn it all," I suddenly said, "I'm glad I went to that funeral."

With an effort Jeff pulled his eyes back from the Capital Transit buses and the passengers who awaited them.

"Why, George?"

"I wanted to be sure they would really plant him there. I couldn't believe they'd have the guts."

"Come on, George. He had a President's Commission just like you did."

"I'm finding myself a new boneyard and I advise you to do the same," I told him.

"That's one place they don't let you into on a press pass," he said.

331

Well, this shocked me. "You wore the uniform, Jeff," I reminded him, "just like everybody from Eisenhower down. Don't forget that."

"Except that Eisenhower's arm didn't have a green brassard with a white C on it," he said.

"What do you think this Beeman wore," I asked him, "plumes and a red-white-and-blue cockade?"

"They needed procurement men in a hurry. He knew the hardware business inside and out. He did his duty. And it cost him plenty."

"Cost him what? I always thought he made his living sticking up silk trains," I said. "At least his face had the look of it."

"This is not like you, George, this misanthropic, dog-in-the-manger stuff."

"Well, maybe it isn't but I'm getting to be a mean old man. I'm just remembering that he killed your wife before she was born."

"No," Jeff said, "I killed her. Some time after she was born."

The cab thereupon made an intricate and gallant passage of shining wet streetcar tracks and stopped under the vast canopy of the Union Station.

"We'll have to take our chances on seats," I said. "You call your Eileen in New York. The Friend ought to be either eating supper or getting washed up or on her way to bed by now. Skip her. Margaret has that detail. What the hell did that sister of yours—"

"Never mind, George," Jeff said.

When Jeff came out of the telephone booth he found his elder kinsman in a restless mood. I guess that I was muttering something about the fake Baths of Caracalla that this fake railroad shed represented and pushing exploratively with my cane not only about the columns of the rotunda but among the magazines displayed within a kiosk of the Union News Company.

"See this stuff?" I remember asking him, pointing exactly to the navel of a four-color print of a young woman on a magazine cover. "No good," I told him. "Like the whole corrupt building. Twenty-five years ago they'd have put you in jail for trying to send that sort of pornography through the mail."

"They don't send it through the mail, George. It has to go by express." Jeff pressed us onward toward the train gate. "If you ask me," he said, "I think you're going down with your generation." That sort of stopped me.

When we got to the bar car (Elks Club was the rowdy name of it and it pleased me for I have always had a taste for low life) I fell into my seat and rang the nearest bell. Nothing for a long time happened. Jeff gave me a copy of the *Star* which he found on a near table.

Suddenly the *riposte*, as one might say, came to mind: "As to that last crack of yours, I may be going down, but I'm holding my nose!"

To his credit, Jeff amiably nodded. Then you could hear the long tin-drum spatter of the rain on the roof of the motionless car. Soon the car would begin to take Jeff to his elder Eileen.

That thought was an agreeable one. Somebody young in our family, just once in a while, just on the actuarial basis, ought to be happy—at least once in a while.

The rain, the Pullman seat's prickly olive- and arsenic-colored upholstery, the finicky-patterned stencil in blood and gold enlived on the cornice above the car's smooth mud walls—all this was somehow restful and familiar as we sank back and then looked at our watches to see if the train would get off precisely on the hour.

How much of one's whole family's life, I suddenly thought— its defeats and victories, its promises and penalties—had been almost wholly experienced within whistle cry of the main line of the Pennsylvania Railroad System: Washington to New York; North Philadelphia to St. Louis.

The four o'clock got off on time.

The muted disks of the undercarriage of the car Elks Club picked up a sure beat from the rail joints as the train outreached the terminal shed, and instantly twilit hachures were architec-

333

turally drawn across the sooty faces of the windows by the exactly slanting rain. Now, as the rhythm of the wheels accelerated, almost everyone in the Elks Club simultaneously began stabbing at the little bell buttons on the putty-colored steel walls outboard their gently rocking chairs. The porter came first to us to take our order.

"Spring water for me. Soda for the other gentleman. Both Scotch, both big glasses."

Jeff's eyes followed the porter as he went back up the aisle to his galley and as they did so Jeff's gaze perfunctorily began to fall upon fellow travelers.

I looked up the aisle with him at a woman and her young child. The eyes of the woman, a rather young woman, were tired but complacent. The eyes of the child, I was startled to observe, were fixed on mine. And, I at once recognized, their regard upon me held an immutable neutrality. This little girl had not yet passed over into the warring country of adulthood. She was taking no sides. She was, I guessed, about nine years old. That made her about the age of young Jeff's Eileen.

Jeff, young Jeff—but why do I have to keep calling him that, his father Jeff so long in his grave? And Mary, his sister, *little* Mary, Jeff's mother being named Mary, too. Call the latter *Mother* Mary? Well, scarcely, if you put any store by the great Christian significance of that name.

"Was that really why you called her Eileen?" I suddenly asked.

"What?"

"Did you really have the guts to make your wife name your kid after your girl friend?"

"No. I just thought it was a lovely name. Carol did, too."

"Well, it's a great tradition in the family," I said, "double names."

"Be's a dollar and eighty cents," the porter said at my shoulder.

"Here's one for the road," Jeff said, picking up his change.

This was such an old ceremony between us that Jeff did not even look around at me, merely and alone lifting the frosting glass from the round face of the aluminum stand.

"What road?" I asked.

334

"I guess the Pennsylvania will do."

"Suits," I agreed, watching the night come down outside.

The railroad conductor simply took our first-class tickets. But the Pullman man, taking our returning but unassigned passages, was grave.

"You got no reservation here, you know. You just have these seats till Baltimore."

"Yes," Jeff said, "we know that."

"Well, I don't know yet about seats for you," the Pullman conductor said, a kind of institutional peevishness springing automatically to his lips.

"That's all right," Jeff said. "We're already sitting in them," Jeff said, very patiently. So gently, in fact, that the man went away and left us alone. Christians, I reflected, far-traveled Christians, have a quiet flair for this kind of thing.

"Baltimore!" the club-car attendant shouted from the corridor.

Baltimore. Jeff and I knew something of Baltimore. The tall brick lofts of the Calvert distillery came darkly past the train windows. So then it must be off on about a course 110 from here that the hospital was where Carol died.

I am not so primetive [yes, she wrote it primetive] that I do not understand my need for all the modern medicine. I am not aboriginal. You must have some sort of hole in your head if you think I have.

Carol's last letter, the one that brought Jeff down for his last trip to Baltimore to see her, had read about the same as all the ones before that one that had made him go there month after month. But this last one, this last letter from Carol, I suppose, he would remember longest:

I think you may think that you are very smart about putting me here and about having Eileen and George and Margaret and Mary your sister to yourself. That's just holes in all of you. I'm not primetive. You see?

How you spell X?

335

They had said at the sanitarium that there was nothing to worry about. Mrs. Hanes' letter to Mr. Hanes, the one of that week, was not at all irrational—she was just seeking a child's and husband's love. Jeff had said that it seemed to him that he had found Carol looking all right that week. The nurses had interested her in taking some care of her skin and when she came out of the shadows of the portico of the institution, even in the anachromatic light reflected from the snow, she looked remarkably younger and fresher than when she had so long ago been committed.

The snow beside the suburban roads was banked almost up to the level of the rented car's top as Jeff and Carol drove back down toward the center of town.

"Would you like us to find one of those great seafood places downtown?" he asked. "Most of them are open on Sunday."

"Yes, did you get my letter?"

"I'll say I did. It was lovely, dearest."

"How you spell X?"

Down the long deserted snow-packed narrow street all the traffic lights went red. Jeff braked the little rented car to a squeaking stop.

"How you spell?" Carol asked.

"Well, of course," Jeff said. "Like this." He leaned over and kissed her. After a few moments she drew away, sorrowfully.

"No," she said. "That's not the way you spell X." She looked all around the snow-banked street corner outside the car and then suddenly gave him a delighted smile. She pointed to a drugstore. "There," she said, letting herself out of the car door. "You wait just here. X, X, X," she whispered.

The cross-street light went green, then red again and then green again. No traffic had crossed. When the signal light had alternated six times Jeff pulled into the snowed-up curb and got out and went into the drugstore. A young woman in a starched mesh replica of an overseas cap was the only one he could see in the place. She was leaning across the marble top of an old-fashioned soda-water counter.

336

"There was a lady who just came in here," he said. "Where is she now?"

"What was that in reference to?" the girl asked. "A prescription?"

Jeff looked down the long high cases of proprietary medicines, winking brightly behind their glass enclosures from the light from the snow outside. The place was empty of anything like humanity except for himself and the soda-fountain girl. But poised in fiery flight above them flew a colored life-size silhouette of a smiling young woman in scanty bathing dress about to be burned to a crisp except for the ministrations of Unguentine. And then, higher up, as Jeff looked distractedly around him, he found another large human image eying his panic. This was a bloated Kodak boy baby who was also perpetually smiling down upon the miracle which the Norwich Chemical Company assured his flaming cardboard associate.

"Look," Jeff asked, "is there a toilet here?"

The young woman shook her overseas-capped head with an expression of almost genuine mercy. "You got to go up the street to the bakery," she said. "She opens about this time Sunday afternoon."

It was then that Jeff saw the entrance to the drugstore from the side street and he started out through it, slamming the door against the harsh cold and slipping on the frozen pavements going up into a kind of wide park and looking for Carol.

After a long time running in the paths of the park he saw a saloon cheerfully lighted in the dusk down a side street entering the park. He phoned the police from there and the police found Carol. The Baltimore police had been very efficient and even very kind and understanding about it. There are a number of great hospitals in Baltimore, and the police had taken Carol to one of them, not knowing about the nursing home where she had been staying.

Poor old Jeff, my nephew, sat on a steel chair tinted apple-green to match the apple-green walls (a color much in fashion with

337

interior decorators of private homes a decade before, and much in fashion now in private hospital rooms) and tried to smile at Carol through the wrinkled glinting cellophane of the oxygen tent which covered her hard-mattressed white-enameled bed (not apple-green, for white has never been out of fashion for hospital beds). I had come over to Baltimore from Princeton.

Most of the rest of this time I spent sitting in one of those nice hospital sun parlors with cretonne on the bamboo seats and sofas where you can take it easy while your relatives or friends try to live or die, or, if female and reasonably young, try to procreate. And all the antlike activities of the staff swarmed about me. Antlike; I mean it. The colony desperate to save the life of one of the colony. These strangers would do anything in their personal power to deliver back into life this faltering life of Carol, whom they knew merely as a name on an aseptic door. But she was of their own colony; she was another human and of every skill of humans she mutely demanded the right and the will from them to save her, dying though she was. The ants in white skirts and the ants in white tunics glided quickly but quietly up and down the slick clean halls, into and out of the aseptic door, white-enameled trays of all sizes in their hands, instruments and containers of every shape upon them. But the ants lost in the end. The procession of them faltered and then, dispiritedly, began to break. Carol's nurse let me into her room where Jeff was sitting on his steel chair beside her shinily canopied high narrow bed.

She never recognized me, and I had always been a pretty good friend of Carol's.

She sighed, we saw with panic, more from her abdomen than her chest. The attending doctors had told Jeff that this was a bad sign in pleural pneumonia, and that of course with the psychological and therefore physical stresses in a recent medical history such as that of Mrs. Hanes, maybe he'd better stay over until Tuesday. And so on and so forth—but what good did that do poor Carol? The ants had already gone away. Who were they kidding?

Then Carol murmured something about the children with holes

338

in them and suddenly she turned toward Jeff and their eyes met. Her face no longer looked like a face, as most faces do, done for example in natural-colored paints. It was, it seemed, a face done in charcoal, and the deepest dead black had been applied to her eye cavities all the way from brows to cheekbones. This killingly terrible caricature of Carol spoke out of an equally large and monstrous black mouth: "I'm going to die, Jeff."

"No, no, my dearest! Don't talk like that!"

Her voice was faint, and yet it still seemed so recognizable that I found it almost possible to believe his agonizing lie.

"Yes I am, Jeff."

"No!"

"And I hate it so."

"No, dearest! You mustn't—"

"Hold my hand, Jeff."

He rose from the apple-green steel chair. "How— We're not supposed to raise the tent for a while yet."

"Damn it! Through the zipper, you fool!"

Then Jeff saw it, obviously the place through which the nurse or physician could attend the patient. He opened the zipper in the cellophane oxygen tent and when he put his arm in through the crackling clear fabric she somehow managed to find the strength to meet his hand halfway on the way to hers. When the weak tears began to run down across her lower lids I found myself for a moment surprised that they did not smudge the charcoal.

"Poor little boy," she sobbed. Her feeble contortion shook her head and her thin shoulders in the hospital smock and then her pale thin arm made Jeff's hand rattle against the zipper opening in the oxygen tent. And then she rolled her head away from him so that she must have been looking beyond the bright plastic onto the nearest apple-green wall. "Poor little girl."

Baltimore is another bad-luck town for our family.

Jeff never forgot the kindness of Mrs. Cox's coming over from Washington and "arranging" everything. I expect that was why he gave her, later, the flag. Women do most of these obsequy jobs best. Well, not all of them: I bought the coffin. You have to haggle a little bit about coffins, I have discovered, beginning with my brother Jeff's. The carrion crowd think that they have you over a sentimental barrel and can make you pay any price. Carol's father, the big hardware man, who later got his own bier at government expense, was not, as I recall it, of much use on this occasion.

Where had that funeral parlor, that cemetery really been? The hospital—of course we knew its address; we were back and forth from there often enough. But where, in what part of the city of Baltimore, was it? Where were the places that Jeff and I and Mrs. Cox had to go to after poor Carol died? And then on the day after that until the day that we buried the poor girl? I just don't know. Which way do the big streets really run in Baltimore?

Jeff once told me that he had been less than twenty minutes in Camaguey in all his life. That, in fact, it was the only time that he had ever set foot on Cuba. And yet, from that brief midnight visit on his way by air to South America, he believed that even from the airport he knew more in the mesquite-smoke, the dark honeyed night, of Camaguey and even of Cuba than he would ever know about Baltimore, where he had spent so many long days while Carol was in that sanitarium and before Carol had died in that hospital.

There was an infinitude that he would never know about Baltimore. Call it trauma or syndrome or whatever the scientific name for his not knowing or his forgetting was. He didn't know Baltimore very well.

He had probably learned this, however, about himself and Carol during the long Baltimore time: that there was an enormously important thing called courage and constancy. That you had to have bravery and enterprise to make your life, and, almost always (and here was where Jeff faltered in not giving himself a good enough mark) the kind of physical co-ordination (did not that help with most kinds of courage?) that, well, a farmer like Truman enjoyed or a football player like Trippe. Or a correspondent who would go up to visit the Kachin partisans?

Down the cliffside of the railway station at Baltimore, down that

340

long dirty open iron staircase, Jeff had once descended almost defeated onto the railway platform which, from the car Elks Club, we now were about to see.

Walking down those steps after Carol was dead, he had the terrible and defeated sense of having almost lost control of his future. I suppose that he *had* lost control of it. Let's not kid ourselves.

That, believe me, had not been a good day. But he had survived it.

His father, it had seemed to me at this time, had never had to put up with the kind of ordeal young Jeff had faced and in his own way mastered.

When the train had come to a slow sighing sorrowful abdication of its might between the passenger sheds beneath the long smoky undercut of the new Baltimore station and the rain on the windowpanes of the Elks Club began dispiritedly to curve downward, and after another belated soapy sigh escaped from the airbrake mechanism beneath the car, I swung myself around in my chair to face the window. "Hey, look," I said, "they've got your book out there."

Jeff looked quite quickly. There they were, about a dozen of them racked on the top of a traveling magazine and confectionery cart. There was not much business going on (nor, gratifyingly, for the neighboring works of other contemporary American fiction), but each copy of this book of his that he saw, each one with its never to be too familiar end-title of *The Pier and the Arch* and the author's name, Hanes, each one was absolutely as dear to him, as much of him, as the product of an incredible multiple birth to an incredible mother. And of course there was some additional special delight for Jeff in looking down upon them, even through the rain and even though there were no purchasers in view. There had already been enough purchasers to make it a resounding popular success. Until now his work had largely escaped the attention of the American reading public.

Does a mother truly love her blasted cripple as much as she

341

loves her fighter pilot? Jeff may have doubted it, and yet I knew that he had a pathetic affection for those other earlier books of his. They had brought him some bad days one way and another; days of unsureness and doubt and disillusion when he was writing them, of course; and then hope when they were published; and then, twice, disaster.

Mischance overcome makes gratifying reminiscence. That first Hanes opus, as I recall, was of such nature that the kindest critic on earth could rate it no higher than "quite unusual." It had to do with a Park Avenue matron who awakened one morning much embarrassed by signs on her pillow which, to her dismay, derived from veritable stigmata. This thoroughly unclassifiable work of fiction was entitled A *Protestant Miracle* and involved a panorama of characters (the thing got very big and very international) so huge that few readers and absolutely no reviewers bothered to pursue the story farther than the first couple of chapters.

Then there came *The Three Dollar Raise*, by Thomas Jefferson Hanes. That was also hard for anyone outside our immediate family to appreciate, largely concerned as it was with the conflict of an officeboy against a lot of bosses and their underlings all of whom Jeff knew and hated much too well when he worked on the Scotchman's miserable little magazine.

Then he wrote one about something he knew about and also of something he was not angry about and also mainly about just one person, it having finally occurred to him that if you have a story about even two people you had better throw one of them away, or maybe both. No reader, he told me, could with much real interest follow the vicissitudes of more than one central character.

"Nice wrapper, I continue to believe," I casually observed as we both stared out of the Elks Club's window. "Now. Look. Now there's a man with a great lot of brains. He's buying one. God, how I like to see real sound appreciation for writing show itself in this republic. It lifts up the heart."

The train began to glide forward between the sheds.

"Yes," I said looking backward, "there he goes. A man of big,

342

broad intellect. He knows three dollars and seventy-five cents worth of value when the right merchandise is put before him. Hope he goes to see it in the movie, too, when it comes out. Wouldn't want him to miss anything."

"He only bought it for your jacket design."

"He only bought it to read about the art of building and me and your father, kiddo," I said. "But you did quite well by us." And I could have bitten my tongue off.

"Let's have one for the road," Jeff said quickly.

I swung my seat back to face my nephew. "Jeff, my dear old Jeff, I said something wrong. You did a beautiful story and it's all your own. You must forgive my foolish age and long memories." I figured that this would sound soothing and venerable enough.

"What road, George?"

"Sixty-six, that's where they get their kicks, isn't it, in that colored song? That's the one that you and your Eileen are taking to California tomorrow?"

It was night now, and as we were passing the Martin bomber plant, its old peeling camouflage a kind of a weary bad joke beneath the floodlights of the well-lit new armament race, I thinking to do my best, lifted my glass toward the end of the train. "You're kind of glad to get by there, aren't you, Jeff?"

"Where? Oh, Baltimore. Yes."

"He was *such* a son of a bitch, her old man was. Don't kid me, we lived in the same town together. He wasn't nice to Carol's mother and he wasn't nice to Carol. She had to be the way she was with an old son of a bitch like him for an old man."

"Let's talk about something else," Jeff said.

"That's all right with me, kiddo. What?"

"What's your opinion of self-pity?"

"I thought we must have gone over that a time or two in your life, Jeff," I said with some surprise. And then, sensing that this was no time for the gruff stuff, I said, "I'm all for it. If you're not going to pity yourself, who's going to do the pitying for you?"

"When did you do yours, George?"

343

"Oh, hell, lots of times. You remember, when I didn't get that tenure at the University."

"No, not when you didn't get that tenure at the University. You were disappointed but you weren't sorry for yourself."

"Well, then at the Open in Minneapolis in 1916. I sure felt bad that time. So did you, for that matter. Threw up all over the clubhouse, and not even four years old. Yes sir, all over the good old Minikahda Club."

"Cut it out, George."

"In the old war plenty of times. I mean the old old war, or rather the old old old war. They've got one going in Korea now, haven't they?"

"How about when father was killed?"

"Yes, of course," I said. "That was badder than hell."

"But you weren't sorry for yourself."

"Listen, let's drop this subject, what do you say?"

"And about you and Margaret, and about you and mother."

"*Wilmington*, Wilmington next station stop!" the porter yelled out.

"E.I. Du Pont de Nemours," I said. "Did you ever stop to think what a lovely-sounding name that is?" I asked my nephew. "And so many other really spine-tingling names that American industry has? Western Union; just let that one roll off your tongue. Anaconda. Very sharp, very frightening, Anaconda. The Aluminum Company of America, lots of rhythm there. And how about just General Electric?"

But I had lost my nephew's attention. He was looking down on the platform where he had first laid eyes on Eileen Maben. And I knew all about that scene. This was the time that Carol Beeman had come down from Smith for a Christmas—or was it Easter?—holiday party at the home of one of the Du Ponts, and Jeff was to be her escort. When Carol got off on the railroad platform—now, as then, a story above the street—Jeff was of course there to meet her and she of course was accompanied by Eileen Maben, a schoolmate. Carol was by nature hesitant. Not Eileen. Eileen the fair beamed at Jeff, reminded him that he was a friend of her brother's, and told him to give the Pullman porter a dollar. His reaction—mind you, he was a Midwestern boy and not used to Eastern ways—was to get drunk that night in the locker room of the country club with a midshipman from Annapolis and neglect both Carol, the woman who was his dear good friend, and also Eileen, the woman who had stunned him. This I learned, of course, many years later. It was naturally nothing that was known to me on the back porch of Bob Mayer's house at Rumson on the evening of young Jeff's marriage to Carol—when Jeff and Eileen and her brother Peter and Eileen's new husband Mr. George had breezed by each other so diffidently—but one can guess; could always have guessed.

There was this other scene—no, there were three more in all, one of which I was myself a witness to. Anyhow, this next one was at Princeton on the Saturday night of house parties, so that must have been at least a year after Jeff had first met Carol. Maybe two. He would have had to be a junior at least, maybe a senior.

He remembered how, he told me, after he had taken Carol across the street to the Observatory, where she was to sleep, he had come back to his club and, not now being sleepy at all, he had gone into the little anteroom outside the main floor washroom, and taken one of his books from its shelf.

He had taken it with him down the solemn, dark hall to the billiard room where the light was suddenly so bright across the long red leather window seat. The wide blossoms of the tulip trees outside reflected a soft illumination of their own into the room, for this was still May and they had not yet had to give up their swift and lovely lives.

He was reading, he remembered, for perhaps the tenth time the lyric in the book which at that particular period he most esteemed for style and content when Eileen came into the far corner of the room. She stood in the high dark oaken doorway, caressing the neweling of the applied columns of the opening, and she rocked in the tender shadows as though in an absolute embrace of the beauty of the spring morning.

"Hello," he had said. "Hello, Wilmington."

345

"Hello."

"Come on over. We seem to be the last of the party."

She swung slowly around the pool table and came to rest at the opposite end of the window seat from him. It was one of the years when skirts were blessedly long. She tucked hers up, long legs and pleats and all, upon the window seat with two generous arms and asked: "Where is your young woman?"

He nodded toward the Observatory. "Over there. Sleeping."

"My young man is not sleeping," she said. "He is down in the basement shooting craps. Or do you call it crap? I can never remember."

She seemed to him the most beautiful thing that he had ever seen. Up until that exact moment the most beautiful thing that he had ever seen was the body of the Bugatti which had without success raced the June before on the new board speedway at Egg Harbor. The deep, iridescent, chemical dark blue of the Bugatti reminded him of the same color, depth, and shine of his first Christmas horn. And looking into the golden face of this girl he had the same instant sense of ecstatic recollection. She was the superb, the totally recollected fairy princess of his never to be forgotten and never to cease to be beloved storybooks.

At which point he had then said to her: "You must be here with Famine Murch."

And she had said: "No, I'm afraid I don't know him. In fact, my young man's from Yale University. And now you must say: a great school."

"Where were you all night?"

"We were what is called going up and down the street. What do you hear from my brother Pete?"

"From Pete? Nothing."

"What's in your book?"

He had moved a little toward her; now he slid back on the leather. "Some lyrics," he said.

"Let's hear the one you like best. Who did them, by the way?"

"Some people who went here a few years ago and wrote poetry for the *Lit*."

346

"Do you?"

"Of course, what do you think? Oh, I'm sorry—"

"Let's hear your favorite."

"Okay. It's by Niv Busch. I'll give it to you in part."

"Okay, in part," she agreed.

By now the rising light and the blossoms of the tulip trees outside the windows and beyond and behind her pale hair had made of her, to him at least, a creature of sublime radiance.

> *"Since that midsummer morning now long past*
> *When the poor princess, with a dwindling cry,*
> *Saw the red drop that from her finger leapt,*
> *This place, whose lease Time holds, has slept."*

"Pretty rich stuff, don't you think?" Jeff had asked Eileen.

"I like the words and I like the music," Eileen had said, moving over toward him. *"The Sleeping Princess, is it called?"*

"Sleeping Castle."

"Proceed."

> *"She sleeps and you have seen her. Now go forth.*
> *Journey what roads you will in tears and rain*
> *The heart out of your breast will travel back*
> *As mine has traveled along the secret track*
> *To see, in this sad place, her face again. . . ."*

Eileen was looking out of the window as he finished, he remembered.

"Where does a princess sleep around here, I wonder," she whispered. "Everywhere? Is it really enchanted, this place?"

And then Jeff had (he often later thought) grossly overbid the hand. "I have two very quiet rooms in Campbell."

She had then bent upon him the utmost look of forgiveness. "I'm staying with lots of other young women in a long room way upstairs in a place called Cap and Something. I guess you had better show me to the door of that place."

Arching up from the not too distant blue sea the early sun shone

347

down upon the topmost young maple leaves, making them bright green as parrot feathers, then silver down upon the walks of Prospect Avenue. And it was out of this enchantment that Jeff had taken Eileen through the oaken door of Cap and Gown. And had tried to kiss her.

"I don't think that would be a very good idea, do you?" she said.

"Not for good night? Not even for good morning?"

"Go on home now, Jeff," Eileen had said.

Eileen did not stay for the house parties beyond the next morning, somebody later told Jeff. By herself she had taken a train for New York.

I myself saw them together when I suppose it must have been their first meeting after his marriage and hers. Carol was of course in the nursing home. Eileen's husband, this boy George, was dead in the war. It was the last game of the season—against the Dartmouth people, as usual—but a bright fine day. I was lifting up the wire for Margaret and myself and Jeff to get under and go on up the lawn to Cannon and I guess all our eyes turned, like a camera you might say, and there were Eileen and a couple of other people doing the same thing. Well, when we all straightened up on the other side of the wire the other two people, her escorts, turned out to be Tom Hightower, a young chemist from the Whitney Institute, and a friend of his named Murch. We shook hands all around, agreeing that it was a near thing to have beaten Dartmouth, but as usual, and Hightower and Murch urged us up to a Whitney Institute station wagon where they pulled down the tail gate and we all had a sandwich and a drink.

"This is sort of like drinking in church," I remember Jeff saying, and we all laughed.

"You mean you feel guilty about it?" Eileen asked.

That's all that I remember about that scene. But I began to get the idea.

Then the next time that Jeff saw Eileen, the most important time, perhaps—although the time after *that* may have been what you would call the really important time—the next time that they came together after their autumn meeting was when Jeff ran into Eileen at Schwarz's. F.A.O. Schwarz's.

He was sitting at one of the three writing desks next to the cashier windows on the second floor and was trying with a bad pen to address a card to little Eileen which would accompany the gift of a rubber raft, a tent, a cot, light blankets and mosquito netting (so woodsy had she now become and so well-off, now, had he) when he slopped ink over the card and reached forward to the well-scarred rack for another. There was just one card remaining and two hands reached for it at the same time. Well, maybe that was meeting cute.

"Excuse—"

"Please—"

Phonographic musicboxes filled the top of the air with tidings of seasonal good will; howls of dismay, pleasure, interrogation, search, and demand provided a deeper commercial sonic background. And yet Jeff quite clearly heard her say "Jeff" and Eileen heard him say "Eileen."

He stood up and looked at her. It was just the same, except maybe the loss or need or whatever it was made his throat oh just barely perceptibly tighter this time. And yet he was quite able to say, "I'm in the tent and raft business. What business are you in?" As easy as that.

"I'm in the microscope business, and very expensive business it is, this model of ours. Suitable for P and S, I should think. He's going to be a pathologist." She, he noted a little enviously, also sounded all right.

"Well, that's fine."

"I rather think not. Next year he's almost made me promise him a cadaver."

"What?"

"They're quite cheap, didn't you know? About fifteen dollars."

"Let me find us both a card," Jeff said hurriedly. "Then a pretty fast drink."

"Well. . . ." Eileen hesitated.

"In the interest of pathology," he insisted.

Where had they gone? Oh, sure, the Plaza. Right across the street. The Oak Room.

They had looked at each other with speculation, I suppose: two kinds of speculation. At any rate, Jeff knew that he had wondered if he would ever stop loving her and, he had guessed, she must have looked at him wondering, speculating just what the hell he was up to.

The purple evening light fell almost lifelessly down upon the dull snow of the park and then, miraculously, jumped and danced upon the happy sparkling fingers at the edges of the enormous silver-tinseled wreaths hanging in the great windows of the room, bringing into its russet richness, bringing privately to each table, a bright holiday intimacy.

"This is nice," Eileen said quietly. "A nice pre-Christmas treat."

"God knows I think so," Jeff said. And then: "Well. To the potato chips. Have some?"

"What are you going to get for Christmas, Jeff?"

"Not much, I guess. No. That's not right. Uncle George is going to give me a whopping big aneroid barometer. He'll hang it up in the hall in his own place in the country. That's where my kid lives now."

"Oh."

He cleared his throat. "Er—who's, I mean, what's being given to you, do you suppose?"

"My boy's coming home from school tomorrow."

"That's fine."

"You've said that before."

"Okay. What school?"

"Exeter. His father went there."

"That's fine."

"I'm going to leave." And she actually stood up, he remembered. And he remembered it still with dismay.

"Please sit down, Eileen. Please stay here just for a minute. I mean a few minutes, please."

She still stood there, looking out the windows into the park. "That's the north that way, isn't it?"

350

"Yes."

She shook her head helplessly, and, even in their silver and oaken privacy he saw that a few nearby people were beginning to notice her, not that he could possibly care.

"*And face the North.* That's the end of the poem, isn't it?" She sat down again, dispiritedly. "What do I know about you? Oh," she swept some useless saucers and silverware just gently, just impatiently but gently, aside, "what do I really know of you. After years and years and years and you had your wife and I—oh, what? *Poems.* No, a *poem.* Not even yours. Worse."

A waiter, hovering outside their small bright orbit, blessedly brought to the table another pair of highballs. Manfully, he hoped, Jeff took advantage of the pause to state some small case of his own.

"I've written a few things recently," he said. "All my own, too."

And, great God, here suddenly came the divine face from long ago in front of the Japanese tulips. And yet all she did was to nod her bright head and say, "Yes, Jeff. And that was good." And then, "And now I *really* must be going."

Well, if you were supposed to be articulate you'd damned well better be articulate at a time like this, when the whole bloody show of your life might be going over the dam. And, God and experience with dialogue helping him, Jeff did it as fast as he could talk: "Look, you asked me what I was going to get you didn't ask me what I wanted did you?"

"No."

"Well what I want is to kiss you."

"Jeff, after all these—"

"It's not my fault damn it if it's after all so you say these—"

"Jeff."

"Waiter for dear Christ's sake let's have a check will you please?"

"Next station stop, *Trenton!*"

"Wouldn't you like to have a little something to eat, George?" my nephew asked me.

351

"I sure would," I said.

And so we went up to the dining car, rocking and rolling with the train's momentum. He was the first one of us to be given the Pennsylvania's rather limited menu. When he ordered I said, "For two."

For two indeed, I thought. He also had been kept for so long from the one he loved. Not as long as I had been, I thought, looking across the table at him; but long enough. That, at least, we had in common.

"Off to California then, tomorrow?" I said.

"You'd have loved it yesterday, George," he said. "My agent turned up with a Mark IV Jaguar. That's what Eileen and I are supposed to get to California in."

"Well, what's wrong with that?"

"He brought us a wedding ring, too."

"Well, I still don't get it. What's wrong with that?"

"He said we'd need it going through the Plains States. We don't want to seal it officially until we get to the Pacific Ocean. Or do you understand that?"

Of course I did. Romantic, of course, but understandable. You cleanse yourself by moving from one ocean to another. And they, poor kids, had been a long time waiting for the cleansing process.

"Did I ask you about Mother?"

"What about your mother?"

"How did she take it?"

"You mean about the disposition of the building?" He was so free now. He was as free as a bird. He and his Eileen, he and his long-earned success. He who was at last doing exactly what he wanted to do. I, believe me, was the last person in the world who would tell him about how his mother reacted to the disposition of the Tower. But I could scarcely withhold the recollection from myself at that time. Nor forever in all time to come.

"*Newark!* Next station stop *Newark!*"

His mother, young Jeff's mother and my former wife, had indeed spoken to me about the disposition of the building. She, too,

352

had summoned me to New York. Well, maybe not summoned. I was putting up a house out at Sands Point for a man who had made a lot of money during the war out of sugar—the trustee who had slipped me the bad news, as a matter of fact—and I was in and out of New York every week or so. I had gone to see Mary at my own convenience, to tell the truth. But of course all the family owners of the building had a report coming to them.

So there she was to receive me, and I must say looking very well. She had on one of those golden pleated things that fitted her very well and there were lots of places for the things to fit her. Her face was pretty much all of a sort of paste that the movie actresses wear, but in the low evening light of this apartment of hers and Bob Mayer's she looked pretty good.

The apartment itself, a co-operative duplex of course somewhere in the Seventies on Park Avenue, was to me an atrocity: no natural light, a half-dozen lianas perched here and there, a Sandy Calder mobile, and a lot of new and unrememberable furniture.

"You took your time getting here, George," she said.

"I've been busy."

"Busy doing what? Giving away our building?"

"Yes," I said, "I've given it away."

"For God's sake why?"

"Because they raised our taxes and all that was left were the few stores on the street level. I think Nat Pierce wrote you that even the movie house was condemned."

"That's another dope, that Pierce. Why do you think you can give the Tower away?"

"I can. I have. To keep it from being torn down I've given it to the city."

"What about the rest of us, you God-damned philanthropist?"

"Mary's married to all the tea in China," I said. "Jeff's doing all right. You certainly are doing okay, too, Mary."

She wriggled a bit on one of those unrememberable couches. "A girl likes to have a little pin money of her own, George," she said.

"Have you ever talked to Bob about this?" I asked her.

353

"Do you think that this is the kind of thing that you talk about to your *husband?*"

I got up to go.

She got up, too.

"This is the last of what you've got to say, George?"

"Yes," I said, "although I haven't said very much."

Then the maliciousness on that painted face had really appalled me. "You better listen to me, then, big boy," she said, "because I've got big fat news for you." She walked toward me even as I was walking toward the door.

"Trondheim? Remember?"

"Where my brother was killed."

She now began to shout. "Where he wanted to kill *me!*"

"Yes, you've told me that before."

"It was a hot day, do you understand? Even in Norway in the summer it gets hot. They've got inns and joints like that all along the roads. We stopped at a couple, me and that brother of yours. Then I told him about Ed Reagan. Don't you understand!"

"I guess I understand," I said.

Then I really wanted to go. I was on my way to the door now, truly.

"What a great joke on you, George, you bloody martyr, protecting my good name all these years!" she yelled at me as I got myself into the elevator hall of the Mayers' duplex.

"Penn Station next station stop!"

We went into the tubes, the familiar old pressure stopping our ears and, always, stopping conversation, and then a few minutes later Jeff and I bustled out ahead of the people who had baggage.

At the higher escalator level, just below where you reach the rotunda, we came upon a man and his wife and three kids who were in the middle, it appeared, of a great tired quarrel. The children wanted to do something that the parents didn't want them to do; they were all wrangling with each other; I don't know what. A mess. The rest of us, at any rate, who wanted to go up the escalator were for the time held there.

354

Jeff looked at me with a happy, good-natured, and absolutely honest smile. "Well," he said, "at least you brought *me* up right, George."

For a moment I think that my heart stopped. "I've got to get some cigarettes," I said. "Good-by, Jeff. Good luck." I had to turn away from him.

He was on the escalator going up, but I could hear his voice calling down: "We're going to be seeing you in California, George!"

"You bet," I said, but I was going in the other direction.

Eighteen

This is the end of the story.

I spent the night following my departure from young Jeff in one of those dingy crypts at the Princeton Club and Margaret, to save money also, had stayed with a woman friend of hers in the friend's apartment. We met at the Airways Terminal on Forty-second Street—just diagonally across the street, by the way, from where I had, or at least I thought I had, joined the Seabees.

When we were in the airplane bus to Newark, Margaret asked me: "Do you really want me to take this trip with you?"

"I certainly don't want to take another one of these drag-ass trips to St. Louis by myself again as long as I live," I said.

"What language," she said, and cracked open a paper-bound volume of Josephine Tey. "The Friend should hear you."

We got to St. Louis a little after lunchtime and, the Lambert Airport being as far as it is from town, arrived at the Teutonia Bank at about the end of the business day. This, however, was on schedule.

There they were, the four of them: old Mr. Neidlinger, older than God now I should imagine but you can bet that he was still very much the master of that great gray Middle-European cube of a banking office of his; Nat Pierce, the tiny but oh (on occasion) so effective legal counsel; Mrs. Adams of the dear sharp eyes and the dear big nose; and City Councilman Adams. This was my first meeting in all my life with Mr. Adams, and of course it was Margaret's, too. The councilman looked awful good in there to me. He looked like, I thought, any one of three great National League baseball umpires. He had the same white hair, the same blue suit, the same absolute assurance and confidence. This was another kind of tribune of the people. He was the one, of course, who with Mr. Neidlinger and Nat Pierce had rigged it up, if that is not too sporty a phrase, for me to give the Tower to the city for a municipal college. I got out from under the taxes, the city got a place where kids could learn something.

They couldn't have been nicer to Margaret. Mr. Neidlinger addressed her as "Miss Carton," but of course that was an affectionate salute and for very old times' sake. Then little Nat produced from that valise of his (I wondered, was it possible that it could have been the same one that had held the currency that had once bought control of the Tower?) a great pile of papers. At least on this occasion of changing the Tower's ownership they had not been all spread out before I got there.

"Well, that's about the works," Nat said, pushing his documents across about a quarter of the area of Mr. Neidlinger's black morocco leather desk top.

Mr. Neidlinger held up a hand so fragile that even with the dying western light coming in from the Grand Avenue windows behind him the hand was almost transparent, like a large old moth's wing. "I want to say here something," he said. He looked about at us, settled as we were in the big black leather chairs on the big Kirman rug. "Mr. and Mrs. Adams deserve great credit for bringing about this project. Municipalities are sometimes—their government, their interests, I mean—it requires great skill to reorganize their attitudes. . . ." The pale old hand fluttered into the air again. "What am I trying to say?" I saw a tear come down, crookedly, from the corner of one of the old raddled eyes. None of this made any of the rest of us feel any better, but for some reason everybody had always shut up until Mr. Neidlinger had

357

finished speaking, and he hadn't yet. "You are a very good boy, too, George," he said. "You always were. Now you must all excuse me." By golly, he got up and walked out of that room as straight as a grenadier.

We all, I guess, took a breath. Nat Pierce, I know, lit a cigarette and turned to me and Margaret.

"If I get any more clients like you two," he said, "giving property away without any kick for the lawyer, I'm going to the poorhouse."

I hadn't thought of that.

"Well," I said, "that's not fair to you, Nat. I think I can pay—"

And then we got the little jockey's smile. "Sign off," he said.

"There's just one thing," I then said, and I had to say it. "We've got to see one more person before we sign these papers."

Not a protesting sound from any of them—Nat or the Adamses —about who or why or where. What nice people.

"Would tomorrow be all right?" I asked.

Everybody got up, so I did, too. We more or less came together at the high old door that led from Mr. Neidlinger's office into the hall that led into the rotunda, you might call it, of the bank itself.

"The rooms of the hotel are so spacious, of course you know, Mr. Hanes," Mrs. Adams said. "Admirably fitted for classrooms."

"Yes, of course."

"Good kitchen facilities," her husband the councilman said. "Place for a whole hotel school, like Hopkins in Miami, we thought, if not Cornell."

"And the atelier," Mrs. Adams said.

Then nobody said anything.

"Tom?" Mrs. Adams prompted her husband.

So Mr. Adams was not only Mr. Adams the councilman who wanted to make a college for the city, but Mr. Adams also had a first name—Tom.

"We've got to have a first-rate architectural section to the college," Councilman Adams said. Mr. and Mrs. Adams looked at me, but I swear to you that it was not a *quid pro quo* look, if you know what I mean.

358

"I'm sorry I won't be able to be there, Mr. Hanes," Mrs. Adams, however, said.

"Well," I said, "I've got my eye on a girl named MacKenzie from Evanston. We were in the Navy together."

"I'm sure I will be glad to meet and talk to her, Mr. Hanes," said the boss handmaiden. Hanes & Hanes was back in business again, so obviously.

We all went out into the twilight of South Grand Avenue together. Nat got himself a cab. The Adamses begged to take us where we wanted to go, but I convinced them that it was impossible.

The last thing that Mrs. Adams said was said to Margaret: "It must be so good for you and Mr. Hanes to come back to where you came from." Then she and the baseball umpire drove off in their medium-large Buick sedan. Margaret and I took a cab and went out to the address that Nat Pierce had already some weeks ago found for us. He was always such a nice sharp little rascal.

At the southwest corner of the Park, Bill Medart, another friend of younger days, had built a very impressive eating joint—for St. Louis, anyhow. And there Olive was one of the headwaitresses. It was a place of various artificial levels, fake fieldstone fireplaces, old flintlocks hung here and there on the walls, but nevertheless a resort to which a sort of Missouri carriage trade was attracted. I was glad that this was the kind of spot whither we were directed to find Olive. Where she might otherwise have worked could have been a lot worse, I thought. She was the lady, as it turned out, whose job it was to greet us at the door. A modified Old Home Week was the type of her greeting to me. Margaret of course she had never seen, but she certainly was not afraid of her.

Olive took us over to a table near one of the appallingly unfunctional fireplaces—one of the best spots in the house, of course—and asked us what, if anything, we wanted to drink. I looked up at her as she seated us, and she looked so very well, I must say— cinctured into what the girls, I believe, call a very good black

359

dress—that all I could say was, "Please, Olive, sit down. Just sit down."

And she did.

"Well," she said, of course, "long time no see. So nice to meet Mrs. Hanes."

"So very nice to meet you," Margaret said.

I think they liked each other. Olive chased a waitress off for some drinks for Margaret and me. She wouldn't have one.

Well, no use mincing words. "It looks like I am going to have to give the Tower away to the city," I said. "Otherwise it would have to be torn down."

"Oh," she said, "Junie would never have liked that. He *loved* the Tower. You know that."

"But if we tore it down we'd have a valuable lot, and I'd want you to get some dough out of it. This way we all give it away and the city makes a college out of it."

"But *Junie* was a college man. Didn't you know that?" she asked. "Yale College. I think that's what he'd like the very best."

"You're sure? There's dough in it for you the other way, Olive."

"I don't suppose they would call it the Neidlinger College? No."

"No, I don't think so, Olive."

"Well, anyway—"

"But are you sure you want to do this? There's money in it for you if you don't."

She got up.

"I'm quite sure." And I am convinced that she was.

"Can't you have dinner with us?" Margaret asked.

"No. Mr. Medart would never like that. But I'll see you get a couple of good steaks."

"Thanks, Olive," Margaret said.

"I wish I could say they were on the house. But you'll like them, I'm sure."

The Tower was black against the evening sky. I mean really black. Limestone that hasn't been cleaned for fifteen years, suf-

360

fering from the soot of St. Louis, becomes as black as carborundum.

It looked even better black to me that evening; more powerful in silhouette. And of course there were no more badges of illuminative disgrace upon it. In the dark, in its death, the old building looked pretty good, I thought. In fact, magnificent. Like some great ruin out of the Middle East—but a lot better because, by God, it was no ruin. The owl would be no trumpeter here.

I led Margaret to the theater and office side, wanting to take a last long and of course sentimental journey up to see the campanile in its final desolation before its rebirth and reform. But under Jeff's beautiful arches she halted.

"No," she said. "I'll wait here. You go on up by yourself. It's your baby."

"You come along," I said, and she did.

My old key worked in the center door—good brass key, good brass lock—and we went across the lobby without the need of light. How often had I walked these spaces; I'd built them. And then I saw a working light beside the Tower elevator entrance. We went toward it and there, sitting on a stool just inside the central car and reading an evening paper, was Barney. He was not as surprised to see me, the one reluctant to come to this place for these past years, as I was to see him, the man who would never give up a job.

"Let's go up," I said. "We thought we'd have to walk."

"Oh, you'll never have to walk," he said, as though we'd last made the trip that afternoon.

I had another old key and I opened the doors of the old atelier where the crooked insurance firm in later years used to be, and then we made our way out to and through the door of the West portico, where my brother's office had faced. Mine had been toward the south and east. I looked out into the night, toward the long, long strings of lights along Lindell, toward the hazarded road lights through the Park.

I suppose I should say that I underwent a long soliloquy about all the chances I had missed; how throughout my life, year after year, event after event, every time that something seemed to be

361

going good it fell apart; that I had been cheated. But I didn't. Why should I? There wasn't much money in the cash register, but as Jeff used to say, who cared? And how could this great building be now put to a more magnificent—well, functional—use than for a school?

The Tower held its head high, as a tower should.

But oh, my brother, how lonely I had been. . . . But, no, no. That wasn't either what I felt or wanted to say. I was so immeasurably glad to get this almost interminable, almost lifelong, prop-turned-burden from my back—honorably, of course. Now I could almost rise up and hold myself straight like a tower, too. The custodian's job, with all its limping implications, was over. And suddenly I was very glad.

Margaret was at my side on the portico, of course, looking out with me into the westward night.

"Are you sorry, darling?" she asked.

I reached for her and took her solidly in my arms. Here was something important and really mine; only she could take this away from me. We went down in the elevator with Barney to the Chestnut Street door. Margaret and I arm in arm walked the half block east to Eighth to look for a cab to take us to a hotel.

Set in Linotype Electra
Format by Marguerite Swanton
Manufactured by The Haddon Craftsmen, Inc.
Published by HARPER & BROTHERS, *New York*